And Not a Penny More

And Not a Penny More

Penny More

Kathryn R. Wall

Coastal Villages Press
Beaufort, South Carolina

Tabby Manse ™

Published by Coastal Villages Press,
a division of Coastal Villages, Inc.,
2614 Boundary Street, Beaufort, SC 29906
843-524-0075 fax 843-525-0000
email: info@coastal-villages.com
Visit our web site: www.coastal-villages.com

Available at special discounts for bulk purchases
and sales promotions from the publisher
and your local bookseller
2 4 6 8 10 9 7 5 3 1

Cover illustration by Matt Bogart
Cover design by Ryan Kennedy
ISBN 1-882943-12-0
Library of Congress Control Number: 2002100153

First edition
Printed in the United States of America

For Norman,
the rock and safe harbor of my life

Acknowledgements

I wish to thank my first readers Shirley Wall, Mark Woodruff, and particularly Erik Woidtke (whom some of you may recognize, thinly disguised, in the ensuing pages), for their invaluable input and advice. As always, my sister-in-law, Dr. Barbara J. Everson, gave me excellent editing critique, as did my writing group partners, Linda McCabe, Peg Cronin, and Vicky Hunnings. Peg was especially helpful in sharing with me her marketing expertise which made promotion of *In For a Penny*, the first book in this series, more of a joy and less of a burden than I ever imagined possible.

I would also like to express my profound gratitude to the many bookstores, gift shops, and other outlets who took a chance and helped *In For a Penny* achieve a critical and commercial success beyond my fondest hopes. The same thanks extend to all those readers who were willing to expend both their money and their time on an unknown writer, and who were also kind enough to express their sentiments to me in person, by letter, and via the Internet. Fan mail! Does life get any better than that?

Finally, to my family, to my old Ohio compatriots, and to the wonderful new circle of friends we've been fortunate enough to acquire since moving to the South, thank you all for your continuing love and support.

Prologue

He stood beside her bed, marveling at how sleep and the deep satisfaction of good sex had smoothed the lines from her face. For these last, few precious moments, she looked as she must have on so many other nights, long since slipped into cherished memory.

Back then there would have been a husband curled in beside her, one arm tossed possessively across her shoulder, his measured snores the cadence of her dreams. And down the hall, their children might have slumbered, waiting to claim her attention, give meaning to her life.

He reached into the pocket of his tuxedo jacket and snapped on the surgical gloves. He hated the necessity of them. They tainted this act of ultimate intimacy—this joining of souls—making of it something sterile and impersonal.

He removed the pillowcase and set it aside. Not that she would struggle. They almost never did. A few grains of Valium dissolved in a celebratory glass of champagne usually took care of that. Still, he had survived a long time by paying attention to just such small details. The quiet rage was coming upon him after ever shortening periods of calm. He would need to be doubly careful from now on.

Pausing then, the pillow poised just above her head, he smiled. Fine and striking in repose, his face became dangerously irresistible when he smiled. They all said so.

"It's almost over now," he whispered, in English this time, for she was American. He liked to believe they could hear him, would carry the soft caress of his voice with them, into the dark. "You should have been true to him, *mutti*. He did love you, you know, despite the others. You have only yourself to blame . . ."

Ten minutes later he stood at the door surveying the suite to be certain he had overlooked nothing. The diamond-and-emerald necklace she was to have worn that evening lay tucked securely in his pocket along with the matching earrings. His eel-skin wallet bulged with the ten thousand dollars in *reais* he had urged her to cash out of her travelers' checks for their planned night out at the casino.

He never took everything, only what he truly believed they'd want him to have. After all, hadn't he restored their youth, made them feel beautiful and desirable again? What price could be put on such things? But, in the end, they always disappointed him, forced him to administer the final, tender justice their transgressions deserved.

His call to the front desk, posing as an American doctor and ordering undisturbed bed rest, would keep the hotel staff at bay for at least a couple of days. Plenty of time for him to claim his aging Alfa Romeo from the lot at the train station and put several hundred kilometers behind him. If all went as usual, her death, when discovered, would be put down to natural causes, a tragic ending to a dream vacation.

He cracked open the door and glanced quickly up and down the corridor. At three in the morning it was as deserted as he'd expected. He flipped the *Nao Perturbar* sign into position and turned off the lights. Looking back, his dark, empty eyes fastened on the soft glow bathing her lifeless body. Others might claim it was only the reflected lights of the city, filtered through the slight gap in the heavy drapes, but he knew better.

"I forgive you," he whispered and slipped quietly into the hallway.

He had to constrain himself from whistling as he strode past the double row of closed, silent doors. Anyone peeking out would have noticed a tall, dark man in impeccable evening clothes, walking innocently toward the fire stairs.

1

"Damn it, Bay, you're not concentrating! Get your arm up and aim at the center of the target. You're not trying to shoot the guy in the kneecap!"

"Why not? I thought the idea was to stop him. Taking a bullet in the leg would definitely slow someone down."

My brother-in-law, Sergeant Redmond Tanner of the Beaufort County Sheriff's Department, ran a hand through his straight brown hair and scowled at me in frustration.

The truth was, I didn't want to be there, and I wasn't doing a very good job of disguising the fact. Learning to shoot a handgun and thereby obtaining a concealed weapon carry permit was not the top item on my list of things to do that day. I had been badgered into it by Red and by my father, retired Judge Talbot Simpson. An avid sportsman, the Judge would have been the logical one to introduce me to the joys of armed combat. But a series of strokes had left him wheelchair-bound, his legs and left arm virtually useless. His iron will, however, had survived intact.

So there I stood, on a perfect mid-September morning with the sun just beginning to radiate the heat that would send the temperature well into the eighties by afternoon, sighting down the barrel of a Glock 9-millimeter pistol at an imaginary assailant.

"Look, you know why we're here." Red's patience, along with my own, had started to fray a little around the edges. "You agreed this was necessary, so quit wisecracking and pay attention. I'm trying to help you stay alive here, okay? And you're not going to do that by aiming at the guy's legs."

I raised my hands in surrender, pulled the ear protectors back onto my head, and picked up the weapon. I had been surprised at how heavy it was when Red first slapped the clip into the handle and passed the dull-gray handgun over to me.

"Okay, now take your stance," he mouthed.

I planted my feet slightly apart, gripped the Glock, and folded my left hand around my right, the way he'd shown me. I resisted the urge to close one eye, a mistake I'd made the first time I'd stepped up to the firing line.

"Now don't 'pull' the trigger. Squeeze it. Gently. That's it, squeeze . . ."

The sharp report, muffled by the ear protectors, startled me nonetheless. My hand jerked upward, and the bullet whizzed by the target, barely nicking the upper right-hand corner.

"Now you're overcompensating, aiming too high."

I slipped the orange plastic earmuffs down around my neck, popped the clip and the chambered round, and handed Red the gun—butt first as I'd been instructed. I turned and stalked back into the shade. The chilled bottle of iced tea I'd brought along had reached the temperature of bath water, but I gulped it down anyway. Beside me, Red silently unscrewed the top of his thermos and drank.

I stared out over the target range, amazed at the number of people who were learning—or perfecting—how to blow away their fellow citizens. Not that I have a problem with the bad guys getting theirs, especially not after everything I'd been through in the past year.

"If you could duplicate that scowl on your face, you wouldn't need a gun. People would just die of fright."

Like his older brother, Red had an uncanny knack for making me laugh when I really didn't want to. Shorter than Rob, but still a couple of inches over my five-foot ten, Red had my dead husband's slightly crooked smile and boyish good looks.

"Go to hell," I responded cheerfully, then sobered. "Here's the problem, Red. Every time I pick that thing up, I remember what it was like being on the other end. Hearing the bullets smash into the wall over my head, knowing that in a split-second my brains could be splattered all over the woodwork. I'm not sure I could do that to another human being, so what's the point of all this?"

"The point is, you never know what you're capable of until the situation presents itself."

We both turned toward the deep, booming voice.

"Hey, Matt," I said as the compact, heavily muscled homicide cop stepped up to us, "how's it goin'?"

Detective Matt Gibson and I had gone to grade school together thirty years ago and had recently become reacquainted under circumstances I was trying hard to put behind me. "Fine, just fine, thanks," he replied. "More importantly, how are you? You're lookin' good, all things considered. I like your hair."

"Thanks." My hand went automatically to where my red-tinted, dark brown hair lay softly around my ears. I still felt naked without the mass of curls hanging on my shoulders, but it couldn't be helped. They'd had to cut it off in the emergency room.

"Didn't mean to butt in on your lesson, Sergeant." Matt mopped his nearly bald, black head with a bright red bandanna. "Couldn't help overhearin', though. Miss Lydia givin' you trouble?"

"Nothing I can't handle." Red grinned at Matt's use of my hated first name.

Lydia Baynard Simpson. I was seven when I shortened it to "Bay". The Tanner came later, a couple of years after I'd set up practice in Charleston with two other CPAs. My life had been idyllic for the next fourteen years—until the day just over a year ago when I'd stood on the tarmac of a tiny country airstrip and watched Rob's plane disintegrate before my eyes. As always, when thoughts of that horror managed to force their way past my mental defenses, my hand went to my left shoulder. Struck by a burning piece of metal after the explosion, I would carry the scars for the rest of my life.

"Have fun, boys," I said, hefting my oversized tote bag onto my good shoulder. "I'm heading for the showers."

The army-green, epauletted shirt and khaki shorts I had donned that morning, along with heavy boots and socks, were sweat-soaked and plastered to my skin. At the time, the outfit had seemed appropriate for learning survival skills. But now I felt a little ridiculous, like some sort of Safari Jane out of an old Tarzan movie. All I lacked was a pith helmet.

"What about your next lesson?" Red called as I waved at Matt and clomped down the wooden walkway that led to the parking lot.

"I'll call you," I yelled back, not sure if I could be heard above the crack of gunfire and not really caring all that much if I couldn't. I had a lot of thinking to do about whether or not I wanted to pursue becoming armed and dangerous—possibly to myself as well as to others.

I'd left the top down on my sea green BMW convertible. When I'd unexpectedly found myself in need of a new car, I'd fallen in love with the little Z3 two-seater and now couldn't imagine being without her. Parked under the spreading limbs of one of the largest—and probably oldest—live oaks I'd ever seen, the cream leather seats felt only marginally like a griddle as I slid behind the wheel.

I eased down the rutted dirt track that serviced the target range and turned right onto Route 17. Had I gone left, another fifteen minutes would have found me approaching the Savannah River bridge and the lovely antebellum city that the greatly reviled General William Tecumseh Sherman had so graciously spared as a Christmas gift for President Lincoln. Instead I was headed for another jewel on the southeast Atlantic coast, Hilton Head Island.

Free of the hordes of tourists that clogged the highways from May to early September, the drive down nearly deserted, two-lane roads overhung with oaks, sweet gums, and the ever-present Spanish moss brought a welcome relief from the stifling heat and noise of the shooting range. I had only recently come to a fuller appreciation of the simpler joys: of salt-scented wind blowing through my cropped hair, of the gentle warmth of the South Carolina sun on my face. Of just being alive.

For months after Rob's death and my recuperation from my injuries, I had hidden out at the beach house, wallowing in my grief and pain. Being dragged from my safe cocoon against my will had been terrifying, but strangely liberating as well.

Get a life, they used to say.

Well, I was trying to get mine back.

* * * *

An hour later, showered and dressed in a white, sleeveless float and strapped sandals, I pulled open the door of the Carolina Café to a rush of blessedly cold air. Tucked into a corner of the luxurious Westin Hotel, its understated elegance and extensive seafood menu made it a local favorite. Beneath softly whirring ceiling fans, I spotted a thin arm waving in my direction. I made my way through the maze of sea foam green covered tables to where my best friend of thirty-three years sat fidgeting in her high-backed chair.

"Bay, honey, where have you been? It's almost five past one. I thought you were never gonna get here!"

Elizabeth Quintard Elliott—*Bitsy* because of her five-foot, three-inch frame—is a blonde, blue-eyed bundle of nervous energy who eats everything in sight and still remains a perfect size six. As I bent to touch her tanned cheek with my own, I noticed she had already made a considerable dent in the basket of sweet potato biscuits on the table.

"Am I that late?" I asked, seating myself and draping the soft napkin across my lap. "I thought we were meeting at one."

"Well, we *were*, but you're *always* early, you know you are. I was countin' on havin' a few minutes to talk to you first."

A waiter appeared, and I ordered iced tea as he handed me an oversized menu. Bitsy rooted in her bag while I lit a cigarette and studied the choices.

"I thought you were givin' those up," she drawled without looking up from her digging.

"I am. Eventually. This is only my third one today," I snapped. "How about you?"

"Cold turkey, two weeks ago." She tried to keep the superiority out of her voice and failed. "I figured what with all the trouble with the kids, I should set a good example."

Two of Bitsy's four children—the teenagers—had become entangled with drugs, one directly, the other only peripherally, but it had scared the hell out of all of us. The family was working through their problems now with the help of my old college room-mate, child psychologist Dr. Nedra Halloran.

I adjusted my attitude. "Good for you. Just give me time. I'll get there."

"I know you will, honey, but cuttin' down is not the way."

I was still staring straight at the top of Bitsy's head bent over her handbag. "What in God's name are you looking for in there?"

"Here it is," she announced triumphantly and thrust a crumpled newspaper clipping at me. "Hurry up and read that. I'll order. Crab salad okay?"

"Sure," I replied, smoothing the clipping out on the table and staring quizzically at my friend. "But what . . .?"

"Just read it, okay? It'll save time."

I concentrated on stubbing out my cigarette, avoiding the sharp black letters on the crinkled paper. The last time I had been directed to a seemingly innocuous article in the *Island Packet* it had unleashed a chain of events that nearly cost me my life. With a sigh of resignation, I picked it up.

Widow of local businessman found dead in hotel room

Rio de Janeiro, September 5. Leslie Mayne Herrington, 68, wife of the late John T. "Jack" Herrington II, founder of the Bi-Rite hardware stores and local civic leader and philanthropist, was found dead last night in her suite at the exclusive Rio Palace Hotel in this South American city. While local authorities have yet to rule officially, preliminary indications are that death was from natural causes.

Mrs. Herrington, who had resided in her native Natchez, Mississippi, since the death of her husband six years ago, was apparently traveling alone when she was stricken. There was no evidence of foul play, according to unnamed sources in the Rio de Janeiro police department, and the presence of a large amount of cash and jewelry among Mrs. Herrington's effects tends to support this theory.

Mrs. Herrington is survived by two sons, John T., III, of Los Angeles, and Justin of Dallas, and one daughter, Jordan Mayne von Brandt of Atlanta and Geneva, Switzerland.

Mrs. Herrington was preceded in death by her husband and by her parents, Franklin and Elizabeth Boothe Mayne.

A brief memorial service will be held tomorrow at 10:00 a.m. at St. Helena's Episcopal Church in Beaufort, with interment in Riverdale Cemetery immediately following. The graveside service will be private. Memorial contributions may be made to the Beaufort County Historical Society.

I finished reading the lengthy obituary just as the waiter approached with our salads.

"And some more of these yummy rolls," Bitsy announced, handing the empty basket to him with a generous smile. "Thanks so much. Well?"

"Well what?" I asked.

"Don't you remember them? The Herringtons?"

"No. Should I?"

"Oh, Bay, of course you do! Jack T. built all those hardware stores? You can't drive five miles without runnin' across one of them. And Leslie and your mama were in the Historical Society together. And surely you can't have forgotten Jordan?"

Bitsy attacked her plate then as if someone would take it away from her. Wiping a drop of creamy dill mayonnaise from the corner of her mouth, she swallowed and plunged back in.

"Jordan Herrington. Tall, black hair, gorgeous? Sort of exotic looking? She got boobs before any of the rest of us. You two got kicked out of school for smoking our freshman year. There was heavy bettin' as to who would raise a bigger stink with the school board, her daddy or your mama."

Jordan. I had her now. Exotic was an accurate description. A sharp widow's peak and slightly almond-shaped eyes, as if there might have been a drop or two of oriental blood somewhere generations back. Which was ridiculous, of course. Both sides of her family, all the Maynes, the Boothes, and the Herringtons, were of pure, well-documented Anglo-Saxon stock. My mother would not have tolerated them otherwise.

"Yes, I remember her now. Didn't she leave school early?"

"Middle of the year," Bitsy said, nodding. "Seems to me there was some scandal, hushed up, at least in front of our tender ears. Her daddy shipped her off to boarding school in Europe, and she never came back."

"So what's this all about? Why the urgency? I mean, I'm sorry about her mother, but these things happen. I'll send a check to the Historical Society."

"*Sshhh!* There she is!"

Bitsy rose from her chair and waved toward the doorway. I turned, as did most of the male occupants of the restaurant, and a murmur of appreciation rippled across the room.

Jordan Mayne Herrington von Brandt paused dramatically just inside the entrance. Her short, jet-black hair lay plastered against her beautifully shaped head, a style that accentuated her widow's peak and dark green, uptilted eyes. The black silk suit was obviously hand-tailored, probably in an exclusive little shop on the Rue de Faubourg St-Honoré, and clung to her tall, willowy frame like a second skin. Full, copper-colored lips parted over even white teeth as she spotted Bitsy. Her progress to our table was slow, unhurried, like a model slinking down the runway at a Paris couturier's.

"What is this all about, Bits?" I whispered, mesmerized like everyone else by the gorgeous creature approaching.

"She wants to talk to *you*, honey. That's why she's here."

"Me? What on earth for?"

"She thinks somebody murdered her mama."

2

There had been too many years and too little contact for spontaneous hugs and exclamations of delight as Jordan von Brandt joined us at the table. Besides which, her aloof manner and chic mourning clothes proclaimed loudly that she had not returned to her hometown on some nostalgic pilgrimage. Her mother's death had brought her here, that and nothing else.

We shook hands, and Bitsy and I mumbled our condolences. Our waiter moved immediately to her side, taking her order for coffee.

Jordan crossed one long, elegant leg over the other, extracted a slim, gold Dunhill lighter and matching cigarette case from her black Gucci bag, and blew a long stream of smoke across the table.

"Well, this is awkward, isn't it?" she said into the lengthening silence, and her deep, smoky laugh broke the tension.

"A little," I answered, lighting my own cigarette and settling back into my chair. "So what have you been up to for the last twenty-five years?"

Jordan stirred cream into her coffee. "Married, two daughters, divorced, filthy rich. How about you?"

Bitsy and I exchanged raised eyebrows. Neither of us answered. How could we hope to top that?

"Actually, I've heard quite a bit about your recent adventures from my friends in Beaufort," she went on. "Pretty impressive. I'm sorry about your husband."

"Thanks. So, where are you staying? Will you be in town long?" Trite questions, but I wanted the conversational spotlight away from me.

"Yes, how long are you here for?" Bitsy chimed in. "You didn't say when you called, and I'd love to have you to dinner some evening."

A guarded look snapped down on Jordan's face. "I'm not really certain. It may depend on Bay."

The reappearance of our waiter stifled the sharp protest ready to burst from my lips. With practiced ease Jordan snatched the check from his outstretched fingers and scrawled her name and room number across the face of it.

"I'm a guest of the hotel," she said, slipping a twenty-dollar bill from her bag and handing it, along with the check, to the startled young man. "Thank you."

"Yes, ma'am. Thank *you*, ma'am." He scurried off, beaming. I wasn't sure if his delight came from the generous tip or the dazzling smile that accompanied it.

"Oh, Jordan, honey, you don't need to do that! You're *our* guest. And you didn't even eat! We couldn't possibly accept! Truly we couldn't, could we, Bay?"

Bitsy tends to babble when she's nervous or embarrassed.

Jordan waved the protest away with a hand burdened by the weight of a diamond the size of a large walnut.

"Bits is right. We may not be 'filthy rich', but we can damn well pay for our own lunch." I'd had about enough of her highhanded behavior. Who the hell did she think she was?

Jordan looked startled, and Bitsy blushed.

"Oh, I'm sure she didn't mean it *that* way, did you, Jordan? Y'all probably do things differently in Europe, isn't that true? It must be so excitin' livin' over there. I mean, Paris, London, Rome . . ."

My furious, knock-it-off look finally registered, and Bitsy ran down.

"Sorry. I didn't mean to offend." Jordan delivered her feeble apology with all the sincerity of a used car salesman.

"Well, this has been *such* fun," Bitsy lied as she rose abruptly from the table.

"And just where do you think you're going?" I spluttered.

"Oh, I have a dozen errands to run before I pick the troops up at school. You know how it is with kids, never a moment's peace."

"No, I don't know," I snapped.

"Well, of course not, honey, but Jordan understands, I'm sure. Thanks *so* much for lunch. I'll be in touch. Bay, I'll call you."

Like a startled rabbit she scurried around the tables and out the door.

The silence left in the wake of Bitsy's hasty departure was finally broken by the almost simultaneous clicks of two cigarette lighters and two deep exhalations of smoke. I rattled the melting ice cubes around in my glass and sipped at the diluted tea in the bottom.

"I really am sorry. I don't know what gets into me sometimes."

I looked up in time to catch Jordan's rueful smile. It was the first honest expression I'd seen since she'd sat down at the table.

"That's okay. Bits isn't usually that ditzy, either."

Jordan laughed. "I remember her so well. My mother used to throw her up to me all the time. 'Why can't you be more like little Elizabeth Quintard?' "

"You, too? I thought I was the only one getting beaten over the head with Bitsy's perfection."

"Oh, no. I used to hear it daily. I dreamed of strangling her."

"Bitsy or your mother?" I reached out to snatch the words back the second they were out of my mouth. "Damn, Jordan, I'm sorry. I didn't think . . ."

Again the huge diamond flashed as Jordan von Brandt dismissed my stumbling apology. "Actually, the answer is both of them. But I got over being mad at Bitsy a long time ago. She couldn't help being perfect. Leslie is . . . was another story."

I tried to conjure up a picture of Leslie Herrington as her daughter lit another cigarette and re-crossed her perfect legs. No good. I couldn't distinguish her face from the dozen or so elegant matrons who had comprised the inner circle of my mother's coterie. Leslie would have been younger, my mother having unintentionally stumbled into parenthood well into her forties. But still I couldn't place her.

"Look, why don't we go up to my suite and have a drink?" Jordan tossed her napkin onto the table and began gathering up her things. "I'm dying to get out of these shoes. And what I want to talk to you about is . . . well, I'd rather discuss it in private."

Bitsy's words came back to me with a jolt. *She thinks someone murdered her mama.*

"Jordan, I'm not the one you should be discussing this with. If you seriously believe your mother . . ."

"Bay. Please." Her voice caught, and a look of naked vulnerability filled her dark green eyes. It reminded me of that day we'd gotten busted by Millie Adams, the guidance counselor, for smoking in the restroom. Jordan's usual teenage bravado had been reduced to quivering, childish fear as the call was placed to her father. And then to mine.

"Okay, sure," I capitulated, dropping my cigarettes into my bag, "but I need to be out of here by five."

"Got a hot date?"

I hoped I was imagining the hint of contempt in her tone.

"In a manner of speaking," I said airily, wondering not for the last time what the hell I was getting myself into.

We rose, and I trailed Jordan von Brandt out of the dining room. Nearly the same height, we must have made an interesting counterpoint, she in her mourning black, and I in virginal white. She walked with that sure, animal grace beautiful women seem to acquire. She looked straight ahead, totally ignoring the small cluster of tourists gathered in front of the elevators. The cold imperiousness was back. Money—and the power it inevitably conveys—radiated from her like heat off a woodstove. Maybe the others could feel it as well, and that was why they kept back, leaving an empty semicircle around the two of us.

We stepped off onto the top floor, and I followed her into the sunlit suite of rooms. The facing wall was entirely glass, and Atlantic rollers foamed on the wide beach far below. Off toward the horizon, a shrimp boat was hauling in its massive nets.

Jordan kicked off her shoes and shed her jacket as she headed for the bedroom. "Help yourself," she called, "everything's by the bar."

I opened the small refrigerator and finally managed to locate a can of Diet Coke shoved in behind bottles of French wine and champagne. I poured it over ice in a thin crystal glass and carried it out onto the balcony.

A few locals and some late-season tourists strolled the sand. Gulls wheeled in a cloudless sky, their mournful cries echoing off the pale stone walls of the high-rise hotel. Farther out, a flock of pelicans flew in precise formation, the lead bird scanning the ocean for the telltale silver flash of a school of fish. Just at that moment he banked and dived, and the others followed suit. They were too far away for me to tell if their run had been successful.

I turned at the sound of a cork popping and watched Jordan fill a tall flute with pale, foaming champagne. She had changed into cream-colored linen shorts and a shimmering copper silk tank. Even barefooted she managed to look chic and elegant. Bitsy was right. Living in Europe made people different. Not better necessarily, just different.

Jordan folded herself onto a white sofa in one of two groupings that didn't begin to fill the huge room. I pushed open the glass door and settled into the facing loveseat. We both got cigarettes going. Bitsy was right about that, too. Cutting down was definitely not working.

"Champagne?" Jordan topped off her own glass from the napkin-wrapped bottle on the table between us.

"No thanks, I'm fine."

"Iced tea for lunch, and now soda. I take it you don't drink?"

"Nope."

"Not at all? God, how do you survive?"

"I manage."

We sipped and smoked. Jordan played with the huge diamond, twisting it around on her finger in a gesture of nervousness now reflected on her face. I sneaked a look at my watch.

"I'm sorry," she said, "I know you have an appointment. It's just . . . now that it's come down to actually putting it into words, I feel a little foolish. You'll probably think I've lost my mind. Or turned into one of those neurotic, middle-aged women with too much money and too much idle time on their hands."

"Hey, watch it, girl. We're the same age, remember?"

The perfunctory smile didn't reach her eyes. She took a long swallow of champagne, and a little shiver shook her slender shoulders. Apparently I was going to have to get the conversation moving.

"Bitsy said you have some questions about your mother's death. Have you talked to the authorities in . . . Rio, was it?"

"Yes. I mean, yes, it was Rio de Janeiro, and yes, I have tried to talk with them. Unfortunately, Portuguese is not one of the languages I'm fluent in."

"Surely someone there must speak English. Did you try the U.S. Embassy?"

"Yes. Well, actually it was the consulate. The embassy's in Brasilia, the capital." I shrugged, and Jordan smiled, genuinely this time. "You were always better at math than geography, as I recall."

"So what did they say?"

" 'We believe the Rio police to be very competent, we really can't interfere in an internal process, so sorry', *blah, blah, blah.* The coroner, or whatever he's called in Brazil, ruled death by natural causes, the body was shipped back here for burial, end of story."

"So what makes you think otherwise?"

"Do you remember when my father was killed?"

The abrupt change of subject threw me, and for a moment I floundered around, not knowing how to respond. "No, actually, I don't," I finally managed. "I've been living mostly in Charleston until just recently. And what do you mean, *killed?*"

The hair tingled on the back of my neck, and the room seemed suddenly colder.

Jordan rose and carried her glass to the windows. For a long moment she stared unseeing at the ocean spread out before her. Then, without turning, she spoke, her voice tight with barely suppressed emotion. "It was an accident, they said. No other car involved. He'd been drinking, as usual. I was in Geneva then, right in the middle of my divorce. I couldn't come home. Klaus and his family were fighting me for custody of the girls, and I had to be there. I had to!"

Jordan gripped the stem of the crystal with such force I half-expected it to crack in her hand.

"I'm sure your mother understood."

"Saint Leslie? Hardly! Not attending your own father's funeral is considered a serious social gaffe in her circle. But she had her precious 'boys' with her, so it wasn't as if anyone really missed me."

I assumed Jordan meant her two brothers, the ones mentioned in the obituary. I had no recollection of either of them.

"I'm sorry, Jordan, but you've completely lost me." I was beginning to lean heavily toward the neurotic, middle-aged woman theory she had half-jokingly advanced.

"When I finally managed to get back to the States, there were rumors flying around Beaufort about some kind of cover-up surrounding the accident. Even Leslie was beginning to wonder if maybe there wasn't more to it than she'd been told. But nothing ever came of it, and eventually the talk died down. I've just never gotten over the feeling that there was something more to his death, something . . ."

She let the unfinished thought dangle there and sloshed more champagne into her glass. The neck of the bottle rattled against the rim of the delicate crystal.

"Okay," she said around a deep sigh, "Leslie. Three things. First, she had a checkup just before she left on her trip. I talked to her doctor in Natchez. Except for a minor cholesterol problem and slightly elevated blood pressure, she was in good health for a woman her age." Jordan had begun to pace, her brightly painted toenails flashing against the white of the thick pile carpet. "Second, I think there's some jewelry missing. All her effects were sent on to me, and several pieces weren't there. They were among her favorites, and I'm sure she wouldn't have traveled without them."

It sounded pretty lame to me, but then I was certainly no expert. Again I asked myself why she had chosen me as her sounding board.

"And third," she continued, pausing to reach behind the sofa, "there's this." Solemnly she handed me a white, rectangular dress box with a large, violet 'M' in flowing script with 'Rio Palace Hotel' printed beneath. "Open it, and tell me I'm wrong."

I placed the innocuous-looking package across my knees and studied Jordan Herrington von Brandt quizzically. Her face was flushed, and she was breathing heavily.

"Go on, open it!"

Gingerly I removed the lid. Tissue paper crackled as I peeled back the layers. And lifted out a black silk negligee, the fabric so fine, so transparent, it weighed almost nothing. Trimmed in soft lace, the garment whispered through my fingers.

"It's a nightgown. So what?" I'd had just about all of this farce I was going to take, and my annoyance rang clearly in my voice.

"Don't you see?" Jordan cried, her flailing arm sloshing French champagne across the expensive upholstery. "It's hers. It's Leslie's. And we both know there's only one reason a woman buys something like that. My mother . . ." She spat the word as if it were an obscenity. ". . . the woman who drove my father to one disgusting affair after another with her aloofness, her damned frigidity . . ." Jordan paused dramatically, and her eyes glittered with a cold hatred that made me shudder. "My oh-so-sainted mother picked the wrong man to shack up with, and it got her killed."

3

Of course I was late for the poker game. Being the epitome of Southern courtliness, my father and his cronies started without me.

By the time I got Jordan von Brandt calmed down, she had already gone through one entire bottle of Moët-Chandon and was well into the second. I left her slumped on the deep, white sofa while I dialed room service. The brawny young man who delivered the coffee and club sandwich eagerly accepted my scrawled forgery and a five-dollar tip.

Jordan was by then bordering on incoherent and wanted no part of trying to sober up. I am, however, not without experience in this area, and I soon had her upright enough for me to feel comfortable in leaving her alone.

I finally made my getaway amid slurred apologies and reassurances that I would call her the next day. I had no intention of keeping that promise. I could only hope that her alcohol-soaked brain would have forgotten all about it by then.

So it was close to eight o'clock by the time I skidded to a halt in the semi-circular driveway in front of my childhood home on St. Helena Island and trotted up the sixteen steps onto the wide verandah. *Presqu'isle*—so named by my Huguenot ancestors for its site on the peninsula of land that jutted out into Port Royal Sound—is a magnificent example of Lowcountry, antebellum architecture with its arched foundation of tabby and its square white columns supporting a hipped roof.

The interior was cool and dim. An elaborate air conditioning and humidity control system kept the temperature constant even in the steaming heat of the subtropical summers. My late mother had spared no expense when it came to safeguarding her collection of beloved art and antiques.

Lavinia Smalls, my parents' longtime housekeeper and the woman who had all but raised me, had apparently retreated to her suite on the second floor of the massive house. My sandals made little slapping sounds on the heart pine floor as I followed the smell of expensive cigar smoke and the ring of raucous laughter down the hallway to the Judge's study.

". . . so the hooker says . . ." Charlie Seldon stopped in mid-sentence as I paused in the doorway.

"Go ahead, Charlie, don't let me interrupt. So the hooker says . . . what?"

The former county solicitor blushed to the top of his bald head and ducked his face to his cards. "Nothin', Bay, honey. Really. It wasn't that good a story anyway."

"Where have you been? Nat had to go to his grandson's damn-fool birthday party so we're shorthanded to begin with."

The booming baritone that had swayed juries, then intimidated lesser attorneys after my father's elevation to the bench, still carried the ring of authority despite his wasted body. Looking at him now, his wheelchair pushed up to the round mahogany table, it was difficult to believe that he could no longer tower over me, the stern presence I remembered from my childhood. He still had a full head of snow-white hair, and his piercing gray eyes still commanded respect for a sharp intellect only partially dulled by time and illness.

"Hello, Father. Nice to see you, too. Gentlemen." I pulled out a chair, threw a twenty on the table, and picked up my chips. "So what's the game?"

"Straight poker, five-card draw." Lawton Merriweather, another attorney well past retirement age, but still practicing, dealt the hand. "It'll cost you the usual dollar to get in."

I lit a cigarette and anted up. Boyd Allison, the only one of the group not associated with the legal profession, pushed an ashtray in my direction. Boyd had founded Beaufort's first bookstore and had just recently—and reluctantly—passed the business on to his daughter and son-in-law.

"So answer the question," my father growled, tossing down three cards and studying the replacements Law dealt him. "Where have you been?"

Jordan hadn't specifically asked me to keep our discussion private, but still I hesitated. "I went shooting with Red," I hedged.

My father tossed a chip onto the pile and glared at me over the top of his reading glasses. "Two bucks," he said, glancing again at his cards. "That was this morning, and you walked out on him before you even got started. You in or out?"

So Red had reported back to the Judge. Apparently I was still on a short leash.

"Cards?" Law Merriweather interrupted.

"Nope, I'll play these." I threw in a couple of chips. "Your two and raise two. I also had lunch with Bitsy at the Westin."

Charlie, Boyd, and Law all folded, leaving the Judge and me to slug it out. Some things never changed.

"Must have been some lunch. That girl could flat-out talk the ears off an elephant. Never did have an *off* switch."

I bristled on behalf of my lifelong friend. "It wasn't Bitsy that held me up. You in or out?" I mimicked, and Charlie Seldon snickered.

The Judge flipped in his two-dollar chip and slapped his cards on the table. "Call. Two pair, aces and kings." He grinned and reached for the pot.

"Three deuces," I announced smugly and scooped the chips out from under his grasping hands.

"Damn it all," he muttered, "can't think why I ever taught you this damnedable game."

" 'Profanity is the last refuge of a limited vocabulary'," I quoted him, and he laughed.

" *Touché*. How did I ever manage to sire such a smart-alecky, disrespectful child?"

"Just lucky, I guess," Boyd Allison replied, grinning at me.

"So what—or who—did hold you up?" my father asked as we took a break to freshen drinks and replenish plates from the buffet Lavinia had set out on the sideboard. I could see he wasn't going to leave it alone.

"I spent some time with Jordan Herrington after lunch. She's in town for her mother's funeral. She's staying at the Westin."

"Jack T.'s girl?" Charlie asked as he juggled a plate piled high with rare roast beef, Lavinia's famous red-potato salad, and several cheese biscuits. "Wasn't that a shock about Leslie? I couldn't hardly believe it when I saw it in the *Gazette*."

All the men seated around the table had been contemporaries of the Herringtons, members of that moneyed elite who had been the movers and shakers in our little corner of coastal South Carolina. My parents, older and with a more aristocratic lineage, had been the leaders of the pack.

"Little Jordan sure fell into it and came out smellin' like a rose, didn't she?" Boyd sloshed Kentucky bourbon over the ice in his tumbler.

I had worked up a thirst for something cold and non-alcoholic, but I didn't want to leave the room to go get it. I knew this bunch well. Once the reminiscences started flowing, they would be impossible to stop. Here was a chance to get the scoop on Jordan's father's death. All I had to do was sit quietly and listen, and I would learn more than if I asked a thousand direct questions.

"Yup. Jack T. sent her over to Europe to get her away from that crowd she was runnin' with, and she ends up marryin' some duke and livin' in a castle."

"I believe it was a count," my father corrected Charlie. "Austrian, I think, or maybe German. Hard to imagine that wild little girl a countess. Divorced now, isn't she?"

"So I hear, but she got a pile of money out of the deal. Flies back and forth between Atlanta and Switzerland like we'd drive up to Charleston." Boyd Allison lit a cigar and blew smoke at the ceiling fan. "Can't say that Jack T. shouldn't have expected trouble out of her, though. Blood will tell. He was quite a heller in his day, if you recall."

"Didn't much change when he grew up, either," Charlie Seldon said with just a trace of malice. "If it hadn't been for ol' Sheriff McCray, he'd have spent a whole lotta nights sleepin' it off in the back room of the jailhouse."

I picked up the deck and absently shuffled the cards, fanning them out as the Judge had taught me.

"Yessir, the world has sadly changed." Law Merriweather exhaled and studied the glowing end of his contraband Cuban cigar. "Way the press is these days, there'd be no way Mike McCray coulda kept it out of the papers, the way Jack T. died. I still believe Leslie went to her grave never knowin' the truth of it. Leastways, I hope so."

The other three men murmured agreement and nodded sagely. I swiveled my head back and forth, waiting expectantly for one or the other of them to expound. When the smoky silence had finally stretched my patience to the breaking point, I slapped the cards down on the table. All four of them jumped.

"So is someone going to enlighten me here? What's the big mystery? I thought Jack T. died in a car wreck."

Four pairs of white-browed, faded eyes sought each other, glanced briefly at me, then slid away.

"You gonna deal those cards or just wear the spots off of 'em?"

I looked down to see my fingers unconsciously riffling the deck as the Judge's harsh words hung in the air.

"You gonna tell me what the hell the big deal is about Jack T.'s death?" I mimicked his sarcastic tone. "Seems to me if you four know all about it, it can't be much of a secret."

"I thought you might have learned your lesson in the past few weeks about stickin' your nose in where it doesn't belong."

Charlie, Boyd, and Law looked as taken aback as I was by the steel in the Judge's voice.

"Aw, come on, Tally," Boyd Allison began, "no call to be . . ."

"You boys stay out of it," the Judge snapped, "the subject is closed. Now deal the cards, daughter. We're here to play poker, not sit around gossipin' like a bunch of old Beaufort hens."

I glared at my father, unsure of whether to take up the challenge or let it drop. I had believed we were making our way back, he and I, to the superficial, but comfortable relationship we had carved out for ourselves since my mother's death. The fragility of it had become all too apparent during our confrontation on the verandah outside this very room just one short month ago.

This attack was unwarranted and unfair, and we both knew it.

But did I want to be right, or did I want to have peace? With my father there was never any middle ground.

I took my time lighting a cigarette. I set it in the ashtray, then picked up the cards.

"Seven-card stud," I announced, flipping cards expertly around the table. "Ante up."

There was a deep, general sigh of relief that female histrionics had been averted as the four septuagenarians tossed their chips into the center of the table. I pushed the mystery of Jack T. Herrington's death to the back of my mind with a brief flash of sympathy for Jordan. Could she possibly be right? Could *both* her parents have died under questionable circumstances? Was there a connection?

Maybe I would call her tomorrow after all, just to see how she was dealing with her hangover. Maybe we'd do lunch again. It was just possible her suspicions merited more consideration than the casual dismissal I'd given them this afternoon.

Or maybe I was losing *my* marbles, too.

At any rate, I turned my concentration to the game with a determination to clean all their clocks. It took me until well past midnight, but eventually I leaned back with a smirk of satisfaction on my face and every one of the poker chips in neat little color-coded piles in front of me.

I left them then to their post-game cigars and trudged wearily up the curved oak staircase to my old room. My last thought before drifting off was of who I could badger into telling me the truth about how Jack T. Herrington really died.

4

I took my time the next morning, letting Lavinia talk me into hot biscuits smothered in creamy sausage gravy before I got on the road. I made a mental note to swim an extra half-mile to make sure all those fat grams didn't get a chance to settle permanently onto my hips. Thanks to the intensive rehab needed to make my injured left shoulder function again, and my subsequent manic obsession with staying fit, I was in the best shape of my thirty-eight years. I intended to keep it that way.

As I negotiated the Broad River bridge, the outer islands shimmered in the distance under a cloudless sky. It was a magnificent fall day, the humidity having dropped overnight, and the temperature hovering in the mid-seventies. I loved my little corner of the Southeast coast. I had spent most of my college and graduate school days on the frigid shores of Lake Michigan where the advent of autumn brought brief, pleasant days along with a heightened awareness that they would give way all too soon to another brutally cold winter. Here, September glided into November with an audible sigh of relief for the departed tourists and joy in the jewel-like perfection of mornings like this one.

The soft wind whipping through my hair failed to blow away the confusion I felt about Jordan von Brandt. I still couldn't decide whether or not to contact her. As I sped along the two-lane black-top, I felt again the ambiguity her drunken accusations had aroused in me. A sexy negligee made pretty flimsy evidence—*Pardon the pun*, I chuckled to myself—that Leslie Herrington had been having an affair, let alone that it had led to her murder. On the other hand, my old college roommate, Neddie Halloran, would not have been so quick to scoff.

"Trust your instincts," she had told me when, all evidence to the contrary, I had been convinced that someone had been systematically searching my house. The fact that I had let logic override my gut feeling had nearly gotten both of us killed.

So why couldn't I bring myself to believe *Jordan's* gut feeling that her mother had not died a natural death?

My little Z3 crested the first of the two bridges that would carry us onto Hilton Head Island, and still I had no answer. The mud flats, exposed now at low tide, glistened wetly on both sides of the road. Their sweet, dank odor was the one I most closely associated with home. Blue and white herons, along with egrets and a few curlews, picked their way daintily among the tufts of marsh grass. Their long beaks poked and prodded, searching for any unfortunate shrimp, clams, or tadpoles left stranded by the tide shift.

Ten minutes later I cruised through the security gate in Port Royal Plantation, past the golf course, and into my driveway. The concrete apron in front of the garage was jammed with pickup trucks and vans festooned with ladders, and my heart sank.

Damn! They were supposed to be finished today. From the number of vehicles clogging my yard and the sharp whine of power tools making my teeth rattle, it was a pretty safe bet that wasn't going to be the case.

I pulled the Zeemer up onto the pine straw and strode toward my house, ready for battle. I stood at the foot of the steps leading up to the kitchen for what seemed like forever before someone finally realized I was there.

"Hey, Miz Tanner," he shouted over the screech of an electric saw, then touched its operator on the shoulder. "Knock it off for a sec, okay, Eddie? Go take a break."

The bronzed, muscled young man clicked off the saw, grabbed a battered thermos off the counter, and headed for the stairs out to the garage.

"What's going on here, Andy? I thought you were wrapping it up today."

Andy Petrocelli, the part-time paramedic who had ridden the ambulance on the night all this damage got done, grinned and shrugged expressively. The remodeling firm he and his brothers operated had been low bidder on the reconstruction of my shattered kitchen and the garage beneath it.

"You know how it goes," he said, "Murphy's law."

I turned, and he followed me out onto the open deck that wrapped around three sides of the house. I flopped down onto a cushioned chaise. Andy took the matching chair.

"So let's have it," I said as I lit a cigarette and lay back. "How much longer?"

"Well," he began, ticking the disasters off on his fingers as he named them, "the sink isn't the exact dimensions they said in the brochure, so we had to enlarge the opening in the counter. That's what Eddie was doing. The tile came in okay, but it's the wrong color. I was pretty sure lilac wasn't what you picked out, so I had to send it back. Doesn't really matter, though, 'cause the tile installers are hung up on a job out at Sun City. Then the humidity got to some of the sheetrock tape in the garage. The painters were pulling it off every time they ran a roller over it. So I sent them home and called the drywall guys, but . . ."

"I know, they're hung up on a job out at Sun City."

Andy grinned and spread his hands in a what're-ya-gonna-do gesture that made me smile along with him. I found it hard to be angry at those snapping black eyes and finely molded Italian cheekbones.

"Okay, I get the picture. Give me a date, can you? I'm going to have to scrounge someplace to stay until y'all get done."

"Oh, you don't have to do that, Miz Tanner. We're about finished here for today. Can't get too much outta the boys on a sunny Friday afternoon, ya know? We'll be back bright and early Monday mornin'. Everything goes according to plan, we should be outta here Wednesday, Thursday tops."

So, another week of sawdust and paint fumes, I thought as I walked Andy back into the house. I should have stayed at the Judge's. At least then I would have had Lavinia to feed me.

"Oh, I almost forgot." Andy Petrocelli stopped in the middle of the great room. "That came for you awhile ago." He pointed to a large, padded brown envelope on the glass-topped coffee table. "Lady dropped it off, said there was a letter inside explaining."

"Did she leave her name?"

"No, but she sure was a looker. I had to go pop the eyeballs back in on every guy workin' here."

"Tall, black hair cut really short?"

"That's the one." Andy whistled softly through his teeth. "Looked like someone outta one of those fashion magazines."

Jordan von Brandt, I thought. *Now what's this all about?*

"Came in one of the airport shuttles, said she'd be gone for a while. I hope it was okay. Taking the package in, I mean."

"Of course it was, Andy. Thanks."

I picked up the envelope, bulging with papers, and carried it into my office. I closed the door, shutting out the excited chatter of Andy's men packing it in for the day. The letter rested on top. Not surprisingly, Jordan's handwriting was bold and erratic. She rambled a lot, apologizing again for passing out on me yesterday, but the main gist of it was that she was on her way to Rio. She realized, she said, that she couldn't hope to convince me or anyone else of the validity of her theories without more proof. She had gone to get it.

Nuts, I thought, tossing the crested bond paper onto my desk, *the woman is nuts.*

Upending the envelope, I spilled the contents out in front of me. Jordan had instructed that I examine everything she had of her mother's papers. Maybe I could see something that Jordan had overlooked, some clue to her mother's death.

My first instinct was to say the hell with it, grab my swimsuit, and head for the beach. It was pretty damned presumptuous of her, dumping this mess on someone that, until yesterday, she hadn't laid eyes on for twenty-five years.

I picked Leslie Herrington's passport out of the jumble and idly riffled through it. Lots of entries, I noticed, most of the pages nearly filled up. This woman had been on the move. I checked the front cover, looking for the expiration date. The passport had another seven years to run, so all this traveling had been done in only three.

The small picture was, like most official photos, hardly flattering. Still, there was a look of Jordan about the smiling mouth and the arrogant tilt of the chin. Even in her late sixties, Leslie Herrington must have turned heads.

I flipped back to the exit and entry stamps. They were scattered, with no rhyme or reason to their placement. I remembered from my own limited overseas travel that harried immigration officials merely looked for a blank space on a page and slapped a stamp on it. If I wanted to bring any order out of her trips, I would have to record each one separately, then sort them out according to date. I could build a database on the computer, let those wonderful little chips do most of the work.

I slipped off my sandals and rummaged in the pocket of my dress for a cigarette. My finger hung poised over the ON button of the terminal when I brought myself up short with a laugh.

Okay, Tanner, admit it. You're hooked. So much for 'who the hell does she think she is'.

The passport had piqued my curiosity, and I knew I would eventually plow through every single piece of paper in the pile.

But not right now, I decided, pushing back from the desk and stepping out of my dress. First things first. I had about 150 fat grams of sausage gravy to work off. I crossed to the bedroom, pulled on one of my specially designed swimsuits and an old, sloppy T-shirt and trotted down the short path to the beach.

No use wasting this gorgeous weather, I rationalized, plunging into the still-lukewarm surf. *After all, tomorrow is another day,* the ever-present Scarlett whispered in my ear as I stroked out into the Atlantic.

Sergeant Red Tanner lay sprawled on the chaise as I mounted the steps up to my deck. The bill of his Atlanta Braves baseball cap rested on his nose, and soft snores bubbled from his slightly open mouth. In tattered, cutoff Levi's and a faded, olive drab T-shirt with the Marine Corps insignia nearly worn off, he was the picture of my dead husband, his older brother. Even the shape of his long, bony feet was the same, the second toes about a quarter-inch longer than the big ones. I slipped past him and through the French doors into my bedroom.

When he finally woke himself up with a particularly noisy snort, he found me stretched out across from him in a nearly identical getup, my damp hair just beginning to dry in the late afternoon breeze.

"Hi," he said, wiping the sleep from his face in an all-too-familiar gesture. "How long you been sittin' there?"

"How long you been catnapping on my porch?" I countered and held out a cold beer.

"Thanks." Red drained about a third of it in one long pull. "That hit the spot. Since when'd you take to keepin' beer in the house?"

"I stocked up when they started working on the remodeling. I thought maybe a little liquid reward at the end of the day might spur the boys on to greater effort."

"Obviously you were in grievous error." Red grinned and cocked his head toward the chaos of the kitchen.

"So, what can I do for you?"

I realized how abrupt that sounded the minute it was out of my mouth, but Red's resemblance to Rob tended to unnerve me, especially since he had made plain his feelings for me. Not in words, I don't mean that. He respected his brother's memory—and me, too, I hoped—too much to be pushy about it. But I knew, the way any woman over the age of thirteen knows, that all it would take was the slightest encouragement from me and our relationship would be kicked up several notches on the intimacy scale.

With a sigh, Red reached under the chaise and slid out a black nylon zippered bag. "Here," he said, holding it out to me.

"What's that?"

"Your weapon. You left it at the shooting range yesterday morning."

"*My* weapon? I don't think so."

"Sure is. The Judge got it for you. Well, he paid for it anyway. Even took care of the permit. It's right inside. You need to have it on you whenever you're carrying."

I fastened on the least offensive part of their incredible presumption. "And just how did my father get me a carry permit? I've only fired the damn gun a total of three times."

His eloquent shrug spoke silently of power, connections, and influence undimmed by age or infirmity. The Judge still had it.

"Well, I'm not keeping it, so you can just go get the big man his money back."

"Hey, come on. You know why he's doing this. He'll sleep a lot better knowin' you've got a way to defend yourself. Tell the truth," he went on as I squirmed in my seat and lit a cigarette, "wasn't there a point back there when you wished you had a gun and had been trained how to use it?"

He was dead on, of course, and we both knew it. It didn't make my father's interference any more palatable.

"Okay, I'll keep the damn thing. But I'm locking it up, and that's where it'll stay. You can't make me carry it, either one of you."

"Fine. It's all cleaned and ready to go. All you have to do is slap in the clip and release the safety." Red looked so pleased with himself I had to smile in return. A little of the tension seeped out of the air.

"Did you include a warning label?" I asked as Red downed the rest of his beer.

"A what?"

"A warning label. You know, like on cigarettes. Something like, 'Caution! Confronting this woman could be hazardous to your knees!'"

Red's laugh was out of all proportion to my little joke, but it had served its purpose. We seemed to be back to our old, comfortable relationship.

"Cute, Tanner, real cute. Hey, you hungry?"

"Yeah, actually, I am. What'd you have in mind?"

"Want to run down to the Shack?" Red checked his watch. "The boats oughta be in by now. We could shuck a few oysters, peel a few shrimp."

"Sounds great. Just let me change and put this thing away." I picked up the gun case, gingerly, between two fingers.

"It's not a snake, Tanner. It won't bite you."

I ignored him and carried the weapon into the bedroom. Despite my joking, I had been perfectly serious about refusing to have a gun. I needed no reminders of my own close brushes with death, but running around armed to the teeth was not my answer. I worked the dial on the concealed floor safe in my walk-in closet and slid the bag in beside the sheaf of stolen papers I thought of now as my insurance policy. Once I figured out how to get them unobtrusively to a more secure hiding place as I had threatened to do, I felt reasonably sure my enemies would see the wisdom of leaving me alone. Carrying a gun would become unnecessary.

At least that was my plan.

The Shack, a dilapidated frame hut at the foot of the Skull Creek docks, looked precisely like its name. A scarred wooden bar ran along two sides of the dim interior. Four tall, round tables were jammed into the remaining space. Mismatched bar stools completed the ambiance.

Most of the cooking was done outside in huge kettles fashioned from whittled-down oil drums over an open fire. The town fathers had been trying—at least publicly—to shut the place down for years, citing health, safety, and sanitation ordinances. Privately, most of them were regular customers.

Several familiar faces hailed us as we walked into the steamy bar. No air conditioning here. If the ceiling fans and windows open to the breeze off the water didn't cool you off, then you just had to sweat.

"Cheese it, the cops!" The booming bass of the Shack's proprietor rattled the flimsy walls with his customary greeting to Red.

"Hey, Bubba, how's it goin'?"

We snagged the one empty table and climbed up onto the high stools as Damon "Bubba" Mitchell lumbered over to us. A standout defensive tackle for the old Cleveland Browns, he had been felled by a chop block that destroyed his knee and his career one

snowy November afternoon ten years before. Since then, the
bull-necked giant had been running the family fishing and shrimp-
ing business his granddaddy had started right after the war. Long
before there was a bridge out to Hilton Head, in the days when a
white face was as rare as a hump-backed whale in these waters, Mit-
chells had been netting a living from the sea.

Bubba wiped his huge, black hands on a stained, gray apron that
barely spanned his middle and favored us with a rare grin. "How
you been keepin', Bay? Seems like dog's years."

Rob and I had been Friday night regulars, the Shack one of our
first stops after traveling down from Charleston for weekends at
the beach house. After Rob's murder, my self-imposed seclusion
had kept me from even this haven of old friends and wonderful
food.

"Around," I answered noncommittally, thankful when Bubba
let it go at that.

"So, what'll it be, Sarge?" he asked.

Red ordered a dozen oysters and a couple dozen shrimp.
Dwight, Bubba's equally mammoth brother, brought a frosty draft
for Red and set a Diet Coke in front of me. Then he dropped a battered metal pail into the ragged hole cut in the center of the table.

"So where'd you run off to yesterday morning?" Red took my
lighter and touched the flame to my cigarette.

"I had a lunch date with Bitsy. Didn't the Judge fill you in when
you called him to report my going AWOL?"

Red's smile was unrepentant. "He just likes to be kept abreast of
local happenings."

"Right. Anyway, we ran into Jordan Herrington. Well, von
Brandt, now. Do you remember them at all?"

It had suddenly occurred to me that I was sitting across from a
probable source for the details about Jack T. Herrington's mysterious car crash.

"I used to see the old man around town. He was some sort of
wheel in local politics, wasn't he?"

"Never elected to anything that I recall. But I'm sure he was one
of the 'boys' who kept the wheels greased."

"One of the Judge's pals, huh?"

Dwight Mitchell loomed up between us and slapped a bucket of oysters and a steaming plate of jumbo shrimp onto the table. A stack of paper napkins followed, along with a shuckin' knife, a bowl of sizzling melted butter, and another of Bubba's world-famous red cocktail sauce. I remembered that sauce well. It had enough horseradish in it to take your breath away. Rumor had it you could also use it to strip varnish off old furniture.

"The boys were talking about Jack T. last night at the poker game," I said as I peeled the shell off a shrimp. "They seemed to be hinting there was something fishy about his accident. You remember anything like that?"

Red expertly pried apart an oyster, flipped the top shell into the metal pail, and loosened the meat in the bottom one. With a deft twist of the short-bladed knife, he popped the oyster out into the butter. While fingers are definitely acceptable utensils at the Shack, Red used a fork to spear the little delicacy and carry it, dripping, to his mouth.

"So, do you?" I pressed, drowning my shrimp in the butter. In deference to my vocal cords, I avoided the red sauce.

"Do I what?"

"Remember anything screwy about the accident that killed Jack T.?"

"I don't think so. That was what, six, seven years ago? I was just a rookie then. All's I recall, he ran off the road on his way back from some meeting or other. Late, like maybe two, three in the morning. Probably fell asleep. Put 'er nose down in the river, and that was that. You want one of these?"

Red held the shucked oyster out toward me, and I wrinkled my nose.

"No, thanks. I don't like them."

"You don't like oysters? I think that must be illegal in this county. I may have to run you in."

"Was there anyone else with him in the car?"

"Hey, what's with the third degree?" Red's eyes narrowed suspiciously. "What are you up to?"

I shrugged nonchalantly and popped another shrimp into my mouth.

"Bull," he said, "I know that look. Your nose is twitching, and you're about to stick it in someplace where it doesn't belong. Haven't you learned your lesson?"

His question echoed the Judge's of last night. Both of them should have known me well enough by now to answer it for themselves.

But Red stood his ground, so I told him the whole story. Of Jordan von Brandt's conviction that her mother had been murdered, of the Judge and his cronies' thinly veiled hints about her father's death, of my own peripheral involvement at Jordan's request. Red scowled through the whole recitation as oyster and shrimp shells rattled into the pail, and the pile of wadded-up paper napkins grew on the table.

"The lady is obviously paranoid," he pronounced as I concluded with a request to see the police report on Jack T. Herrington's accident, "and you're just as nuts as she is. Even if it were still around after all these years, you know I couldn't let you see it. It's not public information. My advice—not that you'll likely take it—is to put as many miles between you and this bimbo as possible, and mind your own business."

I let it drop then, and we finished our meal in relative peace. Dusk had fallen by the time we argued over the check and wandered back up the dock.

"Could you at least get me the exact date?" I asked as we stood beside our cars in the gravel parking lot. A spectacular, fiery orange sunset, diffused through high, thin clouds over the mainland, reflected off the smooth waters of Skull Creek. "I could go blind trying to find the story in the paper without a date."

The county library had all the back issues of the local newspapers on microfilm, but they hadn't been indexed since the first Roosevelt administration.

"Why can't you just leave it alone?" Red asked, his voice plaintive now rather than angry. "Why do you want to get mixed up in this crazy woman's fantasies?"

There was no point in trying to explain it to Red when I really didn't understand it myself. Maybe it came from having been a victim of violence, of having stood by helplessly while my husband's body was blown to pieces in front of my eyes. I just felt that, if Jordan were anywhere near the truth, I had to help her find it. Maybe her father's death had nothing to with her mother's. Maybe his had just been a drunken accident; hers, a heart at last given out. I didn't know. And, damn it, I wanted to.

"No, Bay, I won't help you. I'm sorry, but I think you're way off base here. Please just leave this alone. I don't want you in any more danger. Haven't you had enough of death?"

Of course! That was it!

"Do you have a flashlight I can borrow?" I ignored Red's pleading eyes, the hand that halted near my cheek, checking what might have been the start of a tender caress.

"Jesus, I give up!" he snapped, reaching into the restored Ford Bronco that was his pride and joy. "Here." He shoved a battered old Eveready at me and climbed behind the wheel. "I don't know what you're up to, but for God's sake be careful. I have to get to work."

"Thanks!" I called to his retreating taillights. I hopped into the Zeemer and let down the top. It was a beautiful night for a drive, not to mention a leisurely stroll through a cemetery.

I didn't need Red's help to find out when Jack T. Herrington had died.

It would be on his tombstone.

5

It took me longer to find a way into the cemetery than it did to locate the grave. The ornate, wrought iron gates were secured with a rusty padlock that, despite its age, didn't budge when I tugged on it. I was forced to walk the perimeter until I stumbled—literally—into a gap in the wire fence. The thin mesh had been flattened, probably by a foraging deer. I brushed off my knees and followed the flashlight beam across the uneven ground.

It was an old cemetery, many of the tilting stones predating the Civil War. Had I stopped to examine them, I would have recognized most of the names synonymous with our Lowcountry history: Fripps and Jenkinses and Chaplins, cotton planters and farmers, forever covered by the dirt of the land their descendants had abandoned after the Union Navy won the Battle of Port Royal in 1861. The hated, blue-clad troops had continued to occupy their beloved Sea Islands until the end of that bloody conflict four years later.

I skirted a crumbling brick mausoleum, its tenants long since removed to more stable surroundings. Up ahead, the pale light of a half moon sparkled off the pearl-white marble wings of an angel standing watch over the long-dead Cooper twins. I'd wandered here as a child, drawn invariably to the serene guardian that towered over the tiny graves. "Annabelle and Abigail Cooper", the marker read, "Too sweet for this Earth, Called home to their Father, On the Day of their Birth. Rest in peace, our little lambs".

The plot was always perfectly tended, no blemish permitted to mar the pristine sculpture. Even now, some ninety years after their deaths, I had to blink back tears.

The raw mound of turned earth heaped with wilted flowers rose starkly in the next row. Leslie Mayne Herrington had been laid beside her husband, her date on the dual headstone not yet chiseled in. His read "Aug 27, 1994".

I stood there a moment, debating with myself whether or not to move the few steps over to where my mother's impressive monument loomed in the darkness. Honesty won out over hypocrisy, and I turned back toward the fence.

The screech of a barn owl shattered the stillness. Startled, I quickened my pace. Far out on the river, a horn sounded, the running lights of the big cruiser seeming to float on the pine-scented air. By the time I reached the car, an intense quiet had settled back over the night.

Brown twigs of pine straw and some brittle, yellow sycamore leaves had drifted onto the seat of my convertible where it rested just off the highway. I was reaching down to retrieve them when the spotlight hit me. I froze, like a rabbit in the road.

"Stay where you are! Hands out where I can see them!"

The voice, amplified by the speakers on the roof of the sheriff's car, reverberated off the trees and bounced back, surrounding me.

"Red, damn it! That wasn't funny!" I yelled, stepping out of the glare. "Turn that damn thing off!"

"I said, stay where you are, ma'am. Both hands on the trunk. Now."

The deputy who unfolded himself from the cruiser, one hand resting lightly on the butt of his sidearm, was shorter and thinner and much too young to be Red. I spread my palms on the Zeemer and prepared to backpedal.

"Sorry, officer," I said meekly as he approached the front of the car, "I thought you were someone else. Sergeant Tanner. Red Tanner. Maybe you know him? He's my brother-in-law."

I tried out my best *aw-shucks-I-feel-like-an-idiot* grin on him and got stony silence in response. The deputy pulled a long, silver flashlight from his belt and played it over the car.

"I need to see some identification, ma'am," he demanded, directing the beam at my face.

I put up my arm to shield my eyes, and he barked, "Hands back on the car!"

As I slapped my palms back onto the trunk, fear was fast giving way to anger. I tried to keep it out of my voice. "What's the problem here, officer? Am I blocking traffic or something? I was just leaving."

Over his shoulder I caught the flashing blue lights of another cruiser approaching fast in the opposite lane.

My God, did he call for reinforcements? I wondered, and the fear was back. My baby-faced deputy had just picked up my bag from the front seat when his backup wheeled off the road in a spray of gravel and pulled up in front of us. This time it *was* Red Tanner who eased slowly out, stretching as he tucked his nightstick into his wide leather belt. I could see the gleam of his grin from twenty feet away.

"Evenin', Tommy," he drawled, taking his own sweet time ambling up to us. "What seems to be the problem?"

I stood then, wiping my sweaty palms on the seat of my pants.

"Got a call, Sarge, a few minutes ago, 'bout lights in the cemetery. Found this lady here rummaging in this open car. I was just checkin' it out when you come up."

"You can just put that bag back on the seat where you found it, sonny, unless you've got a search warrant," I snapped, proud of how steady my voice sounded now that Red stood by to back me up.

"Knock it off, Bay. Okay, Tommy, I'll take it from here. You get back on the road." Red clapped the smaller deputy on the shoulder and gently steered him towards his cruiser.

I snatched up my tote bag and fumbled for a cigarette. I was exhaling deep, satisfying clouds of smoke when Red waved his colleague off and sauntered back in my direction, shaking his head.

"Don't even start on me, Tanner. I wasn't doing a damn thing to warrant getting shaken down by some gung-ho rookie looking to boost his ticket count."

"Tommy's okay. Maybe a little over-zealous at times, but he'll learn. You shouldn't have threatened him."

"*Me?* I wasn't the one swaggering around with my hand fondling my gun like some redneck Wyatt Earp," I spluttered. "And how did you get here so fast? He didn't even know my name, let alone have time to call it in."

Red laughed and leaned his long torso against the side of my car. "Minute I heard the squawk over the radio about a light in the cemetery, I put two and two together and came up with Bay Tanner and my borrowed flashlight. Find out Herrington's date of death, did you?"

I crushed the cigarette out under my sandal and swung open the car door. "You're not as dumb as you look, Sarge," I grinned. "Keep this up, and you'll make detective before you know it."

Red shut the door as I cranked the engine to life. "Listen, I know you don't want to hear this, but you need to stop doing fool things like this," he said. "On the off chance that somebody's still got an interest in you, you're makin' it awful damn easy for them to get to you."

"Relax, Tanner, nobody's looking for me. And, even if they were, I'm through hiding out. I'm not going to live the rest of my life like that."

Red raised his hands in mock surrender as I eased the car off the grass verge. "Thanks for the rescue, anyway," I called and pulled out on the highway.

I was pretty sure the headlights that stayed in my rearview mirror until I turned into the Port Royal entrance gate were Red's.

The story had made headlines in *The Beaufort Gazette* and remained on the front page for several days thereafter. The obituary itself covered two columns. All of Jack T. Herrington's philanthropic and civic contributions along with his business successes made for impressive reading.

What the story lacked were details. The initial account of the accident was sketchy, understandably so since the paper went to press in the wee hours for early morning delivery. Still, subsequent articles proved no more enlightening. Law Merriweather's assessment had been accurate: if there were any dirt or scandal attached to Jack T.'s death, it had been swept neatly under the carpet by the influence of his high-placed friends.

With no way to generate copies from the antiquated microfilm reader, I had to content myself with my own scribbled notes.

Stripped of all the fulsome praise and lamentations over a good life cut short, however, the remaining facts were few and far from helpful. If I were going to find the truth behind Jordan's father's death, I was going to have to pry it out of the people who had helped conceal it at the time: the Judge and his poker-playing pals.

I emerged from the quiet dimness of the library into the bustling brightness of downtown Beaufort on a Saturday afternoon. Mothers balancing shopping bags and the sweaty hands of whining toddlers moved briskly about their errands. Tourists wandered aimlessly, their attention occasionally caught by a gallery's clever window display.

Two blocks over, the historic district slumbered in the mid-September sunshine. The stately antebellum homes—most privately owned, a few converted to bed-and-breakfast inns—rested majestically on high, arched foundations, their wide verandahs across two- and three-storied facades angled to catch the breeze off the Beaufort River. One hundred and fifty years ago, they had been the treasured summer retreats of wealthy planters anxious to remove their families from the deadly miasmas of their swampy Sea Island homes. Today, restored and modernized under the watchful eye of the Historical Society, they seemed indifferent to the hordes of curious who trooped their streets, littered their yards, and snapped endless photos in front of their pineapple-topped gates.

I stepped back to allow a couple pushing a stroller to edge by me on the narrow sidewalk. I was wavering, undecided whether to drive on out to St. Helena Island and confront my father or head back to Hilton Head and forget the whole thing. The beach would be deserted this late in the season. I could probably risk sunbathing in one of my old bikinis. No pitying stares or quickly averted glances at the scars that crisscrossed my back and shoulder. The plastic surgeons had done the best they could repairing the mangled tissue and skin shredded by burning debris. There would be no more operations. I would just have to live with the results.

A low rumbling in my stomach decided the question for me as I checked my watch. At a little after one, most of the crowds would be gone from the Fig Tree. I opted for lunch.

I plunked two more quarters in the parking meter and strolled down Carteret, turning right on Bay Street at the foot of the bridge. The front door of the Fig Tree opened almost directly into the low-ceilinged bar. I paused to let my eyes adjust to the sudden darkness.

"Hey, Lydia!" a raspy, disembodied voice called from out of the gloom, and I cringed at the use of my despised first name. Gilly Falconer materialized at my elbow, her long, gray-streaked black braid swinging jauntily across her back. About 5' 1" and thickset, with the *café-au-lait* skin that proclaimed her mixed heritage, the sixty-something dynamo had been a fixture at the local hangout for as long as I could remember.

"Where you been keepin'?" she asked as she led the way through the smoky bar and out onto an awninged deck. Slapping a plastic-coated menu on the table, Gilly pulled out a chair and plopped down opposite me.

"Around," I answered for the second time in as many days. I touched the flame of my lighter to a cigarette. "You?"

"Hell, where else would I be but here?" Gilly Falconer had been drawing beer and keeping order at the Fig Tree since she was old enough to step legally through its doors. "Lemme see that lighter."

I handed over the plastic disposable as she pulled a long, black cheroot from the pocket of her stained smock. "Them Herrington boys ever catch up with you?" Gilly asked, exhaling a stream of foul-smelling smoke.

"Herrington boys? No. I talked with Jordan yesterday, but she's left town already. What's this all about? I didn't even remember that she *had* brothers until I saw it in the paper. What would they want with me?"

"No clue. All's I know is, Cissy Ransome over to the bookstore come in for lunch today and said them two'd been in there, lookin' for you. Said you wasn't to home, nor at your daddy's place neither. Seemed real hot to track you down, or so Cissy said."

Cecilia "Cissy" Ransome, Boyd Allison's daughter, and her husband, Quinn, had both been born and reared in Beaufort. Between them, they probably knew everyone in town. The East Bay Book

Emporium, with its back-room coffee bar reserved for locals only, had been a Lowcountry gathering place for more than fifty years.

Gilly Falconer stubbed out her cigar in the pink plastic ashtray. "So, you eatin' or what?"

"Wait a minute. Why were the Herringtons looking for me? What else did Cissy say?"

"Nothin', just what I tol' you. You could go ask her, but I think she's closed up for the day. What're you havin'?"

"Okay, give me a couple of crab cakes and a small Caesar salad. And iced . . ."

"Tea. Lord, don't I know? Ain't no liquor gonna pass the lips of Miz Lydia Baynard Simpson."

"Tanner," I added. Gilly knew my name as well as I did. "And quit calling me 'Lydia', will you? You're the only one who still does it, except for the Judge or Lavinia when one of them is ticked at me."

"I don't like your nickname, honey. Never did. *Bay.* Sounds like some la-di-dah eastern snob. Ain't the name your mama gave ya."

"Well, does anyone call you Virgilia?" I countered.

"Not and live to do it again," Gilly tossed over her shoulder as she disappeared inside.

6

It didn't take long to find out what the Herrington brothers wanted from me.

When I pulled up to the security gate later that afternoon, the duty officer, instead of waving me through, stepped out of the gatehouse and flagged me down.

"Hey, Mrs. Tanner, how's it goin'?" he asked, leaning down to my low-slung car.

"Fine, Jim, just fine, thanks. What's the problem?"

"Two fellas here lookin' for you a while ago. Got real nasty when I wouldn't give 'em a pass. Told me to give this to you when you came in. Said they'd wait for you up at the Westin."

The hotel could be reached by taking the road just before the checkpoint.

"Thanks, Jim," I said as he handed me one of the temporary paper passes, folded in half. "Sorry if they gave you any trouble."

"Nothin' I ain't seen before," he answered with a grin and touched his finger to his cap.

I made a sweeping U-turn and headed back toward the hotel access road. Pulling off onto the grass verge, I opened the scribbled note. *Imperative that we speak with you immediately re: Jordan. Will wait in the bar at the Westin.* It was signed "John T. Herrington III".

I wadded the paper up and tossed it into the seat beside me. It seemed all the Herringtons had inherited the family arrogance. I was getting just a little tired of one or the other of them ordering me around. The roar of the Zeemer's compact, but powerful engine reverberated off the walls of the short tunnel under the overpass as I whipped the car around the tight turns and squealed to a halt in the hotel parking lot.

The Westin bar is dark, with the deep glow of burnished mahogany reflecting the soft light of green-shaded lamps. The atmosphere is at once elegant and homey. A couple—both blonde, both

52

in T-shirts and tennis shorts—perched on high stools, chatting with the young woman behind the bar. All three turned as I hesitated in the doorway, scanning the dim recesses of the spacious room.

"Help you?" the bartender asked.

"Yes, I'm looking for two gentlemen I was supposed to meet here."

"Is one of them a tall, dark hunk? Looks sort of like Pierce Brosnan?"

"I haven't a clue," I answered truthfully. It wouldn't surprise me if Jordan's brothers were as attractive as she, but I wouldn't know them if I fell over them.

"Back wall, last booth," she said, jerking her thumb over one shoulder.

"Thanks."

"Lucky you," the bartender added with a wicked grin, and the blond couple snickered.

I ignored them and wove my way through tightly packed empty tables to a row of raised banquettes covered in dark red leather.

John T. Herrington, III lounged gracefully against the gleaming upholstery as if posing for a magazine ad for some outrageously expensive men's cologne. I don't know why I was certain which one he was. I suppose something about his poise, and the casual, trendy clothes just said *California.* As I approached, I saw that he owned his sister's best features molded into masculine form, down to the black widow's peak and exotic, almond-shaped eyes. His were a different green, paler and less direct. The touch of silver at his temples could have been artificial, but I didn't think so.

All I could see of his brother was the back of his head, a pronounced bald spot right at the crown where it rested against the back of the booth.

"Mr. Herrington?" I asked from about five feet away when it became apparent that the suave, James Bond look-alike was not going to acknowledge me.

John T. Herrington, III made no effort to rise. The banquettes sat high off the floor, so, seated, his strange, opaque eyes were almost at direct level with my own. Our gaze held: his languid and assessing, and mine turning from initial anger at his rudeness to a confusion touched with an unexpected flicker of fear.

The word *dangerous* flashed through my mind.

Then his brother broke the spell by leaping to his feet, hand extended. "Bay Simpson! Hi! You probably don't remember me, but I'm Justin, Jordan's brother? And this is Trey. We really appreciate your coming."

Justin Herrington was short and bluff, and he pumped my hand as if he were trying to coax water from a dry well. His broad, open smile crinkled his chubby cheeks. He couldn't have looked less like his older brother. "Please, join us," he said, sliding over on the bench to make room for me.

Trey had still not spoken.

I set my bag next to Justin, stepped up, and sat down, tentatively, on the edge of the seat. I couldn't have said why, but I felt the need to be ready for flight.

"What would you like to drink?" Justin Herrington said into the awkward silence. "We're having wine. It's a quite respectable Merlot, for domestic. Here, let me pour you a glass."

"No, thanks, really. I don't care for anything."

"Sure? Maybe you'd prefer a cocktail. Let me get the bartender for you. Miss?" he called, twisting around in his seat. "Miss?"

"Shut up, Justin, for God's sake. You're making an ass of yourself. This isn't a social occasion." Despite the stinging words, Trey Herrington's voice was low and well modulated. As with his sister, no trace of his native Southern accent remained. In fact, his precise diction sounded almost British.

Justin's blush turned his round face a mottled pink, and I squirmed in embarrassment for him. I hid my discomfort by lighting a cigarette. I didn't bother to ask if anyone minded. Frankly, I didn't really give a damn.

"What did you want to see me about?" I asked, looking pointedly at my watch. "I have another appointment."

"Well then, we're honored that you could squeeze us into your busy schedule." Trey's sarcasm was as childish as it was baffling.

"God, Trey . . ." Justin began, but I cut him off.

"No, that's fine. Cards on the table. I prefer it that way. Have your say, Mr. Herrington, and make it quick. You've got three minutes."

"It's about Jordan. We're very . . . worried about her." Justin Herrington spoke hesitantly, his soft voice full of what sounded to me like genuine concern.

"I'll handle this," his brother interrupted. "Look, we know you spent a lot of time with our sister day before yesterday." He leaned in, narrowing the distance between us, his opaque eyes locked on mine. I stared right back. "We also know you discussed this hare-brained notion of hers about our mother having been murdered. Now we find out that Jordan's left the country on some kind of wild goose chase to prove her theory."

If Trey Herrington thought his unwavering gaze and rapid-fire delivery would intimidate me, he was sadly mistaken. I'd done battle with countless IRS agents in the course of my years as an accountant and financial advisor. Compared to them, this guy was a rank amateur.

"Tell me something I don't already know, Mr. Herrington, and make it soon." Again I consulted my watch. "You've already wasted one of your minutes."

"You tell me something I don't already know, *Ms.* Tanner," he snapped back, any pretense of courtesy now completely gone from his tone. "What's in this for you? Is Jordan paying you for this half-assed advice? Looking for a cut of the action? My sister is already a very wealthy woman, and she always was a fool with her money. It wouldn't be the first time some slick operator had . . ."

I slammed my cigarette into the glass ashtray on the table between us, spraying a cloud of ashes that caught him right in the face. By the time a spluttering Trey Herrington had recovered from the shock, I had slung my bag over my arm and was halfway across the room. The bartender raised an inquisitive eyebrow as I stomped past her and flung open the door to the lobby.

Justin caught up with me in the parking lot. I heard him wheezing behind me as his short legs pumped with the effort to catch up to my angry stride.

"Bay, wait!" he puffed as I yanked open the door of the Zeemer. "Wait! Please!"

"What?" I barked, my attempt to get control of my temper a total failure.

"Look, I'm sorry about Trey. My brother is . . ."

"An arrogant bastard," I finished for him, tossing my bag into the seat.

"Exactly." Justin's lopsided grin made him look like a chubby schoolboy, the effect enhanced by his having to squint up at me from his five feet four inches. "Always has been, actually."

I expelled a long breath, and, with it, a lot of my anger. I smiled back, unable to resist his open, ingenuous face.

"So how did you escape the family curse?" I asked, and Justin laughed.

"Well, look at me. I mean, it's hard to be too overbearing when you're the resident midget, right? The Herrington changeling, that's me."

I marveled at this deprecating little speech delivered with good humor and not a trace of self-pity. You have to admire someone who, surrounded by stunningly attractive siblings, can still laugh at himself.

I could like this man, I thought.

His expression sobered as we both leaned against the side of my car. "Listen, about Jordan. We really are concerned. Oh, not about you, of course. I don't know where Trey got that screwy idea from, but it's just nonsense."

"Thanks," I said, unable to keep a trace of sarcasm from sneaking into my voice.

"You see, Jordan has a history of this sort of thing. Running off half-cocked without thinking things through. All we really wanted to know is if you have any idea what she's up to. She left us a very cryptic note at the hotel saying she was off to Rio and that you were helping her. That's why we wanted to talk to you, see if you could shed some light. That's all."

I reached back for my cigarettes and got one going. "Then what was all that crap about 'slick operators'?" I asked. "Why would your brother think my interest had anything to do with Jordan's money?"

"Trey thinks *everything* has to do with money," Justin replied, "probably because he never seems to have any." He correctly interpreted my look of skepticism and hurried on. "Trey's an actor. Not a very good one, I understand, but he has the looks. He also writes screenplays. In L.A. He's always mounting some avant-garde production, some experimental film project or other. He hasn't been wildly successful at that, either. Our parents were always having to bail him out."

"What kind of productions?" I asked, intrigued in spite of myself. *Hollywood.* Who can resist its lure? "Anything I might have heard of?"

"I doubt it. I seem to remember something about a rap version of *Hamlet* a while back."

"You're kidding!" I spluttered, and he grinned widely.

"Yeah, actually, I am. Seriously, though, I don't really keep up with all that artsy stuff. My wife, Diane, is the refined one in our family. She's always dragging me and the kids off to museums and gallery openings and the ballet."

"How many kids do you have?"

"Three. Two girls and a boy. I won't bore you with pictures, though thank God they take after their mother. Besides they're all teenagers now. Can't get 'em to sit still long enough for family portraits."

"And what do you do?" I asked, warming more and more to him the longer we talked.

"Investment counseling. Boring, huh? Mostly I work for Diane's family. They're oil," he added, as if that explained everything. I remembered then the last few lines of his mother's obituary: Justin lived in Dallas.

The sun had slid behind the loblolly pines, bringing an onshore breeze redolent with the sharp smell of the ocean. I reached in and crushed out my cigarette in the ashtray of the convertible.

"Well, Justin, I've enjoyed talking to you. I wish I could help you with Jordan, but I don't know any more about her motives than you do. As long as she can afford to indulge her whims and doesn't get herself into any serious trouble, I think you just have to back off and leave her alone. Maybe this is her way of dealing with her grief."

"I kind of doubt that," he said, a cloud passing over his previously open countenance. "None of us had the best of relationships with Leslie."

"I'm sorry."

"It happens." Justin shrugged and shoved his hands into the pockets of his rumpled Dockers. "Look, if you hear from Jordan, will you let me know? Tell her we need her back here so we can settle the estate. It's a bit tangled, and there's lots of decisions to be made. I'd like to get it all handled and head back home as soon as possible. Just tell her that, okay?"

"Sure. If she calls, I'll pass along your message."

"Thanks. It was nice to see you again, Bay Simpson. You take care now, hear?"

"You, too, Justin," I replied, meaning it.

I backed out of the parking space and glanced up toward the hotel as I shifted into drive. Trey Herrington lounged against the warm stone, one long leg crossed casually at the ankle over the other. The fading sun glinted against his straight black hair and flashed off the gold ring on his raised right hand.

I wasn't certain if the gesture was intended for me or exactly what it meant, but I ignored him as I gunned the engine and sped out of the parking lot. I had a strange feeling that his eyes followed me all the way down the winding driveway.

The house lay blessedly still in the soft light of falling dusk. Most of the birds had settled in for the night, leaving a profound silence broken only by the distant *sshussh* of ocean rollers breaking gently over the beach a short distance away through the trees.

I ignored the accusing red eye of the answering machine, slapped peanut butter between two slices of nearly-stale bread, and pulled a lukewarm can of Diet Coke out of the melted ice floating in the cooler. If they didn't get my kitchen straightened around soon, I was moving into a hotel.

I carried my "dinner" out onto the wide deck and sat down at the white, wrought iron table. I half expected Mr. Bones to come leaping into my lap, although I knew full well the battle-scarred tomcat was staying with my housekeeper while the renovation was going on. I missed them both.

Dolores Santiago, with her wide smile and bustling efficiency, normally came very weekday to see to the house and badger me gently in her colorful, broken English, sprinkled liberally with the Spanish of her native Guatemala. Her help had been invaluable during the weeks of my recuperation when even raising my arms to brush my hair had been an agony almost beyond bearing. Now, of course, I could take care of myself, except for cooking, my ineptness in the kitchen being the stuff of local legend. But the bond between Dolores and me had been well forged, and she had become more friend than employee. Besides, she had three kids to put through college and would have refused any gesture that smelled the least bit like charity.

Mr. Bones had quite literally saved my life, and I missed the warmth of his furry body sprawled across my feet in the otherwise wide and empty bed.

I pushed the half-eaten sandwich away and propped my bare feet up on the chair opposite. I resisted the urge for a cigarette, determined to get back on my program of cutting down. The light was almost gone now, and faint rustlings announced the rousing of the night creatures: raccoons, owls, and other predators on the hunt for their own dinners.

Trey Herrington's handsome face floated up out of my reverie. What was his problem, anyway? He seemed to have taken an intense dislike to me even before we met.

Why? I wondered, scrunching deeper into the padded chair. What business was it of his what Jordan did with her money? And why would he assume I was trying to scam her out of it? I had a hard-earned reputation for both personal and professional integrity. What had he heard to make him think otherwise? And from whom?

The telephone shrilled inside the house, and I welcomed the interruption of these pointless questions. I caught it just before the machine would have picked up.

Jordan Herrington von Brandt sounded as if she were in the next room instead of several thousand miles to the south. "Where have you been?" she snapped, setting my teeth immediately on edge. "I've been calling all day! Don't you ever pick up your messages for God's sake?"

I glanced guiltily at the blinking red light, then rummaged in my bag for my cigarettes. No way was I facing this call without some form of tranquilizer. I let the silence stretch while I lit up.

"Bay, are you there? Can you hear me?"

"I'm right here, and I'm about two seconds from slamming this phone down in your ear, *Countess*. If you want to talk to me, do it in a civilized tone of voice, or go to hell. I'm not one of your damned subjects."

A short pause was followed by her smoky laugh. "You're right. Sorry. I've been doing battle ever since I got here, and I guess I'm still in attack mode. Can we start over?"

"Sure," I said, carrying the portable phone back onto the deck and flopping down onto the chaise. "What's up?"

"Well, to begin with, the police have been very cooperative, much more so in person than they were on the phone. They seem to be impressed that I came all the way down here just to talk to them."

I shifted into a more comfortable position and reached for the can of warm soda. "So what did you find out? Anything useful?"

"Well, the first thing I did was to hire an interpreter from the consulate. The officials there just brushed me off, so I knew right up front I'd be operating on my own. Then we went to see the officer who originally handled the call. Took some digging to find him, but I threw my weight around and finally prevailed. Unlike Americans, these people are still impressed by a title. I can be very imperious when I put my mind to it."

"Tell me about it," I quipped, and Jordan laughed.

"Anyway, he told me everything he knew, which wasn't much. The coroner estimated Leslie had been dead about forty-eight hours when she was discovered. Apparently the hotel staff is very conscientious about honoring a "Do Not Disturb" sign. No one entered the room until her checkout time had come and gone."

I wondered why the idea of Jordan's mother lying dead in a hotel room for two days bothered me more than it apparently did her. "Does he stand by the original cause of death?"

"Yes, adamantly. I couldn't shake him on that. He says her heart just stopped, that she died peacefully in her sleep."

I swallowed hard and asked, "Was there an autopsy?"

"No. Apparently it's not required by their law like it would be in the States for an unattended death. As long as there was no evidence of foul play, the coroner rules and that's that."

I knew Jordan was waiting for a reply, but what was I supposed to say? *Sorry your mother wasn't murdered? Too bad they didn't cut her open from neck to pelvis and poke around inside?* How could Jordan speak of these things so dispassionately? The mental images the words conjured up were making me nauseous.

"Bay?"

"I'm still here. I don't know what you want me to say, Jordan. I'm sorry you wasted your time and money, but at least now you can put your suspicions to rest and get on with your life. When will you be back?"

"You don't understand. There's more." Her voice rose, and I could feel the edge of excitement beneath her words. "I'm staying at the hotel, the Rio Palace? In fact, I've got the same room. And this morning . . ."

"You're what?" I exploded, certain I must have misunderstood. "You're staying in the same room as Leslie did? Sleeping in the same bed your mother died in? That's really sick, Jordan, absolutely disgusting! How could you?"

"For God's sake, Bay, it's not the same bed. They replaced it right after . . . And what's so disgusting about it? What do you expect, her ghost to be hovering nearby?"

I was speechless. I couldn't even drive by the road that led to the private airstrip where Rob's plane and the rest of my life had exploded on that sunny August day. And that had been more than a year ago. Leslie Herrington had been dead less than three weeks.

"Anyway," she continued, "I spread a few hundred *reais* around the housekeeping staff and finally hit pay dirt."

"What do you mean?"

"There was a man!" Jordan announced triumphantly. "One of the maids saw them together, in town, on her day off. They were getting into a cab."

"How can she be sure it was your mother?"

"Leslie had a habit of personally handing out generous tips to the cleaning people every couple of days. Felt it assured her of superior service, which it probably did. Besides, I showed her a picture. She was certain it was Leslie she saw."

"Are you sure she wasn't just saying what she thought you wanted to hear?"

"I've dealt with enough servants to be able to tell when one of them's lying to me. And I'm a damned good judge of character. I picked you to help me, didn't I?"

There was nothing I could say to that. "What about the man?" I asked.

"She really didn't see his face. He was bending over, helping my mother in. All she can remember is that he seemed tall and had graying hair. And he was wearing a dark suit."

"That narrows it down to a couple of million Brazilians and tourists. And how do you know he was her lover? It could have been just a passing acquaintance or someone she ran into from home."

"Then why hasn't whoever it was come forward? Her death made the papers here. I've seen the article."

"I don't know, maybe he didn't want to get involved. Maybe he'd already left Rio."

"No, Bay, I'm right about this. I'm certain of it. Besides, you seem to have conveniently forgotten about the negligee. It was charged to her room. Two hundred and twenty-five dollars, American. You don't spend that kind of money on something to sit around alone in while you watch Brazilian soap operas. And then there are the flowers."

"What flowers?"

"A dozen white roses, delivered every day she was at the hotel. She didn't send them to herself, I checked. And no card, or so my little informant tells me. She threw out the wilted ones every morning."

"Okay, you seem to have collected a lot of circumstantial evidence, but what does it prove? Have you shared all this with the police? What do they think?"

"That I'm a rich, kooky American who watches too much television. They aren't going to do a damned thing. No, Bay, it's up to us."

I rubbed my temples where a throbbing headache was setting in and chose my next words carefully. "Jordan, why don't you come back now, and we'll sit down and discuss this rationally. I admit you have more than you did before, but it's still not enough to be one hundred per cent certain. Besides, your brothers are anxious to see you. There's a lot to be settled about your mother's estate."

"How do you know that? Have you been in touch with them?"

"We met this afternoon. Justin is particularly concerned. He asked me to tell you that if you called."

"What about darling Trey? I imagine he was furious. He can't wait to get his hands on his share of Leslie's money."

"They both want you to come back as soon as possible."

"I'll bet. Well, they'll just have to stew a while longer. I'm off to Switzerland tomorrow to visit the girls. They've been so upset about their grandmother's death. I want to reassure them that I'm doing everything I can to get to the bottom of it. With your help, of course. You can't know how much that means to me, Bay. Have you found anything in Leslie's papers?"

"Not yet, but I'm working on it," I lied.

"Good. Oh, one other thing, sort of strange, I thought. Constanza, the little maid who was so helpful? She told me a story about her cousin who works in a big hotel in Caracas. Seems the cousin told her a few weeks ago about a lady who died in one of her rooms. The poor thing came in and found the woman dead in her bed. So sad, Constanza's cousin said, because the woman had been so pretty and such a generous guest to the staff. An older woman, French, the cousin thought. It was ruled a heart attack. I think it might be worth checking out."

"Jordan, I don't know . . ."

"Listen, I have to run. I put in an overseas call to the girls, and it's coming through now. Tell my brothers I'll be back in the States in a few days. *Ciao!*"

"Jordan, wait . . ."

The soft hum of the international dial tone buzzed in my ear.

7

Sometimes the Internet drives me crazy. Search engines and I apparently speak different versions of the English language. Nevertheless, as I logged onto AOL and typed in my password, I felt that flutter of anticipation I always get when I'm about to make a right turn onto the information superhighway. The thought of all the little gems just waiting to be culled from the mountains of cyber trash floating around out there gives me a rush. I admit it: I'm a knowledge junkie.

I have wandered the stacks of the Library of Congress, checked out the FBI's Ten Most Wanted list—complete with photos—and stumbled on a really great recipe for Peking duck, which would be great if only I could cook.

My problem is always in defining my search so my screen doesn't announce "Top10 of 726,942 matches". So in attempting to track down Jordan's story about a death in Caracas similar to her mother's, I put a lot of thought into how to structure the search. I finally settled on "caracas venezuela daily newspaper", and clicked *Find.*

"Hey, girl, you're getting good at this," I congratulated myself as the first batch of only 2,259 possible entries popped up.

El Nacional and *El Universal* were both in Spanish. I can stumble through that language, but my French is much better. I tried VENEWS which was printed in English, but only provided headlines, most of them business-related. This was getting me nowhere fast.

Just out of curiosity, I opened up a travel site with information provided by the U.S. State Department. Scanning down, I caught the name *Daily Journal.* Published in English, it was recommended as a source for tourists to acquaint themselves with the latest alerts about areas to be avoided. Apparently the countryside was rife with roving gangs of modern-day highwaymen eager to pounce on wealthy visitors who strayed off the beaten path.

Below that I found another warning, this one highlighted so as not to be overlooked: "Tourists, Americans in particular, are cautioned against leaving cash or jewelry in their rooms. Even in the most exclusive Caracas hotels, burglaries are not uncommon, and some recent incidents have involved violence against foreigners. Be certain to use deadbolts on doors and windows and store all valuables in the hotel security area."

Fun place, I thought, stretching the kinks out of my neck and shoulders.

I scrolled through a few more pages, trying without success to find the *Daily Journal* online. By then I was down into the 50% match area. My watch read 10:15, and I decided to give it up and see if I could catch the last innings of the Braves game when an entry caught my eye.

"HELP! WHO MURDERED MY . . ." the title read, then "Summary: none available" underneath.

Unable to resist, I clicked on the intriguing words.

Gradually the screen filled with a color photo of a very attractive older woman, probably somewhere in her sixties. Beneath the picture, WHO KILLED PENELOPE WHITESIDE? glared in bold, black print.

I lit a cigarette, barely conscious of the action, my concentration riveted on the story unfolding before me.

Penelope Whiteside, seventy-year-old widowed grandmother, had left her home in Charlotte, North Carolina, on January 23 on the dream trip she and her late husband had always planned to take together. Flying to Los Angeles, she had embarked on a cruise that took her down the west coast of Mexico and through the Panama Canal, ending up in San Juan. From there she island-hopped around the Caribbean, then flew to Venezuela. Her itinerary called for her to board another ship at La Guiera, the port for Caracas, and cruise down the South American coast to Patagonia and Tierra del Fuego.

Caracas! Now I understood why this link had shown up on my list of matches.

I squirmed around in the chair, tucking one bare foot up under me. *Curiouser and curiouser*, I thought, unconsciously quoting Alice and her reaction to Wonderland.

Penelope Whiteside had been religious in adhering to the schedule worked out with her family. Every other day she mailed a postcard back to the States. Once a week she called. When she failed to check in on the Sunday following her arrival in Caracas, her son contacted Venezuelan police. Two days later authorities discovered her body in a room at the Intercontinental Hotel. She appeared to have been the victim of a heart attack.

"Boy," I said out loud, "this is getting freaky."

The balance of the posting detailed the family's efforts to convince authorities that Penelope had not died naturally. Chief among their reasons was the disappearance of an extremely valuable ruby-and-diamond ring, a gift from her husband shortly before his death, and a clean bill of health from her physician just days before her departure.

I sat back and ran a hand through my tangled mop of hair. It was Leslie Herrington's story, almost down to the last detail. Except for the cruise part. Jordan hadn't mentioned anything about her mother's having been on a ship at any time during her journey, but that didn't mean she hadn't been.

I pulled open the deep drawer on the right-hand side of the desk and retrieved the envelope Jordan had left me on her way to the airport. As I dumped the contents onto the already cluttered desktop, motion on the screen caught my eye. The AOL timer had popped up, reminding me I had been idle for awhile and asking if I wanted to stay online. Quickly I clicked on the heart icon, bookmarking this site so I could reconnect without going through the whole search process again.

I rummaged through the pile of papers, receipts, customs declaration forms, and odds and ends of foreign currency that had been returned to Jordan along with her mother's body. I riffled through a narrow, leather portfolio that seemed to contain her travel documents.

And there it was. Royal Scandinavian Cruise Lines, the tissue-thin paper printed with a trident symbol supporting what I thought was the Norwegian flag.

So Leslie, too, had been on a cruise prior to her arrival in Rio de Janeiro.

I glanced up just as the AOL server logged me off for non-participation. Damn! I had wanted to make a note of the e-mail address appended to the article. I definitely wanted to connect with whoever had created this bizarre website.

The wind had kicked up, rattling the sharp palmetto fronds and sending the mini-blinds clattering up against the open window. Storms were common at this time of the year, though few, thank heaven, turned into full-fledged hurricanes. I turned off the computer and shoved Leslie Herrington's papers back into the drawer. Then I toured the house, locking windows and doors, and arming the newly installed security system.

It was a little past midnight when I finally crawled into the king-size bed, my mind whirling with the implications of all the information I had gathered in such a short time. I made a mental note to call Justin Herrington first thing in the morning to let him know I had heard from Jordan. My Internet surfing had driven the promise right out of my head.

Maybe now her brothers would have to reassess their contempt for Jordan's suspicions about their mother's death.

Maybe we all would.

Sunday morning broke dull and overcast, clouds lingering from the previous night's storm. Humidity saturated the air, making everything feel damp and sticky.

I woke up with a screaming headache. Even the hot, steamy spray of the shower couldn't dispel the chill that sent goose bumps running up and down my arms. For the first time since late April, I shut off the air conditioning.

Maybe I'm coming down with something, I thought as I plodded out to the kitchen. I cursed the workmen who, in their haste to get out of there on Friday, had left more than their usual mess. By the time I'd blown the woodchips off the electric teapot and retrieved a tea bag from the box of supplies I kept stashed in the half-bath, I was working myself up into a pretty foul mood. Having to wipe a layer of sawdust off the bottoms of my bare feet didn't improve things either.

The hot Earl Grey revived me a little. I settled myself at the table in the screened-in area of the deck and dialed the Westin.

"Justin Herrington's room, please," I requested of the switchboard operator.

The phone rang a long time before a breathless voice gulped, "Yes?"

"Justin, it's Bay Tanner. I just wanted to let you know . . ."

"Justin's not here. Hold on. You got me out of the shower, and I'm dripping all over the furniture."

He must have dropped the receiver onto the table. The crash sent little shock waves of pain shooting through my already pounding head.

Great, I thought, *just what I need.*

Trey Herrington. Mr. Personality.

I'd almost decided to hang up on the rude s.o.b. when he snapped, "Okay, what is it?" in my ear.

"When do you expect Justin?" I snapped right back. "I'd prefer to talk to him."

"I have no idea, since he didn't deign to inform me of where he went. Whatever you have to say to him, tell me, and let's get this over with. I'm expecting some calls from the Coast, and I don't want this line tied up all day."

If I'd felt better, I would have told him where he could stuff his "calls from the Coast". Was I supposed to be impressed? At any rate, I wanted this conversation over as much as he did.

"Jordan called me from Rio last night. She's on her way to Geneva to visit her daughters. She'll be back in a few days."

"Geneva? Didn't you tell her we need her here to settle the estate?"

"Look, Herrington, I'm not your damned secretary. You got a problem with your sister, tell her yourself. Just let Justin know I called, okay?"

I hung up without giving him a chance to reply.

I rummaged in the medicine cabinet and found an old bottle of pain pills left over from the excruciating agony of the healing skin grafts. The prescription was probably outdated, but at that stage I didn't really give a damn. I tossed two into my mouth and washed them down with the dregs of cold tea in the bottom of my cup.

I knew I should eat something, but the thought of it made my stomach roll. I threw back the dust cover on the wide, white sofa and flopped myself onto its soft cushions. I grabbed the remote control, then pulled the sheet back over me. Despite the heavy sweat suit I'd thrown on that morning, I couldn't seem to get warm.

Damn the Herringtons, I thought, running through the eighty-plus cable channels, looking for something to distract me. *They can go to hell, all three of them!*

I paused at the Weather Channel, depressed to learn that this bleak, ugly day showed no signs of improving. Another tropical wave had moved off the west coast of Africa and would bear watching as hurricane season neared its peak. I finally fell asleep to the steady dripping of moisture off the live oaks and the husky voice of Barbara Stanwyck plotting her husband's death with Fred Mac Murray in *Double Indemnity*.

8

I awoke Monday morning to bright sunshine and a head that had shrunk back down to its normal size. I showered and, dressed in my tennis whites, was just pulling out of the driveway as the first of the workmen began to arrive.

A huge breakfast at Frank's, the narrow diner that grilled the best home fries in the world, restored my body as well as my soul. So did two matches—one singles, one with my standing doubles partner—both of which I won. I put the entire Herrington mess out of my mind, lounging by the pool and cooling off with periodic dips in the ocean until I had managed to while away most of the afternoon. By the time I cruised back up the drive a little before four o'clock, I felt ready to face just about anything.

I found the house strangely quiet, the yard devoid of pickup trucks and vans. The only vehicle in residence was Dolores's battered blue Hyundai. I could hear her soft humming amid the clatter of pans as I mounted the steps. When the sharp *meow* of Mr. Bones greeted me at the door, I dared to hope that we were almost back to normal.

"Dolores?" I called, reaching down to stroke the scraggly tomcat as he wove, purring, in and out of my legs. I rounded the corner and stopped dead in amazement.

Gone were the sawhorses and plastic drop cloths, the snaking cords and whining power tools. My new kitchen, gleaming in the late afternoon sun, stood spotless, risen like a phoenix from the ashes of the old.

"I don't believe it!" I cried, running up the three steps onto the shining oak floor. "Andy said he wouldn't be done 'til the end of the week!"

Dolores beamed, nodding and smiling at my astonishment. "*Señor* Andy, he tell the little fib. We wish to make for you the surprise. It is good, no?"

71

My housekeeper's face registered a moment of anxiety. After the explosion that destroyed this part of my house, along with my car, I had turned the remodeling project over to Dolores. The kitchen was her domain, after all, and I wanted her to arrange things to suit herself. All I needed to know was how to find the refrigerator and the teakettle.

"It's wonderful," I said, "perfect. It's so much lighter than before."

I wrapped my arms around the little woman, and, briefly, she hugged me back before squirming away in embarrassment.

We took a tour then, Dolores pointing out to me the marvelous new appliances, the island with built-in grill and retractable fan. Even the new breakfast table with its glass top and wicker chairs had been delivered while I frittered away the day at the beach.

"But are you satisfied with it?" I asked after admiring the honey oak cupboards and green slate countertops.

"Oh, *si, Señora, es muy bueno.*" The pride ringing in her voice made all the mess worthwhile. "Oh, I am forgetting. There is the message. I write it here."

Dolores handed me a paper with her own peculiar brand of phonetic English printed carefully in block letters. She had spelled it *Haryten,* but I knew who she meant.

"Which one?" I asked.

"*Señora?*"

"Which Herrington called? Did he leave a first name?"

"Oh, no, it was not the man. A *señorita.* She say call at hotel, please, right away."

Jordan? But she was in Switzerland.

I glanced at the local number Dolores had written down. That was the Westin, all right. What had happened? Why was she back already?

Well," I said, stuffing the paper in my pocket, "what shall we do to celebrate? If either one of us drank, I'd say we should crack open a bottle of champagne."

Black eyes sparkling, Dolores whipped open a lower cupboard door and unfolded a set of collapsible steps. She climbed up and retrieved a pair of crystal flutes from the topmost shelf while I applauded this clever innovation. We filled the delicate glasses with fresh iced tea and toasted the return of our lives to normality while the cat groomed himself in a soft patch of sunlight falling through the sparkling windows.

"Now, *Señora*, you must relax while I make the dinner," Dolores said. "I have the special treat for you."

She turned from the refrigerator holding aloft a huge lobster. Its antennae quivered at the sudden change in temperature.

"Yuck! It's still alive!" I cried, sending Mr. Bones scurrying for cover.

"*Si,* "Dolores said, looking bewildered.

"Can't you kill it first?" I asked, unconsciously moving away from the waving claws.

"No, *Señora*. He must go live into the pot."

"At least wait until I get out of here," I called as I retreated down the steps toward the bedroom. Thank God it would not be *my* hands that had to drop the wriggling crustacean into boiling water. I did my best to pretend that *all* my food, including the meat, was harvested from a field, like carrots and potatoes.

As I stripped off my shorts, I pulled the paper with Jordan's message from my pocket and tossed it on the dresser. She could wait. I deserved at least part of a day that hadn't been spoiled by the Herrington family, and I intended to have it.

That resolution lasted until Dolores and I had devoured the doomed lobster, stacked the plates in the new state-of-the-art dishwasher, and I had waved her off down the drive. Mr. Bones, who had been treated to a few morsels of the succulent meat, slept curled up contentedly on the rug in front of the sink.

Jordan, when I finally bit the bullet and called, was not in her room, so I left a message with reception and wandered into my office. I decided I might as well check out the Penelope Whiteside website while I waited, and flipped on the computer.

Again I watched in fascination as the lovely, serene face materialized on my screen. My mother always said true beauty was about bones, and here was a woman who proved her point. Despite the inevitable sags and wrinkles, the perfection of her features still shone through.

I scrolled down through the body of text I had already read. Two paragraphs remained. The first held a request for anyone with information relative to Mrs. Whiteside's death to contact the Venezuelan authorities. An international telephone number was provided.

The last few sentences contained a personal appeal from the designer of the site, the dead woman's grandson. Erik Whiteside wrote of his love for his "Granny Pen" and his unshakable determination to find the truth behind her death. He asked anyone who had lost a loved one under similar or other unusual circumstances, or knew of someone who had, to contact him at the e-mail address given.

I copied it carefully onto my desk calendar.

This kid either has a lot of guts, or he's missing a few bolts, I thought as the cat padded through the doorway and leaped up onto my lap. I wondered how many responses Erik Whiteside had gotten and whether any of them had been legitimate. He had certainly left himself open to all kinds of weirdos and crackpots, many of whom seemed to prowl the Internet. All you had to do was drop in on a chat room sometime to find all the proof of that you needed.

I clicked on the PRINT icon and leaned back while the printer warmed up, then began to whir as the photo and article slid out onto my desk. Absently I stroked the purring cat as I mentally composed and discarded messages to the young man. In the end I settled on noncommittal and, I hoped, intriguing: *Dear Mr. Whiteside,* I typed in the message box, *I am aware of one, possibly two, cases similar to your grandmother's. Does Royal Scandinavian Cruise Lines figure into her story? Please reply at your earliest convenience.*

I signed it "Bay" only, and appended my e-mail address even though he could pick it up from the header. That way, if he wasn't for real or had some whacked-out agenda I hadn't picked up on, he wouldn't be able to track me down personally through the nether regions of cyberspace to my little office/bedroom at the beach.

At least I didn't think so.

The phone rang just as I logged off AOL, and the noise in the soft evening quiet made me jump.

"Finally!" Jordan's voice exploded in my ear halfway through my hello. "Your line has been busy for hours."

"I was online. And what are you doing back here? I thought you were in Switzerland."

I figured the best way to deal with Jordan was just to yell right back at her. Apparently *her* fancy, French finishing school had skipped the section on telephone manners, or else she had cut that class.

"The damned headmistress told me I couldn't see the girls, not for another week. They're in the middle of exams, and she didn't want the whole school disrupted. God, you'd think I was planning a terrorist attack rather than a simple visit to reassure myself of the well-being of my children."

I had to smile at Jordan's histrionics. My sympathies lay entirely with the headmistress.

"The old battle-ax!" Jordan spluttered when I didn't respond. "German, you know, just like Klaus and the rest of his stiff-necked family. If it weren't part of the custody agreement, I'd yank my babies back here so fast, it would make his Saxon head spin. I think she must be a descendant of Himmler or Goebbels or one of those other bloody Nazis!"

"Who?"

"*Frau* Kreutzer, of course! She runs that school like a boot camp!"

"Jordan, why did you call me?" I could feel the faint drums of yesterday's headache beginning to pound in the back of my head.

"We need to talk to you, the boys and I. We'll meet you in the bar in, say—what? Twenty minutes?"

I glanced at my watch. A little past eight-thirty. "Why?" I asked, then mentally kicked myself for not just flat-out refusing. I wasn't usually this easy to manipulate. Why did I keep letting the Herringtons jerk me around like a balky puppy on a leash?

"I'll explain when you get here. Come on, Bay, we'll buy you dinner."

"I already ate," I said, sounding like a whiny brat even to my own ears.

"Well, then you can watch us. Look," Jordan said, her tone sobering, "we've got big trouble. With the stores. The boys spent all day with the attorneys. We really need your advice."

I heard her huge diamond clank against the receiver as she covered the mouthpiece with her hand. It didn't quite muffle her insistent hiss. "Shut up, Trey, for God's sake, will you? I'll handle this."

So, dissension in the ranks, I thought, brightening a little at the prospect of crossing swords again with the arrogant Trey Herrington.

"Sure, why not?" I heard myself saying. "Twenty minutes. In the bar."

I hung up and went to arm myself for battle.

9

I had the satisfaction of causing more than a few heads to swivel as I snaked my way through the surprisingly crowded bar a little after nine o'clock. The white knit dress clung to me in all the right places, and my tanned skin still glowed from a day spent entirely in the sun. Even my cropped chestnut hair had cooperated, lying in soft curls around my barely made-up face.

Justin Herrington nearly knocked over his chair as he jumped to his feet at my approach. "Here, Bay, sit here." He offered me his seat, then stumbled into the one next to it. "Thanks for coming," he beamed, his round face crinkling with the width of his smile. "You look fabulous."

"Thank you," I said, retrieving cigarettes and lighter from my bag. "Jordan. Trey."

I risked a quick glance from beneath partially lowered lashes. Trey Herrington regarded me silently, his face registering the same look of mild amusement he'd worn as he watched me pull out of the parking lot a few days before.

"Yes, thanks, Bay. Let me get you a drink."

Even in the dim light of the bar, Jordan looked awful. As she turned to signal the bartender, her face in profile looked drawn and haggard. Pouches sagged under green cat's-eyes, and her skin seemed dull and pale against the jet black of her close-cut hair.

"Diet Coke," she said as the waiter approached, "and another mimosa, please."

The men waved off refills.

"So, what's up?" I asked.

"Trey has something he'd like to say before we get down to business." Jordan regarded her brother steadily as she sipped from her fresh orange juice-and-champagne cocktail.

"Trey?" Justin said as the silence lengthened.

His brother shot him a withering look, then turned back to me. "It seems my siblings here think I've been unconscionably rude to you in our brief encounters, Ms. Tanner. If so, I humbly apologize and beg your forgiveness."

He extended a well-manicured hand across the table. His dazzling smile belied the mocking formality of his words and completely altered his usual sullen expression. Hard muscle rippled along his arm from beneath a pale yellow polo shirt that accentuated his dark, California tan. I gripped his hand and shook it, not a wimpy, fingers-only handshake like so many women use, but firm and strong, the way the Judge had taught me.

"Accepted," I said and sat back.

"Good," Trey Herrington replied, raising his glass to me before he drank.

If he was faking it, he was a much better actor than his brother gave him credit for.

"Our mother's estate is a mess," Justin began, apparently satisfied that the air had been sufficiently cleared. "Her investment portfolio is sound. I've handled most of that for her myself over the years. The real problem is with the stores."

"It seems Leslie took very little interest in the business after Father died. Left it in the hands of the manager he'd had for years," Jordan interrupted.

"The returns just kept dropping off, year after year, but always enough for our mother to live well on, so she just shrugged it off. The attorneys have examined the books, but they can't make heads or tails out of them." Justin sighed and shook his head. "I don't know if we're looking at fraud here or incompetence, or . . ."

"Embezzlement?" I offered. "So you want me to go over the records and see if I can determine which it is, is that it?"

"Exactly!" Justin beamed. "We can't value the estate until we have a handle on the finances of the stores. Would you do it, Bay?"

"We'll pay you, of course. Or rather, the estate will." The mockery was back in Trey's voice, but his eyes held mine steadily.

Two waiters appeared, their hands balancing huge bowls of steaming crab legs. Silence descended as they set about distributing plates and utensils along with shiny, metal "crackers" and sizzling dishes of melted butter.

"We weren't really that hungry," Jordan explained as she draped a linen napkin across her lap and reached for a crab leg. "Go ahead, Bay, dig in. There's plenty."

I declined, sipping on my soft drink while the three Herringtons attacked their food. Amid the crunching of shells we worked out a game plan. Justin would inform their attorneys—Brandon and Phelps in Beaufort—that I was to have access to all the records of the hardware store chain. He would then make an appointment for us to go over the books. I warned them that I was a little rusty, having totally abandoned my profession for the better part of the last year.

"I'm not worried about that." Jordan dismissed my reservations as she wiped her chin daintily. "We don't need a full-blown audit right now, just an idea of where we stand. If it comes down to tearing everything apart, you can hire someone to help you."

I smoked and watched them demolish the seafood delicacies while heaps of mangled shells piled up in front of them. We talked desultorily of the old days in Beaufort, playing "do you remember?" until Jordan yawned widely and reached for her bag.

"I think I must have terminal jet lag," she said, rising from the table. "If I don't get to bed I'm going to pass out right here on the table."

Both her brothers rose with her. Their goodnights were perfunctory, no hugs or even Hollywood-style air kisses. Jordan paused by my chair as Trey said, "What about the check?"

Jordan cocked a finely shaped eyebrow at him. "I'm sure Justin will take care of it, won't you, dear? We all know *you* never pick up a tab, Trey."

The venom in her voice broke the peace of what had become almost a cordial gathering of the remaining Herringtons. Far from being offended, Trey grinned at his sister and brought his hands together in mock applause.

"Bravo, Jordan, well said. I was beginning to fear you'd gotten mellow on us."

"Go to hell, darling," Jordan replied and turned to me. "Lunch tomorrow? We have quite a lot to discuss."

I thought briefly of the e-mail I had sent off to Penelope Whiteside's grandson, and wondered whether or not I should wait for a reply before mentioning it to Jordan. I was trying to remain open-minded about any connection in the death of the two elderly women until I had a chance to check it out more thoroughly. Jordan, on the other hand, seemed ready to mount a full-scale attack, though against whom was still the paramount unknown.

I decided on silence.

Then another thought popped into my head. "Tomorrow's Tuesday, right?"

Trey's snort of derision wiped out his pretty apology and put us right back in the adversarial relationship we'd first established. "Easy to lose track when you don't have to get up and go to work every day, I guess," he sneered.

"You should know, brother dear," Jordan fired back, leaping to my defense unasked. "When was the last time you had a *real* job? Somewhere around the first Reagan administration, wasn't it?"

The reappearance of the waiter cut off Trey's rejoinder. Justin signed the check, produced his room key as verification, then pushed back his chair. "I think I'll turn in, too. I need to call Diane and make sure everything's under control at home. I'll be in touch tomorrow, Bay, and set up an appointment for us with Chris Brandon."

"Fine," I said, "only make it in the afternoon, okay?" I turned to Jordan. "That's what I started to tell you. About tomorrow. I have a lunch date with Adelaide Boyce Hammond. I've sort of adopted her recently, and I hate to disappoint her by canceling."

"I see. Well, call me when you find a break in your schedule." It was Jordan Mayne Herrington von Brandt at her haughtiest. She spun on her heel and stalked out of the bar before I could reply.

Justin, obviously embarrassed by his sister's rudeness, shook my hand, mumbled a hasty goodnight, and retreated in her wake.

I threw my cigarettes into my bag, determined finally to wash my hands of the entire family, when Trey laid a restraining hand on my arm. I jerked away, half rising from my chair, when he said quietly, "Bay, please. Don't go yet."

It was the first time he'd called me anything except *Ms. Tanner.* I glanced across the table and encountered pale green eyes filled with entreaty.

"Please," he said again, and I found myself sitting back down. "Good, that's better." He raised a hand at a passing waiter. "I'd like coffee, please, with cream. Bay?"

"Nothing for me, thanks."

"Bring the lady some hot tea," Trey overrode me.

The young man bustled off, leaving me to puzzle over how he knew I never drank coffee. And then I wondered whether I was finally facing the *true* Trey Herrington, or if this was just another of his many roles.

"It's late, Trey," I said when he made no move to initiate conversation, "even though I don't have to get up and go to work tomorrow."

His laugh sounded genuine, devoid of its customary mocking undertone. "That *was* a pretty rotten crack, wasn't it? In my defense, let me just say that neither of my siblings seems to bring out the best in me. They're both so damned sure of themselves," he went on, sobering. "Some people have no concept of what it's like having to struggle to make a living."

"And you include me in that privileged group as well?"

He shrugged as cups appeared in front of us. Now that it was here, the tea seemed just what I needed. We performed our separate rituals and sipped before Trey sidestepped my not entirely rhetorical question.

"I suppose. Hey, you're the talk of the old hometown, did you know? Everywhere I went in Beaufort, people were gossiping about that Grayton's Race thing."

His pause seemed to invite me to elaborate. I lit a cigarette and exhaled smoke toward the ceiling.

"Justin doesn't seem very sure of himself," I said, steering the conversation away from myself and back to the Herringtons. "In fact, he seems downright intimidated by you and Jordan."

"Ah, a tactful change of subject. So be it." Trey smiled and ducked his head. "Not to sound too incredibly vain, but I think that's somewhat understandable, don't you?"

I was sure his ego didn't need any stroking from me, so I let his feeble attempt at humility slide. "He appears to be quite successful at what he does," I ventured.

"And why shouldn't he be?" Trey fingered the coffee spoon, his expressive mouth once again curled in contempt. "He married his biggest—hell, his *only*—client, except for Leslie. Little Diane is used to the finer things, so Daddy makes certain Justin rakes in enough to keep his little girl in tennis bracelets and Land Rovers."

"Why do all of you call your mother Leslie?" I asked. Although I often referred to my father as *the Judge*, the tone in which the three of them invoked Leslie Herrington's name always sounded harsh and disrespectful.

"She liked it that way. Once we grew up, she didn't want to be reminded of how old *she* was getting. The Herrington vanity is genetic."

I sneaked a quick look at my watch and downed the last of the tea. Whatever Trey's reason for wanting me to stay, I couldn't wait all night for him to get around to it.

"Thanks for the drinks," I said, rising again from the table. "I really should be getting on home."

"No, wait!" For the first time since we'd stared each other down in the red leather booth right behind us, I saw uncertainty flicker across his movie-star handsome face.

"What?"

"Well, it's about Jordan. Damn it, Bay, I don't understand what she's up to, do you? What's the point of all this jetting halfway around the world, playing amateur detective? I mean, even if Leslie *was* murdered, what difference does it make now? It's not going to bring her back. And if the police are satisfied it was natural causes, why can't Jordan just leave it alone?"

"Why don't you ask her? Why interrogate me?"

"You think she'd tell *me* anything? It can't have escaped your notice that we can barely manage to be civil to one another."

"Why?"

That stopped him. He gazed up at me in genuine puzzlement, as if he'd never really considered the question before. "I'm not exactly sure," he said after a long pause, during which I settled back into my chair. "I guess it's always been that way. Justin's the youngest, you know, and Jordan always looked out for him. It's always been the two of them against me." He shrugged eloquently. "That's just how it is."

"What about your parents?"

"What about them?"

"Well, I mean, did they play favorites?"

"At times, I guess. But then, we all turned out to be a disappointment to them, one way or another. Neither Justin nor I wanted to run hardware stores for the rest of our lives, and Jordan . . ." He laughed, not unkindly this time. "Jordan got into every kind of trouble you could think of before she was old enough to drive. It sent Leslie right up the wall. She was thrilled when Dad packed Jordan off to Europe."

Trey accepted a refill of coffee before continuing. "She almost redeemed herself, marrying old Klaus and becoming a countess, although a minor one. Imagine the mileage Leslie got out of that with her high society friends."

I cringed a little at his sarcasm. My mother had, after all, been the doyenne of Leslie's social circle.

"But then Jordan wouldn't come home, even when my nieces were born," he went on. "Just flying visits once a year, here and gone again like a flash. Didn't even stay long enough to be flaunted around town. It drove Leslie nuts."

Trey's original question drifted back into my mind. What *was* Jordan up to? If the relationship between mother and daughter had been as strained as Trey described it, why was Jordan so hell-bent on playing avenging angel?

"I think you need to talk to your sister about her motives," I said, intent this time on making my escape. "I'm glad we had a chance to talk, though."

"Me, too," Trey said, standing with me and throwing a ten-dollar bill on the table. "Let's do it again."

He *was* incredibly good-looking, and he could definitely be charming when he set his mind to it. I have to admit I was tempted. But my confidence in my own judgment had been recently—and nearly disastrously—shaken, so I just smiled noncommittally and let the implied invitation pass.

"It's late," Trey said, cupping my elbow with a strong, warm hand as we made our way out to the nearly deserted lobby. "Let me walk you to your car."

"No thanks," I said, easing away from him as I retrieved my keys. "I'm fine. Goodnight."

"Goodnight, then," he answered.

I left him at the bank of elevators with a casual wave. Again I had the feeling that his eyes followed me all the way out the door.

For some reason it gave me the creeps.

10

Adelaide Boyce Hammond was seated at our usual table when I walked into the dining room at the Cedars, the upscale retirement community on the marshes of Broad Creek. Her pure white hair formed a soft halo around sunken, wrinkled cheeks that creased into a triumphant smile as she noticed me across the sea of tables. The age-spotted hand she raised in greeting was her left one, and I realized that the cast had been removed sometime in the last week.

I leaned over to kiss her gently, then pulled out the white wicker chair opposite. "Congratulations," I said as she beamed back at me. "When did you get liberated?"

"Friday morning. I can't tell you how thrilled I am to be rid of that cast. The itching was getting almost unbearable."

"I know," I said, remembering the torment of the healing burns on my hands and knees. Thank God that was over with, the ordeal having left only the faintest of scars behind. "How does it feel?"

Miss Addie maneuvered her mended wrist in a circular motion and wriggled her fingers. "Just like new. Maybe even better. I don't know how to thank you, dear."

Injured in an attack by an unseen intruder into her apartment, Miss Addie's recovery had been touch-and-go for a while.

"I had nothing to do with it," I said as a pretty blonde waitress approached the table. "Thank Dr. Winter."

"Hello, Debbie," Miss Addie acknowledged her. "Lovely day today, isn't it?"

"Yes, ma'am, it sure is. Soon as my shift is over, I'm hittin' the beach."

"Take care with your complexion, dear," Miss Addie cautioned. "You don't want that lovely fair skin of yours to start looking like old shoe leather."

"No, ma'am. I'll remember to use lots of sunscreen," she said, then turned to me. "Have y'all made up your minds?"

"What's the fish today?" I asked.

"Grouper. You can have it grilled, broiled, or blackened."

We both decided on broiled, with rice and a fresh vegetable mélange. Without asking, Debbie had brought two glasses of iced tea.

"I've dismissed Mrs. Monaghan," Miss Addie said, looking guiltily up at me. "She's getting her things together now."

"Are you sure you're ready?" I asked, and she nodded vigorously.

I had engaged Patsy Monaghan to look after Miss Addie on her release from the hospital. Large, competent, and cheerful, the practical nurse had come highly recommended by the hospital staff. She had been occupying the guestroom, seeing to Miss Addie's medication and helping her with whatever tasks she'd been unable to manage with only one useable arm.

"I'm quite recovered, as you can see, dear, and the expense . . . Well, I fully intend to reimburse you, Lydia."

"We'll argue about that later," I said as Debbie set our lunch in front of us.

"Perhaps we could arm-wrestle for it," Miss Addie replied with a charming, ladylike little chuckle as she waved her left arm once again.

Adelaide Boyce Hammond, like Leslie Herrington, had been a member of my late mother's inner circle, though much closer to Emmaline Baynard Simpson in years. While I couldn't be certain of her exact age, I knew she had to be at least eighty.

As if intercepting my thoughts, Miss Addie said, "I was saddened to read of Leslie Herrington's death in the paper last week. Such a lovely woman. Do you remember her at all, Lydia?"

I swallowed a bite of the flaky grouper. I had become resigned over the past weeks to Miss Addie's use of my formal name. "Not really," I said, "but of course I remember the family. In fact, I've spent quite a bit of time with her three children over the past few days."

"How sad it must be for them," the older woman replied. "I remember little Jordan so well. What a trial she was to her dear parents. Quite a beautiful child, but so willful!"

"She hasn't changed much," I said archly, the memory of last night's grand exit fresh in my mind.

"The older boy was very attractive, too, as I recall."

"Yes," I said noncommittally. Then an idea struck me. "Do you remember when their father was killed? Jack T.? Wasn't there some scandal attached to it at the time?"

Miss Addie pushed her plate away and dabbed delicately at the corners of her narrow mouth with her white linen napkin. For a moment I thought she was going to ignore my question.

"Well, dear, there were always rumors, you know. Beaufort, devoid of tourists, is, after all, just a small town. I'm certain it's unwise to put any faith in the veracity of common gossip."

She sounded so much like my mother just then that a little shiver of *déja vu* slithered down my spine. I felt eight years old and properly rebuked for my unladylike curiosity.

"However," she went on, a conspiratorial twinkle in her faded blue eyes, "my daddy always said there's no smoke without a little fire."

Debbie cleared away the plates and refilled our glasses. We both reluctantly declined dessert.

As with the Judge, the best tactic was probably not to push too hard. I resisted the urge for an after-dinner cigarette and waited.

"I seem to recall that Jack Herrington had something of a reputation with the ladies," Miss Addie began, her gaze wandering past me to the live oaks swaying lightly just outside the wide windows. "Even after his marriage. He was considered something of a catch in his younger days. Wildly handsome, with that jet-black hair slicked back against his head. And a sharp eye for business. An 'up-and-comer', that's what Daddy called him. He and Leslie Mayne were the match of the season that summer she accepted him."

She was far away now, lost in a time when debutantes were still presented on the arms of their doting fathers to be paraded past an assembly of "acceptable" suitors like so many cattle in a show ring. It was a part of our glorious past I was thankful to have missed. I fiddled with a heavy teaspoon and remained silent, afraid to break the rhythm of her memories.

"The children came quite quickly, one right after another. And Leslie was always delicate. Mama used to say that a well brought up lady had to overlook a certain . . . inconstancy in her husband from time to time, men being what they are."

So Jack T. had cheated on his wife, and society had expected her to look the other way. I wondered if she'd been able to do that. I certainly couldn't have, nor could most of the women I knew. It had, however, been a different time.

"How did Leslie handle it?" I asked.

"Not well, I'm afraid. There were scenes, or so one heard. Leslie developed an unfortunate fondness for sherry as she grew older, you know. She remarked once that she had made herself *unavailable* to her husband's attentions."

So Leslie had cut Jack T. off, to state it baldly. I remembered then Jordan's remark about her mother's frigidity.

"What about the night he died? The night he ran his car into the river? I've heard he wasn't alone. Is that true?"

It was only a small exaggeration, a logical conclusion to draw from the hints and innuendo bandied around by the Judge and his cronies.

"One heard," Miss Addie said, her voice dropping nearly to a whisper as she leaned closer to me across the table, "that he was not."

"Who was she?"

Miss Addie's eyes behind her wire-rimmed bifocals smoldered with an indignation I had never seen there before. Then she seemed to come to some inner realization, shook her head slightly, and sank back against her chair.

"What?" I said a little too loudly. "Surely you're not going to leave it there? Who was with Jack T. the night he died?"

"I'm sorry, Lydia. I should never have started down this road. Mama always said an unguarded tongue was the Devil's favorite tool. Let the dead rest in peace. I'm afraid I have never adhered to the biblical notion of the sins of the fathers being visited upon the children."

". . . 'unto the third and fourth generation of them that hate me'," I finished the passage for her. "Exodus, Chapter Twenty, I believe." Appropriate Bible verses had been one of my mother's weapons of choice. I knew when I was beaten.

"Are you very angry with me?"

"No, of course not," I said, swallowing my frustration with a smile. What was it to me, after all, except a desire to satisfy my own morbid curiosity?

"Good," she beamed, "because I'd like to ask you a little favor. Not that I'm unmindful of what you've already done for me, Lydia. I wouldn't want to appear ungrateful."

I cringed, remembering the twisted path of deceit and death her last request had set me upon. "What is it?" I asked, with not a little trepidation.

"Well, all this recent dredging up of the past has put an idea into my head. I'd like to find my brother. I'd like to see Win once more before I die. Will you help me?"

Edwin Hollister Hammond, a dashingly handsome scoundrel, or so I'd been told, had disappeared more than twenty years before after being disinherited by his straitlaced father. To my knowledge, no one had heard from him since.

"How can you be certain he's still alive?" I asked. Better to get the tough questions out of the way first. "He'd be—what? In his sixties now?"

"Sixty-three, next month," Miss Addie replied. "He's the baby, you know."

"Yes, I remember your telling me that. But even if he's still living, where would you begin to look? I mean, he could be anywhere, couldn't he?"

Miss Addie's eyes once again sparkled with the mischief that so endeared her to me. She reached into her tan leather handbag and produced a picture postcard, which she slapped triumphantly onto the table between us. I recognized the sweet curve of palm-fringed beach ringing crystal blue water. Rob and I had vacationed there early in our marriage.

"Megan's Bay on St. Thomas in the Virgin Islands," I said quizzically as the old woman nodded.

"Turn it over," she said.

The block letters were neat and straight as if someone had used a ruler to insure their evenness. *Hope you are much recovered,* the message read. *I think often of rainy afternoons, of you and I and Grandma's trunk.* It was signed simply, *Win.*

"When did you get this?" I asked, studying the postmark. It was blurred, unreadable, as was the date. It bore a standard, U.S. twenty-cent stamp.

"Saturday. Isn't it wonderful? Win is alive!"

I tried to share Miss Addie's elation, but my cynical side kept asking uncomfortable questions. The card had been addressed correctly, down to the proper apartment number. She had lived here only a little more than three years. How had her wayward brother gotten her current address? And his reference to her recovery. Surely such a local scandal hadn't made the papers any farther south than Savannah. So who had informed him of her injury?

But the most nagging mystery of all was the anonymity of the whole thing. If Win Hammond wanted to make contact after two decades of silence, why had he not provided a return address, some way for his sister to get in touch with him? It seemed to me the height of cruelty for him to drop this little bombshell and then retreat behind the security of his self-imposed exile.

"What's all this about a trunk?" I asked to cover what was becoming an awkward silence.

"It belonged to Grandmother Boyce," Miss Addie said, her face alight with fond memory. "It was stored in the attic, and Win and I used to dress up in the old clothes we found in it and act out books and plays. Win especially liked Shakespeare. Even as a little boy one could see the talent, sense the presence. Imagine his remembering that after all these years."

"Did he contact either of your sisters?"

"No, he didn't. Of course I called Edwina right away, and she was as shocked as I. Daphne was having one of her 'spells', but the administrator at the home assured me she had received no mail in the last several weeks."

Edwina, the oldest, suffered from crippling arthritis, and Daphne was in the late stages of Alzheimer's disease and rarely coherent. Neither had been able to come to Miss Addie's assistance in her recent troubles.

I hated being the one to burst her bubble, but a reality check was in order. "Have you considered the possibility that your brother doesn't want to be found?"

Miss Addie had once described herself to me as a tough old bird, and she proved it now. "Of course I have, Lydia. Otherwise he could have just called me on the phone. Or left his address on the card. The point here is not what Win wants, but what *I* want. And I want to find him. Will you help me?"

I had no clue how I was going to go about it, but her entreating eyes left me little alternative. "Of course I will. At least, I'll try."

"Wonderful! Now, I know this will cost money, at least I assume it will. I want no expense spared." Her blue eyes flashed with humor once again. "At my age, I can't afford to waste any time."

"You'll outlive us all," I said as we rose and walked arm in arm out of the dining room.

"Perhaps," she replied, squeezing my hand as we touched cheeks, "but let's not leave *everything* to Providence."

I sat in my car and watched the old darling walk jauntily toward her apartment. I lit a cigarette and backed the Zeemer out of the parking space.

What have you gotten yourself into now? I wondered, jerking the gearshift into drive.

I hoped Red had some ideas about how to begin searching for someone who had dropped out of sight twenty years before and apparently wanted to keep it that way. If not, I was going to have to take a crash course in private detecting—and soon.

* * * *

As promised, Justin Herrington had left a message suggesting a meeting at the attorney's office at ten o'clock the following morning. If that proved inconvenient, I was instructed to call him at the Westin.

I slipped out of my low-heeled pumps and deposited my pale green, sleeveless dress in the hamper. Much more comfortable in faded denim shorts and a tank top, I fired up the computer and checked my e-mail.

No response from Erik Whiteside.

Although it had been less than twenty-four hours since I'd posted my reply, I had hoped to have some input from him before I was forced to confront Jordan von Brandt. While my lunch with Miss Addie had postponed her proposed council of war, I fully expected Jordan to be pounding on my door—either literally or figuratively—before the afternoon was out.

While I was online, I decided to take an initial foray into the possibility of tracking down Win Hammond via the Internet. The search engine revealed scores of websites relating to missing persons, as well as several offering international telephone listing and locator services. Most of the former involved adopted children seeking their birth parents. I clicked on a few of these, but the pain and confusion evident in so many of the pleas for information left me tired and depressed. As for the phone numbers, I didn't know for certain where Win lived. I tried St. Thomas, but drew a blank. Maybe he had just been passing through when he mailed the postcard.

I logged off, retrieved a cold Diet Coke from my shiny new refrigerator, and wandered out onto the deck.

Who was luckier, I wondered as I stretched out on the chaise, *children who had been chosen by strangers who desperately wanted them, or those of us who knew our real parents, but were never certain we had been truly welcome?*

Probably it was a "the grass is always greener . . ." kind of thing, I decided, every one of us convinced that the other guy's life was perfect and, if only we could be in his shoes, ours would be, too.

The late afternoon sun, filtering down through the swaying clumps of Spanish moss, cast rippling patterns across my bare legs. The effect was mesmerizing, and I felt my eyelids begin to droop.

The deck lay completely in shadow when the strident voice jerked me suddenly awake. For a brief moment I thought Jordan must be standing right next to me, so clearly could I hear her angry words. Then I realized the stream of invective was issuing from the answering machine.

I flung open the French doors and sprinted across the white carpet. I snatched up the phone and yelled, "Hold it!" into the receiver.

Blessed silence followed as I drew a breath, preparing to counter-attack. Then Jordan's voice, no longer angry, but agitated and frightened, close to tears, "Thank God! Bay, I don't know what to do! It's just unbelievable!"

"Jordan, what is it? What's happened?"

I could almost feel the shudder pass through her. "A letter," she said, choking on the words. "I got a letter. From my mother."

11

Two voices from the grave, all in the same day, seemed a little too coincidental, at least to my mind. However, my friend Neddie, a red-haired, Boston-Irish child psychologist, was a firm believer and had gone a long way toward convincing me that sometimes things just happened.

Still, for Miss Addie to have heard from her brother after twenty years of silence, and now Leslie Herrington . . .

Jordan arrived a few minutes after her phone call, roaring into my driveway in a black Jaguar convertible that made my stomach drop into my shoes for just a second.

Nice car, bad associations.

Her white silk shirt, soaked in perspiration, clung to her breasts and back, and her black linen trousers were creased and rumpled. She carried a napkin-wrapped bottle of champagne in one hand.

"The goddamned air conditioning doesn't work," she snapped as I met her at the top of the steps. "A hundred and twenty-five dollars a day for this bucket, and I'm sweating like a pig."

I led her into the kitchen where I retrieved a champagne glass from the top shelf while she wrestled with the cork. I replenished my Diet Coke, and we settled into the soft cushions of the white sofa.

"Can I see it?" I asked as Jordan drained the first glass and poured herself another with less than steady hands.

She pulled the letter from the top of her Gucci tote and handed it over without a word. The original postmark read 'Rio de Ja" and was dated September 3.

"Was that the day . . .?" I began when Jordan interrupted.

"That she died? Yes, according to the coroner."

So this truly was a message from the dead. My fingers trembled slightly as I turned back to the envelope. Originally addressed to what I assumed was Jordan's home in Geneva, it had been redirected to her fashionable Buckhead residence near Atlanta. That explained the delay.

"How did it get here?" It really didn't matter, but I was postponing looking at the actual letter as long as I could. The thought that the woman who penned it had done so with no idea that within a few hours she would be dead made my skin crawl.

"My secretary sent it on to me, in a package with other mail that had accumulated in Atlanta. I don't think he realized its significance, or he might have prepared me. I can't tell you what a shock it was to be leafing through a stack of meaningless correspondence and come upon this . . . this," she finished lamely.

"What does it say? The letter."

Jordan gulped champagne and fumbled in her bag for her cigarettes. The silence deepened while she lit up and inhaled greedily. She ran her long, slender fingers through her half-inch of black hair and stared out the window.

"I don't know," she said at last, avoiding my eyes. "I haven't opened it yet. I want you to do it."

I flipped the envelope over, verifying that the flap did, indeed, remained sealed.

"Jordan, I'm not sure . . ."

"Oh, open the damned thing!" She jumped to her feet and began to pace, striding back and forth in front of the empty fireplace, pausing only long enough to flick ashes into the blue porcelain bowl on the coffee table.

"Had you heard from her before? I mean while she was traveling?"

"No, not directly." Jordan stubbed out her cigarette, then immediately lit another. "She'd sent a few postcards to the girls, from some of the more exotic places she was visiting. Christianne, my oldest, collects stamps. But Leslie always included some little sop to my vanity, something like, 'Regards to your mother' or something equally impersonal. This . . ." Jordan stumbled over her next words, "this is the first letter in years she'd written specifically to me."

I laid the unopened envelope on the table. "Jordan, come sit down here a minute, will you?"

"Why? Just open the damned thing, and let's get this over with."

"Humor me," I coaxed, and patted the cushion. "Come on. You need to get control of yourself."

Jordan dropped reluctantly onto the sofa with an exaggerated sigh of impatience. "Okay, I'm calm. See?" She held up her nearly empty glass with a steady hand.

"Explain something to me," I began cautiously, unsure how my questions would be perceived, but certain I needed to ask them. "All I've heard from you and your brothers over the past few days is what a rotten relationship you've all had with your mother. Look, I'm not judging," I added quickly as Jordan's head snapped up. "God knows my parents could have written the manual on raising a dysfunctional kid."

"Couldn't everybody's? I don't think I could name one single person I know who came out of childhood completely normal, whatever that is."

"Exactly. So what I'm saying is, your situation isn't unique. What's troubling me is this . . . *obsession* you seem to have with proving that Leslie was murdered. Trey and Justin seem satisfied to leave things alone and get on with their lives. Why aren't you?"

For a long moment I thought she was going to refuse to answer. Or tell me to go to hell, which would have been all right, too. Somehow I had gotten sucked into the emotional morass of the Herrington family neurosis, and I would welcome almost any excuse to walk away from it.

"I'll be thirty-nine in a couple of months," Jordan said with a trace of a smile. "I'd lie about it, but we're the same age."

"Thank you for reminding me."

"The point is I suddenly realized that, here I was, pushing forty, and my life is pretty much worthless. Oh, I've got a lot of money. And, if you knew Klaus, you'd know I earned every penny of it. And the girls are wonderful, probably the only important thing I've ever done. Both of them are bright and beautiful and surprisingly well adjusted."

"You must be very proud of them."

"I am, but, because of the custody restrictions, we're practically strangers. Klaus and my Nazi mother-in-law have them for two months during their summer holidays, and I get the rest—Christmas and so on, plus regular visitation. I've let them be taken away from me—just like Leslie let Daddy send *me* away. I've done the same damned thing I've hated *her* for all these years!"

I had no idea where this was going, but I wanted to let her talk. It seemed to me a real human being was emerging from behind the brusque façade Jordan von Brandt presented to the world. I didn't want to do anything to scare this new, fragile personality back into hiding.

"I wrote to Leslie, just after she left on her trip. In care of the cruise line." Jordan poured more champagne, emptying the bottle. Despite all she'd drunk, she appeared relatively coherent. "I told her I had set my lawyers in Switzerland to work on breaking the custody agreement, that I wanted to bring the girls permanently back to the States."

Her voice dropped so low I had to strain to catch her next words.

"Over the years, Leslie had made overtures, hints that she'd like to repair our relationship. I'd rebuffed them all. But in my letter I told my mother I was going to find a place in Natchez so we could all be together, the four of us Herrington girls. I wanted to put all the animosity and the endless arguments of the past behind us. I wanted us to be a family again."

Jordan sighed deeply and set her empty glass on the table.

"And you think this is her answer," I said, gesturing at the envelope before us, "and you're scared to find out what it was."

"Yes," she said simply, "scared to death."

We smoked in silence for awhile, the four-by-six envelope seeming to expand in importance, like a tumor. Benign or malignant, that was the question.

"What does her response have to do with anything now?" I asked, picking up the letter by one corner as if it might explode in my hand. "Maybe it would be better just to put a match to it."

"No!" Jordan cried and snatched it out of my grasp. "If Leslie was willing to make an effort at reuniting our family, then the girls and I have been cheated. It does no good to rail at God or fate or whatever. I learned that a long time ago. No, I need someone to blame for what we've lost. I want the s.o.b. to pay. I want revenge."

"And if the answer was no?"

Jordan shrugged and crushed her cigarette in the blue ashtray. "Then, I guess you're right. It really doesn't matter," she said softly.

She rose then, the letter from her dead mother clutched tightly in her hand. I watched as she walked silently through the French doors and onto the deck. She collapsed onto the chaise, her eyes wandering out toward the sea. Then I saw her hook a copper-painted thumbnail under the flap and rip open the envelope.

I gathered the dirty glasses and the empty champagne bottle and carried them out to the kitchen. That took only a second. I wanted to give Jordan some privacy, so I pulled out the chair from the built-in desk and tried to get Red Tanner on the phone.

My brother-in-law was off duty, and there was no answer at his spartan, half-furnished apartment. I rang the dispatcher back and left a message for Red to call me.

By the time I had wiped down the already spotless counter and added a few items to Dolores's running grocery list, I heard the French doors open. Jordan stood trembling, the letter clasped to her breast like a shield of armor. Tear-tracks streaked her careful makeup, but her slanting green eyes glittered with anger.

"His name is Ramon. She met him on the ship. She thought the murdering bastard wanted to marry her!"

12

I found the law offices of Brandon & Phelps in the same building that used to house my old enemy, Hadley Bolles. Located one floor above his now-empty suite, their space, while similar in layout, couldn't have been more different.

I gave my name to a pretty, blonde receptionist and took a seat in the uncluttered, chrome-and-glass waiting area. The furniture was leather, but it was the sleek, black, modern variety, not the cracked and faded red I remembered from Hadley's office. The walls, a stark white, held only two paintings, bright splashes of abstract color that captured the eye and held it. And, unlike Hadley's cigar-ash strewn surroundings, here discreet little "Thank You For Not Smoking" signs adorned the end tables alongside current issues of *Time, Newsweek,* and *Sports Illustrated,* as well as today's *The Wall Street Journal.*

I barely had time to mourn the absence of anything like Hadley's battered grandfather clock that always ran twenty minutes fast before the inner door swung open. Christopher Brandon was my height and almost cadaverously thin. His light brown hair flopped onto his forehead, and he continuously flicked it away with a left-handed gesture I'd bet was so automatic he didn't even realize he was doing it.

"Mrs. Tanner? Hi, I'm Christopher Brandon. Won't you come in?"

His smile lit up his pale blue eyes, magnified by thick, heavy, horn-rimmed glasses. I followed him into a wide corner office so obsessively neat not a single piece of paper or client file marred the smooth shine of his glass-topped desk.

He was far too young to have been Jack T. Herrington's attorney, couldn't have been more than four or five years out of law school. He grinned engagingly when I remarked on it.

"Right. A lot of folks are surprised. You probably remember my dad. He's retired down in Fort Myers Beach. He and my mother spend their days on the golf course now. So," he said, folding his hands in front of him, "I understand you're going to check out the Herrington books for us."

"I'm going to have a crack at it, Mr. Brandon."

"Please, call me Chris."

"Fine. I'm Bay."

"Oh, you don't have to tell me anything about yourself. You're pretty famous around here. A lot of folks have you to thank for saving their bacon on that Grayton's Race thing. And your father—well, the Judge is pretty much a legend in this town."

I blushed under his steady, admiring gaze. *My God*, I thought, *I've acquired a groupie.*

I wasn't sure I liked the idea of being old enough to be looked up to by this earnest young lawyer. I glanced quickly at my watch and changed the subject.

"Mr. Herrington must be running late this morning," I said.

"Oh, he won't be able to join us. He called me yesterday afternoon to say he'd been called out of town on business. He said we should proceed without him."

"I see. So, what have we got?" I asked, sliding my reading glasses onto my nose. "What sort of records do you have?"

"Well, that's the problem," Chris Brandon said, settling into his high-backed, swivel chair. "We have a lot of paper, but most of it isn't in any kind of order. I'm not really sure what we've got."

"Did you request tax returns from their accountant?"

"It appears they were doing the accounting and taxes themselves. Dudley—that is, Dudley Macon, the manager—and his wife, Marilee. She runs the office."

"You mean there hasn't been any kind of outside audit? For how long?"

Chris Brandon bristled, sitting up straighter in his chair. His voice told me he'd taken my question as some kind of criticism. "My father strongly advised Mrs. Herrington to have the books checked by a professional, for her own protection. I repeated his warnings when I took over the practice. Did you know Mrs. Herrington well?"

"No," I replied, "not well at all. She was a friend of my mother. Look, Chris . . ."

"Well, I can tell you that she was a very strong, opinionated woman. When I tried to push her about an audit, she basically told me to butt out."

I tried unsuccessfully to suppress a smile, and a few seconds later Chris Brandon joined me. "It's tough trying to fill your father's shoes, isn't it?" I asked, and he nodded.

"Especially when a lot of your clients remember you as a two-year-old nuisance with a runny nose and messy pants. I think sometimes I'd have been better off to start out someplace else and build my own practice from the ground up."

I thought fleetingly of Geoff Anderson, of his obsession with breaking out of the old Southern traditions of his upbringing, and of what grief that bid for independence had ultimately brought him. "No," I said, shaking my head, "I think you made the right decision. Cut the old-timers some slack. They'll come around."

"Thanks, I hope you're right. So, what would you like to look at first? I've set aside a conference room for you. Figured you'd need some privacy, plus room to spread everything out."

"Actually," I said, consulting my watch, "what I'd really like to do is take it all with me. I have a couple of computer programs I want to use, and they're loaded on my hard drive at home." When the young attorney didn't respond right away, I asked, "Is that a problem? You can check it with the other Herringtons if you like. I don't think they'd object to my removing the records, but . . ."

"Oh, no, it's not that. Really. I'm sure there'd be no problem. It's just . . . well, maybe you'd better see for yourself."

Puzzled, I followed him out a side door that gave onto a narrow hallway. We passed two other offices, smaller and with fewer windows than Chris's. Inside each, a woman sat before a terminal, fingers flying across the keyboard as characters flashed in neat lines onto the screen. One wore the headset of a dictation machine.

Chris Brandon held open the wooden door at the end of the hall and gestured for me to precede him. The decor was probably similar to that of the sleek reception area, but it was impossible to tell.

Nearly every square inch of carpet was stacked with cardboard boxes overflowing with computer printouts, invoices, bulging envelopes stuffed with canceled checks, and the green columnar sheets of journals and ledgers.

I stood speechless in the doorway as I surveyed this paper disaster area. These were not neat, carefully labeled bankers' boxes like the ones I had used to store old records in at my office in Charleston. Instead I faced sagging, brown shipping cartons, their tops ripped away and names like Pittsburgh Paint and Mr. Coffee stenciled on their sides. The contents of several filing cabinets appeared to have been stuffed willy-nilly into every available space.

"Tell me this is a joke," I said.

"I wish it were," Chris Brandon replied. "When I asked Dudley for the records, I expected bound computer sheets and maybe the tax returns for the past six years. My secretary nearly had a coronary when one of the Bi-Rite delivery vans pulled up, and two guys started carting all this stuff up three flights of stairs."

"This could take the rest of my natural life," I said, approaching the nearest box and leafing through a stack of dusty paid invoices. The top one was dated 1994. "Why on earth would they think you needed all this?"

"I have no idea. I've been trying to get hold of Dudley for the past few days, but he seems to be out of touch. So what do you want to do?"

"Gasoline and a match are my initial choices," I said, and he laughed.

"I can have it messengered over to your house, unless you want to go through some of it first, maybe mark the ones that look most promising?"

"No, I guess I'd better have it all. Murphy's Law pretty much guarantees that the one thing I really need will be in the one box I don't have."

"I'll have Cheryl get right on it. Will you be home this afternoon?"

"No, actually I have a lunch meeting with Jordan Herrington on Hilton Head," I said. My watch warned me that I needed to get on the road soon if I were going to make it on time. "But I'll alert my housekeeper to expect a delivery."

I turned, and we walked back to the big corner office where I offered Chris my hand. "Thanks—I think," I said, grinning. "Better give me a couple of days to get this mess organized. Then you can tell me exactly what you're looking for in the way of documentation. I'm assuming a current balance sheet is the first order of business."

Chris Brandon held the handshake a little longer than was strictly necessary and moved toward the door. "That would be great. We need to value the stock so we can get the process started." He paused, one hand on the doorknob. "You're sure you have to rush off?" He swallowed and studied the tassels on his shiny cordovan loafers. "I mean, I hoped . . . I thought maybe . . . we could have lunch or something."

His awkwardness was endearing, but hey, I was old enough to be his . . . well, his much older sister, anyway. Still, his stumbling invitation seemed sincere, and, truth to tell, I was flattered.

"Sorry, that would have been nice. Some other time, perhaps?"

"Sure," he said brightening, "great. I'll make sure everything is at your house before five this afternoon."

"Thanks again, Chris," I said as he trailed behind me past the receptionist's desk.

"My pleasure, Mrs. . . . I mean, Bay."

The little blonde looked distinctly disapproving as I waved at the gawky attorney and let myself out.

I smiled as I trotted down the steps and out into the late morning glare. Any forty-ish woman who says the admiration of a younger man, no matter how inappropriate, isn't damned ego-boosting is a liar.

Then I sobered, remembering the purpose of my lunch with Jordan. I'd had no response from Erik Whiteside on my computer that morning, and I was beginning to think the whole thing had been some kind of elaborate hoax. Somehow I had to convince Jordan that this scheme of hers was ludicrous, that her best course was to grieve for the lost opportunity to reconcile with her mother, and get on with her life. Maybe she should still fight to bring her girls back to the States. I had to believe she'd be happier with them close by. Regardless, I had to dissuade her from this harebrained idea that two slightly faded flowers of the old South had any business setting out in hot pursuit of the mysterious, and probably innocuous, Ramon.

How this had become my responsibility, I wasn't sure. I only knew that it was.

I strode through the doorway of the Carolina Café ten minutes late to find Jordan von Brandt stubbing out a cigarette in an already overflowing ashtray and glowering at her diamond-encrusted watch. Across the table, dazzling in a white polo shirt and shorts, lounged her brother, Trey. He rose as I approached, pulled out a chair, and seated me with a flourish.

"At last," he said, his eyes once again alight with that mocking amusement I wasn't sure how to read.

"Sorry," I said, flipping the napkin onto my lap, "traffic from Beaufort was horrendous. They're working on the bridge again."

Neither of the Herringtons responded. Trey signaled a passing waiter, and I ordered a grilled shrimp Caesar salad. Jordan had already made a considerable dent in a chilled bottle of Pinot Grigio while her brother nursed a glass of orange juice.

"I just came from seeing Chris Brandon," I said when no one else appeared eager to initiate conversation. "The records from the hardware stores are a disaster. It's going to take me days to wade through all the mess, and I can't guarantee what I'll find. You might want to consider hiring an accounting firm instead of just me. This is going to require some serious man-hours."

"No!" Jordan snapped. "I don't want anyone else poking around in our business. I want you."

Trey picked up his sister's gold Dunhill lighter and held the flame to my cigarette. "I agree," he said. "The fewer people who know what a mess things are in, the better."

Jordan nodded. "We don't want potential buyers getting scared off by rumors."

"You're going to sell then?" The waiter set my salad in front of me, and I speared a plump, rosy shrimp.

"Of course." Trey dug into his crabmeat omelet. "You didn't seriously think any of us wanted to become the hardware king of Beaufort County, did you?"

"But your mother . . ."

"Left it in the hands of a fool, and look where that's gotten us. Besides, my father's will prohibited her from selling. We don't have that problem." Jordan stared at her heaping bowl of steamed mussels. "Anyway, if you need help, hire someone you can trust to keep his mouth shut. Otherwise, this stays strictly between us."

Maybe I'd gotten used to her imperiousness, or maybe yesterday's glimpse of the vulnerable side of Jordan von Brandt had mellowed me. At any rate, I shrugged in agreement and turned my attention to my lunch. We ate in silence for several minutes, Jordan concentrating more on the wine than on her food. The mid-September sunshine bathed the table in a soft light. Through the nearby windows I watched late-season sunbathers stretched out beside the sparkling pool below.

"I've told Trey about Ramon." Jordan's voice startled me out of my reverie.

Oh great! I thought, pushing the remaining shreds of romaine around in my bowl. *Now I've got* two *of them to convince.*

I took a minute to gather my thoughts and marshal my arguments as the waiter cleared the table and left us at last alone. I'd worked on this speech in my head during the interminable, stop-and-go drive back from Chris Brandon's office. I wanted to get it right the first time. I might not get a second chance.

"I have something I want to say. And I'd like to get through it without interruption or contradiction," I added hastily as Jordan opened her mouth to break in. "Please, just hear me out."

I leaned forward, elbows on the table. "Your mother is dead. Whether she had a heart attack or whether someone—deliberately or inadvertently—contributed to her death is not something you'll ever be able to prove. Not conclusively."

I raised my hand as Jordan again seemed on the verge of challenging me. Trey, on the other hand, slouched back in his chair appearing completely disinterested.

"The point is, you have no proof whatsoever, other than the most tenuous circumstantial evidence, that your mother was murdered. One," I pushed on relentlessly, "you have Leslie's letter, in which you tell me she mentions having made the acquaintance of a man named Ramon on the ship. Maybe he was her mysterious escort in Rio, maybe not. Maybe she never had one at all. Either way, there's no hint from her about anything intimate in their relationship, right?"

After she'd steeled herself to read Leslie's letter on my deck the day before, Jordan had been strangely reluctant to show it to me. So I had been forced to make deductions about Leslie's death based on the sparse bits of information her daughter had been willing to share with me.

Now she poured the last drops of wine into her glass and flagged our waiter for another bottle. She toyed with the huge diamond on her ring finger, much as she had on the day she'd first propounded this outlandish scenario to me.

"No one ever actually proposed to her. It was just a feeling she had, right?" I persisted, and Jordan allowed me a brief inclination of her head in acknowledgment.

"Okay, second, the nightgown. It was still in the box. Never been worn. Even though you say it's Leslie's size, it could have been a gift for someone, even you. As I recall, you and your mother were about the same height."

"Don't be ridiculous. It's a full two sizes too large for me."

"But that doesn't say it couldn't have been for someone else. A close friend, another relative?"

Jordan's lack of rebuttal gave me hope.

"Then, there's the missing jewelry. You said she wouldn't have traveled without it. Do you know that for a fact? Have you checked out her house? Her safety deposit box? You can't assume it's been stolen until you verify she had it with her." Another idea struck me. "Have you filed an insurance claim? Surely they'll require proof of loss before they pay off."

I could see Jordan's certainty wavering. It didn't make me feel good. I gulped down some iced tea and forced myself not to reach for the pack of cigarettes. I was taking no pleasure in knocking down her carefully constructed house of cards, but I honestly believed it had to be done. In fact, I should have kicked it over that first day.

I glanced over at Trey, but his back was turned to me, his attention apparently captured by the row of hard, bronzed bodies lounging around the pool below.

"I hope we're not boring you," I snapped, and his head swiveled deliberately around to face me.

"I didn't think you required my assistance. You seemed to be doing a bang-up job on your own."

I ignored his smiling condescension and plunged back in. "The last thing is Leslie's health. You said you talked to her doctor, and she'd had a checkup just prior to leaving on her cruise. How extensive? I mean, did he do an EKG and all sorts of tests, or was it just a blood pressure and tongue depressor, everything looks fine, have a nice trip kind of thing?"

Jordan shrugged and sipped Pinot Grigio. "I didn't ask. But he's been her physician for years. Surely he would know if something were seriously wrong with her."

"Not necessarily," I replied, succumbing to the persistent nicotine cravings and lighting up. "An hour before she died, my mother was putting the finishing touches on the menu for a dinner party for eighteen and haranguing poor Lavinia about finger smudges on the leaves of the dining table. Then she went out back to cut flowers for the centerpieces. Lavinia found her, face down in her prize Queen Elizabeth rosebush. A massive coronary."

Incredibly, I felt my eyes misting over. Despite the total deterioration of our relationship, I still remembered how shocked I'd been by the news of my mother's unexpected death.

"Dr. Gwinnet, who'd attended her for years, said he'd seen no indications of heart trouble in any of his recent examinations." I cleared my throat self-consciously, hoping to cover the slight quaver in my voice. "So you see, it could have happened that way with Leslie, too."

"So what you're saying is, you're backing out of helping me get to the bottom of this. You'll be pleased to know my brothers are in complete agreement with you." Jordan stabbed viciously at the ashtray, breaking her half-smoked cigarette in two.

"I think I can make better use of my time by straightening out the Bi-Rite books and helping you get your mother's estate settled. Don't you?"

"Absolutely," Trey answered. "The sooner, the better."

Jordan shot him a venomous look, then leaned over to pull a cellular phone from her bag. "We all know getting your grubby hands on the money is your only interest in Leslie's death, darling. But you might try being just a trifle more subtle about it, for appearances' sake."

She jabbed numbers into the phone with a well-manicured nail. Trey shrugged, his gaze drawn once again to the window.

"Philippe? Get your notebook. I have instructions for you. My secretary," Jordan announced, covering the mouthpiece with her hand. "What?" she barked back into the phone. "Who gives a damn what the weather's like down here? Listen carefully. In the safe in my bedroom is a file marked 'Mother'. In it you'll find a set of keys. I want you to bring them to me in Natchez. Tomorrow. Hold on."

I turned to follow Jordan's surprised look as Justin Herrington pulled out a chair and joined us at the table.

" 'Hail, hail, the gang's all here'," Trey mocked as Jordan resumed her rapid-fire conversation.

"Yes, Philippe, Natchez is in Mississippi. Book me on a flight out of here that gets us in at approximately the same time. I'll meet you at the airport. And call Doctor . . . wait a moment."

She reached in her bag for a calf-bound address book and riffled through its pages. Her brothers and I could only watch in wonder, a silent audience to this naked display of the power of wealth.

"Valerian. Dr. John Valerian. Get me an appointment for to-morrow afternoon. Tell him I only need half an hour. And I'll be wanting to inspect my mother's medical records."

Jordan lit a cigarette and listened intently as her beleaguered secretary apparently read back her instructions. She nodded, seemingly satisfied. "Call me here with the flight number. Right. *Ciao.*"

She scribbled her name across the check the waiter had left on the table and rose to stand beside me. "I'm going to prove you wrong, Bay, on every count. When I get through, you'll be as convinced as I am that Leslie was murdered by this gigolo she picked up. You'll have to help me then."

In a swirl of Chanel, she was gone.

Justin reached across for his sister's glass and poured himself some wine. "What was that all about?"

I deferred to Trey. "She's off on another tangent, this time to Natchez." He gave his brother a quick rundown on the lunch table discussion as I collected my things and pushed back my chair.

"How'd it go with Chris Brandon?" Justin asked.

"Fine. Trey can fill you in on the details. I'll be in touch when I have something to report."

"Do you think you got through to Jordan?" Justin studied me anxiously.

"No," I said and headed for the door.

13

The boxes were stacked neatly around the perimeter of my spare bedroom-turned-office. Someone had used heavy, black marker to print a number on the side of each one, and they had been arranged in ascending order. Hopefully this meant they were at least somewhat chronological.

Dolores had lingered past her usual quitting time, certain I'd need her assistance in dealing with this paper invasion of my normally orderly home. Had her English been better, she would have been the perfect choice to help me sort through the mess. I was practically pushing her out the door when inspiration struck.

"Is Angie still planning on a business major in college?"

Angelina, Dolores's oldest and a senior at the local high school had "shadowed" me last year as part of a Careers Day project. For some reason, she had found my profession fascinating and had determined on following in my footsteps.

"*Si, Señora, es verdad.*"

"Do you think she'd be interested in helping me out here? I promise I won't let it interfere with her schoolwork, and I'll see that she's well paid."

Dolores looked torn, unhappy at the thought of refusing me, yet uncertain about the wisdom of anything that might adversely affect her daughter's straight-A performance. Barely literate in English herself, my housekeeper was fiercely determined that her children would become well-educated Americans.

"It'll be good experience for her," I coaxed, "hands-on stuff she won't get out of a book. It'll only be for a couple of days."

"*Si, Señora.* If her papa, he says *no problema.*"

"Great! Have Angie call me tonight, okay?"

I quickly shed my business clothes. In my favorite cutoffs and ragged T-shirt, I sat down at the kitchen desk and checked my messages. Red had returned my call. Off duty at eight, he said he'd try to stop by. Bitsy wanted an update on "the Jordan thing". And some earnest young man wanted to send me a platinum Visa card with a fifteen thousand dollar credit limit if only I'd call him back at his 800 number. I deleted that one. I hate junk phone calls almost as much as I hate junk mail.

Which reminded me that I hadn't checked my computer since I'd gotten home. I settled myself in front of the monitor and logged on. When the little red flag popped up on the mailbox icon, I jumped. A click, and the header was displayed.

A reply from EWhiteside.

Damn.

Having convinced myself that the whole thing was probably a farce, I had lectured Jordan on the folly of her fantasy. I had purposely left out all mention of Erik and his bizarre website, certain nothing would come of it. And now . . .

Bloody hell! I didn't want there to be any connection between the deaths of the two women. I wanted Erik Whiteside to be a crackpot, a loony who got his kicks from luring gullible people like me into replying to a totally phony come-on. For what purpose I hadn't worked out yet, but it didn't really matter.

I wanted to bury myself in the familiar tangle of debits and credits, deposits and withdrawals, a puzzle that would eventually yield up a solution I could see and defend. Numbers have an order, a beautiful logic that defies interpretation, innuendo, emotion. Put the right combination in, and the correct answer will always pop out, perfect and indisputable. Not like people, with their messy problems. Not like Jordan or Leslie . . .

My finger hovered over the <Delete> key.

Curiosity and a need to know, the same damnedable things that made me itch to get my hands on the boxes of chaotic records, won out. I should have known they would. I opened the file.

Erik Whiteside had been out of town on business, which explained his delay in replying. Yes, his grandmother had been on a Royal Scandinavian cruise ship, the *Crystal Countess*. What information did I have about other mysterious deaths? Where? When? What was my interest? Was I with law enforcement?

A lot more questions than answers. He appended both his work and home phone numbers this time, closing with a plea for me to call him collect, day or night. I was the first real lead he'd had, and his desperation to make contact was evident throughout his e-mail.

I pulled the manila envelope with Leslie's papers out of the drawer and located the cruise ticket. The *Crystal Fjord,* not the *Countess.* So much for that.

I sat staring at the glowing monitor for a long time, vacillating. Finally, I saved the message and logged off. I needed time to think this through.

Mr. Bones wandered in and curled himself around my bare feet. I leaned over to scratch his ears and noticed absently that he'd managed to wriggle out of yet another flea collar. I hoped I had one left. If not, the scruffy tom would be banished to the outdoors.

As I gathered the scattered receipts and documents from my desktop, a splash of color caught my eye. Stuck to the back of one of the ship's daily programmes, the tiny card had slipped by unnoticed in my first hasty perusal. Gently I tried to pull it off, but it was melted against the softer paper.

About the size of a gift enclosure card, it immediately brought to mind the dozens of roses Jordan had said her mother'd received during her brief time in Rio. I worked at it patiently, but all I succeeded in doing was ripping the programme.

I disentangled myself from the sleeping cat and headed for the kitchen. I filled the teakettle and set it on the cook top, cranking the heat up to HIGH.

At last some justification for my misspent youth, I thought, drumming my fingers on the counter in barely controlled impatience. All those nights huddled under the covers with a purloined flashlight and Edgar Allan Poe or Agatha Christie for company had not been in vain.

When steam began to rise from the little hole in the spout, I took the kettle off the stove and gingerly moved the paper back and forth across it. Slowly the edges began to loosen. I had to reheat the water twice, but fifteen painstaking minutes later the card lay face up on the counter. Some of the bold, black ink had run, but enough remained for me to make out the message: "Until tonight, darling. R."

That single initial dominated, formed with a flourish at once dramatic and slightly ridiculous. "R" . . . for Ramon.

I left the card to dry and carried the programme back into the office. I logged back on to AOL and pulled up Erik Whiteside's message. "I prefer to remain anonymous at this time for reasons I may be able to explain later", I typed. "Do you have a passenger list for the *Crystal Countess?* If not, can you obtain one? Look for anyone named 'Ramon' traveling by himself, and get back to me."

As an afterthought, I added, "This is not a joke."

I clicked <Send>, and, determined to put the mystery on the back burner for the time being, turned and hauled the first box of the Bi-Rite records over to the desk.

When the doorbell rang a little after seven, I prayed it was the pizza man. I'd ordered almost an hour ago, intending to be showered and presentable by the time my dinner arrived. But, as usual, I had gotten engrossed in the puzzle, and now had to wipe my grimy hands on dusty shorts as I made my way to the front door. The records had obviously been stored in an attic somewhere. They smelled as grungy as they looked.

I pulled open the door to the acned young delivery kid, exchanged cash for food, and graciously accepted his apology for the delay: he'd gotten lost. My tip was still generous even though I'd probably have to reheat the pizza. As he turned to go, he nearly collided with the trim young woman trotting up the steps.

"Hey, Jer," Angelina Santiago greeted him, "how's it goin'?"

Her perfect olive complexion glowed around a dazzling smile, and her cascade of waist-length black hair shimmered in the soft light of the fading sun.

"Jer" gulped, apparently awestruck by the beautiful creature before him. "Hey, Ange," he managed to mumble, then, "Gotta go", as he nearly sprinted for his Giuseppi's Pizza delivery car.

I laughed as Angie joined me in the kitchen. I washed up as best I could at the sink, then opened the box. Not exactly piping hot, but I was too hungry even to wait for the microwave.

"You want some?" I asked, pulling napkins out of the holder.

"No thanks, Mrs. Tanner. I've already had dinner."

"How about a Coke?"

"Sure, that'd be great."

I flipped her a can and got a diet out for myself. "So your mom told you about my job offer, huh?" I snagged a wayward piece of pepperoni and piled it back on top before taking a huge bite of the fragrant slice.

"Yeah. I mean, yes, ma'am. I had to drop my brother Bobby off at a friend's house, so I thought I'd just stop over. I hope that's okay?"

"Sure, if you don't mind talking while I eat. I'm starving."

"No problem. I'm really excited. Do you think I'll really be able to help? You're not just doing this to be, you know, nice or something?"

The Santiago pride had obviously been passed down to the next generation. Dolores was a firm believer in earning her own way.

"You may not think it's so nice of me when you see the mess we've got on our hands. Literally." I held my fingers up, displaying grimy nails that hadn't yielded to my quick wash-up.

"Oh, I don't mind getting dirty. When can I start? You want me to do anything now? I've got an hour or so before I have to go pick Bobby up."

"Why don't you go take a look at what we're up against while I finish eating?" I suggested, wiping mozzarella off my chin. "In the office, down the hallway there."

"Cool," she said, leaping up from the table.

"Don't move anything around yet," I called after her. "I've started to make piles."

"Okay," Angie hollered back.

Cool? I didn't know kids still said that.

"Wow, what a mess!" Angie wandered back into the kitchen, dusting her hands off against each other. "What do you want me to do, exactly, Mrs. Tanner? I can come after school tomorrow, around four, if that's okay."

"Four will be fine. Well, first, everything has to be separated into categories—invoices, payables, checks, and so on. That's what I started on tonight. Then each category will have to be organized by date and document number so we can see what's missing. If you can tackle that part, I can start dropping numbers into the computer."

"Great! Why don't I do some now? I mean, you've already made a start, and I can just follow your lead. If I have any questions, you'll be right here."

I saw no reason to squelch this youthful enthusiasm, so I nodded my agreement. "One thing, though," I said, checking Angie's eager bounce down the steps from the kitchen. "Two things, actually. Don't try moving any of those boxes by yourself. They're heavy."

Angie pulled herself up to her full 5'5" and probably 110 pounds soaking wet. "I'm pretty strong, Mrs. Tanner. I'm a cheerleader, plus I work out in the weight room at school."

"I'm sure you're a tough cookie, but just the same, call me, okay? Your mother will murder me if I let you get hurt."

"Sure, no problem."

"And, most importantly, no discussing what you see here with anyone. Not your family, not your best friend, not your boyfriend. Nobody."

Angie blushed. "I don't have a boyfriend."

"You will. But the rule holds. If you want to get into this business someday, you might as well learn now that confidentiality is the heart of the profession. People trust us with some of the most private information they have—their finances. So, nothing of what you're doing or whose records you're working on. Agreed?"

"Oh, absolutely, Mrs. Tanner. Not a peep. I swear."

Angie raised her hand solemnly as if she were being sworn in to the witness box.

"Okay. And Angie?" I called as she headed for the office.

"Yes, ma'am?"

"When we're here working, why don't you call me Bay? It'll make things a lot easier."

"But Mama . . ."

"Doesn't have to know. It'll just be for when we're alone, okay?"

"Cool. Bay."

She flipped her curtain of hair back over one shoulder and bounded down the hall.

What a delightful kid, I thought, lifting another slice of pizza from the box. All Dolores's offspring were like that: bright, attractive, mannerly. The times when I regretted Rob's and my decision to postpone a family became fewer the older I got. But when they hit, like now, it felt as if a huge hole had opened up in my gut, an emptiness nothing could fill.

I shook off the encroaching depression, wrapped up the remaining pizza, and straightened up the mess I'd made at the table. I was just stuffing the greasy box into the trash when the doorbell rang.

I hadn't heard a car pull in. Puzzled, I opened the front door to find Trey Herrington leaning casually against the railing.

"Hi," he said. "I guess this is the right place."

"What are you doing here? How did you get in?" I glanced around him toward the driveway, but only Dolores's Hyundai was pulled up in front of the garage.

"Nice to see you, too," Trey said with a mocking smile.

I felt my face flush in embarrassment. "I'm sorry. Come in. Please."

I held the door open as he edged past me into the house. It was probably accidental that his tan, muscular arm brushed against my left breast.

"Nice place," Trey remarked as he wandered into the great room and plopped, uninvited, onto the white sofa. "Great view of the beach."

"It's better from the bedroom," I blurted out, then bit my tongue in anger at his raised eyebrows.

"Really? I'll have to check that out."

Now that I'd made a complete idiot of myself, there was no point in carrying on the pretense that this was a welcome visit. I remained standing.

"What can I do for you?"

"Oh, nothing. I took a walk up the beach and suddenly realized I could just follow one of those narrow paths and wander right into the plantation. Kind of makes all your uniformed guards and security gates sort of pointless doesn't it?"

"How'd you find my house? Or did you just wander around knocking on doors?" His calm assurance, the way he had simply made himself at home, was beginning to piss me off.

"You're in the phone book. If you don't want people to have your address, you should get an unlisted number."

"You carry a phone book with you? Or did you by chance happen to look it up *before* you started on your 'aimless' walk on the beach?"

Trey's laugh lit his face, crinkling the skin around his pale green eyes, making him look younger, more human, than the sullen, cocky expression I'd become used to.

"Okay, Nancy Drew, I'm busted. Since I couldn't storm the walls of the castle directly, I decided on a sneaky, backdoor incursion. Maybe not strictly honorable, but it worked, didn't it?"

"So what can I do for you?" I repeated.

"For starters, you could sit down."

"I think that was supposed to be my line," I said, settling into one of a pair of wing chairs by the fireplace.

"*Touché.* Sorry if I violated any long-standing traditions of Southern protocol. Things are a little more relaxed out in lotus-land."

"So I hear," I said, smiling in spite of myself.

"Well, at least in L.A. the hostess would have offered me a beer by now."

"Hostess implies a guest, which implies an invitation," I shot back. Despite my annoyance at Trey's unexpected appearance, I was beginning to enjoy this verbal battle.

"Damn, I like you. I didn't want to, you understand. I figured any longtime friend of my sister was probably as overbearing and pushy as she is. But you're okay, Bay Tanner."

"Thank you, I'm so relieved. Want a beer?"

Trey followed me up the steps to the refrigerator where I managed to locate the last of the bottles I had stocked up on for the workmen. He twisted off the cap, took a long pull, and surveyed my remodeled kitchen.

"Nice layout," he said, running his hands over the slate counter. "I like the color contrast. Must have been a real mess after the explosion."

I flinched, remembering the smoking ruin of my car, the total destruction of this room and the garage beneath.

"Sorry. Didn't mean to scare up bad memories. Mind if we sit out on the deck? It's a beautiful evening."

Without waiting for a reply Trey crossed to the French doors. I trailed along behind, grabbing up my cigarettes and warm Diet Coke on the way. I squared my shoulders as I stepped outside, determined to regain control of the situation.

"At the risk of repeating myself . . ." I began as we sank onto the cushioned chairs.

"You mean what do I want now that I've barged in on you uninvited and made myself at home?"

"Something like that," I replied as I lit up. "I'm really kind of busy right now."

"Got a date, is that it? Hope you're gonna clean up a little first," he said with a grin.

I looked down at my filthy shorts, blackened nails, and grubby knees, and had to laugh. "I got like this in your employ, I'll have you know. The Bi-Rite records look like they've been stored in a gravel pit."

"Think you'll be able to make sense out of them?"

"Eventually. It's going to take some time, though."

"Well, hire someone to help you. I'm sure the estate can handle the expense."

"Already did," I replied.

As if on cue, Angelina Santiago appeared in the doorway. "Oh, I'm sorry, Mrs. Tanner. I didn't know you had company."

"That's okay, Angie. Did you have a question?"

"No, I didn't have any problem following your system. But I have to pick up Bobby now. We're supposed to be home by nine."

Trey Herrington cleared his throat loudly. He left me no choice but to perform introductions. His dazzling smile, turned up to full power, mesmerized poor Angie. Usually poised and confident, she stumbled over her replies to his polite questions.

I finally rescued her by the simple act of taking her by the arm and guiding her back through to the great room. "I'll walk you out," I said, adding pointedly as Trey moved to follow, "I'll be right back."

"Nice to meet you, Mr. Herrington," Angie called dreamily over her shoulder as I headed her toward the front door.

"What a hunk!" she whispered when we reached the porch. "He looks just like James Bond!"

"Yes, he does. But he's also old enough to be your father, and he has a nasty disposition."

"He's not too old for *you*," she said with a mischievous twinkle in her deep brown eyes.

"Out, dratted child!" I ordered in mock severity. "See you tomorrow at four."

"I'll be here. Thanks, Mrs. Tanner. Goodnight!"

"Drive carefully," I called after her.

I turned on all the outside lights and watched until she made the left out of the driveway. I found Trey stretched out on the chaise, one hand tucked behind his head, his shoes discarded on the deck beside him.

"This is great," he said while I lighted a few citronella candles to keep the no-see-ums at bay.

I couldn't help noticing that he had great legs, long and tanned, and perfectly proportioned. I mentally slapped myself and resumed my seat a few feet away.

"Sort of reminds me of Malibu," he continued, "except the sunsets are better out there."

"That may be because we're facing east," I said dryly. "The sun sets over the mainland here."

Trey swung his legs over the side of the chaise and rested his elbows on his knees, the nearly empty beer bottle dangling loosely from his hands. "You don't like me very much, do you?" he asked softly.

"You haven't exactly gone out of your way to make a good impression, have you? I mean, you have to admit, ever since our first meeting, you've been a little . . ."

"Rude? Obnoxious? Overbearing?"

"*Caustic* was the word I would have chosen."

Again his laugh made me smile in return.

"Generous," he said and downed the last swallow of beer.

"What was that all about, the first time we met? I could almost feel the animosity pouring off of you in waves."

I could barely make out his shrug in the growing darkness. "I don't know. Like I said, Jordan had been singing your praises for two days. Plus all the stories around Beaufort about how you saved everyone from the big, bad developers and almost got yourself killed. I guess I like my women a little less intimidating."

"*Your* women?"

"Sorry. Bad choice of words. I'd really like us to be friends, Bay. Think that's possible?"

"Probably," I said. "I'll give it some thought. But speaking as your 'hostess', I need you to get the hell out of here so I can get back to work. The estate isn't going to get settled until I get those records straightened out. I know that's a priority for you."

"Not really. That's just Jordan's bitchiness talking. I did pretty well on my last film. I don't need the money nearly as much as she'd like to think I do."

I assumed he couldn't see my raised eyebrows in the flickering light of the candles.

"So, what do you say? One more beer?" he asked.

"Sorry, that was the last one. You've cleaned me out."

"Next time I'll bring a six-pack," Trey said, rising reluctantly as I did.

I led the way back into the house, flipping on lights as I went. "Listen, do you want me to drive you back to the hotel? It's pretty dark out there."

"No thanks, I'll be fine. Maybe I could borrow a flashlight, though. Not much of a moon tonight."

"Sure." I rummaged around in the hall table, finally coming up with a small Eveready. "And the batteries are still good," I announced, flicking it on and off.

"Thanks. I'll return it tomorrow night at dinner. Will you call me in a pass? Unless of course you'd rather pick me up at the hotel. That might be easier."

"Slow down a minute," I said, backing away from the unfamiliar look in his eyes. "Who said anything about dinner?"

"Oh, did I forget to mention that? I'm taking you out tomorrow night. Pick a really nice place. Something that faces west, so we can watch the sunset."

"Look, Trey, I don't think . . ."

"Bay, come on. Take pity on a poor, stranded exile. Jordan's heading for Natchez tomorrow, and Justin plans to drive up to Charleston to get together with some old college pals. I'll be all alone. What do you say? Just a nice dinner, between friends?"

He sounded so sincere, so earnest. He had been good company tonight, funny and charming.

Oh, what the hell, I told myself, *it's only dinner.*

"It'll have to be late," I said. "Angie's coming over to work on Bi-Rite."

"Great! Eight o'clock okay?"

"Fine. I'll meet you at the hotel."

"Thanks, Bay. I mean that." His fingers brushed my cheek, and his smile sent little shivers skittering up my spine. "I'll even pick up the check."

"What a guy!" I laughed as he let himself out and trotted down the steps.

"Eight o'clock," he called as he rounded the corner of the house and disappeared into the dark.

"You're an idiot," I chided myself as I locked up and set the alarm. "The man is trouble with a capital 'T'."

Even so, I found myself humming as I headed back into the office.

14

By the time I shooed Angelina Santiago out the door and shut down the computer the next night, I knew I would have to hustle to get cleaned up and dressed for my *date* with Trey. I had stripped down to my lavender briefs and had one hand on the shower knob when the doorbell rang.

I cursed loudly and snatched up the sweaty, dusty T-shirt I'd just pulled off. I skidded to a stop at the end of the hallway, remembering just in time that I'd left the inside door open with only the screen on the latch.

I peeked around the corner. Red Tanner, one hand shading his eyes, peered through the mesh.

"Bay," he called, rattling the door against its hook-and-eye closure, "you in there? It's me."

"Red, go away!" I hollered from behind the wall. "I'm not decent. I was just getting into the shower."

"If that's supposed to discourage me, it's not working," he laughed.

"I'm serious. I'm getting ready to go out."

"Where?" he snapped, the humor gone from his voice.

"None of your damn business," I said lightly, but meaning it.

"I'm only here because you left me a message. I thought you wanted to talk."

"I did. I mean, I do, only not right now. Seriously, you're making me late."

"Who's the lucky guy?" Red tried for nonchalance and failed.

"It's business. Now will you get out of here? I'll call you."

"What do you mean 'business'? You haven't been to work in a year."

I could have left him standing on the porch and gone back to the shower. Somehow though I knew he'd still be waiting there when I got out.

"Okay, turn around."

"What?"

"Turn around! I'll come and unhook the screen."

He made an elaborate show of covering his eyes, like a kid playing hide-and-seek. "Will this do?"

I tiptoed to the door, flipped up the latch, and bolted back down the hallway. I slammed my bedroom door and twisted home the lock, then leaped into the shower.

One good thing about having my hair shorn off was that it took a lot less time to dry. Fifteen minutes later I dashed into the kitchen to find Red sipping a Coke at the glass-topped breakfast table.

"You're out of beer," he said, then, "wow!" Slowly he surveyed me from head to toe and back again. "What kind of business did you say this was?"

I'd almost changed my mind about the simple, black silk dress in order to avoid just such a comment. The back was cut high, to hide my scars, but the front dipped low enough to expose a fair amount of tanned cleavage.

"Red, look, I only have a couple of minutes. I hate to rush out on you like this, but you should have called first."

"Sorry. Next time I'll make an appointment." He scooped his hat up off the table. He stood ramrod straight in his sharply creased uniform, his face reflecting more hurt than anger. "Have a nice time."

He turned and marched to the front door.

I stumbled a little in the unaccustomed two-inch heels, but managed to catch up to him on the porch. "Why are you acting like this?" I asked, plucking at his sleeve to make him stop.

"Like what?"

"Like I just confessed to the Oklahoma City bombing or something. You and the Judge and Lavinia are always harping at me to get out of the house. And when I do, you act as if it's some sort of betrayal. It's a business dinner. That's all."

"You don't owe me any explanation," his voice said, but his eyes told a whole other story.

"Damn right I don't," I fired back, "but I'm giving you one, anyway. As a courtesy. You remember courtesy?"

"Okay, you're right," he said, the stiff set of his khaki shoulders relaxing. "I'm being an asshole."

"No argument here," I replied, and we both laughed. "You off at seven tomorrow, too?"

"Yup."

"Why don't you stop by? Maybe we could grab a burger. I really want to pick your brain about something."

"Not the Herrington thing again, I hope."

"No." I had almost forgotten about my quest for the truth about Jack T.'s death, so much else had happened since then. "Nothing like that."

"Okay, deal. You gonna wear that dress again?"

"In your dreams," I said and shoved him playfully toward the steps. "Now beat it."

Even though it was already past eight, I waited until I saw his taillights disappear before I snatched up my black bag and keys and sprinted for the car.

I told myself it was only because I hate being late, but that couldn't fully account for the pounding of my heart as I squealed to a stop under the canopy in front of the Westin. One of the young bellmen, dressed charmingly like an old-time golfer in plus fours, vest, and knee socks, hustled up to the car.

"Sorry, son," a voice said from out of the darkness, "you'll have to find your own date. This one's mine." Trey Herrington leaned over and kissed me casually on the cheek. "Want me to drive?"

"No . . . thanks," I stammered. "I've got it."

"You're the boss." He crossed in front of the headlights, his white silk turtleneck a gleaming contrast to the black linen blazer draped over his arm.

God, he is gorgeous, I thought as he slid effortlessly into the seat beside me.

"Sorry I'm late," I said as we roared back down the drive. "It's not far, though. We should still be able to catch the sunset."

Quit babbling! I ordered myself.

"You were worth the wait."

At least I thought that's what he'd said. By then we were out on the highway, and the rushing wind snatched away his words.

Ten minutes later we pulled into the entrance of the north end r.v. park and marina. Trey turned to me, a quizzical look crinkling his eyebrows.

"Trust me," I laughed.

The Sunset Grille was something of a local secret, one we hated sharing with the tourists. They'd eventually discovered it, of course, but on a Thursday night in mid-September I'd had no problem reserving the best table in the corner overlooking Skull Creek.

We barely had time to settle ourselves on the high, swivel chairs before the sun plunged to earth in a fiery display of reddish orange, tinged with trailing wisps of pink and mauve.

"Great timing," Trey said as our waitress set his Dewars and water in front of him.

"We aim to please."

"Don't you ever drink?" he asked, watching me sip Perrier and lime.

"Your sister asked me that same question," I said, scanning the menu to make certain my favorite dish was still being offered.

"And?"

"No, I don't."

The waitress approached, and we both ordered the salmon.

Trey had apparently gotten the message and changed the subject. "How's it going with the records?"

"Actually a lot faster than I anticipated. Angie's been a big help."

"She's a beautiful girl. Hey, I'm human," he added as I cocked an eyebrow at him. "A lot of hearts are going to get trampled under those pretty little feet."

"She's seventeen. I hope it's a lot of years before she worries too much about any of that."

"Don't count on it. There're kids younger than she is—and not nearly as attractive—raking in big movie bucks and sleeping around with each other."

"This isn't Hollywood," I snapped as our dinners arrived. "Don't go putting any screwy ideas in her head. She's already got her life planned out. And it doesn't include a movie career."

"You were right. This is wonderful," Trey said around a forkful of the tender fish. "So when do you think you'll have some results for the attorneys?"

"Anxious to get back to lotus-land?"

"I was," he said, and his eyes riveted on mine left no doubt as to his meaning.

I could feel the flush spreading upward from the base of my throat. "Tell me about Hollywood," I said to cover my confusion.

We finished our meal as the lights of a slow parade of returning pleasure boats cast their twinkling glow against the calm water below us. Trey tried to downplay the glamour of the movie business with tales of the incredible competition for work and the backbiting and maneuvering that was an integral part of every project. But his stories were also laced with familiar names, thrown out casually as if everyone did lunch with Bruce, took a meeting with Stephen, and hobnobbed over cocktails with Michael and Catherine. How much was true, and how much meant simply to impress me, I had no way of knowing, but it fascinated me nonetheless.

Over tea and coffee and a wickedly wonderful chocolate raspberry torte, the subject came back to Bi-Rite.

"What have you found out so far?" Trey asked, trying to sound unconcerned, but not quite succeeding. Or maybe, despite his protestations to the contrary, I was reading things into his questions simply because of Jordan's less than subtle hints about his financial situation.

"Too early to tell," I said as Trey handed his gold card to the waitress. True to his word he was picking up the tab. "All I know for certain is that record keeping does not seem to be the Macons' strong suit. What do you know about them? Personally, I mean."

We had strolled down the steps and out onto the small dock that serviced the marina. The sky seemed ready to burst with stars, glowing more brightly the farther we moved away from the artificial lights. Except toward the east, where distant lightning flashed in a heavy bank of dark clouds.

"Looks like a storm coming," I remarked as the wind freshened, and I shivered involuntarily.

Trey draped his blazer across my shoulders, his hands lingering in a gentle caress along my arms. "You've got a big one brewing out there somewhere. They're just about to give it a name, I think."

"A hurricane? I haven't heard anything about it."

"Just a tropical storm now, way out in the Atlantic. Or so the Weather Channel said. Nothing to worry about."

"You wouldn't say that if you'd ever been in one." I shuddered, remembering the devastation Hugo had wrought on the antebellum treasures along the Battery in Charleston. Luckily the condominium that had been Rob's and my home during the workweek had escaped major damage.

"Beats the hell out of earthquakes. At least you get some warning."

We turned and ambled back toward the parking lot. Trey's hand on my elbow felt warm and much too comforting.

"So what about the Macons?" I asked, moving out of his grasp.

Trey dropped his hand reluctantly. "I don't know the first damn thing about them," he said with a trace of irritation. "Dad hired Dudley long after I'd headed west. His name would come up once in awhile in casual conversation. Dad apparently trusted him enough to make him manager."

"What about the wife? Marilee, I think it is."

"Must be his second. I seem to remember his first wife died a few years back."

The wind continued to rise as the storm moved onshore. "I think we'd better head for the car before we get drenched," I said. "We'll need to get the top up, too."

I moved to slip Trey's jacket off my shoulders when a buzzing vibration sounded against my left breast. I jumped, nearly dropping the expensive sport coat into the murky water beside the dock. Trey snatched it up, reached for the inside left pocket, and removed his cell phone.

"Sorry," he said, grinning as he flipped open the small device. "Herrington," he spoke into the mouthpiece.

I turned my back to give him some privacy and stared out toward the mainland. To my left, a steady stream of headlights flowed across the graceful arch of one of the bridges onto the island. Lightning continued to crackle through the clouds, and a continuous rumble of thunder reverberated across the open water.

I could hear Trey's low voice in the background from a few feet away. This was why I refused to carry one of the damned intrusive little gadgets, and why I wouldn't have one in my car. There had to be a few places where the almost Pavlovian reflex to pick up a ringing phone could be avoided. Just because someone wanted to talk to me didn't necessarily mean I wanted to talk to them.

His voice at my shoulder startled me. "Here, it's Jordan. She wants to speak to you."

Puzzled, I took the thin phone, only certain which end was up by the way he handed it to me. "Hello, Jordan."

"My, my, isn't this cozy? Having a good time with darling Trey? He certainly didn't waste any time once I was out of the way."

"Did you call just to be bitchy, or is there some point to this?"

Unlike me, Trey did not move discreetly away, but hung at my elbow taking in every word.

"Look, Bay, I'm just trying to watch out for you. My brother can be damned charming when he sets his mind to it, but he can't be trusted. Leslie learned that a long time ago, and so did I. You need to be careful . . ."

"I'm a big girl now, Jordan. What is it you wanted?"

"Let's not argue," she said after a lengthy pause. "There's been a robbery. Here in Natchez. All Leslie's jewelry is missing, along with most of her personal papers and records. The police have been and gone, but there was no sign of forced entry. Either someone picked the locks, or he had a key."

"My God, Jordan, that's unbelievable! Was the place trashed?" I shot a look at Trey, but he had obviously absorbed the news with much more equanimity than I was able to muster.

"No. Whoever it was knew exactly what he was looking for and where to find it. The police dusted for fingerprints, but they don't expect to find anything. It looks like a professional job."

I leaned against the railing, totally stunned by this turn of events. "Was her obituary in the local papers there? Maybe someone saw that and figured the house would be empty and vulnerable."

"It's a possibility. The detectives mentioned it. But why steal her papers? That's what I don't understand. Her financial records and stock certificates would be useless to anyone but us."

"Did she have a safety deposit box? Maybe she transferred all those things there without telling you."

"She did have. I had a duplicate key and a power of attorney for it. But I checked with the bank. She closed it out a few months before she went on her trip." Another long sigh escaped, and I could hear the sounds of a cigarette being lighted. "I swear to God I don't understand what's happening."

"You're thinking it's related to her death," I said, and Trey frowned.

"Of course I am, but I don't see how. Do you?"

"No, not right off the top of my head. Did you see her doctor?"

"I went there right from the airport, before I came here to the house. She had nothing wrong with her, Bay. No indications of heart disease or anything else life-threatening. She had a major physical in June."

"I'm sorry, Jordan. I know how upsetting this must be for you."

"It's really going to screw up settling the estate, isn't it? Without those records, how are we supposed to know what kind of investments she had?"

The storm was almost directly overhead now, the fierce stabs of lightning causing sharp bursts of static. "Doesn't Justin have that information? He told me once he handled all that for your mother."

Trey took my arm and pointed to the sky. The first dime-sized splatters of rain began to plop into the water as we moved toward the parking lot.

"I don't know. Maybe."

"Jordan, I've got to go. It's starting to rain. When will you be back here?"

The line crackled, making her response nearly inaudible. I thought she said, "Saturday."

"Call me then. Here's Trey."

I shoved the phone at him, kicked off my pumps, and broke into a trot as the skies prepared to open. I managed to get the top and windows up just as the downpour burst.

"That was close," Trey said, running a hand through his thick, wet hair. "You okay?"

"A little damp around the edges, but otherwise fine." I cranked the engine and flipped on the defroster to clear the steamy windows. "I'm going to wait a few minutes and see if this lets up a little. I don't think I can see well enough to drive."

The rain pelted us from all directions, bouncing off the hood of my sports car and cascading over its sides. Thunder broke all round us, and the wind whipping through the loblolly pines sounded like the creaking of old bones.

Tucked inside the gradually warming car, I felt a growing sense of isolation and intimacy, as if we had crawled inside a dry cave to escape the storm. When Trey reached for my hand, I let him take it without resistance. Neither one of us seemed inclined to break the spell with words.

The storm fled as quickly as it had pounced. There was no gradual tapering off. The rain suddenly ceased as if someone had thrown a switch.

"Looks like it's over," I said, disengaging my hand from the warmth of Trey's.

"Too bad," he said with a smile.

Parts of the driveway were flooded, and I held the straining engine down to a crawl until we had gained the highway. I could feel

Trey's eyes on the side of my face, but I kept mine determinedly on the road.

"What do you make of the burglary at your mother's?" I asked to break the tension his concentrated gaze was building inside me.

"I think your assessment is probably right. Someone read about her death and decided to take advantage of the situation. Leslie liked to flaunt her possessions, especially her jewelry. It wouldn't take a mastermind to figure out the house would be loaded with goodies. You have wonderful hair."

The *non sequitur* startled me almost as much as his long fingers, now gently twining the damp curls that lay against my neck.

"Stop that," I ordered, afraid to take a hand off the wheel to slap his away. Deep pools of standing water stretched across the road in places, sending off towering sheets of spray as we passed. My low-slung car needed all my attention.

Traffic slowed, then stopped completely as we approached the intersection where the cross-island highway spilled out all the traffic from the south end of the island. I could see ahead the flashing blue lights of sheriff's cars intermingled with the rotating red glow from emergency vehicles.

"Oh great, an accident. We'll be stuck here half the night."

"Damn," Trey said with a wicked grin as I took the opportunity to disentangle his hand from my hair.

"You think I'm joking? This is an island, remember? With only one main road. Unless we can make it to the on-ramp for the by-pass, there's no alternate route."

I lowered the window and lit a cigarette. The sweet smell of rain-washed air mingled with exhaust fumes as traffic began to stack up next to and behind us.

"You seem pretty calm about the break-in," I said. "Doesn't it bother you at all?"

"Nothing I can do about it. Besides, everything's probably insured."

"Is that all that matters to you? The money?"

In the dim light from the dash I caught the flash of anger that deepened his strange eyes to a smoldering emerald.

"You know, I'm getting pretty damned sick of all the snide cracks about my interest in Leslie's money. What right do you or anyone else have questioning my motives? All I want is what's legally mine, and not a penny more."

Bright red brake lights began to flick off in front of me as vehicles started crawling forward. I pulled the gearshift into drive and inched after them.

"You're right. I'm sorry." I stubbed out the cigarette and avoided his gaze.

"You know, it seems to me you ought to step back a little and apply some of that famous accountant's objectivity here." His voice, no longer tight with anger, still held an edge.

"What do you mean?"

"You've been taking everything Jordan tells you at face value. Did you ever stop to wonder about *her* motives?"

"Did you read the letter she received from Leslie?" I fired back. "I think that pretty much tells her story."

"You think so? Work through the logic of it. Jordan's lifestyle depends on keeping old Klaus happy. If she challenges him for custody, what do you think's going to happen to her cash cow? She lives like a Rockefeller because she sold her kids to the highest bidder."

My head whipped around so abruptly, my hands followed, and I had to fight to keep the Z3 from slithering off the road.

"What a despicable thing to suggest!"

I whipped into the left lane and took the turn into Port Royal much too fast. I was gratified to see Trey Herrington reach out to brace himself against the dash. I jumped a stop sign and raced around the curves, pulling up in a sheet of water in front of the hotel.

"Thanks for dinner. Goodnight," I said through clenched teeth, my hands gripping the steering wheel as if I thought it might get away.

"Bay, look, I'm sorry. I didn't mean to tick you off." When I didn't respond, he went on, his tone now soft and reasonable. "But think about what I said, okay? How well do you really know my sister? You haven't laid eyes on her in over twenty years. Should you accept everything she says as gospel just because you went to school together half a lifetime ago?"

I held fast to my indignant silence as Trey extricated himself from the bucket seat, then leaned in through the open door.

"I'm sorry the evening had to end like this. I had a great time. Mostly."

I caught the flash of his killer smile out of the corner of my eye.

"Something else to think about after you cool off a little," he said. "Did *you* read the letter from Leslie?"

I turned then and stared him straight in the eye.

"I didn't think so," he said softly. "You ought to ask Jordan for it. You might find it very enlightening. Goodnight."

He closed the door with exaggerated care and sauntered slowly into the lobby, the black jacket slung over one shoulder. I sat for a moment, unable—or unwilling—to grasp the significance of his last sally. I was still frozen, staring after him through the wide glass doors, when Trey Herrington turned and waved. With a guilty start, I gunned the engine and sped off down the drive toward home.

The word *bastard* kept playing over and over in my mind, like a litany.

15

At 2:26 I gave up, tossed back the rumpled sheets, and rolled out of the king-sized bed. I pulled on a T-shirt and shorts and plodded wearily into the kitchen to put the kettle on for tea. A confused Mr. Bones mewed loudly from the hallway, then padded up to join me at the table.

"I know, old friend," I said, scratching lightly behind his ears, "but I just can't sleep. Might as well do something constructive, don't you think?"

He followed closely behind as I carried the teapot into my office. The cat had decided the neat piles of documents stacked around the floor had been put there for his convenience. After sniffing out several likely candidates, he selected a stack and curled himself onto it. In seconds he was fast asleep.

"Lucky beast," I said and flipped on the computer.

I hoped the tangle of the Bi-Rite financial records would banish the fruitless thoughts I'd been chasing around in my head for the past three hours. Much as I hated to admit it, the seeds of Trey Herrington's attack on his sister had found a small, fertile patch in my brain and had begun to put down roots.

It was true I had pretty much taken Jordan's statements at face value. Why shouldn't I? While she had aroused a series of conflicting emotions in me—from pity to white-hot anger—I'd never once stopped to question the truthfulness of her statements. Trey had thrown words like *objectivity* and *logic* at me as if they were epithets.

Okay, pretty boy, I snarled to myself, *let's see where that gets us.*

Ignoring the computer screen, I pulled a legal pad toward me. List making is a way of life for me, and Rob and I had refined it to a science in the days when I had played Watson to his Holmes as we plotted against the drug traffickers and money launderers that polluted our state.

Twenty minutes later I sat back to review my pathetically short list, flicking long, gray ash off the cigarette I didn't remember lighting.

FACT: Leslie Herrington died on or about September 3 of apparent natural causes in an expensive hotel room in Rio de Janeiro, Brazil.

Proof of that was in the newspaper's obituary Bitsy had shown me over lunch.

And that was as far as I'd gotten. Because every other piece of information I had, I'd gotten secondhand—from Jordan. The missing jewelry. Leslie's health. The proposed reconciliation. The burglary. Even the mysterious Ramon. Everything.

What stung the most was that Trey had been right on target. My face flushed in humiliation as I recalled my impassioned, if perhaps now unfounded, defense of his sister.

"And this is why you're a number cruncher instead of a psychologist, my girl," I mumbled, pushing the pad away and reaching for the computer mouse. "People are just too damned unpredictable."

As I waited for the connection with AOL to go through, I wondered how I could go about independently verifying the other "facts" about Leslie Herrington. I was trying to figure out why I felt this compulsion to stay involved in something that was essentially none of my business when the little red flag popped up on my cyberspace mailbox.

It had to be Erik Whiteside.

I poured myself a fresh cup of tea and opened the file.

> *Bay— I do have a passenger list, although it isn't an official*
> *manifest. Just a roster for fellow passengers so they could*
> *correspond with new acquaintances if they liked, so I don't*
> *know how complete it is. There is no one named Ramon.*

I sat back, surprised at the sharp stab of disappointment. So much for that theory. Then my heart quickened as I read the next line.

> *There were, however, five men traveling alone, three of whom*
> *had Spanish-sounding names—Carlos Montoya, Edgardo*
> *Ruiz, and Luis Araujo. And none of these has a hometown,*

> *just their names. Of course, other people chose not to list*
> *their addresses, so that in itself doesn't prove anything.*
> *Okay, I've done as you asked. Now I think you owe me some*
> *answers. It's cruel to dangle this kind of bait at me if you're*
> *just some crackpot playing games. And if you are, I'll track*
> *you down somehow and beat the crap out of you!*
> *This isn't a joke to me either. Respond, damn it!*

Once again I picked through the envelope of papers Jordan had left with me. No passenger list. I knew it was the logical place to start, but how would I go about getting one?

I saved the mail file and clicked onto the Internet. I hit it on the first try. Royal Scandinavian Cruise Lines had a website. Quickly I scanned the options on the home page, opening "Passenger Services" as the most promising. However, it turned out to be simply a three-line address in Miami with a phone number appended. I made a note of it on my desk pad.

I browsed through a few more areas, one of which included a layout of the ship. Converted from service in Europe, the *Crystal Fjord* was a luxury liner in the old tradition. Wide, open promenades circled three of the top decks, and the cabins appeared spacious and well appointed.

I pulled Leslie's ticket from the jumble and checked her stateroom assignment. Cabin A-6 was a suite on the topmost passenger deck with a sitting room, mini bar, and a small, private balcony. The view from there must have been spectacular. Leslie had indeed gone first class. The price listed for these accommodations on the eleven-day cruise portion of her trip was over ten thousand dollars.

So, I thought, *even though cruising was touted as being affordable for the average traveler, anyone who knew her cabin number would know this was a wealthy woman.*

I ran through the list of amenities this floating palace offered: two dining rooms, three nightclubs, a casino, movie theater, and show lounge. A fully equipped fitness center featuring sauna, massage, and Nautilus machines. A complete beauty salon. Eight gourmet meals a day, from breakfast and morning bouillon to afternoon tea and a lavish midnight buffet. Not to mention round-the-clock room service.

Not a bad little getaway, I thought, wondering why Rob and I had never taken advantage of this hedonistic travel option. Probably because we could never plan far enough ahead. Our vacations had tended to be spur-of-the-moment jaunts sandwiched around Rob's drug investigations and subsequent court dates.

I rubbed my eyes. They were dry and finally growing heavy. Maybe I could sleep now. My finger moved on the mouse, ready to click off, when an unfamiliar box popped up in the left-hand corner of the screen.

"Instant Message" was displayed across the top, then my e-mail address in red letters, followed by

> *This is Erik Whiteside. I know you're online and can read this.*
> *You've picked up my message. Please respond.*

Below this was a blank box labeled "Reply".

Real-time communication! I vaguely remembered Rob's mentioning this capability when he set up the system, but I'd never seen it in action. Probably any kid over the age of six could have explained it to me, but right then, flustered and caught off-guard, I didn't know what to do.

The screen flashed again and another message rolled up.

> *Come on, don't jerk me around. Let's talk, whoever you are.*

I studied the layout, fixed the cursor in the empty space below Erik's words, and typed,

> *I'm here.*

I located a square labeled <Send> and clicked on it.

> *Good. Who are you?* shot right back. It was working!
> *Let's just leave it at 'Bay' for now.*
> *Why all the secrecy? What are you hiding?*

It took a few seconds for each response to go through which gave me a chance to try and order my thoughts.

> *Nothing,* I typed, *Just being cautious. How do I know* you're *not*
> *some nut case?*
> *Good point. How do you propose we resolve this conundrum?*

Conundrum? What was this guy, an English professor?

> *Are you a teacher?* I typed.
> *Why, 'cause I use big words? No, I'm in retail. Run an electronics*
> *store. Mom was a teacher. How about you?*
> *Early retirement, but accounting and finance before that.*
> *You sound okay. Not many ax murderers in the bean-counting*
> *profession. How am I doing?*

I laughed in the chilly silence of the air-conditioned room. What was I afraid of, after all? Secure behind the anonymity of cyberspace I really had nothing to lose in leveling with Erik Whiteside.

> *I guess you pass. But it's a long story. Sure you want to do it here?*
> *Rather talk than type. Can I call you tomorrow?*

Again suspicion—or caution—flared in my gut. And I had his phone number from his previous e-mail.

> *I'll call you. What's a good time?*
> *Still don't trust me, huh? Store's open late on Fridays. Make it*
> *after ten.*
> *Okay. Talk to you then.*
> *Thanks. G'night.*
> *You too,* I typed, then logged off the computer.

Seems like a nice enough kid, I thought as I deposited the tea things in the sink and shuffled toward the bedroom. Mr. Bones darted ahead of me and settled himself onto the bed. Through heavy-lidded eyes I noted the red, glowing numerals on the bedside clock: *3:57.* With a groan, I threw myself onto the cool sheets.

In ten seconds I was out.

By the time Red Tanner leaned on the doorbell a little after eight that evening, I had pretty much recovered from my restless night. Dolores had tiptoed around all morning, sensing somehow that I needed the sleep. By ten, showered and stuffed full of French toast, I was hard at work in the office. I had managed to sneak in a short catnap before Angie showed up around four.

The sorting completed in short order, we had then tackled the daunting task of enumerating the missing documents. The list staggered me. Most disturbing was the lack of any tax returns for the most recent three years. I thought they had to have been filed, otherwise I should have been awash in demanding IRS notices. Unless they, too, were among the missing.

I paid Angelina Santiago in cash, adding a generous bonus for having deprived her of that most precious of teenage rites—Friday night out with her friends. I could see visions of new compact discs and clothes-shopping sprees dancing in her eyes as she hugged me and bounced down the steps to her car.

I met Red at the door, my tote bag and a light jacket already slung over my arm. We both started to laugh as I set the alarm and locked the door behind me.

"No one will believe this was accidental," I said, surveying Red's white polo shirt, crisply pressed jeans, and bare feet slid into scruffy Birkenstock sandals.

I was dressed exactly the same.

"Maybe they'll think we're tourists who always go around looking like the Bobbsey twins," he said holding open the door of his restored green Bronco. "Where to?"

"How about Jumpy's?"

"Ah, got a craving for a *real* burger, huh?"

Jump and Phil's was another local hangout, popular with visitors as well. It was jammed as usual on Friday night, but we managed to snag a just-vacated table in the back of the bar, not far from the empty fireplace. The Braves' game flashed from several muted, large-screen TVs, and autographed photos of sports and movie celebrities covered the walls.

We ordered cheeseburgers and fries, and Red sipped a draft. Seated next to each other, we still had to raise our voices to be heard above the clatter of crockery and the din of sixty or so people all talking at once.

"How'd your date go last night?" Red asked, then raised his hands as I shot him an exasperated look. "Okay, okay. Forget I asked."

I lit a cigarette and added my smoky contribution to the haze already hanging under the low ceiling. "I had lunch with Miss Addie this week," I began.

"How is the old girl? Still in a cast?"

"No, she got that off a few days ago. She's fine now, I guess. She asked for my help."

Red's face clouded over. "That's what got you into the last mess, as I recall."

"I know, but this is different. You familiar with the family at all?"

"Nope. Didn't even know Miss Addie until you got mixed up with her."

"Well, she has a brother. Younger, early sixties. Sort of a charming scoundrel, the way she tells it."

The burgers arrived then, thick and medium-rare, smelling faintly of the open fire they'd just been flipped from and adorned with oozing Monterey Jack cheese and big slabs of onion. We gave ourselves over to eating, glancing up every now and then to check out the game. I thought the Braves were losing, but it was hard to tell with no sound.

Red polished off the French fries I couldn't finish and ordered another beer. "So what about Miss Addie's brother?" he asked.

"Win. His name is Edwin, but they call him Win. Well, he disappeared, twenty years ago. She wants me to help her find him."

"Oh no, you're not trying to worm another confidential file out of me, are you?"

"No, nothing like that. It was never reported to the police. He just took off on his own. No one's heard from him since, until last week."

I told Red about the postcard mailed from St. Thomas and the lack of any return address or phone number.

"Sounds like he wants to stay disappeared," Red observed, and I nodded.

"That's what I said. But she wants to see him once more, before she dies."

I couldn't quite control the tears that welled up suddenly behind my eyes.

"You've really gotten attached to the old girl, haven't you?"

Again I nodded.

"Well, what does she think you can do? You're not a P.I. or anything like that."

"I know. She sort of thinks I walk on water, I guess."

"Lot of that going around." Red grinned and lightly touched my hand. "It's not a police matter, you know. Unless there's some suspicion of foul play?"

"No, nothing like that. He just got ticked at the family and took off."

"But why make contact after all these years? Did he say?"

"Nope. How would you go about locating someone like that? If it were a police matter."

"Gosh, I don't know. After twenty years? I'd say it was pretty close to impossible. Check with last known associates maybe, old friends. See if anyone has heard from him. You used the word 'scoundrel'. Was he ever in trouble with the law?"

"I don't know. He could have been."

"Let me ask around the department, see if any of the old-timers remember him. Maybe we can scare up a couple of leads for you."

"Thanks," I said, overriding his efforts to pay for dinner by handing my credit card to the harried waitress.

"Don't get your hopes up, though. This is about as cold as trails get. I hope you didn't make any promises."

"Only that I'd try. I'll ask Miss Addie for a list of his cronies from the old days, too. Maybe some of them are still around."

I glanced at my watch, startled to discover it was nearly ten. "Gotta go," I said, rising from the padded chair.

"Another business meeting?" Red asked snidely.

"Phone call," I said, moving toward the exit.

I stopped to pat the dry, brown nose of Waldo, the massive moose head mounted next to the fireplace. It was a ritual among the regulars, sort of like rubbing the distended stomach of a Buddha statue, for luck. During the holidays his incredible rack of antlers was draped with tiny, white Christmas lights that twinkled in the dim coziness of the bar, while a wide, red bow encircled his neck.

The drive back from the Sea Pines Circle passed in silence. Once again I had managed to make my brother-in-law angry. Maybe I shouldn't do this anymore, I thought, try to maintain a relationship based on our shared love for Rob and grief at his loss. Red wanted more than friendship, and that was all I was prepared to offer. At the moment.

Our goodnights were strained, but he did promise to let me know if he came up with anything on Win Hammond. It was almost a relief when he let me out in the driveway, then pulled away without a backward glance.

I kicked off my sandals and carried a Diet Coke into the office. With a fresh pack of cigarettes and a clean legal pad, I was ready for action.

Erik Whiteside answered on the first ring. "Is that you, Bay?" he asked, in place of 'hello'.

"Yes."

"So you're a woman. Interesting."

"I guess my name is kind of generic. Why is my being a woman interesting?"

"Had I known that up front, I probably would have been less suspicious about why you wanted to keep your identity a secret. I take it you live alone?"

I let that question hang.

"Okay, I guess some things are still off limits," he said. "Where do you want to start?"

"I'm going to tell you a story," I began, "about a friend of mine. No names. Not because I don't trust you, but because it's not really my life I'll be revealing, and I haven't said anything to my friend yet about your Granny Pen. I'm sorry for your loss, if I haven't mentioned that before."

"Thanks. Why haven't you talked about me to your friend?"

"I think you'll understand after I've finished."

I'd taken the time that afternoon to make some notes, primarily to insure I didn't forget anything, but also to be able to present the facts in as clear and concise a manner as possible. For the next fifteen minutes I laid out the scenario of Leslie Herrington's last days as Jordan and I had reconstructed them. I left nothing out except for Jordan's hoped-for reconciliation with her mother. That seemed too private to share, even anonymously. I ended with the burglary at the Natchez mansion, pointing out that it might not even be related to the rest of it.

"Wow," Erik said when I finally stopped for a breath. "Except for the break-in and a couple of other details, it's almost exactly what happened to my grandmother."

"I know. That's why I contacted you in the first place. When I stumbled on your website, I couldn't believe the similarities myself."

"One of the discrepancies, though, is a big one."

"What's that?"

"Granny Pen never mentioned meeting any particular man. No 'Ramon', like your friend's mother."

I thought a moment about that. "How long had she been widowed?"

"About a year, maybe a little more."

"Maybe she was embarrassed to say anything to the family, thought they might disapprove."

"That could be. My dad was devoted to his father. He probably would have had a fit if he suspected Granny Pen had found another man."

"So we can't rule it out," I said.

"Right. But where does that leave us? I mean, it looks like a pattern, but how do we prove anything? No one's going to take us seriously without evidence."

"I need to get hold of a passenger list for the *Crystal Fjord*. Where did you get yours for the *Countess?*"

"It was in with Granny Pen's stuff they sent back with the . . . with her. Didn't your friend's mother get one?"

"I don't know. I have all her papers, but it's not with those."

"Do you have the sailing date?"

"Sure," I said, puzzled. I pulled the cruise ticket from the envelope. "August 20. Why?"

"Maybe I can get that list."

"How?" I asked.

"Well, everything's computerized now. I'm sure they keep passenger records, for follow-up and marketing for repeat business. You know, stuff like that."

"But how . . .?" Then it hit me. Erik Whiteside managed an electronics store. Electronics. Computers. "Are you going to hack into the cruise line database? Can you do that?"

"Bay, I don't want to sound immodest, but there's just about nothing I can't do with a keyboard and a modem."

I remembered then how my own system had been compromised, how simple it had apparently been for someone who knew what he was doing.

"Is it legal? I mean, could you get in trouble?"

Erik's laugh rippled down the phone line. "They'd have to catch me first."

"Okay, you've made your point. You'll let me know if you find Ramon?"

"You bet. In the meantime, maybe you could check out the story about that French woman that supposedly died suspiciously in Caracas. I'd work on that too, but I don't speak Spanish. Do you know anyone . . .?"

"God, I'm an idiot!" I cut him off. Angelina Santiago was totally bilingual, and I'd had her ensconced right here in this office for two entire days! Not only could she translate, she could run the computer, too. "Sorry," I said into the mouthpiece. "It just occurred to me that I do, in fact, know someone who could help. I'll handle that."

"Great. So, we each have an assignment. When can we get together and compare notes? I'm off on Sunday. Maybe we could meet halfway, say, in Columbia? Or, if you like, I could just drive on down there. I can't be more than a four-hour trip from Charlotte. I could bring . . ."

"Hold it!" I barked. "What do you mean, 'down here'? I never gave you my address. For all you know I could be calling from Idaho!"

The silence stretched out to a full minute before Erik Whiteside said meekly, "Sorry. Caller ID. I plugged your number into this cross-reference program I've got. You're calling from Hilton Head. Port Royal Plantation. Eight Eagle's Point."

"Did my shoe size pop up by any chance?"

He laughed. "No, but the phone's listed to L. Tanner. Where'd you get the name Bay?"

I tried to hold on to my righteous indignation and failed. "It's a scary world out there, Erik Whiteside. Especially for those of us without your obvious talents."

"Yes, ma'am, I guess it must be."

"Let's postpone a meeting until we have some more to go on, okay? Besides, I think it's time I let Jor . . . my friend in on what we're up to. After all, this is her ballgame. She should be the one calling the shots."

"Okay, I guess you're right. But I would like to meet you sometime."

"You'll e-mail me if you find anything out about Ramon? Or you can call—now that you have my number."

He ignored the sarcasm. "I'll call. It'll be late, though. Work."

"Fine. I'll look forward to it."

"Thanks, Bay. I really mean that. For the first time since Granny Pen died, I feel like I just might be able to see that she gets justice."

I didn't have an answer for that, so I said goodbye and hung up.

In a little more than forty-eight hours, I seemed to have done a complete one-hundred-and-eighty-degree turn, from pointing out to Jordan all the fallacies in her arguments to jumping full-tilt back into the game. Erik Whiteside's enthusiasm was contagious, as was his unwavering conviction that he was right. But the deciding factor had been the theft of Leslie Herrington's personal papers. The more I thought about that, the more it seemed as if it had to be connected to her death. What other reason would someone have to steal them? Somewhere in those missing documents had been a clue. Somehow or other we had to find out what it was.

16

The insistent ringing dragged me out of a black, dreamless void. I pried open one bleary eye long enough to pick out the six on the digital clock, then collapsed back onto the pillows with a groan. I could barely hear the faint sound of my own voice from the kitchen, inviting whoever this idiot was to leave a message.

When I found out his identity, I would track him down and kill him.

I rolled over onto my stomach and burrowed back under the covers. Then the breath was expelled forcefully from my lungs as the full weight of Mr. Bones landed squarely in the middle of my back. His deep purring vibrated against my neck. He rubbed his chin through the messy tangle of my hair while his barely sheathed claws kneaded my skin through the sheet.

The soft brush of his whiskers against my ear was the last straw. I dislodged him by turning slowly onto my side, and he leaped over me to nestle snugly into the curve of my arm.

"To what do I owe the pleasure of all this affection?" I asked, stroking his furry head.

His green eyes regarded me solemnly, as if he were considering his answer.

Wide awake now, I pulled on a T-shirt and went to find out who the inconsiderate moron was who had screwed up a perfectly good night's sleep. I stopped on the way and let Bones out the French doors onto the deck.

"I found him!" Erik Whiteside's excited voice boomed from the answering machine when I pushed the PLAY button. "Ramon Escalante! His address is listed only as the Bahamas, and there's hundreds of islands, but at least it's a place to start. If you get this before eight o'clock, call me at home. After that I'll be at work. We're rollin' now!"

146

I listened to his enthusiastic recitation while I set the kettle on and dropped two bagel halves into the toaster. I smiled when the flow of words stopped abruptly.

"Oh, God," he resumed, "I just realized it's only six o'clock! I'm really sorry, Bay. I was so psyched, I guess I got carried away. It took me all night to gain access—those cruise people have some pretty sophisticated security protocols. Anyway, call me after you talk to your friend so we can plan our next move. I'll keep working on this bozo Ramon, see if I can coax an address or phone number out of the 'net. I'm online at the store, too, for the customers, you know? I'll get . . ."

A loud click was followed by the soft whir of the rewind. Erik had used up the entire tape.

I set out food for the cat, then decided on an early morning swim. No one I needed to contact would be up yet. I did call the Westin and leave a message for Jordan, who was due back from Natchez sometime during the day.

I got in a good hour of much-needed exercise. Too many lunches and dinners out, and too many hours at the computer were beginning to show. I punished myself a little, and was rewarded by the loosening of my injured shoulder, grown stiff over the last few days of inactivity. I jogged back to the house from the beach, noticing a little bite in the wind blowing directly off the ocean, reminding me that autumn was fast approaching. Soon I would be able to fall asleep to the soft night sounds through an open window instead of to the incessant drone of the air conditioning.

By the time I'd showered and dressed, I felt safe in making a few calls. Miss Addie assured me she'd been up for hours, an inability to sleep for long stretches being one of the curses of old age.

"I'm going to have to think about that a bit, Lydia," she replied when I asked for a list of her brother's former friends. "One of the reasons Daddy got so angry with Win was that he tended to associate with what Mama always called a 'low element'. Not our sort of people, you understand."

I smiled. Anyone who thought class distinctions were a thing of the past had only to study the social hierarchy of the modern

South. Up North, folks tended to ask, "Where are you from?" or "What do you do?" when introduced to someone for the first time. Down here, the questions, especially for a married woman were always, "Who *were* you?" or "Who are your people?". Knowing your family background allowed a new acquaintance to place you in the proper slot in the pecking order.

"Perhaps Edwina would remember," I suggested, thinking the oldest sister might have been more aware of the family undercurrents.

"I'll check with her and call you back, shall I?"

I hung up after again cautioning Miss Addie that the search might prove fruitless, while she continued to assure me of her complete faith in my abilities. I hoped she wouldn't be too disappointed if I failed to deliver.

I next tried the main offices of the Bi-Rite Hardware chain in Beaufort where a perky young thing with an almost unintelligible drawl informed me that Dudley and Marilee Macon had been out of town, but were expected back later that morning. I left my name and number, purposely not stating my business in case the Macons were trying to avoid dealing with the fallout from the discrepancies in their records.

Dolores was surprised to hear from me on a weekend, immediately assuming that something must be wrong. I calmed her down and asked for Angie.

"Ah, that one, *Señora*," she said with a laugh. "Already she has done her *tareas*—her chores?—and her studies. Roberto and Alejandro, them I must pull from the bed by the *pies*."

The image of tiny Dolores dragging her tall, lanky sons out by the feet made me smile. Not that I doubted for a minute her ability to do it.

Angie, when she heard my proposition, was thrilled at the prospect of earning some more spending money. She made only one suggested change to my game plan.

"Why don't I do it from here, Mrs. Tanner? Papa bought the three of us a computer for Christmas last year, and we're online. That way you won't have to worry about being there to let me in."

I agreed, giving Angie all the information I had scratched down on my desk pad. I told her to check the Caracas papers starting in July and work forward. I theorized that the maid's reference to a mysterious death "a few" weeks ago might mean anything from two to twelve.

"Make sure you keep track of your time," I added, and she promised to get started right away.

Having set in motion all the wheels I could at this point, I busied myself straightening up the house and paying a few bills. I flipped on the TV in passing and checked out the weather. There was indeed a tropical disturbance lurking far out in the Atlantic Ocean. Thanks to El Niño or La Niña or whatever, we'd had a relatively quiet hurricane season so far. The next name up on the list was Flora.

When the phone rang a little after eleven, I made a mental bet with myself as to which one of the seeds I'd planted that morning was bearing fruit. I lost.

Dudley Macon had a low, semi-sexy voice with a rolling drawl that made even the most mundane statements sound like the lyrics to a country-western song. Either he'd purposely cultivated this youthful sound, or he was a lot younger than I'd envisioned him. Introductions and social pleasantries out of the way, I got right down to business.

"Whoa there, Miz Tanner," he said after I'd launched into my laundry list of missing documents, "slow down a mite. You're settin' the dogs on the wrong scent here. I packed everythin' I could lay my hands on off to that lawyer fella, just like he asked. Anythin' else, you need to be talkin' to the little woman."

Oh, please! I thought, *'the little woman'*?

"Do you mean your wife?" I asked through clenched teeth. If Rob had ever referred to me in that manner, I would have rearranged his dental work.

"Oops, sorry, ma'am. I didn't mean no disrespect. I know you high-powered, female business types don't take well to that kind o' thing. What I mean to say is, Marilee handles all the paperwork and taxes and stuff. I'm just the good ol' Georgia boy that keeps the customers happy and the wheels greased."

I wasn't sure I was buying all this self-deprecating, redneck innocence routine of his. There had to be more to Dudley Macon than just his backwoods charm and cracker dialect. An astute businessman like Jack T. Herrington would never have put an empty-headed backslapper in charge of his hardware empire.

"Maybe I'd better speak to Mrs. Macon then," I said.

He didn't respond right away, and I wondered who he was conferring with in the muffled tones filtering through the covered mouthpiece.

"Mr. Macon?"

"Sorry, ma'am," he drawled back into the phone. "I was just checking with the little . . . with Marilee. We'd be honored if you'd join us for lunch. Sort of get to know each other and all that? Then you could ask whatever you need to right face-to-face, so to speak. Whadda you say? We'd be real pleased if you would."

This guy was sounding more and more like some character out of "The Dukes of Hazzard", but it wasn't a bad idea. I agreed to meet them at the Fig Tree at 12:30.

I selected black linen trousers and a cream, silk tank top. Downtown Beaufort on a Saturday afternoon didn't call for any special attire, but I thought it incumbent upon me to look something like the "high-powered, female business type" Dudley Macon would be expecting. I rummaged in the back of the closet and hauled out the gleaming calfskin briefcase Rob had given me on our last Christmas together. Lovingly I wiped a thin layer of dust from it, then used the tissue to dry my suddenly streaming eyes.

Damn! I hated it when the pain pounced like that, from out of nowhere.

I blew my nose and stuffed papers and a clean legal pad into the briefcase. Almost out the door, I trotted back into the kitchen and snatched up a laminated card from next to the phone. I could never remember how to retrieve my messages off the answering machine from long distance without the instructions.

I fired up the Zeemer and roared out of the driveway. Maybe I would have to reconsider one of those annoying cell phone gadgets.

No, I decided, turning onto the highway, I'd resist as long as possible. Anyone who needed to contact me could just wait until I checked in. Nothing was so important that it couldn't wait a few hours, was it?

Gilly Falconer, her gray-streaked braid draped over one shoulder, greeted me as I stepped into the Fig Tree, almost as if she'd been watching for me out the window. Her first words confirmed my suspicions.

"Hey, Lydia, hold on a minute," she whispered, pulling me to one side of the narrow entryway.

"What's up, Gilly?" We had to turn almost sideways to allow a couple of heavy, sweat-drenched tourists to pass by us into the restaurant.

"You really meetin' with them Macons?" she asked, jerking a coffee-colored thumb over her shoulder.

"Yes. Why?"

"That's what I wanna know. What business you got with the likes of them?"

"Gilly, what's this all about? I'm doing some work for the Herrington estate, and I need to discuss some things with them about the stores, that's all."

I wanted to ask what business it was of hers, but her creased, unsmiling face set off the first stirrings of alarm in my gut. Bartending in a small town hangout gave Gilly Falconer access to a lot of secrets, a lot of indiscretions spilled out over one too many scotches-on-the-rocks. She'd kept her job and her reputation by forgetting everything she heard.

"You just be careful, you hear me? He's as slick as they come, underneath all that smilin' and drawlin'. And her!" Contempt dripped from Gilly's voice. "Nothin' but poor Arkansas white trash. Thinks havin' money can make up for havin' no class."

I didn't know what to say. It was so unlike Gilly to talk about her customers this way.

"It's only lunch," I managed to splutter. "I'm not going to marry them."

Her wide, spatulate fingers fastened painfully on my upper arm. "You just watch your back, hear? Them two could bamboozle a snake-oil salesman. You ask your daddy if I ain't right."

Gilly relaxed her hold on me and shooed me toward the bar. At a back table in the farthest corner, a man rose and waved tentatively in our direction. Gilly marched ahead of me, slapped a menu on the scarred, oak surface, and stomped away without a word.

"Well, here she is, honey, right on time. It's a pure pleasure, Miz Tanner, ma'am."

"Bay," I said and took the offered hand, which closed around mine in a surprisingly firm grip. He was shorter than I, but not by much. Brown hair, thinning in the front, much too long in the back, and muddy brown eyes, everything about Dudley Macon was *medium*. He was sort of good-looking in a rough, motorcycle-gang kind of way. In an open-necked sport shirt and too-tight jeans, I guessed his age at late forties, trying to look ten years younger.

"Nice to meet you," I said, pulling out a chair and settling my briefcase onto the one next to it.

"And this here's Marilee. My wife," he said proudly.

"Hey," Marilee Macon said with a smile as fake as the dull finish on her over-teased, jet black hair.

I ordered an iced tea and the Macons opted for draft beers. Under cover of removing papers from my briefcase, I studied Marilee Macon while we exchanged get-acquainted pleasantries.

She'd obviously taken Dolly Parton as a role model. Whether she'd been born with the massive chest that spilled out over the white, scoop-necked jersey or whether it had been surgically assisted, she flaunted her hourglass figure with defiant pride. I could sense the swiveling of every pair of male eyes in the room every time she leaned forward. But behind the heavy eyeliner and patently false lashes, her dark eyes glittered with a native shrewdness that made me think she might just be the brains of the outfit.

My guess was confirmed as we chatted about generalities over lunch. Dudley deferred to his wife on almost every question. The table cleared, I spread my list out while Dudley lit a cigarette and ordered another beer.

"Now, here's what I need," I said, passing the list across to Marilee.

She retrieved rhinestone-studded glasses from her bag and skimmed the three sheets of paper. "I got all this," she said, tossing the list aside. She'd barely taken enough time to absorb even a tenth of the hundred or so items I'd compiled.

"Are you certain?" I asked skeptically. "I'm especially interested in the federal and state income tax returns. You did file them, I hope."

"Of course I filed them," she snapped, and Dudley laid a restraining hand on her arm.

Battle lines had been drawn. Marilee Macon and I stared across the table at each other while her husband stroked her as if she were a skittish mare.

"Excellent," I said briskly, shoving my copies back into the briefcase. "I'll expect the documents at my home by Monday."

I scribbled my address on the back of one of my old business cards and shoved it across the table as I pushed back my chair.

"Whoa now! Hold on here." Dudley's voice held an edge of panic. "No cause to go rushin' off. We were just gettin' acquainted. Marilee didn't mean no harm, did ya, honey?"

I watched as his wife struggled to get her anger under control. When she spoke, her words belied the fire still flashing in her eyes. "Yes, please stay. I didn't mean to get my back up. Sorry."

"There now, that's better." Dudley signaled for refills all around and leaned over to light my cigarette as I settled back in. "Marilee tends to get a might sensitive sometimes." He draped his arm across the back of her chair and squeezed her shoulder. "Thinks folks don't take her serious just because she's so gorgeous. You prob'ly have the same trouble."

Marilee's smile was almost a simper. She'd obviously bought into this phony line of his, since she'd married him, but I was trying very hard not to gag.

"I understand you were out of town for a few days," I said, heading back to what I thought of as safe conversational ground. "Vacation?"

"Nope. Had to run Marilee up home to Texarkana. Her mama took sick."

"Nothing serious I hope?" I asked politely.

"Female troubles." Marilee nodded sagely at me, acknowledging my membership in that exclusive sorority of balky uteruses and uncooperative ovaries from which her husband was automatically excluded. "Dud came back, but I stayed on for a few days. That's why all those papers are such a mess. If I'd been here, you woulda gotten everything proper."

Dud didn't look the least bit contrite. "Did the best I could, sugar. I couldn't make heads or tails outta most of it, so I just packed up everything in sight when Mr. Brandon called. Sorry if I caused you a lotta extra trouble," he added, turning the full force of his grin in my direction.

"It did take some doing to come up with that list. How long have you worked for the Herringtons?" I asked. Now that we were all pals again maybe I could wring some useful information out of this otherwise pointless trip.

"Ten—no, eleven years now, right, honey?"

Marilee nodded and sat up a little straighter. I watched the wariness creep into her eyes. "Been around eight for me. Right after Dud and I got married."

"So you were both there when Jack T. got killed. That must have been difficult."

"Saddest day of my life," Dudley said with a heavy solemnity that rang less than sincere. "'Cept of course for when Ellen, my first wife, passed," he added quickly.

"Such a shock," Marilee said, hand to her bulging chest with what she probably thought was an impressive display of stunned disbelief.

Really, I thought, *if these people are going to try and bullshit me, the least they could do is practice in front of a mirror first.*

"The family was fortunate to have two such devoted employees to keep things together," I said. Both of them missed the sarcasm. "The business probably never missed a beat."

"Well, Jack had pretty much turned everything over to me by then anyway," Dudley said with a total lack of humility. "You know, I started out working in the paint department. Got to be assistant manager at the Ridgeland store, then manager there. Pretty soon I was in charge of the whole shebang."

"A real American success story."

"No one knows more about the business than my husband." Marilee leaped into the fray, claws out and fangs bared, ready to protect her man. She'd gotten it this time. "Without Dudley, there wouldn't be any Bi-Rite Hardware chain. The Herringtons are damn lucky to have him, even if they don't appreciate it."

"Shush now, honey . . ." Dudley began.

I overrode him. "Really? What makes you think they don't appreciate him?"

"All Mrs. La-Di-Dah Herrington of Natchez, Mississippi, ever cared about was gettin' her damn check on time. And always whinin' about how it wasn't enough."

With my back to the room, I couldn't tell for sure if Marilee's rising voice was attracting stares, but I did notice that the hum of other conversation had dropped off. Dudley's grip on his wife's wrist was no longer gentle, but she ignored him.

"And what did she do to deserve all that money every month, huh? Answer me that! Dud tried to tell her it was tough goin' up against the new Wal-Mart and that big Home Depot they just put up out on the highway. But did she care? If she'd of had her way, she would of sold the whole damn thing right out from under us. Thank God Jack knew who his real friends were. Fixed it in his will so's we'd be taken care of. He knew which side his bread was buttered on."

"Will you shut up?" Dudley's voice, though pitched low, crackled with anger.

Marilee's face, contorted in fury, suddenly crumpled in pain. I watched deep, red welts in the exact shape of her husband's fingers rise on her arm. She raised her bruised wrist and rubbed it tenderly.

"What's Miz Tanner gonna think of us, you carryin' on like this?" The languid drawl he apparently thought appealing was back. "I apologize for my wife, ma'am. We're both just a little skittery right now, not knowin' what's gonna happen to the stores. You wouldn't by chance know what the young folks got in mind, would ya?"

"They're gonna sell it, of course. Why wouldn't they?" Marilee's decibel level had dropped, but the anger still vibrated in her voice. "They don't care any more about it than their mother did."

"Now, honey, we don't know that for sure." Dudley tried to take her wounded hand, but she snatched it away.

"I really couldn't say what plans the Herrington heirs have," I said, gathering my belongings together. This seemed like the perfect time to make my exit before an out-of-control Marilee Macon decided to come across the table after me. "You'd have to discuss that with them. Or with their attorney, Mr. Brandon."

"But you have some say in it, right?" Dudley persisted. "I mean, after you check out the books and stuff, you'll be able to tell 'em what a great business it is. I mean, hell, they'd be fools to let . . ."

"I really have no influence in this matter, Mr. Macon," I interrupted him. "I've been engaged merely to prepare accurate financial statements to allow the estate to be valued."

I tapped my finger on the list and stared straight into Marilee Macon's smoldering eyes. We were definitely never going to be buddies. "I'll look for these records on Monday. Thanks for lunch. If there's anything else I need, I'll be in touch."

The heels of my black leather flats clicked against the bare wood floor as I marched out of the Fig Tree. Out on the street the heat and glare hit me like a slap. I took a deep breath and relaxed the tension that had bunched up in my shoulders.

Well, I said to myself, pulling the sunglasses down off the top of my head, *that was interesting.*

A flickering hand about a half-block down caught my eye, and I realized it was Cissy Ransome signaling to me from the doorway of the bookstore.

"Bay," she hollered, waving frantically, "in here!"

I walked briskly along the deserted sidewalk and ducked into the door she held open for me.

"Hey, Cissy, what's up?"

"Come on," she said, leading me behind a tall display holding the latest bestsellers.

"What are you doing?" I asked as she peeked around the edge.

"Wait. They'll be goin' by in a minute."

"Cissy . . ."

"Sshh! There they are."

I peered out over her frosted hair, cropped short like a man's, as Dudley and Marilee Macon stormed past the wide front window. Neither of them spared a glance into the bookstore, so intent were they on the argument obviously raging. I glimpsed Dudley's face, mottled bright red with anger, then they disappeared from view.

"Whooee, girl, you must have stirred up some hornet's nest," Cissy said with a grin.

Her pixie haircut matched her narrow face and pointed chin. Wide-set brown eyes danced under her fringe of bangs.

"What's this all about?" I asked as we stepped out of hiding.

"You tell me. All I know is Gilly called a second ago and told me to drag you in here until they got past. Said otherwise you might get attacked in the street."

"That's ridiculous," I said, following Cissy into the reading area and dropping down into one of the chintz-covered wing chairs.

"Okay, give. What happened? Does this have anything to do with Leslie Herrington's estate? Are the kids gonna throw those two losers out on their ears?"

Her eagerness made me laugh. Gossip was a staple on the menu at the locals-only coffee bar in the back room, and Cissy was the reigning doyenne.

"You know I can't discuss that," I said.

"Come on, Bay, you're not in business anymore."

"I still have an ethical responsibility . . ."

The jangle of the bells over the front door interrupted me, and Cissy jumped to her feet. "Oh, damn! Customers. Don't move. I'll just be a minute." She returned in less than that, shepherding Gilly Falconer in front of her. "I'll get coffee," Cissy said. "Don't anybody say a word until I get back."

Gilly took the chair across from me and flopped down wearily. "I purely do hate this heat," she said, taking a crumpled tissue from the pocket of her apron and wiping her wide brow.

"You should be used to it by now. You've lived with it all your life."

"I know, but it should be coolin' off by now. We could be in for a good storm 'fore long."

I thought of baby Flora whirling out in the Atlantic somewhere, maybe gathering strength for a run at the mainland.

"What'd I miss?" Cissy carried in a tray laden with three steaming mugs. "Tea for you," she said, handing me mine.

"Nothin' here, but it was a fair old shoutin' match next door," Gilly offered. "What'd you say to send Miss Dolly into such a snit?"

I spluttered with a mouthful of hot tea and nearly choked over the laugh rising in my throat. "That's exactly who I thought of the minute I saw her," I gasped.

"Do y'all believe that hair?" Cissy chimed in. "Nobody's worn a rat's nest like that since the sixties. And nobody's gonna convince me that those boobs of hers aren't ninety per cent silicone."

Gilly laughed. "Could be. But what was all the yellin' about? I didn't catch it all, but it sounded like she was goin' off on the Herringtons."

"That's pretty nervy," Cissy offered before I could reply. "Jack T. pretty well left them set for life, the way his will was written. Tied poor Leslie's hands six ways to Sunday. She couldn't sell the stores, and she couldn't get rid of the Macons, either. Lots of folks wonderin' what they had on Jack T. to work themselves a deal like that."

" 'Had' on him? What is that supposed to mean?" I asked, suddenly alert. "You think they were blackmailing him?"

"No one's ever used that word, right out," Gilly said, "but there's been talk. I mean, why would a sharp guy like Jack T. just turn over his whole operation to a pair like that? They ain't exactly the brightest bulbs in the chandelier, you might have noticed."

"I'm not so sure about that," I said. "Marilee may not be well-educated, but there's some intelligence there, a certain cunning." I sipped the cooling tea and thought a minute. "So you're saying that the Macons pressured Jack T. into arranging his will so that they couldn't be fired. But I don't get what the point of that was. I mean, he could have lived another thirty years if it hadn't been for the accident."

Cissy and Gilly exchanged a look I couldn't quite decipher.

"What?"

"Well, I heard," Cissy said importantly, "that they were set *either* way. Jack T. couldn't have got them outta there with dynamite. And neither could Leslie."

"But once she died," Gilly jumped in, "all bets were off. The kids can do whatever they damn well please. That's why I warned you to watch yourself. Those two got a big stake in the outcome. If they can't charm you into takin' their side, they may try somethin' else."

"Like what? And what good would it do them to put pressure on me? I have no say in what the Herringtons decide to do. I'm just hired help."

"That's not the way I hear it," Cissy said. "I hear the Countess won't change her underwear without checkin' with you first."

That made me laugh. "When did you turn into such an old busybody, Cissy Ransome?"

"You've been gone a long time," she said with a touch of asperity. "Haven't been around much since you went off to college. Not much excitin' to do around here but keep track of other folks' business."

"Well, I got to get back over to the Tree before them college kids steal me blind," Gilly said, rising. "Thanks for the coffee." She turned to me. "You think on what I said. I wouldn't cross swords with the Macons unless you're ready for a real battle."

The bells tinkled as she closed the door behind her.

"Do you really think they were blackmailing Jack T.?" I asked as Cissy gathered the dirty mugs onto the tray.

"Honestly? No one knows for sure. Jack T. took the truth of it into the river with him that night. But it's sure hard to figure otherwise."

"What was the scuttlebutt after the accident?" I asked, feigning disinterest. "I heard he wasn't alone in the car."

Cissy stared hard at me, her languid brown eyes suddenly alert. Apparently I had touched a nerve. "There was some talk," she said cautiously, "but nothin' ever came of it."

"What kind of talk? It seems to me it was pretty common knowledge that Jack T. had a way with the ladies."

Did I imagine the flicker of relief that flashed across her face?

"He did have a little problem with keepin' his zipper up," she said with a laugh, and carried the tray into the back. "You goin' out to your daddy's by any chance?"

So that subject's off limits, I thought, trailing along behind her into the tiny kitchen. *I wonder why?*

"I hadn't planned on it, but I could. Why?"

"That new John Grisham novel Lavinia ordered for him came in this morning. He was real anxious to have it."

Cissy dried her hands on a striped towel, and we walked back into the stacks past the used and rare book section that had always been my favorite. I loved the smell of musty paper and mildewed bindings.

"You want me to deliver the book, is that it?"

"If it's no trouble. Your daddy loves those legal thrillers. Lavinia tells me he reads them straight through, then goes back and marks all the places where the lawyer or the judge did things wrong," she laughed.

"That sounds like my father. Sure, I'll take it."

I didn't really want to go visiting, but I suddenly realized it had been more than a week since I'd talked to him. All my entanglements with the Herringtons had been occupying me full-time. Maybe it would be good to run a lot of this by him. While the Judge had the ability to drive me crazy when he chose to, he still had the sharp intellect and eye for detail that had made him so successful in his profession.

I took the bag from Cissy, thanked her for the tea, and headed for the door.

"Bay?" she said, and I turned to face her. "You be careful now, hear?" All the laughter was gone from her eyes.

"Sure."

I stepped out into the waning afternoon sun, puzzled by the whole exchange, both with Cissy and with Gilly Falconer.

Why was everyone suddenly so concerned with my health and well being?

17

My timing couldn't have been better. The Judge, fresh from his afternoon nap, was just taking the first sip of his daily allowance of bourbon and lemonade when I walked into his room.

Lavinia settled a light throw over his useless legs in the wheelchair and went to fetch another glass for me. Though our greetings to each other had been cordial enough, it still hurt me to feel the strain my relationship with her had suffered in the past month. Thanks to my mother's "little problem", Lavinia had had the care of me almost from the time I was old enough to remember. Shunned by the woman to whom my unexpected arrival, late in her life, had been an embarrassing inconvenience, I had found comfort in the soft brown hands and mellifluous voice of the housekeeper.

My father studied my face as I bent to brush a quick kiss across his bristly cheek. He, of course, knew the reason for the breakdown in the formerly close tie Lavinia and I had shared over the years, probably felt himself at least partly to blame. But unpleasantness was not discussed in our family, no more than any other subject that might lead to emotional outbursts. Wounds were left to fester, and heal as best they could on their own.

So his brusque words were not at all surprising as Lavinia closed the door behind her and trudged up the wide oak staircase to her suite on the second floor. "Where the hell have you been?" he growled as I sipped the icy lemonade and regarded him calmly. "I told Vinnie I could have fallen off the face of the earth for all you apparently cared."

"Want a cigar?" I crossed to the cherry highboy and rummaged through the neat pile of pajamas for the slim case of illegal Havanas.

I watched him perform the ritual, then held the crystal desk lighter for him. His deep sigh of satisfaction sent a cloud of smoke toward the creaking ceiling fan. I lit a cigarette, then curled myself onto the sofa opposite him.

"You're really full of it, you know that?" My father chuckled as I continued, "You know Lavinia would have called me if there'd been any real problem. Besides, I've been busy."

"So I hear. That my new Grisham?" he asked, pointing at the bag.

"Yup. Hot off the press. Cissy Ransome tells me you tend to pick them apart."

"You can't believe a damn thing that fool girl says," my father snorted. "Biggest gossip in the county. Boyd Allison's gonna be sorry he turned his store over to his daughter and that pantywaist husband of hers, you mark my words."

"Why do you call Quinn a pantywaist? Because he writes poetry? Some of it's quite good, so I've been told. And he's still teaching at the high school, isn't he? It's not as if they're making a big living selling books. Or poetry."

"Not a fit occupation for a man," the Judge mumbled, "scribbling love poems and such. Damn things don't even rhyme!"

Time for a change of subject. "Guess who I had lunch with today?"

"Dudley and Marilee Macon. At the Fig Tree. You had the crab cakes; they both had burgers."

"How do you do that? It hasn't been more than an hour since I left there."

My father's grin was mischievous and more than a little smug. "I like to keep the lines of communication open," he said, gesturing at the phone.

"You should subcontract your network out to the CIA. I'll bet they haven't got anything nearly as efficient."

"I understand the meeting was less than cordial."

"Oh, he was okay. He's kind of oily and ingratiating, but her! She ripped the Herringtons up one side and down the other. Everyone except Jack T., of course. You knew him pretty well, from what I gathered at the poker game. Why did he keep those two around? Did they have something on him?"

The light faded from his clear, gray eyes. I could feel the stone wall being constructed, brick by brick.

"Come on," I said, leaning forward with my elbows on my knees. "Why do you clam up every time I ask anything about Jack T. Herrington? What do you think I'm going to do, worm all his most intimate secrets out of you and broadcast them to the world? I am capable of a modicum of discretion, you know. Early childhood training."

He flinched at that, but I held my ground. I *had* been taught, as a very young child, that there were things—family things—you just didn't talk about outside. A large part of my growing up had centered around keeping "The Secret". I had proved I could be trusted.

"It's not the whole world I'm concerned about."

"Who, then?"

He rubbed an age-spotted hand across his face in a familiar gesture. He'd used it in court when he needed to buy a few seconds to decide which road he was going to take.

"Seems to me," he said at last, "you've been dancing attendance on her royal highness, the Countess, quite a bit lately."

"And?" He was making me seriously angry now. *Dancing attendance?* Was that what it looked like from his vantage point?

"And," the Judge said, avoiding my eyes, "there are some things children are better off not knowing about their parents. Wouldn't serve any useful purpose. Only cause everyone a lot of grief and unnecessary pain."

"And you think whatever you told me would go straight to Jordan von Brandt? You must have a pretty low opinion of my character."

"Don't be ridiculous," he snapped, "I have no such thing." Then his face softened. "Sometimes you just let your heart get in the way of your better judgment, that's all."

I had no rebuttal for that. We sat in silence for a minute or two, then I decided to let it drop. There was no point in badgering my father. He would either tell me or he wouldn't, in his own good time.

I looked up to find him studying me anxiously. "So," I said, smiling, " ' . . . where ignorance is bliss . . .' ".

" 'Tis folly to be wise' ", he finished.

"Thomas Gray," we said in unison, completing the ritual of a childhood game he'd devised for us when he'd first discovered I shared his love for words.

Despite the haze of mingled cigar and cigarette smoke hovering near the ceiling, the air was decidedly clearer.

"I do want your help with something," I said, refilling our glasses with lemonade.

For the next thirty minutes I laid out for my father all the bizarre happenings of the past ten days, from my initial meeting with Jordan right through Erik Whiteside's jubilant phone message this morning. Part way through my recitation, the Judge closed his eyes and rested his chin on the steeple of his index fingers. I knew he hadn't fallen asleep. It was a pose I'd seen many times, an indication that he was deep in thought, concentrating hard on what he was hearing.

By the time I'd finished, the ice had melted in the cut glass pitcher and my father's expensive panatela lay half-smoked and forgotten in the ashtray at his elbow. "So what do you think?" I asked when he remained silent. "Are we totally nuts?"

Half of me wanted him to say *yes*. Armed with the opinion of someone whose judgment was respected by everyone who knew him, I could blow Jordan and Erik Whiteside off with a relatively clear conscience and get back to—what?

That was the question. It was a decision I had been postponing for the better part of a year: what was I going to do with the rest of my life? Financially I was set. Between my own investments, a trust fund from my late mother, and Rob's multiple life insurance policies, I could maintain my current lifestyle indefinitely. The sale of my interest in the Charleston accounting practice would just be an added bonus.

The beginnings of a plan—nebulous and unformed at the moment—had been scratching around at the back of my mind, but I wasn't ready to put it into words, not even to myself. A lot depended on how this all turned out.

The click of the lighter as the Judge restarted his cigar jerked me back to the moment. "I think you need to contact Interpol," my father said, nodding in agreement with his own pronouncement. "Yes, that's where I'd start."

"So you're taking this seriously. Even with no real evidence?"

"Oh, there's plenty of evidence. Granted, it's all circumstantial, but I've seen plenty of cases prosecuted successfully with less."

"Why Interpol? And how would I go about contacting them?"

"If your suppositions are correct, you've got an international serial killer on your hands. Foreign nationals being murdered in South American countries. Crosses borders. That's how Interpol would get involved."

"How do you know so much about this?"

I couldn't conceive of anything happening in our sleepy little corner of the South that would involve international crime fighters.

"You forget we're on the coast, sweetheart," the Judge replied. "I had a few felons who thought they could get out of standing trial by taking an extended fishing trip to the Caribbean."

"Do you still know anyone there? In Interpol, I mean?"

"I'm not certain. Seems to me there was one young fella, Frenchman, I believe, that I did a little business with, but I can't recollect his name. Let me make a few calls, see if one of the boys remembers who it was."

"But how do I convince them to take us seriously? The local authorities don't seem to see any reason to investigate."

The Judge reluctantly stubbed out the last inch of his cigar in the ashtray. "That's the one big flaw in your scenario. You need to make sure Jordan and this Erik fella are really committed. It could get ugly."

"What does that mean?"

"There's no proof a crime was even committed. The death certificates read 'natural causes'. Without that, you're not going to get Interpol to move. Unless they're already onto it themselves."

"You think that's possible?"

"Could be. They don't broadcast their investigations, but they gather and coordinate crime statistics from all over the world. Someone there many have detected a pattern."

I stretched and crossed to the bay window that looked out over the Sound. The short pier where I'd first learned to fish cast long shadows across the water in the fading afternoon light. "What did you mean that it might get ugly?" I asked as my father activated his wheelchair and rolled across the heart pine floor toward the bookcases.

"Come hand me down that book up there," he said, pointing to one of the top shelves.

"Which one?"

"Third row down, about halfway over. Red binding."

I hauled out the thick volume. Like everything else in *Presqu'isle*, it was spotless, not a speck of dust, although I was certain my father hadn't used any of his law and reference books in years.

"What is it?" I asked.

"Forensic pathology. Probably woefully out of date, but I want to check something. You said there were no marks on either of the bodies, right?"

"As far as I know. If they'd been stabbed or shot, no coroner, no matter how inept, could have ruled natural causes."

"Then that leaves two possibilities: poison or suffocation. Both of them would leave traces, but you'd have to be looking for it to find them."

"But what good would that do now? They've both been . . ."

I suddenly knew what the Judge had been driving at, and the bottom fell out of my stomach.

I had to force myself to concentrate on the road as I sped back to Hilton Head through the falling dusk. So many thoughts clamored for attention in my head, I found my mind leaping indiscriminately back and forth among the various threads.

I'd finally managed to coax my messages from the answering machine after three frustrating tries with the instructions. Erik

Whiteside had called twice demanding to know why I hadn't contacted him all day. I knew I first had to speak to Jordan before I went any farther down this path. Until I had brought her completely up to speed, no decisions could be made. For that reason, she was meeting me at the house in a little less than an hour.

Her voice, when I reached her at the Westin, had been strangely subdued, as if the events of the past few weeks were finally catching up with her. She sounded weak and drained. How was I going to approach her about what had to be done? The thought of it sent hard little stones of apprehension bouncing around in my empty stomach.

Both the Judge and Lavinia had pressed me to stay to dinner, but I'd needed to be on the move. It had been my pattern most of my adult life. Faced with a possible crisis, I preferred to meet it head on and get it over with rather than allowing my fertile imagination to conjure up all the possible catastrophes that might result.

I rolled onto the island, then turned right on Spanish Wells Road, paralleling the route of the intrusive cross-island highway. The Santiago family occupied a modest bungalow near the end of a winding dirt road bordering a wide salt marsh. As I pulled into the short driveway, dozens of wading birds rose in a cloud from the mud flats a few yards behind the house. These little pockets of undeveloped beauty, scattered across the north end of the island, gave lush testimony to what life here must have been like fifty years ago.

Angie waved from the front door as I threaded my way through blazing flowerbeds and thick, abundant greenery. Hector Santiago was a genius with plants, able to coax glorious life from even the most moribund specimens. Dolores's husband had definitely found his niche as a professional landscaper.

Angie's face glowed with the same triumph that had rung through so clearly in her voice on my answering machine. Now she fairly skipped out to greet me with an exuberant hug, a sheaf of papers clutched in her hand.

"Here it is, Mrs. Tanner! It didn't take long at all. July 26, in *El Nacional.* It's not very long, but I printed it out for you. Then I translated it into English and typed that up, too."

"Angie, you're a wonder," I said, taking the papers from her.

I could tell she was bursting to ask why I was so interested in the death of a Frenchwoman in Caracas, Venezuela, but the good manners drummed into her by her mother held her back. I took her hand and pressed a folded-up hundred-dollar bill into her palm.

"Some day I'll explain all this to you, Ange."

"I was glad to help," she said modestly, then, "Wow!" as she checked out the bill. "I can't take this, Mrs. Tanner. It's too much! Besides, mama says you already do so much . . ."

"Hush," I said, "you just take it. It's worth a lot more than that to the people I'm trying to help. Buy yourself something pretty."

"Nope, this is going right in my college fund."

"Good for you. Thanks again, sweetie."

"*Nada,*" she called as I backed out onto the road.

I barely had time to glance over the translation of the brief newspaper article before the front doorbell rang. But I picked up enough to convince me that this was the third in our string of suspicious deaths. Anjanette Rousseau, a sixty-four year-old French widow from Lusignan, had been found dead by the housekeeping staff in her suite at the Caracas Intercontinental on July 25 of this year. Natural causes.

I added the clipping to the pile of documents I'd scooped together after changing my clothes, and went to let Jordan in. My face fell when I saw who was with her.

"Trey insisted on coming along," Jordan explained as she swept past me and into the great room. "I don't understand why, since he's convinced we're both lunatics, but I didn't have the strength to argue with him."

Trey Herrington stood tentatively just inside the door. "Is it safe to come in?" he asked, flashing me that smile that seemed to melt my bones no matter how angry I was at him. "I brought a peace offering."

He held up a three-liter bottle of Diet Coke, an elaborate red ribbon tied around its neck. I had to laugh. In his other hand he carried a twelve-pack of Coors Light. "This is for Jordan and me. Friends again?"

"We'll see," I said carrying the drinks out to the kitchen. Since they were already ice-cold, I poured for all of us and set the tray on the low table in front of the sofa.

Jordan and I lit cigarettes while Trey took his beer and went to stand in front of the French doors out to the deck. "Before you start," he said, not turning around, "I want you to know that I've decided to keep an open mind. No preconceived ideas or automatic opposition. I'm willing to be convinced."

"That's big of you," Jordan snorted. "So, what made you change your mind again?" she said to me. "Last time we met you were hell-bent on talking me out of pursuing this."

Mutely I handed her the article from the Caracas newspaper along with Angie's translation. "This is the woman little Constanza's cousin was talking about," Jordan said, looking up as I nodded confirmation.

"Yes, I believe it is."

"We'd have to get a lot more information about the circumstances before we could be certain, but the initial details are similar to what happened to Leslie."

"I agree."

Jordan handed the papers to Trey who had settled in beside her on the sofa. "Seems pretty vague to me," he said, then threw up a hand as his sister's deep green eyes bored into him. "Hey, just an observation. I'm not passing judgment."

"Then there's this." I passed her the printout of the picture and article about Penelope Whiteside I'd downloaded from her grandson's website.

This time Jordan sat up a little straighter as she absorbed the implications. Some of the weariness eased from her face while she read.

"Is this for real?" she asked.

"Yes, I think it is. I've talked to this young man, Erik Whiteside. He seems to be exactly what he says he is. And what's more, he's a computer whiz. He found out that a man named Ramon Escalante was on the ship with your mother, the same cruise line his grand-mother used. Ramon wasn't listed on Penelope's passenger mani-fest, but there were three men with Spanish names traveling on their own."

"That's it, of course!" All of Jordan's nervous animation was back. "Think about it. If you were a gigolo, preying on elderly women, you wouldn't use the same name, would you? Word might get around. He might even be changing his appearance."

Trey finished reading the printout and set it back on the table. "I don't think so. He could be using aliases, but I'd bet we're looking for a tall, debonair Cary-Grant-type guy. He wouldn't want to do anything to mess up that image. Can you picture Leslie's being at-tracted to anyone who wasn't top drawer, at least in the looks de-partment?"

"Making a believer out of you, are we?" I couldn't keep the smugness out of my voice.

"I'm getting there," he admitted with a grin. "So what's our next move?"

I let the *our* slide. "Jordan, I think you should talk to Erik Whiteside. He's expecting me to call him tonight. He was working on finding an address for our *Señor* Escalante, although I don't think he'll succeed. If the creep is using aliases, he's probably giv-ing phony addresses, too."

"Wouldn't he need a passport?" Trey asked. "He's entering a lot of foreign countries. How is he getting around that?"

"Good point. Do you need a passport for a cruise? I think we need to make a list of these kinds of questions." I got a legal pad from the office and sank back down into my chair. "We need to check out how you get a passport in South America. Maybe it's easy to get hold of phony ones." I jotted that down.

"It could be like Europe," Jordan offered. "You can move around there pretty easily from country to country without much fuss."

"Someone should check on this Rousseau woman, find out if she was on a cruise before she landed in Caracas, and if so, which one."

Trey seemed to have shed all his former objections. His eyes were alight with the zeal of the true convert.

"Anybody besides me hungry?" I asked. The mantel clock read eighty-thirty. It had been a long time since lunch. Which reminded me, before the evening was over, I had to fill the Herringtons in on my strange encounter with Dudley and Marilee Macon.

"Sure. We didn't have any dinner either. Had to powwow with brother Justin before he left for the airport," Trey said.

"Justin's gone back to Dallas?" The youngest Herrington was so unobtrusive, I'd completely forgotten about him.

"Diane crooked her finger, and off he went," Jordan mocked. "Besides, there's nothing more he can do here until the estate is ready to close."

"Did you ask him about Leslie's records that were stolen? Does he have copies?" I asked.

"Some, but probably not everything," Jordan answered. ""He'll check his files when he gets home."

"We should run this by Chris Brandon, too. He could have something." I added my own suggestion to the growing list.

"So what are we eating?" Trey asked. "How about Chinese?"

I scrounged a worn take-out menu from the kitchen desk drawer and called in our order. Trey volunteered to pick it up rather than wait an hour for delivery. He waved away my offer to buy and sped off in Jordan's rented Jaguar.

"You're having such a good influence on my big brother," Jordan remarked with a slight curl of disdain on her generous lips. "Siding with me against Justin, offering to buy dinner. I think he must be trying to impress you."

"Bull," I said as I bent to light a cigarette but the warmth of my throat told me I was working up a blush.

I got Erik Whiteside on the phone and interrupted his litany of failed attempts to track down Ramon Escalante by telling him my friend wanted to speak to him. I gave him a quick rundown on the Rousseau woman, then left Jordan tensely gripping the portable while I escaped to the kitchen to set out crockery and silverware on the breakfast table.

"I'm convinced," she said fifteen minutes later, handing me the phone as Trey bounded up the front steps. "He's legit."

Erik and I agreed to speak again the next day after the Herringtons and I had had a chance to organize our thoughts. I turned my back on them and tried casually to work in the question that had been nagging at me since my conversation with the Judge. Erik's answer made me wince, and I could tell he was puzzled, but thankfully he didn't press me for an explanation. As an afterthought, I asked him to check out Interpol, see if they had a website and whether they had any kind of alert posted that might indicate they were aware of a pattern of deaths similar to those of the three women we already knew about.

Jordan, Trey, and I spread the steaming white cartons out on the table and dived in. I was impressed when both Herringtons opted for the chopsticks included with the meal. Both manipulated them expertly, and the steady click of the wooden utensils accompanied my recounting of my earlier meeting with the Macons and of the strange warnings of Gilly Falconer and Cissy Ransome.

"I wouldn't worry about them." Jordan dismissed my concern with an airy wave. "If it turns out the Macons have been embezzling, we'll prosecute, and they'll be in jail. If they're just incompetent, the new owners will likely can them. Either way they won't be around to cause any more trouble."

I couldn't entirely share Jordan's casual dismissal. She hadn't sat across the table, absorbing the full force of Marilee Macon's glittering hatred for the Herringtons—and their friends.

"So where do we go from here?" Trey asked as I finished stacking plates in the dishwasher while he poured fresh drinks.

"I think that's up to you and Jordan. And Justin, of course," I added, resettling into my wing chair opposite the sofa. I took a deep breath and plunged ahead. "I ran this all by my father this afternoon. I hope you don't mind."

Jordan shrugged. "So long as he can be trusted to keep it to himself. I assume he can, from all I've heard."

I bristled, but let the implied criticism go. "He thinks we should contact Interpol."

Trey's eyebrows shot up as I recounted for them the Judge's thinking. By the end, they were both nodding agreement.

"He's going to try and come up with a contact for us, so we don't get dismissed out of hand as some sort of crackpots with an agenda." I lit a cigarette and gazed out into the night. "There's something else."

The somber tone of my voice must have penetrated. I turned back to find two pair of almond-shaped, green eyes riveted on my face.

"If we want the authorities to get involved, we have to prove that a crime has been committed. We have to prove to them these women were murdered."

I waited for one or the other of them to make the leap, but neither spoke. "There will have to be an official autopsy to determine the cause of death." They were going to make me say it. "Leslie's body will have to be exhumed."

All the color drained from Jordan's face. "No," she whispered.

"Jordan, there's no other way."

"Let them dig up this Penelope woman, then! Or the one in France." Her voice had risen, and I watched the rapid rise and fall of her chest as her breathing quickened.

"We have no idea what happened to Madame Rousseau, Jordan." I swallowed hard and tried to soften the words as best I could. "But Penelope Whiteside was cremated in accordance with her wishes. I'm sorry."

"I said no!" she screamed, jumping up from the sofa. "Never! You will not disturb my mother's grave. It's obscene! I won't have it!"

"I don't think you'd have to be there. Just sign some papers to authorize it. I'm sure it could be done very discreetly and with dignity . . ."

I was talking to her back as she fled across the room, ripped open the French doors, and stumbled onto the deck. I rose to follow when Trey's voice stopped me.

"Leave her alone for now," he said quietly. "Give her a chance to get used to the idea."

I settled back in the chair. "You don't find the thought abhorrent?" I asked.

"Sure I do," he said after a lengthy pause. "But it had already occurred to me that, if we want to find out the truth, it would eventually come to this. I've had a while to come to terms with it."

We sat in silence for what seemed like a long time before the click of the screen sliding back announced Jordan's return. Trey and I watched her lift her glass and drain the warm beer in one long, convulsive gulp. Then she lit a cigarette and resumed her seat.

"I have a better plan," she said, her eyes once again sharp and glittering. "Are your passports up to date?"

Trey and I exchanged puzzled glances.

"Throw your swimsuit in a bag and pack the Dramamine, children. We're going on a cruise!"

18

The stretch-737 banked right, floating down through scattered, puffy clouds toward the sparkling sea below. From my wide window in the first-class cabin I watched the crystal water rush toward us and marveled at the clarity that allowed me to pick out a school of dolphins racing along just beneath the surface. For a moment it almost seemed as if they were keeping pace with the rapidly descending plane. Then we banked again, the pilot lining us up with the runway that appeared to rise up like a highway to nowhere in the middle of the Caribbean, and the graceful animals disappeared from view.

I gripped the armrests of the luxurious, roomy seat and hoped the gray-haired guy in the cockpit knew what he was doing. Not a relaxed flier at the best of times, I hate takeoffs and landings, especially when coming back to earth entails setting such a massive beast down on a strip of asphalt that looks no wider than a two-lane country road, surrounded by bottomless ocean.

I tried to remember what the bored flight attendant had said about using my seat cushion as a flotation device.

Across the aisle, Trey Herrington grinned at my ill-concealed terror. "Relax," he said with an air of superiority. "Piece of cake."

Next to him, Jordan von Brandt ignored the pre-landing instructions and pulled her carry-on bag onto her lap. She stuffed in the paperback she'd been reading, extracted her cigarette case and lighter, and dropped them into the pocket of her white linen blazer.

I already had mine close at hand, my craving for the calming effect of the nicotine almost overwhelming. No-smoking flights are a bitch.

I took a deep breath and held it, willing myself to settle down. As I exhaled, the wheels of the landing gear bounced once, twice, then grabbed. I was thrown back into my seat by the combination of hard braking and the reverse thrust of the engines. Apparently there wasn't a lot of runway to spare.

Palm trees and small, corrugated buildings flashed past, then the big jet gradually slowed, dropping finally into taxi mode as we made our way toward the tiny terminal. Above the sun baked building a blue-on-white sign read, "Owen Roberts Airport. Welcome to Grand Cayman."

I shook my head in wonder. The sixty or so hours from Jordan's dramatic Saturday night announcement to this morning's takeoff had been a whirlwind of frenetic activity. I couldn't yet quite believe we'd actually pulled it off.

Philippe Valois, Jordan's Swiss-born secretary, had been the true miracle worker. With the scantiest of notice from his employer, he had secured a suite on the *Crystal Fjord* for Jordan and me, as well as a stateroom for Trey. The ship had sailed on Saturday afternoon from Miami, which made his feat that much more amazing. After a stop in Key West on Sunday, the ship's itinerary called for a full day at sea. We were to rendezvous with her in Grand Cayman on Tuesday.

Three first-class seats out of Savannah, connecting in Atlanta, had apparently been a snap for the incredible Philippe, for here we were, ready to disembark. I tucked the immigration form into my passport, which I had found, thankfully, still had more than a year to run.

The bulk of the passengers in coach class began to rustle around behind us as the plane eased to a halt. Outside I could see the ground crew scurrying to wheel the rolling stairway out onto the tarmac. No motorized jet way swinging out here, where the sun almost always shone and showers normally lasted less than ten minutes.

While we waited for the flight attendant to release the door, I spared a thought for Erik Whiteside, stuck in Charlotte and frantic to join us, but unable to rearrange his work schedule on such short notice. Jordan had offered to pick up his expenses. If he could work it out, he might catch up with us later in the week at one of the subsequent ports of call.

Over Jordan's strenuous objections, I had insisted on paying my own way. I didn't want to explain why. I simply stood my ground and eventually prevailed.

The Judge was convinced we'd all lost our minds when I'd called him in between loads of laundry on Sunday. He was still working on the name of his Interpol contact and insisted on knowing how to get in touch with me. I gave him the passenger services number of the cruise line in Florida and assured him they would know how to reach the ship. I passed the same information on to Dolores who was as dumbfounded as my father, though less censorious, when I asked her to take care of the cat and look after things while I was gone.

Trey stood aside to let Jordan and me precede him. We nodded to the captain standing just outside the flight deck. He wished us a pleasant stay as we made our way down the steep stairway onto the broiling cement apron.

We were first in line at the customs and immigration desk. Probably because we had valid U.S. passports and nothing to declare, the inspections proved a brief formality. We reclaimed our luggage and were immediately beset by a horde of porters and taxi drivers, all clamoring for our business. Jordan politely ignored them, scanning the area behind.

"There!" she said suddenly and thrust her way through the encircling mob.

With good-natured shrugs, they parted, reforming behind us to lay siege to the next group of unsuspecting tourists.

The man stood next to what appeared to be a genuine, old London taxi, its gleaming black finish throwing off a blinding glare in the midday sun. In a crisp khaki shirt, matching Bermuda shorts, and spotless white knee socks, he looked like Alec Guinness in "Bridge on the River Kwai". A visored, military-style hat was tucked beneath his arm, and his hand held a neatly lettered sign reading "von Brandt".

"I had Philippe arrange for a car," Jordan explained as we approached the waiting driver. Up close, he proved younger than he'd first appeared, his skin wrinkled and cracked more by the sun than by age.

"Countess von Brandt?" he inquired in a clipped British accent, and Jordan nodded.

"Jenkins, mum," he said and snapped a brisk, backhanded salute. "If you'll be so good as to point out your cases, I'll just get them tucked up in the boot."

Trey and I exchanged amused glances. A last, thorny vestige of the Empire, standing smartly to attention, amidst the lush, overblown beauty of the tropics. While Trey went to assist Jenkins with the bags, Jordan and I lit cigarettes and inhaled the heady island fragrance along with the smoke.

"The ship sails at five. That gives us time to have lunch, unpack, and get ourselves oriented." She stepped back into the shade of the building. "You haven't been on a cruise ship before, have you?"

"Nope," I answered. "Nothing near the size of these things."

"It takes some getting used to. You'll be hopelessly lost at first. Fore, aft, starboard, port. I always am, and I've sailed at least a dozen times."

I looked forward to proving her wrong. I watched as the men tried to work out the logistics of fitting eight pieces of luggage into a space designed to hold only four or five.

"Philippe couldn't get us a private table." She said it accusingly, as if the poor man had given it less than his best effort. "So, we won't be able to discuss strategy over meals. I suggest we meet in one of the cocktail lounges around seven. That way we'll be able to scope everyone out."

During the heated argument that had followed Jordan's sudden decision on Saturday, it was her insistence that we could retrace Leslie's steps that had been most convincing. While the passengers would certainly be different, the staff and crew of the ship should be the same ones that had served while Leslie was on board. If anyone had noticed the attentions paid to her by a good-looking Spaniard, it would be her cabin steward, her waiter, her busboy. If she had confided in anyone—a masseuse, a hairdresser, a bartender—that person should be available for us to question.

Jordan's belief that we might actually encounter Ramon himself seemed too farfetched even to consider. But I had to admit that, in general, the plan was far preferable to the alternative—exhumation and autopsy of Leslie Herrington's body. That was being held as a last resort in the event our amateur sleuthing failed.

Trey and Jenkins finally surrendered and placed the largest of Jordan's matching Louis Vuitton pieces on the front seat. I noticed that the car had right-hand drive, just like the London originals. I hung back as Trey and Jordan settled themselves onto the lush upholstery of the roomy back seat, then I slammed the door behind them. Jordan's head immediately popped through the open window.

"What are you doing?" Her annoyance was evident in the scrunching-up of her elegant eyebrows. "There's plenty of room back here."

"I know," I said, "but I'm not coming with you right now." I stepped back as Jenkins slid behind the wheel.

"What do you mean you're not coming with us? Where the hell are you going? The ship sails in four hours!" An edge of panic had crept into her voice.

I had come prepared for this battle, had known it would be waged the minute I decided to accompany Jordan. I would help her as best I could, even though I believed she was only postponing the inevitable. But I also had my own agenda, one that had sprung, fully formed, into my head the second I found out our initial destination.

"I have some personal things to take care of," I said firmly, stepping back onto the curb. "I'll catch up with you later."

"Bay, don't be ridiculous! What 'personal' things? You've never been here before. You told me so yourself."

"If she wanted you to know, she would have told you," Trey interjected. "Leave her alone. Let's get to the ship while they're still serving lunch. I'm starved."

Jordan slumped back in her seat, arms folded across her chest in an attitude of disgust. "Do whatever you like," she snapped. "You always do."

"Can we drop you somewhere, ma'am?" Jenkins asked, his face a mask of indifference as if he had heard nothing of our exchange.

"No thanks. I'll just grab a taxi. And I've got a map."

I had no intention of advertising my destination—to anyone.

"Five o'clock," Jordan growled and rolled up the window, effectively cutting me off.

Jenkins released the handbrake, and the ancient cab rolled sedately away from the curb.

The herd of drivers had thinned as the bulk of the passengers from our flight cleared immigration and were transported into George Town, capital of the three Cayman Islands. I looked around as a group of giggling teenagers, apparently on a class trip, was being shepherded toward a charter bus by three harried adults. They and a dowdy, middle-aged couple, overdressed for the tropical heat, were my only remaining companions. The pair stood stoically just inside the terminal, glancing out occasionally as if waiting for a ride that hadn't shown up yet.

"You be needing a cab, my lady? Ernest can assist you."

He didn't look old enough to drive, but the photo on his license, strung on a ragged leather thong and draped around his scrawny neck, matched the gleaming smile and shiny black face now peering up at me expectantly. We agreed on a price and sped off in an antiquated, but immaculately maintained, Chevy Impala.

I told myself I was just being cautious, but I had Ernest drop me downtown, a couple of blocks from the harbor. If Sergeant Red Tanner had been anywhere near on target in suggesting some of the bad guys might still have an interest in me because of the Grayton's Race deal, I could at least make it difficult for them to track me down.

I shaded my eyes against the early afternoon glare and gazed out across the bustling sea front. The harbor was alive with pleasure craft, from small sailboats to sleek yachts. Farther out, riding at anchor outside the breakwall, three gleaming white cruise ships floated majestically. One of them must be the *Crystal Fjord*, but they were too far away for me to read their names. A string of motorized tenders ferried passengers back and forth between the ships and the crowded docks.

The streets teemed with tourists, gaily dressed and chattering away in several different languages. Apparently the morning shore excursions had ended, and everyone had converged on the shops to take advantage of the duty-free bargains in British woolens, Waterford crystal, and other imported products of the United Kingdom. While many of the Caribbean islands had gained their independence from their original European invaders, the Caymans remained a British Crown Colony.

I snagged a vacant table under a striped umbrella at a nearby sidewalk cafe, ordered a Perrier with lime, and spread out my map. I finally oriented myself by stepping out to check the taller buildings in my vicinity. I was on Harbour Drive, a little north of the docks. My destination, on Dr. Roy's Street, seemed well within walking distance. I plotted my course, mentally converted Caymanian dollars to U.S., and tossed a few bills on the table.

The sidewalks were jammed, and I clutched my tote bag, slung over one shoulder, tightly against my side. It was impossible to avoid being jostled as I wove my way against the tide of cruise passengers, most laden with multiple shopping bags, headed for the pier. The narrow street was clogged with vehicles, their horns and the shouted imprecations from their frustrated drivers adding to the general noise level.

I fought my way to Cardinal Avenue and paused, my attention caught by the window display of a narrow antique store on the corner. Old maps of crinkled parchment rested in intricately carved frames, and a cascade of gold doubloons spilled from an ancient wooden chest. They looked real. I peered through the glass and glimpsed shelves of weathered books and artifacts along the far wall. I checked my watch. Better to get my business over with first, I decided. If I had time, I'd stop here on my way back.

Fifteen minutes later I stood before a pair of carved oak doors that looked as if they had been plundered from a medieval castle. The building itself rose three stories, the top two fronted by white, balustraded porches. A discreet brass plate to the right of the entrance indicated I had found the Gellenschaft Bank of Luxembourg.

I pushed the button beneath the sign as Harry Drayton had instructed me when I'd spoken with him early Monday morning. Harry had been a client of my accounting firm in Charleston, an attorney and an expert on international banking. It was he who had made the initial arrangements for the safekeeping of my "insurance policy". I was here to finalize that transaction.

I jumped as one massive door opened a crack, and a disembodied voice asked for my passport. I placed it in the well-manicured hand connected to an immaculate, white French cuff secured by a gold-and-onyx stud.

I glanced around nervously while unseen eyes scrutinized my credentials. I felt conspicuous, standing on the stoop as pedestrians streamed by me a few feet away, but no one seemed to be paying me any particular attention.

Apparently I passed muster. The door swung soundlessly open, and I stepped into the hushed coolness of an ornate lobby furnished with delicate Louis XIV chairs and tables scattered across a huge, blood-red Persian carpet. My unobtrusive doorman melted away as *Herr* Wagner bustled toward me, hand outstretched.

"*Frau* Tanner, how delightful to make your acquaintance. My good friend, Harry, speaks very highly of you. I am the Director of this establishment. Please, come this way."

His English was perfect, with only a slight roll of the *r*'s to indicate it was not his native language. Short and rotund, with a fringe of white encircling an otherwise bald head, *Herr* Helmut Wagner looked more like a jolly innkeeper than the head of one of Europe's oldest family banks. He ushered me into a surprisingly functional office and seated me in a soft leather wingchair facing his cluttered desk.

"You had a pleasant flight, I trust, *Frau* Tanner?"

I nodded, suddenly overwhelmed by what I was about to do. "Yes, thank you," I managed to squeak out.

"We would have sent a car for you, had not dear Harry empha-sized your wish to remain, shall we say, as inconspicuous as possi-ble?"

The rising inflection invited an explanation, but I merely smiled and nodded once again.

"Well then, let us complete the formalities, and then perhaps you'll join me for tea." He depressed a button on his multi-line telephone and spoke in rapid German. Then he rose, excused him-self, and disappeared through a side door.

I expelled the breath I didn't know I'd been holding and wished I'd asked if it was all right to smoke. I glanced around the small of-fice, but didn't see an ashtray. I re-crossed my legs, nibbled on a ragged edge of thumbnail, and tried not to think about what had led me to this place and this time.

I'd told quite a few lies when I'd sat down to confront my old nemesis, Hadley Bolles, a little more than a month ago. The docu-ments I'd managed to pilfer from the Grayton's Race office had been my ace in the hole. I'd used them to bargain my way into a deal that resulted in the abandonment of the development project and the return of all the local investors' money, as well as a guaran-tee of continued safety for my family and me.

Over the course of that long nightmare which had begun with a plea for help from Miss Addie, I had come to believe that the men who sought to defile our county with their drug-tainted money were the same ones who had caused my husband's death. As a spe-cial investigator for the State Attorney General's office, Rob had been relentless in shutting down their money laundering opera-tions. That tenacity had gotten him killed. I had moved up on their list.

I shivered—from the air-conditioning, I told myself—and pulled my oversized tote bag onto my lap.

The biggest lie I'd told Hadley had been that the incriminating documents were in a secure place, along with instructions to re-lease them in the event of my death or incapacity under question-able circumstances. In truth, they had never left my house. They had been tucked up in my floor safe in the bedroom closet, vulnerable to any determined professional the cartel might have sent after them. As was I.

The door behind me opened, and I swung around in my chair.

"Good day, Mrs. Tanner. I am Liselotte Bergen, *Herr* Wagner's assistant."

Everything about her was cold, from the icy blue of her eyes to the slender fingers she withdrew quickly from our perfunctory handshake. A classic Aryan blonde, her beauty was all hard planes and sharp edges, right down to the severe, gray, man-tailored suit.

"If you will be so good as to follow me, please."

Liselotte Bergen led me back out into the cavernous lobby, then down a narrow corridor to a windowless room at the back of the building. Inside was a small oak table, two armchairs placed on either side. The polished top held several documents, a black ink-pad, and a long, metal box with two keys dangling from its lock. In the corner, on a tall, wooden stand that resembled a lectern, rested a strange-looking device that reminded me of something out of a James Bond movie.

We seated ourselves, and Liselotte explained the purpose of each set of papers, indicating where I should sign. Then she asked for my right thumb, rolled it across the inkpad, and pressed it firmly onto an identity card that already held a duplicate of my nine-year-old passport photo. In her heavily accented, guttural English, she instructed me to provide the bank with an updated picture when I renewed my passport so that the two would always match.

I tore open the packaged towelette she handed me and cleaned the black goo off my thumb. She crossed to the machine in the corner, depressed a foot pedal, and raised the height of the stand several inches. Then she pulled down what looked like the eyepiece on a laboratory microscope, and suddenly I thought I knew what it was for.

"You seem to be right on the cutting edge," I said, advancing on what I now knew must be a special, high-tech camera. "I didn't think anyone but the military and movie spies used retina imaging for identification."

"We guarantee absolute security to our clients," she said with a touch of frost in her voice, "as well as complete privacy." Apparently my figuring out her little gadget had spoiled some of her fun. "That is why you chose the Gellenschaft Bank. That is why you chose the Cayman Islands."

I hadn't chosen this particular institution. Harry Drayton had, but I let the remark go. Her cold hands gripped my shoulders as she positioned me in front of the camera, adjusting the lens until it fitted perfectly over my right eye.

"There will be a brief moment of pain," Liselotte said, "but it will pass quickly. You must not blink."

A little warmth had crept in at the mention of my discomfort. She liked this part.

It felt almost as if someone had jabbed a sharp fingernail in my eye, but I managed not to flinch.

Liselotte Bergen wheeled the stand out into the hall where the same French cuffs from the entry door received it and moved off. As she turned back into the room, I took a tissue from my pocket and dabbed at my suddenly streaming eye.

"That, too, will pass quickly," she assured me.

She opened the lid on the safety deposit box and removed the keys, handed one to me, and placed the other in the file with all my signed documents.

"Your account number is here." She tapped a square, unvarnished nail on a narrow slip of paper with seven digits printed by hand. "We recommend that you memorize it and destroy it here. You will be required to provide the number and to prove your identity in order to access the box. Both your key and ours are required to open it once you have placed your valuables inside and closed the lid." All this was delivered in a monotone, as if she were a recording on voice mail. "Thank you for allowing the Gellenschaft to serve you. Good day, Mrs. Tanner."

The door closed silently behind her, and I was alone.

I flopped down into the chair and decided I would sell my soul for a cigarette. The sooner I got this over with, the sooner I could get out on the street and light up. Besides, I thought, glancing at my watch, time was running short. I didn't dare miss the last tender out to the ship.

From the bottom of my tote bag I drew out yesterday's *The Wall Street Journal* and spread it out on the table. Carefully I removed the documents I had interleaved throughout the daily business news and stock quotes, counting to make certain I didn't miss any. I smiled at the silliness of this cloak-and-dagger precaution, which had proved totally unnecessary. I'd let Red and my father make me paranoid with their constant hints that I might still be in danger from the drug lords I'd so recently thwarted. Thanks to Jordan's sudden decision to meet the *Crystal Fjord* in Grand Cayman, an offshore banking haven that now rivaled Switzerland, I had been able to make good on my bluff without arousing any suspicion. With Harry Drayton in possession of my instructions and authorization to access this box, I was home free.

I memorized the account number, ripped the paper into tiny pieces, and wrapped them in the damp tissue. I snapped closed the lid, tucked the key into my bra, and shoved the now useless newspaper along with my passport back in my bag. Out in the hallway I retraced my steps back to the lobby.

Another Nordic beauty waited to escort me to *Herr* Wagner, who renewed his invitation to join him for tea. I pled the time constraints of catching the ship. The Director bowed low over my hand, thanking me for my custom, and asking to be remembered to "dear Harry".

Back on the sweltering stoop, I lit a cigarette and inhaled greedily. The sidewalk and roadway were still jammed, only more with locals now, most tourists having retreated back to their ships. It was nearly four o'clock. I needed to get moving, assuming that the last transport to the *Crystal Fjord* would probably leave within the next half-hour. I stubbed out my cigarette, kicked the butt discreetly into the tangled shrubbery, and plunged into the throng.

I let the tote bag, now emptied of its dangerous cargo, swing loosely from my hand as I wove my way around slower-moving pedestrians, sometimes being forced off the curb by the crush of people. Back at the corner of Cardinal and Harbour, I glanced longingly into the window of the antique store while I waited with a horde of others for the traffic light to change.

I noticed the green produce truck waiting for an opportunity to turn onto Cardinal, heard the roar of its engine as the driver gunned it through a narrow opening in the streaming traffic. I felt the hands thrust brutally into the middle of my back a second before I tumbled headlong into the street.

19

I heard a long, piercing scream, followed by the high-pitched squeal of the truck's brakes as they locked up.

Stunned, I looked up from where I lay sprawled, face-down in the middle of the road, in time to see my whole world filled with a rusted, peeling bumper bearing inexorably down on me.

In slow motion I closed my eyes, thinking what a stupid way this was to die, when a hand clamped down on the collar of my blouse and literally tossed me back onto the sidewalk.

I registered the rush of fetid exhaust fumes as the big truck slid by just inches from my face.

Then everything faded to gray.

I couldn't have been out long. The sea of black faces hovering over me parted, and I found myself staring into steel-blue eyes at once concerned and angry. I blinked a couple of times, and the rest of him slid into focus: a strong, aquiline nose, square chin with just a hint of a dimple, a stern, yet sensuous mouth.

For one crazy moment, I thought he was about to kiss me. His first words dispelled that illusion.

"Lie still," he commanded as I struggled under his hands. "Damn fool thing to do. What hurts?"

"I don't know," I fired back, stung by the implication that I had thrown *myself* into the street. "If you'll get off me, I'll try to find out."

The hem of my calf-length cotton skirt was bunched up around my thighs, the cloth pinned by his knee to the sidewalk where he crouched beside me. He shifted his weight and flipped the material down, restoring my modesty.

For the first time I saw his smile. It had been worth the wait.

"Who are you?" I asked as he cradled my head like a newborn's and helped me into a sitting position. "Was it you who . . .?" I didn't know how to say it. *Pulled me back? Rescued me? Saved my life?* All of it sounded overly dramatic. And true.

He ignored my question. "Can you stand?"

When I nodded in response, he gripped me firmly around the waist, supporting me as we rose together. Nothing snapped or popped, and in a moment I stood squarely, if a little shakily, on my own two feet, surveying my ripped and filthy clothes. I winced as a few well wishers clapped me on my bad shoulder and congratulated my savior. Most had drifted off when they realized no major drama would be played out—I was not dead.

No thanks to one of you, I thought, studying the group now ostensibly helping the driver collect the fresh produce that had tumbled off the back of the truck. Judging by the bulges in a lot of shirts and pockets, a good many were also shopping for dinner.

No one seemed to be interested in me at all now, and I saw no one in the crowd I recognized. So who had pushed me? Or was it an accident?

No! It had felt deliberate, the timing too precise to be coincidental. But who? And why?

A thin, brown hand tugged at my skirt, and I looked down to find a ragged boy, no more than seven or eight, grinning up at me. My tote bag, battered but intact, hung by one strap around his neck. It looked as if it weighed as much as he did.

My rescuer slipped it over the boy's head and handed it to me. He dropped a handful of coins into the eagerly outstretched palm, and the child scampered off. I did a quick inventory: passport, wallet, travelers' checks, cruise ticket . . .

"Oh, no!" I checked my watch, which miraculously still seemed to be functioning.

"What is it?" the man asked, gripping my arm as he scanned the still-crowded street. "Did the kid steal something?"

"What? No, I don't think so. But I've missed the last tender! How am I going to get out to the ship?"

"They'll wait," he announced and steered me out into the street, his hand still firmly around my arm as we maneuvered through the stalled traffic. "But we'll have to hurry. You up for a dash, Mrs. Tanner?"

His stride lengthened when we gained the sidewalk on the opposite side and turned toward the docks. My wobbly knees protested as he pulled me along. Suddenly it registered, and I dug in my heels, forcing him to a stop.

"Who the hell *are* you?" I demanded in a strident voice that made heads turn around us. "And how do you know my name?"

"Later," he said, dragging me off again in a half-trot that jarred my now throbbing head.

Two white-uniformed officers stood fidgeting beside the bright orange, fiberglass launch rocking gently at the end of the pier. One checked his watch, then spoke in rapid Italian to a blue-clad sailor who began unhitching ropes from the dockside cleats as we hurried up.

"Quickly, please, *Monsieur* Darnay." He gestured us toward the boat where another sailor waited to assist us on board. "She is . . .?"

"*Oui*," my companion interrupted, waving the question away. "*Plus tard.*"

Later. The same answer he'd given me.

I barely had time to stumble toward one of the vinyl-covered benches and collapse gratefully onto it when the crewmembers hopped aboard, and we swung abruptly away from the dock. I watched as the lovely, pastel buildings of George Town faded away and the massive white hull of the *Crystal Fjord* loomed ever larger.

The enigmatic *Monsieur* Darnay had deserted me. He huddled in the front of the narrow cabin with the officer who had first spoken to us. They kept glancing over their shoulders. I didn't need to hear the conversation to know they were talking about me.

"Are you all right, dear?"

The voice, coming out of the dimness almost right at my elbow, sent me about three feet straight up off the cushion.

"I'm sorry. Did I startle you?"

"Please be seated, madam, until we reach the ship. For your own safety," the officer called loudly.

She plopped down opposite me as if someone had yanked on her arm.

"Do I know you?" I asked. I was almost certain I didn't, although there was something familiar about her plain, nondescript face. I was not only tired, but more than a little gun-shy, of being accosted by strangers.

"Oh, no, dear. You just looked slightly . . . well, bedraggled, if you don't mind my saying so. Did you have an accident? Can I help?"

For the first time since Darnay had helped me up off the sidewalk, I took a good look at myself. My palms were scraped and raw and had bled in a few places. Ditto with my forearms and elbows. The blood, along with a considerable amount of filth from the Cardinal Avenue gutter, streaked my once-white outfit. Something brushed against my neck, and I reached up to find the collar of my blouse hanging loosely by a couple of threads. It had barely survived the onslaught of Darnay's considerable efforts to drag me out of the street. I ripped it the rest of the way off and stuffed it in my bag.

I realized the woman was still studying me intently. I mustered up what felt like a passable smile. "No, thank you, I'm fine. Just a fall."

"I'm Joan Keppler. My husband's Lou." She gestured toward the back of the cabin.

I tried to turn my head and found I couldn't. My neck had begun to stiffen up. "Bay Tanner." I didn't offer my hand.

"We're from Ohio," Joan said, settling in for a one-sided chat, "near Cleveland? It's our anniversary. We've been planning . . ."

I was saved by the sudden cutting of the engine and a soft bump as the tender came to rest against the boarding platform at the foot of a metal stairway.

"This way, please." The junior officer extended his arm to Joan Keppler.

She seemed more annoyed than grateful. "Maybe we can have a drink later? We'll look you up. Take care of those cuts, dear . . ."

She was still chattering as her husband took her hand and dragged her toward the gangway. Silhouetted against the afternoon sun as they climbed the steps, I suddenly knew why she'd looked familiar. They were the couple from the airport, the lost-looking pair who seemed to have been stood up. He caught me watching them, and I dropped my eyes.

"All set?" *Monsieur* Darnay's shadow fell across my lap as I rummaged in my tote bag for a comb. My hand closed easily around the cosmetic bag that usually sank like a stone beneath everything else in the canvas monstrosity when it finally dawned on me what was missing.

Yesterday's *The Wall Street Journal* no longer lay folded innocuously in the bottom of my bag.

The suite was blessedly cool and empty when the assistant purser ushered me in. Someone—probably *not* Jordan—had unpacked for me. For the third time I waved off the young man's insistence that I should see the ship's doctor and closed the door politely, but firmly, in his face.

The tiny shower stall compensated for its size with heat and water pressure. In seconds I stood enveloped in rolling clouds of steam as I let the pounding spray knead the stiffness out of me.

Fifteen minutes later, wrapped in a thick, terrycloth robe provided by the cruise line, I lay stretched out on a loveseat as the ocean slid by outside a rectangular, floor-to-ceiling window. I had been expecting a porthole, but apparently they were reserved for the lower-priced cabins on the decks beneath us.

This sitting room and the adjoining bedroom were beautifully appointed, the furniture and decorating simple, but elegant. Maximum effect had been achieved in a limited space by the clever arrangement of the various components.

A soft knock kicked my heart rate up a notch, then the door slid open. I found myself clutching the lapels of the robe to my throat like the imperiled heroine of a B-movie melodrama.

He was tall, dark, and homely. The white, cropped jacket and black bow tie told me he was staff, and I relaxed a little. He set the tray he'd been carrying on the table beside me.

"Mrs. Tanner, is it? I'm Gordon. I'll be looking after you and the Countess."

The accent, I thought, had started out Cockney, but been trained to a more polished, upper class British veneer, sort of like Eliza Doolittle in *My Fair Lady*. I wondered who his Henry Higgins had been.

"Thank you. What exactly does 'looking after' entail?"

The smile changed his whole appearance, making the pale, round face and slightly off-kilter nose almost attractive. "Just about anything you need, mum. Fresh towels, laundry. Keeping the room shipshape, of course. Drinks or a bit of a snack at odd hours. I took the liberty of unpacking your things when I heard you'd been delayed. I hope they're arranged to your satisfaction?"

"I'm sure they are." For the first time since I'd found myself staring at the wheels of a two-ton truck bearing down on me, I felt some of the tension ease, although I couldn't suppress a slight shudder at the memory.

Gordon was perceptive as well as efficient. "I understand you had a nasty fall in town, mum. Don't know what they're thinking, three big ships in port all at the same time. Makes the streets much too crowded and dangerous." As he talked, he set about pouring tea from a brightly flowered pot into a matching bone china cup and saucer. "Lemon or milk, mum?"

"Neither. Just a little sugar, please."

Gordon added a lump and stirred, then passed the fragrant cup to me. He stood watching until I'd taken a sip and pronounced it perfect.

"Very good, then. Are you a good sailor, mum? Tummy-wise, I mean?"

"I have no idea. This is my first cruise."

"Right, then. I've brought you something, just in case."

Gordon pointed out the bright blue seasickness pill on the cloth-covered tray along with a couple of smaller white tablets for any pain I might be feeling as a result of my "accident". He'd also included two highly polished apples, one red, one yellow.

"Good for calming any little queasies," he informed me with a twinkle. He offered to peel them for me if I liked.

I declined, choosing instead a luscious-looking scone from the brimming plate accompanying the tea. Gordon excused himself, and his tuneless whistling drifted out as he tended to the mess I'd left in the tiny bathroom.

While I could definitely get used to all this pampering, I suddenly wished he'd finish up and go. I needed to be alone for awhile. Somehow I had to try and make sense of the attack. I had to get it all straight in my head before I faced Trey and Jordan. They would demand explanations, and right now I didn't have any. For the fall or for my mysterious rescuer.

Gordon emerged carrying damp towels and the remains of my white traveling outfit that I'd dropped on the floor by the shower. "Shall I see if the laundry can salvage these, mum?" He sounded doubtful.

"No, thanks. I think they're beyond redemption. Can you just dispose of them for me?"

"Certainly." He deposited the bundle outside the door. "Anything else I can do for you, mum?"

"No, thank you, Gordon. The tea was a lifesaver."

"Nothing like it to restore a body, or so my old mother used to say."

The kindness in his eyes almost undid me. I felt on the verge of bursting into tears.

"I'll just leave you to rest, then," he said briskly. "Oh, bless me, I nearly forgot! I have messages for you, Mrs. Tanner." He produced two pink slips from the pocket of his jacket. "The French gentleman was inquiring about your injuries. Said he'd ring you back later. And the Countess wants you to meet her in the bar behind the casino as soon as you're dressed."

I looked quizzically at the telephone. "How did you . . .?"

"The phone rings at my station if no one here answers it right away," Gordon explained. "The casino is on this deck, by the way.

Just turn left out your door and walk straight down the passage-way. You can't miss it. Or ring me, and I'll be happy to escort you."

"Thank you, Gordon. For everything."

He smiled and nodded and was gone.

I lit a cigarette and poured myself some more tea. The pink message slip carried no cabin number or name, but it had to be Darnay. My hand hovered over the receiver, then I let it drop back into my lap. I could probably track him down. But then what?

How did he know my name? That question bothered me more than any of the others. Was it chance that had put him there on that sidewalk at precisely the right moment, or had it been design? Had he been following me?

I stubbed out the cigarette and rose to stand gazing out the tall window. The sea rolled soundlessly by as we sailed east, into the deepening night.

There was only one reason anyone would have been interested in my movements today: the Grayton's Race documents. But I'd already delivered them safely into the hands of *Herr* Wagner and the Gellenschaft Bank. Attacking me *afterwards* seemed pointless. As did the theft of my clever hiding place. No one else had known about that. No one! And yet, of all the valuables in my bag, only the newspaper had been missing. None of this made sense!

Tentatively I stretched, relieved to find most of my soreness gone. Even my neck seemed inclined to swivel the way it was meant to. I shook off the aimless speculation and crossed into the bedroom.

As I selected a gown for this evening's festivities, I had a rare moment of regret that I don't drink. I had a feeling that a good, stiff belt might be just what I needed to get me through the next few hours.

Floating folds of silver whispered against my ankles as I made my way past the noisy casino toward the small horseshoe bar. The thin straps and deep décolletage of the slip dress would have revealed far too many of my wounds, past and present, so I was thankful for the long, flowing jacket that matched it. I mourned the passing out of fashion of elbow-length gloves for evening wear, contenting myself with makeup to camouflage my raw, scraped palms.

Trey Herrington in formal black tie nearly took my breath away. I thought again that it should be illegal for a man to be so damned good-looking. I was not alone in my appreciation. As he rose from the bar to greet me with a Hollywood-style air kiss to each cheek, I felt dozens of pairs of mascaraed eyes swing our way. When he took my hands I winced, and he was instantly alert.

"What happened to your hands?" Trey asked, inspecting them under the dim light of the bar. "They're all cut up."

I took the stool he'd vacated and fumbled with my cigarettes to postpone answering. Jordan, her back turned to me, was in deep conversation with one of the bartenders and ignored my presence.

"I fell," I said finally to Trey's insistent expression. "It's nothing. I'm fine."

I'm not sure when I'd decided not to tell them the truth—that I'd been deliberately attacked. It just seemed easier than fielding a barrage of questions, most of which I wouldn't be able to answer with any certainty. The coward's way out, I acknowledged, but definitely easier.

Trey overrode my attempt to order my usual bottled water and lime. "Bring her a virgin Sex on the Beach," he told Roger, the Filipino bartender who responded with a wink. What arrived was a tall glass brimming with a cool blend of several juices, with pieces of their fruit skewered on a long pick floating on top. The featured drink of Grand Cayman, minus the vodka, Roger informed me.

Trey and I munched on bar snacks and sipped our drinks while we watched the parade of elegantly dressed passengers wander into and by the casino. The soft *thunk* of dice against the felt-covered craps table gave rise to a mixture of cheers and groans, and the generally raucous noise level was interrupted periodically by the mad clanging of a slot machine paying off.

"I don't suppose there's a floating poker game," I said conversationally.

"Probably not. The idea is for the passengers to have fun and win a little money. No big stakes here, and all the games are tilted in favor of the player. No one's allowed to win—or lose—too big."

"How do you know all that?" I asked, impressed by his knowledge. "You sound as if you've done this before."

"I have," he mumbled into his drink, "a long time ago. Why did you ask about poker? Do you play?"

I wasn't about to be diverted so easily. "Do you mean you've been a passenger? Or have you actually worked on a ship? That sounded like insider stuff. Oh, damn!"

I whirled around on the stool so fast I almost couldn't stop myself. Roger jumped immediately in front of me, whisking away my empty glass and replacing it with a fresh drink.

"What is it?" Trey demanded, accepting his own refill.

"Nothing. Just someone I don't particularly want to cross paths with."

I had spotted Joan Keppler as she sailed into the casino, her grumpy husband in tow. She would have been hard to miss. Her dress was a hideous, lime green thing that looked as if she'd worn it to her high school prom thirty years ago. Someone must have worked her into it with a shoehorn. The never-smiling Lou sported an equally ill-fitting blue suit along with brown oxfords. I'd bet he had on white socks.

"You mean Ma and Pa Kettle?" Trey offered, and I nearly choked on the laugh caught in my throat. "Where on earth did you run into them?"

"Don't do that when I'm trying to swallow," I gasped, answering his grin with one of my own. "On the launch out to the ship. I saw them at the airport, too."

"New friends of yours?"

"Hardly. She's just one of those busybodies who thinks everyone's as fascinated with her life story as she is. Tell me when they're gone."

Trey swiveled back around toward the crowded room. "They seem to be looking for someone. Probably you. Sure you don't

want me to call them over? Maybe her life story really is fascinating."

"Raise that arm, and I'll break it off."

"Okay, all clear. They're headed off—for the dining room, I'll
bet. She doesn't look as if she misses too many meals."

"Who?" Jordan's voice startled us both.

"Nice of you to join us," her brother quipped, snapping the
lighter as I pulled a cigarette from my small evening bag. "Find out
anything useful?"

He held the flame as Jordan, too, lit up.

"Not really." She blew smoke toward the ceiling and surveyed
the casino. "Not yet. I'm establishing rapport," she said *sotto voce.*
"Lots of women traveling alone, though, at least according to Luis.
Seems it's not all that unusual for them to acquire an 'escort' before
the trip is out."

I noticed that many of the players had begun to drift away, their
places at the tables and slot machines being taken by a new crop of
gowned and tuxedoed passengers. Just then a series of chimes
sounded through the ship's speaker system.

"Second sitting dinner," Trey announced, consulting his watch.
"That's us, ladies."

Jordan signed the bar tab, then pressed a folded bill into the
hand of Luis, the bartender she'd been monopolizing all evening.
We followed the herd down a wide, sweeping staircase to the Four
Seasons dining room one deck below.

Most of our fellow travelers had already received their seating as-
signments and had had a chance to orient themselves the first night
out. They flowed around us, finding their places and allowing
white-jacketed busboys to seat them. We watched the evening's
menu being distributed by well-trained waiters, each of whom
would serve only a small number of diners exclusively for the entire
length of the voyage.

Jordan paused just inside the double doorway and signaled for
the *maître d'.* He stepped immediately to her side.

"May I assist you in locating your table, *Señora?*"

Very dark, very handsome, very Italian, or so I thought from the accent.

"Countess von Brandt and party," she announced loudly, causing a few heads to turn in our direction.

Someone emitted a low whistle, and for the first time that night I stepped outside my preoccupation with my own troubles long enough to check out Jordan's attire and discovered the reason for all the attention we were drawing.

It was meant to imitate a man's tuxedo, I assumed, but, aside from being black and lapelled, any resemblance ended there. The trousers were actually skintight leggings with a black satin stripe up the outside of each leg. The jacket fitted snugly, nipped in at the waist, and flaring only slightly over Jordan's sleek hips. She wore no shirt. One diamond-studded button beneath her obviously unrestricted breasts was all that held the two sides of the coat together.

No wonder she had commanded the undivided attention of Luis, the bartender. Standing above her as she leaned over the bar, he must have had an unobstructed view straight to her navel.

"Ah, *si, Contessa.* I am Rodolfo, at your service. And your companions?"

"My friend, Mrs. Tanner." He bowed low over my hand in delightful continental fashion. "And my brother, Mr. Herrington." Trey received a click of the heels and a brief nod.

"If you will be so good as to follow me, your ladyship."

Our slow procession to the center of the vast dining room was accompanied by a lowering of the general conversational hum and not a few curious glances. The round table, set somewhat apart from the rest, glittered beneath a magnificent chandelier, its crystal drops reflected in the elegant blue-and-gold china and heavy silver cutlery. Two white-coated men rose at our approach.

"May I present our First Officer, Mr. Grunewald? And the ship's physician, Dr. Forbes?"

Introductions and handshakes completed, we were finally seated. I counted three empty places.

"Captain Bjornsen will be joining you as soon as he has completed his duties on the bridge. I trust your other dinner companions will be along shortly. Enjoy your evening."

Rodolfo glided off, and a trio of waiters began immediately filling water and wineglasses. I covered the latter with my hand to indicate I'd skip the alcohol.

So, the captain's table, I thought. I didn't know much about the protocol of cruise ships, but I was pretty certain it hadn't been the commoners, Trey and I, who had earned us this coveted honor. I glanced over at him as First Officer Grunewald hitched his chair closer to Jordan's and began peppering her with questions about her title and the location of Klaus's estates. Trey and I exchanged a grin. Apparently his sister had chalked up another conquest. The dark, vulpine officer with the hooded eyes and slightly hooked nose looked ready to devour her.

"Is this your first trip with us, Mrs. Tanner?" Dr. Forbes—short and round and unquestionably British—toyed with a slim, cellophane-wrapped cigarillo.

"It's my first cruise of any kind, Doctor." I pulled my cigarettes from my evening bag. "Is smoking permitted?" I asked.

"Of course! I mean, if you ladies don't mind . . .?" He had the wrapper off his little cigar and had shanghaied a passing busboy for a light before I could shake a cigarette out of the pack. "Disgusting habit, isn't it?" he beamed, exhaling gratefully. "I know I set a shockingly bad example, but there you are. We all have our little vices, eh, Mrs. Tanner?"

I nodded, pitying the poor man. How boring it must be to sit here week after week trying to make conversation with an ever-changing parade of well-dressed strangers. A maroon, tasseled menu appeared over my left shoulder, and I studied the choices offered. Such difficult decisions. Caviar or escargot to start? Vichyssoise or consommé? The lobster or the *filet de boeuf? Or perhaps the duck?*

I was already making plans for the exercise regimen that would allow me to eat one of everything without turning into a blimp when I saw the two officers pop up out of their chairs.

Captain Lars Bjornsen could have been the poster boy for the benefits of clean, outdoor living and the good fortune of having Scandinavian genes. Blonde, tanned, and ruggedly attractive, his pale eyes crinkled at the corners as he greeted each of us.

The woman on his arm was probably a decade or more older than his fifty-something. She carried herself like a queen, and the diamonds that dripped from her ears and throat were ostentatious enough to have been part of the Crown Jewels. Her somewhat horsy face was saved by a sweet smile and a soft, cultured voice. The captain introduced her as Dame Margo Stanhope.

The announcement was made as if we should all recognize the name instantly. I felt like an idiot, because I hadn't a clue who she was or why she might be famous. I was saved from having to betray my ignorance by the arrival of our final dinner companion at the empty place to my right.

"Ah, there you are, *monsieur*," the captain said genially. "I was afraid we might have left you behind in George Town."

"No such luck, *mon capitaine*," the familiar voice said at my elbow. "Please forgive my tardiness."

I looked up to find the gray-blue eyes of my rescuer gazing intently into mine.

"Mrs. Tanner, Countess von Brandt," the captain continued, "may I present *Monsieur* Alain Darnay, security consultant for Royal Scandinavian Cruise Lines."

20

Sheltered from the wind on two sides by tall, latticed panels, the Aft Bar still offered a breathtaking view of black sky and blacker sea. The only way to tell that one ended and the other began was by the blurred line of demarcation where the stars met the white, foaming wake left by the passage of the massive ship.

Most of the passengers were jammed into the two show lounges where Vegas-style revues, complete with leggy showgirls and live orchestras, would entertain them until the lavish midnight buffet had been assembled in the now-deserted dining rooms. For that reason, our table companions—minus the Captain and Dr. Forbes—made up the entire clientele of the intimate little café at the extreme rear of the ship. There Jordan's favorite bartender, Luis, whether by chance or design, dispensed drinks and light-hearted chatter.

First Officer Rolfe Grunewald had attached himself to Jordan like a barnacle on the bottom of a neglected boat. I smiled to myself—both at the blatant charm he was directing at her full force, as well as at my own, unflattering simile. Somehow during the journey up from the deck below, we had become paired off. While Rolfe, with typical German precision, had cut Jordan out of the herd, Trey had inexplicably fallen into deep conversation with Dame Margo Stanhope. Through a few discreet questions and a little Sherlockian deduction, I had discovered the basis for her celebrity: the lady wrote books. Hundreds of them, to judge by the enthusiastic comments of Dr. Forbes who was apparently an ardent fan. Romances, I gathered, of the bodice-ripper, Fabio-bare-chested-on-the-cover variety. For some reason, Trey found her fascinating.

Which left me with Darnay.

He had made no reference to our previous encounter, so I took my cue from him. We had exchanged banal dinner table pleasantries, but otherwise basically ignored each other. Now, however, with the piano player resuming his seat and launching into a medley of Broadway show tunes, and Trey and Jordan well occupied elsewhere, I felt comfortable in mounting my attack.

As he leaned over the tiny table to light my cigarette, I caught his eyes and held them. "Let's have it, M. Darnay, the whole story. And no more *plus tard*. I want some answers. Now."

His gaze never wavered while he lit his own, unfiltered Gauloises, and his smile held a cat-and-canary smugness. "Before becoming a consultant, I spent some time with the French Sûreté in Paris. And, most recently, with Interpol. But let's keep that between us."

He watched my face as the wheels in my brain whirred and spun, and he chuckled when he saw the obvious answer click into place behind my eyes.

"And how is my father?" I asked, unable to hide the combination of relief and annoyance the realization brought me.

"Ah, he said you were sharp. He warned me, actually, not to underestimate you. Said he'd done it himself a couple of times, to his cost."

"I'll bet. So where did you pick me up? At the airport? Did he ask you to follow me all over Grand Cayman?"

My father knew nothing of my *insurance policy*, the papers that now guaranteed his safety as well as my own. I needed to know if Darnay had tailed me to the bank. I was going to have to come up with a quick cover story if he had.

"Do you believe in fate, Bay Tanner?"

His face told me it was a serious question, so I gave him an honest answer.

"If you mean the kind of thing where we're just pieces on a chessboard being shoved around with no choice in the matter, then no, I don't. And I don't believe in coincidence, either."

"Ah, a true American pragmatist. And yet, had I not left my post on the docks where I was watching for you in order to cross the street for cigarettes . . ."

He let the thought dangle, regarding me with those hard, blue eyes as I relived the moment when his strong hands had snatched me from under the wheels of the sliding truck. His shrug was so typically Gallic.

"But . . . who can say?" He smiled then, softening his expression as he stubbed out the strong, French cigarette. "Think of it. My smoking may have proved very good for your health, *n'est-ce pas?*"

"Alain, I've never properly thanked you . . ."

"Please." He held up his hand. "We will not speak of it again. Except perhaps to explore how such a thing could have happened. And no one calls me by that name. I am simply Darnay, *d'accord?*"

"Okay," I agreed with a relieved smile.

Luis, the bartender, set two more of his fruit juice concoctions in front of us. Already he had learned to leave the alcohol out of mine. I sipped and let Darnay light another cigarette for me.

"Why does your name sound so familiar?" I asked, wanting to savor these quiet moments while the pianist slid into the hauntingly beautiful opening bars of *Für Elise*. Murder and mayhem could wait awhile longer to claim our attention.

Darnay cleared his throat dramatically. " 'It was the best of times, it was the worst of times . . .' "

"Of course!" I cried, making the connection. "*A Tale of Two Cities.* Charles Darnay. He changed places with Sidney Carton on the guillotine. Or was it the other way around?"

"I took a bit of ribbing about that in my school days," the Frenchman said with a grin. "But it's an old French name. Dickens merely borrowed it for his book."

"So you can trace your lineage back to the French Revolution?"

"Farther, I believe. But my sister is the one with the obsession about those things. Ancestor worship has never appealed to me."

"You'd be in big trouble back in my neck of the woods," I laughed. "There it's almost a national pastime."

"Yes, I recall that from my visits to Beaufort when I first consulted with your father." He pronounced the name in the proper French manner, *Bo-for.*

His mention of the Judge brought me rudely back to the business at hand. Under different circumstances I could have enjoyed learning more about this former French policeman with the soft mouth and hard eyes who could quote from nineteenth-century English literature and wore no wedding band. As it was . . .

"How much did my father tell you?" I asked, lowering my voice despite the covering background of the piano. "About Jordan's mother and our suspicions?"

"Everything he knew, I think." Darnay leaned closer. "Although you don't believe in coincidence, you must admit it's strange that I should already have a connection to this cruise line that figures so prominently in your scenario."

He had me there. "So what do you think? About our theory, I mean. Is it possible some madman has been targeting women on your ships, then following them ashore and robbing and killing them?"

Stated baldly like that, it sounded preposterous, even to me. The sudden look of anger that flashed across Darnay's face made me wish I'd been a little more subtle.

"Look, I . . ."

"Take out a cigarette and lean toward me." His harsh whisper startled me.

"What?"

"Do it!" he growled under his breath.

I shook one out of the pack and leaned in as he flicked his lighter.

Over the flame he said, "Now, smile and laugh like we're having a good time." His eyes seemed focused somewhere over my right shoulder. He took the newly lighted cigarette from me and crushed it out in the ashtray. "We're going to get up and walk over to the rail. Keep that screen between us and the bar. Let's go."

His hand closed around mine and nearly pulled me out of my chair. His arm encircled my waist as he guided me none too gently around the latticework panel and into a shadowy pool of darkness between two overhead strings of lights. I couldn't tell we'd reached the chest-high rail until my elbow connected sharply with the metal struts.

"Ouch! Damn it, that hurt!" I hissed over Darnay's whispered attempts to shush me. I tried to pull out of his iron embrace, but he only held me closer. "What's going on?" I tried to ask, but his head bent over me smothered the words.

"Shut up. I'm going to kiss you," he said matter-of-factly.

"Like hell you are," I began, but found the breath squeezed out of me by the force of his mouth on mine. I had a moment to register how really good at this he was before his lips moved abruptly away.

"Is he still there?" Darnay asked, those soft lips now exploring the area around my ear. "To your left a little. Cigar end."

I caught it then, the glowing tip beside the screen we'd used as cover. In the whirling winds at the rear of the ship, the not-unpleasant odor drifted past us. As I watched, the unseen smoker turned and disappeared.

Meanwhile, Darnay's mouth had progressed to the side of my neck as his hands stroked the silver sleeves of my jacket.

"He's gone," I said into the shoulder of his tuxedo.

At least I think I said it. I was having a little trouble focusing at that moment. When Darnay finally stepped back, I had to hook my arm over the rail to keep from folding up like a discarded marionette.

Darnay must have been part feline for he moved with swift assurance through the dark, leading me by the hand until we reached the starboard promenade. It, too, was deserted. We sank into canvas sling chairs placed comfortably out of the wind.

"What the hell is going on?" I gasped, expelling the breath I didn't realize I'd been holding.

"That's what I'd like to know." Darnay lit one of his foul French cigarettes and offered it to me. I waved it away. "What do you have to do with Eddie Brown Shoes?" he demanded.

"Who?'

"The guy who's been tailing you. The one who just came looking for us."

"I have no idea what you're talking about."

"Come on, Bay. Level with me. He doesn't have any reason to be interested in me, so it has to be you. What have you done to attract the attention of a Miami mobster?"

* * * *

The radio room was located on the deck beneath our cabin, but on the port side. Jordan had been wrong about my getting lost. I had oriented myself quite quickly and easily. The difficult part had been disengaging myself from Darnay.

I had to exaggerate the queasiness his announcement had generated in me, but not by much. He led me back to the suite with a minimum of solicitude and a lot of barely concealed annoyance. He wanted answers and seemed prepared to wait outside my door until I recovered from this phony bout of seasickness. I summoned up all my meager high school dramatics experience and managed to convince him I would probably be tossing my cookies until dawn.

We made a tentative date for breakfast, and Darnay left me at the door, muttering as he strode away. I changed into shorts and a sweatshirt and chain-smoked three cigarettes before peeking cautiously out to find the narrow hallway empty. So was the tiny elevator when it finally arrived. Too much traffic on the wide staircase, I'd decided, considering the growing number of the people I wanted to avoid.

Darnay's brief description of the man he called Eddie Brown Shoes was enough for me to identify him as Lou Keppler, the silent *husband* of Joan, the garrulous busybody on the tender who had been so insistent on striking up an acquaintance with me. Was she just a cover for my assailant, or was she, too, trained to violence?

I stepped out into the deserted corridor and made my way to the small door marked Radio Room. A hand-lettered sign hung over the knob read "Back in ten minutes". There were no chairs so I slid down onto the floor, my back against the paneled wall, to wait. Up front here—*forward*, I corrected myself—the side-to-side motion was less noticeable, but the rise and fall felt much more pronounced. If I had to sit there too long, I really would be losing my dinner.

During the time I had procrastinated in the cabin, making sure Darnay really had given up on me, I had worked out the probable scenario for the day's events. It hadn't taken a rocket scientist.

I had played my part too well with Hadley Bolles after the Grayton's Race fire, and the fat, sleazy lawyer had convinced his underworld pals that the incriminating documents I had stolen and threatened them with had been secreted out of their reach. The fact that I had been bluffing—about the secure hiding place, at least—had apparently never occurred to them.

I fidgeted around and checked my watch. *What a stupid sign*, I thought. Ten minutes from when? I fumbled in my pocket for my cigarettes, then decided against it. Where was the guy? I hoped he'd be able to speak English when he finally did show up.

The Judge and Sergeant Red Tanner had obviously been right: someone *had* been keeping tabs on me. They must have panicked when they saw me going into the Gellenschaft Bank after the couple tailed me from the airport. If the papers had been stashed, as I'd claimed to Hadley, then I must be *retrieving* them. Whatever my reasons, they couldn't be good news for the drug dealers whose money-laundering scheme I had managed to thwart.

So. A discreet push in the back, undetected in the tightly packed crowd at the curb, my tote bag ripped away in the process, and they were home free.

Except Darnay had prevented my head from being crushed like a melon under the wheels of the produce truck. And the newspaper—the only item missing from my bag—had yielded them nothing but day-old stock prices.

Their obvious conclusion? The documents had been on my person somewhere. I still had them. I was still a threat.

I jumped to my feet at the sound of the elevator door opening. I rattled the knob of the radio room, but it was locked. I couldn't reach the stairs without passing the group of noisy passengers now moving my way. In a second, they'd round the corner. What if my two stalkers were among them? I tensed, ready to charge through them and bolt down the steps when the two couples appeared, and I sagged against the wall in relief.

Beautifully dressed and obviously drunk, none of them was familiar to me.

"Hey there, little lady," a tall, balding man with more stomach than his cummerbund had been designed to contain called out. "You got any idea where the sam hill we are?" His accent was the flat, Midwestern twang I remembered so well from my college days in Evanston. "I think we've been every place on this damn boat except where we're tryin' to get to."

His deep laugh rattled off the walls of the narrow corridor.

"Where do you want to go?" I asked.

"That little piano bar at the back of the boat. There last night, but damned if we can find it now. Need a little nightcap, don't you know."

I seriously doubted if any of them needed any more booze, but I politely pointed out our location on one of the many layouts of the ship posted on every deck. Then I headed them in the right direction toward the stairs. I had to fight to keep them from literally dragging me along to join them in a drink.

The radio operator came trotting up the steps as the revelers stumbled down the opposite side. He apologized profusely for his absence in a Spanish-accented English that was hard to follow, but decipherable. I gave him the Judge's area code and phone number, and he explained that he would make the connection via satellite, then transfer the call to my cabin. I should hurry back there. It would take only a few minutes.

I asked him to let it ring until someone answered. My watch told me it was well past midnight back home. Both the Judge and Lavinia would be long asleep.

But I had to verify that Alain Darnay was, in fact, the Interpol agent my father had worked with years ago. I had to be certain he could be trusted completely.

My life might depend on it.

21

I awoke next morning to a cacophony of voices and the sound of steel drums being played, it seemed, right outside my window. I listened for a moment, finally identifying the song as "Yellow Bird". I lifted the edge of the lined drapery and peeked out.

Below, on the crowded quayside, early rising passengers streamed out to join their prearranged tours or set off on private explorations. Their gaily colored resort wear mingled with the bright clothing of the locals who touted their wares to the debarking tourists. Small trucks and forklifts, carrying the freight that constituted the other business of the port, wove their way through a horde of taxi drivers, all shouting their rates in the lovely, singsong cadence of the island.

We had arrived in Jamaica.

I glanced over to the other twin bed, separated from mine by a narrow table. All that was visible above the light blanket drawn up around her ears was the gleaming cap of black hair at the crown of Jordan's head. I hadn't heard her come in last night—or rather, this morning. It had been after one o'clock when I'd finished my interrogation of the Judge and fallen almost instantly asleep.

I hurried through my morning routine, eager to keep my breakfast rendezvous with Darnay. Now that my father had confirmed his identity for me, only one niggling question still scratched at the back of my mind. I climbed the stairs and once again made my way aft to the small piano bar. It had been transformed, in the daylight, into a bright, open café, set out for a buffet-style, Continental breakfast.

Darnay, in gleaming white shorts and navy polo shirt, waved to me from a table in a far corner protected from the already brutal sun by a striped awning. I acknowledged his greeting, pausing on my way to join the short line at the food table. By the time I had selected a warm croissant and loaded my plate with an array of fresh fruit, a smiling waiter stood ready to hold the chair for me and take my order for hot tea.

"You look well rested after yesterday's excitement," Darnay remarked as I buttered the flaky pastry. "Stomach doing better, I presume?" He glanced pointedly at my heaping plate.

For a moment I was puzzled, then remembered my feigned seasickness of the night before. I hoped the chagrin didn't show too plainly on my face. The trouble with lying is that it requires a damned good memory.

"Yes, thank you," I said, stuffing the croissant into my mouth to prevent there being any more room for my foot.

"And your other injuries?" His smile told me he didn't intend to pursue my reasons for last night's diversion, only let me know he was well aware of my deceit.

"I'll survive." Actually the bumps and scrapes from my abrupt encounter with the pavement in Grand Cayman had pretty much subsided. The worst was still my shins which problem I had solved by donning a long, cotton skirt in place of more revealing shorts.

"I'm relieved to hear it. Eat up," Darnay commanded, checking his watch. "I have a car waiting for us on the quay."

"Why? Where are we going?"

"We're conducting an experiment," he said, rising and scanning the surrounding tables crammed with fellow passengers. "And it will give us a secure place to talk. You have much to tell me, *n'est-ce pas?*"

"I need to get a couple of things from my cabin, first. Where shall we meet?"

"I'll come with you," Darnay said, taking my arm proprietarily as I rose from the chair. "It will save time."

Jordan had left the room a mess which Gordon, the steward, was trying to put to rights when we walked in.

"Oh, sorry, madam," he said, straightening from a half-made bed. "I'll just pop out until you're finished, shall I?"

"No, that's okay," I said, taking a fresh pack of cigarettes from the carton on the table. "We'll just be a minute."

I retrieved my floppy straw hat from the closet shelf and dropped my black swimsuit into the tote bag, just in case a palm-fringed beach should happen to present itself during our travels.

"Gordon, could I leave a message with you for the Countess?" I asked.

"Of course, madam. Shall I get paper?"

"No, just let her know I'll be spending the morning with M. Darnay, and that I'll be back for lunch."

"Very good, madam. Oh, I say . . ." Gordon's voice stopped us in the doorway. "Did your other friends manage to locate you, Mrs. Tanner?"

"What other friends?"

"Why, that nice couple from Ohio. I was sorry I couldn't let them in. Ship's policy. They quite understood, but I did feel rather bad about it. Were the papers you'd left for them terribly important? I could deliver them myself, if you like. No trouble at all."

"No, thanks, Gordon," I managed to stammer. "You did the right thing." Then to Darnay, "Hold on a second, okay?"

I crossed into the bathroom and shut the door. My makeup bag lay zipped up, but in plain view on the small shelf beneath the mirror. Quickly I removed the safety deposit box key from where I'd tossed it in among the tubes of mascara and lipstick and looked around for a better hiding place. Even though Eddie Brown Shoes, alias Lou Keppler, and his pudgy companion had been looking for papers, I couldn't let the key fall into their hands either. I unscrewed the lid of the jar of medicated gel I used to keep the skin around the burn scars loose and supple. Thick and gooey, it swallowed the metal key like quicksand.

The dark blue Citroen had become obvious as soon as we left the bustle of the port behind.

The road narrowed, winding its way into the mountains in a series of gentle switchbacks that gave a clear view below. Darnay smiled and seemed to relax, his eyes no longer glued to the rearview mirror of the big Jaguar sedan.

"So they're following us. Or rather, *me*, I guess. Was that the experiment you wanted to conduct?" I asked, cracking the window a little as I lit a cigarette.

"Partly." The smile of satisfaction was gone, replaced by a frowning concentration as the curves and the angle of ascent sharpened. His fingers on the wheel tightened, and we seemed to be picking up speed.

"You're not going to try and lose them, are you?"

The tires made protesting squeals, and I looked out across the tops of towering trees to the Caribbean Sea stretching to the horizon on all sides. I couldn't force myself to look straight down, past the narrow shoulder with no guardrail, to the dizzying drop-off just feet from my window.

"Darnay?"

His response was a grunt. All his attention was focused on negotiating the increasingly tight curves, some of them now almost ninety-degree cutbacks. I had to force myself not to brace my hands against the dashboard. Panic was beginning to creep in, that old, out-of-control feeling I hated. I glanced over my shoulder and caught a brief flash of dark blue on one of the switches below us.

"What the hell are you trying to do, Darnay, get us all killed?" I knew I was shouting, but I couldn't help it. "For God's sake, this is an island! Where can we run to?" I drew a deep breath and willed myself to calm down. "Sooner or later we have to go back to the ship, don't we?"

I know it was my imagination that the powerful Jaguar teetered on the crest, like the front car of a roller coaster just before it makes that heart-stopping plunge. But when Darnay said tersely, "Hold on!" his face glowed with that same mixture of fear and exhilaration.

And then we were tearing down the mountain.

The ancient, lumbering bus labored up the narrow road smack in the middle of both lanes. As we rounded the curve, I had a split-second to register the wide-eyed shock on the grizzled black face of its driver before Darnay whipped the wheel sharply to the left and stood on the brakes. The high-pitched squeal of the tires failed to drown out the scrape of limbs on pristine metal as we bounced through the dense underbrush and, miraculously, back onto the road.

When I opened my eyes, I found Darnay's face only inches from my own.

"*Jesu!* Are you all right?" he demanded breathlessly.

Before I could reply, the deep blare of the bus's horn caused us both to whip around in the seat. Eddie Brown Shoes didn't have Darnay's instincts, but he, too, had realized he couldn't go to the right. That way lay nothing but a few thin bushes, then a long, terrifying plunge over the edge to certain death hundreds of feet below. But he had reacted too slowly, and we watched in horror as he locked his brakes into a screaming skid, aimed directly at the stalled bus.

I wanted to look away, but somehow I couldn't. As the scene unfolded in seeming slow motion, I held my breath, waiting for the inevitable crash. But at the last moment my pursuer managed to wrest control of the sliding car long enough to alter its course the fraction he needed. With a sickening crunch, the blue Citroen clipped the sagging front bumper of the battered bus, spun completely around, and came to rest, nose down, in the culvert against the side of the mountain.

With a gasp of relief, I unhooked my seat belt and fumbled for the door handle, but Darnay's hand on my shoulder pinned me firmly to the seat.

"But he could be hurt!" I cried, struggling unsuccessfully against his grip. "We have to help!"

"Wait!" he ordered.

"But . . ."

The distraught bus driver ran to the Citroen, and, as we watched, Eddie Brown Shoes stumbled from the crumpled door. On wobbly legs he moved to collapse gratefully against the back fender. Blood trickled from a cut over his left eye, and he held his right wrist gingerly as if it might be broken.

I turned back to find Darnay pulling a cell phone from the console between us. Tersely he reported the accident, requesting tow trucks and an ambulance. He hung up without giving his name, then, with a last look over his shoulder, he gunned the big Jaguar and sped off down the mountain.

From a distance the quiet fishing village looked like something off a postcard, quaint and picturesque. Up close, the signs of poverty and slow decay became evident. Yet I noticed that the few children we encountered looked reasonably well fed. The sea, no doubt, provided a boundless, though probably monotonous, food supply.

Our more sedate ride down to the seacoast had passed in relative silence. Now Darnay took my arm and steered me into an open doorway, indicating a table set out beneath a wide window that overlooked the empty harbor and a crumbling jetty. Far out, waves broke high against what must be an extensive reef.

Darnay ordered a Red Stripe, the local beer, while I opted for a Diet Coke. The plump, smiling proprietress also brought a warm, fragrant loaf of newly baked bread and a crock of what looked like home-churned butter.

I glanced at my watch, amazed to find that it was only a little past eleven, while my companion sipped his beer and regarded me solemnly.

"What?" His silent stare was making me more than a little uncomfortable. I sliced off a hunk of the yeasty bread and slathered it with butter. I couldn't believe how hungry I was just a scant two hours after breakfasting.

"Will you please say something?" I demanded, wiping warm butter off my chin with a paper napkin. "Why are you staring at me like that?"

Darnay drained the last of his Red Stripe and signaled for another. When he had the cold bottle in his hand, he sat back, shaking his head. "I've been trying to figure out what exactly it is you're up to," he said musingly.

"The Judge . . ."

"Oh, I know what your father told me, about your friend's mother and all. That seems pretty straightforward. But what else have you gotten yourself into, eh?"

His tone was calm and reasonable, as if the questions were generated merely by a mild curiosity on his part. "What do you have that our friend Eddie is willing to risk his life to get? What do you know that makes you worth an attempt to kill you in broad daylight in front of a hundred witnesses yesterday, eh, *ma petite?*"

"What makes you think . . .?"

"That they tried to kill you? Come, Bay Tanner, I am not a fool. Do you think you're the only one who doesn't believe in coincidences? Do you think because I now have this job *très confortable* that I have lost all my instincts?"

He smiled then, and I felt myself relax. The Judge had assured me I could trust Alain Darnay. At that moment, my own instincts, wobbling on shaky ground after several errors of judgment in the past couple of months, firmed up again under my feet. This man could be relied upon. I was sure of it.

So I told him everything.

We ate most of the bread, then carried our bottled drinks out onto the narrow, rocky beach that fronted the harbor. The owner had thanked us profusely when Darnay paid our bill and added a generous tip. We made empty promises to return one day for a taste of the local lobster Mrs. Manley vowed to prepare especially for us.

"Why do you suppose this is such a poor area?" I asked after we had finished our stroll and settled once again into the big Jaguar. The left-hand mirror had been snapped off, and a few deep scratches marred the dark green finish, but the beautiful machine had come through relatively unscathed, considering . . .

"No beach to speak of, I would guess. Plus that offshore reef must make navigating these waters pretty tricky. All the big hotels and resorts are on the other side of the island."

Darnay spoke off-handedly, his mind obviously far away. I gave up trying to make polite conversation and watched the endless inland jungle roll past as we made our way back to town on the modern, three-lane highway that skirted the mountains rather than attacking them. He had said little in response to my recitation of the circumstances that had led to my entanglement with the mob. His few, curt questions had been for clarification only.

A sign announcing we were fifteen kilometers from the docks had just flown past when at last he broke the silence. "I wish you had told me all this last night instead of running off, faking seasickness."

"Who said I was faking?"

"You weren't quite the proper shade of green," he replied with a grin.

"I wanted to," I admitted. "Tell you, I mean. I just wasn't sure. It's been hard to know who to trust lately."

His hand crept across the console and covered mine gently. "*Je comprends, ma petite.*"

I wondered if he realized how comforted and safe his touch made me feel. "Anyway, now you know it all," I said.

"*Eh bien.* However, I fear I have made things worse for you."

"How? You got rid of Eddie, didn't you? I don't think he'll be up to messing with me again, at least not for a while. And now he knows I'm not alone."

I knew it was presumptuous of me the second it was out of my mouth, but I didn't care. Having someone to share the burden with had made me almost light-headed with relief.

"*Bien sûr.*" Under pressure, Darnay's speech had become more formal, the cadence of his native French overriding his easy, idiomatic English. "Of course, that is true. He will be withdrawn, along with his companion. I doubt if we will see them again on the ship."

"So what's the problem?" I asked, puzzled by his glum expression. "That's good, isn't it?"

Traffic had thickened as we neared the port, and Darnay removed his hand from mine to concentrate on his driving. A little chill skittered down my spine at the loss of contact.

"But nothing has been resolved, Bay. They—your enemies—still believe you are a threat to them. They still believe you have removed from the bank the documents that could damage them." Darnay glanced sideways at me as we swept into the port and up to the fence surrounding the docks. "Ergo, . . ."

"Ergo, they'll send someone else, and we won't know who it is."

Darnay shrugged and came around to open my door. "Better the devil you know, eh? I'm sorry."

His strong hand in the small of my back guided me through the checkpoint and up the gangway of the *Crystal Fjord*. At the top of the steps he halted, and I turned to face him. "You go ahead in to lunch," Darnay said, his voice tight and determined.

"Where are you going?" I asked as he trotted back down the stair.

"To put things right," he called with a brief wave, "if I can."

I watched him stop and speak with the officer at the security gate, then stride purposefully toward the car.

"Bay! Where the hell have you been?" Jordan's strident, angry words caused more heads than mine to turn at her approach.

"Didn't you get my message?" I asked.

"Never mind that. He's here!"

"Who's here?"

"Ramon! I've found Ramon!"

22

Because so many passengers were ashore—exploring Dunn's River Falls, touring rum factories, or snorkeling in crystal coves—lunch was served buffet-style with open seating. Trey Herrington and Dame Margo Stanhope were already settled, heads close together, when Jordan and I approached the table beneath the long window on the seaward side of the ship.

Jordan hadn't given me a chance to return to the cabin to freshen up. In fact she had fumed in impatience while I ducked into the ladies room to wash my hands. She'd also firmly refused to elaborate on the bombshell she'd dropped on me, insisting that I wait and draw my own conclusions. "Ramon" was joining us for lunch.

He arrived almost as we did, raising Dame Margo's hand to his lips in a gesture at once formal, yet familiar. The rotund writer, resplendent in a flowing red caftan splashed with gaudy white lilies, tittered like a schoolgirl and batted her lashes.

Too much of this and I'm going to be genuinely sick, I thought.

Dame Margo performed the introductions as we seated ourselves. Obviously this was not her first encounter with *Señor* Diego Reyes, which set off the first alarm bells in my head. If Diego was, in fact, Ramon, why was the novelist still alive and kicking? Happily divorced three times—or so she'd informed us with a self-deprecatory laugh at dinner last night—she seemed the perfect target. Yet here she sat, picking daintily at her lobster salad, while her head swiveled from side to side, sucking up the attention of two very attractive men.

And he was attractive. Diego Reyes was a well-aged Antonio Banderas with languid black eyes that appraised every woman they lighted upon. His features bore the stamp of the pure Castilian, bronzed and finely molded. His smooth black hair was liberally streaked with white. I put his age at mid-fifties, perhaps a well-maintained sixty. His open shirt and linen trousers spoke of Polo by Lauren, and the huge diamond that glittered on his left hand rivaled Jordan's.

He left to fill his plate just as the waiter arrived for our drink orders. I took advantage of the confusion to whisper hurriedly behind my napkin to Jordan.

"Are you nuts? That can't be him! Dame Margo knows him," I hissed.

"So what? What does that prove?" she snapped, ignoring my attempts to shush her. "Everything else fits. I'll show you."

"Where's your sidekick, Bay?" Trey Herrington suddenly addressed me as Diego resumed his seat. Jordan's brother had been so quiet I'd almost forgotten he was there.

It took me a moment to readjust my focus. "Uh . . . in town, I think. He had a couple of errands."

"Where did you two run off to so early this morning? I saw you leaving the dock together in a rather impressive Jaguar. Private tour?"

Trey was baiting me and enjoying it. I stuffed several exquisite little shrimp-filled pastries into my mouth and glared at him.

"One should not be surprised, *Señor* Herrington, when a beautiful woman accepts the attentions of an admirer." Diego's smile would have melted the ice sculptures adorning the buffet table had he turned it on them full power. "One should rather be desolated that *he* is not that fortunate man."

This guy's good, I thought, gulping iced tea in an effort to avoid those mesmerizing black eyes across the table. I spluttered a little, and Jordan clapped me on the back a couple of times before turning the force of her own not inconsiderable weapons on her suspect.

"How charmingly said, *Señor*," she purred, leaning forward so that the tops of her breasts, already straining against the confines of her yellow tank top, rose provocatively.

I watched his eyes flicker briefly down from her face. The long, slow smile told me he knew the game well, and approved of the prize being offered.

"Diego is a jeweler, aren't you, darling?" Dame Margo's cultivated, slightly nasal, British accent was like a splash of cold water. She had apparently tired of being ignored. "He helped me find this little trinket."

She waggled her right hand where an obscenely large, square cut emerald, surrounded by diamonds, glittered on her pudgy ring finger. She practically waved it under my nose when I failed to make the appropriate noises of admiration and awe. The truth is, jewelry has never interested me much.

Trey grinned, enjoying my discomfort, until the Queen of Romance Writers turned her eye on him.

"Be a love and fetch me some more of this yummy lobster, would you, Trey, darling?"

He glared as I tried to turn the laugh that erupted from me into a polite cough. I refrained from making lapdog-type yipping noises as he passed, but he got the message.

"So where is your shop located, *Señor* Reyes?" Jordan was back on the attack.

"Please, you must call me Diego. And I have no shop. I am what you call a broker. I act as liaison between the mines where the stones are dug and the artists who turn them into such pretty baubles for the adornment of beautiful women." His piercing eyes included us all. "Alas, I am but a poor merchant."

He patted Dame Margo's hand, whether in obeisance to her or to the magnificent stone, I wasn't sure. I *was* certain that if she didn't wipe that stupid, simpering look off her face, I would be forced to belt her.

"Don't emeralds come from Brazil?" I blurted it out without conscious thought or any real idea of what I intended to accomplish. I could feel my face reddening as the silence held, and all their eyes seemed trained on me.

"How about it, Diego? Is she right?" Jordan again leaned forward to display her wares.

"Tourmaline is sometimes called Brazilian emerald, but the most beautiful—the most valuable—are found deep in the jungles of Colombia." He acknowledged the resumption of the game with a slight tilt of his head, as if to say, *Over to you.*

"You must travel a lot in your work." Jordan probed as Trey made a show of banging the heaping plate he carried down in front of Dame Margo.

"Yes, mostly in the Caribbean and South America. That is where I have developed most of my contacts over the years."

"And where is your home? When you're not out conducting business?"

I could see Diego Reyes beginning to draw back a little under Jordan's relentless questioning. Perhaps he sensed the undercurrents that the rest of us, except for Dame Margo, had been fully aware of from the start. He couldn't know the reason, unless he really *was* Ramon. I had to admit, at least on the surface of it, he sounded like a good candidate.

Then I saw him relax, saw the joy of the chase rise once again in his eyes. "Here and there," he said dismissively. "I find staying in one place too long confining. I believe you would agree with me, Countess, no? I believe you have not always lived in America. I sense a touch of Zurich in your voice, and Paris sparkles in your eyes."

His outrageous flattery was starting to wear down even Jordan's jaded defenses. I watched her resistance melting under the force of his charm.

"Are you on vacation then?" I asked in an effort to break the spell.

He immediately transferred the intensity of his regard to me. I ducked my head to my lunch as he spoke.

"No, *Señora*, this is how I conduct my business. With so many islands to call upon and air travel sometimes precarious, I find a floating hotel to be the ideal solution. Besides, one always encounters such interesting people."

It made sense. It also made for a perfect cover if he were our still theoretical serial killer.

"Diego has a unique arrangement with Royal Scandinavian, don't you, darling?" Dame Margo chimed in.

Señor Reyes appeared embarrassed. Both Jordan and I pricked up our ears.

"*Es nada,*" he said with a dismissive wave.

"Don't be so modest, Diego." The older woman patted his cheek proprietarily. "How many people do you know who have a cabin kept available for them on *four* different cruise ships so that they can hop on and off whenever they choose?"

How many indeed, I thought. *And how terribly convenient.* I couldn't resist a sidelong glance at Jordan.

"If you'll excuse me." Diego Reyes pushed back his chair and rose to stand beside the table. I put his height at something over six feet, enough so that a little Brazilian maid would consider him tall, at least from a distance. "I must be off to visit my clients. Perhaps we shall meet again?"

"Of course we will! Seven o'clock in the observation lounge. We'll all be there. Now don't disappoint me!"

He inclined his head in acknowledgment of Dame Margo's commandment and hurried off.

I was itching for a private powwow, so I suggested Jordan and I head outside for a smoke. I tried to catch Trey's eye to indicate he should join us, but he seemed once again entranced by his stout companion. Heads close together they were finalizing plans for a shopping expedition into town.

Out on the portside promenade, we both lit up and leaned against the rail. On this seaward side of the ship, the harbor traffic bustled past, mostly pleasure boats and yachts with a few larger cargo ships offloading the goods which kept this populous island in all the necessities it was unable to produce for itself.

"What's with those two, anyway?" I asked, indicating with a jerk of my head the unlikely couple we had just left at the table. "They seemed to be joined at the hip."

Jordan laughed, turning her face up to the sun. "Think about it. She writes books. He makes movies. She's enormously successful; he's not. Trey would suck up to the Medusa herself if he thought she could advance his career."

"How can she help his career? She has nothing to do with Hollywood, does she?"

"No, but I understand she's been approached about turning some of her less lurid tales into made-for-TV movies. You know, the kind they're always running on the women's channels? Can't you just see my big brother playing the dashing leading man? Or perhaps directing? Trust me, Trey's interest is not carnal, although it wouldn't surprise me if he bedded the old bat. Whatever it takes to get the job done."

So I had been thrown over for the possible backer of a Trey Herrington production. I tried to be disappointed.

"So what do you think about him?" Jordan turned and studied my face anxiously. I knew she was not referring to her brother. She seemed so eager for Diego Reyes to be a killer.

"I admit, on the surface, he looks pretty good. His business is a perfect cover for meeting lonely women on board, and he's a familiar face that comes and goes. No one would be surprised to see him here one day and gone the next. So he has opportunity."

"Exactly."

"Who put you onto him? Luis?" Jordan had been pumping the bartender shamelessly ever since we'd boarded the ship.

"No, actually, it was Rolfe."

"First Officer Grunewald? How would he . . .? Oh, Jordan, how many people have you told? For God's sake, we can't have the entire crew . . ."

"Give me a little credit, will you?" She stubbed out her cigarette in the metal ashtray attached to the railing and immediately lit another. "I was discreet. Besides, don't tell me you haven't been spilling your guts to our dashing security consultant."

"That's different. He's an ex-cop. It's what he does."

Jordan's skepticism was palpable in the air between us.

"Look, let's not argue about it," I continued. "What did Rolfe say?"

"That Diego's been seen on several of their ships and with a variety of ladies, both young and old. Some of the crew gets assigned to different ships when they're short of help. Luis told me the same thing."

"Luis specifically mentioned Reyes?"

"Among others. Seems it's not that unusual for single men to travel among the islands hoping to pick up a wealthy patroness. And the cruise line doesn't like to discourage them because they provide dancing partners and escorts for the single women passengers."

"Makes the place sound like a floating bordello—in reverse," I observed.

Jordan ignored me. "Okay, we agree Diego had opportunity. What else?"

"Means. If the Judge is right, it's probably suffocation. Unless they're looking for it, it's hard to detect as a cause of death. Especially without an autopsy."

Despite the warm breeze ruffling my hair, I shivered. The light had gone, too, from Jordan's face. "So anyone with access to a pillow had means."

In silent agreement we stepped back into the shade and found two chaise longues set far enough away from any possibility of being overheard. Before we had finished settling in, a white-shirted waiter hovered over us. Jordan order two piña coladas, one without rum. I waited until they'd been delivered and signed for before I spoke.

"That leaves motive. And unless we're dealing with a seriously disturbed person, I can't figure out what that might be. Can you?"

"The jewelry?" Jordan suggested, sipping the creamy, coconut concoction. "How do we know he's what he says he is? Maybe this is how he gets rid of the stuff he steals from the women he murders. Maybe it's how he really makes his living."

It was a valid point, but I couldn't wrap my mind around it. Despite all I had been through in the past months, I still had trouble believing that evil of the kind we were contemplating really existed. That a man would deliberately woo vulnerable, elderly women, then murder them in cold blood for their jewelry. What kind of monster could do such a thing? What kind of psychopath?

"Do you realize how bizarre this is?" I set the drink aside and lit a cigarette. "We just sat across from this man at lunch and exchanged pleasantries with him. You even flirted a little. Can you honestly picture Diego Reyes suffocating rich old ladies for their diamonds? If it's really him, why hasn't he gotten around to the Romance Queen? That rock she's sporting has to be worth a few thousand pounds sterling. But she says he helped her buy it. Damn it, it doesn't make any sense!"

"We'll just have to dig a little deeper. Maybe your friend Darnay could check out Diego, see if he's who claims to be. He must still have contacts."

Jordan had read my mind. It was what I fully intended to do as soon as Alain returned. *Where the hell is he?* I wondered. He'd left me at the gangway over two hours ago, declaring that he was going to 'put things right'. What did that mean? Surely he knew the ship sailed at four, bound for St. Thomas in the U.S. Virgin Islands. Suddenly it seemed imperative that I see him.

"Where are you going?" I asked as Jordan rose from the chaise.

"I'm meeting Rolfe at the pool. He has a couple of spare hours before we sail."

"Be careful," I said, remembering the dark, hooded eyes of the ship's first officer.

"He is deliciously dangerous-looking, isn't he?" Jordan's smile spoke of challenge and risk.

"Haven't you had enough of brooding Germans?" I asked, thinking of the much-reviled Klaus von Brandt, Jordan's ex-husband.

"Not to worry," she said airily. "I can handle it. Besides, he'll be gone in a few days."

"Where?"

"It depends on where they need him. Don't forget to ask Darnay about Diego. *Ciao.*"

I sat for some time with my eyes closed, partly to discourage any of the strolling passengers from attempting to strike up an acquaintance, but also to try and bring some kind of order to my jumbled thoughts. I was growing seriously concerned about Jordan. What had begun for her as an impassioned quest for the truth about her mother's death now seemed more like a game, an abstract exercise, the outcome of which appeared of less importance to her than the pursuit of her own pleasure.

But murder is not a game. It's not the sanitized, intellectual exercises of Sherlock Holmes or the cozy little puzzles on *Murder She Wrote* with Jessica Fletcher tying up all the loose ends in a two-minute denouement where all is explained and the killer led away in handcuffs.

No, I thought, squirming in my chair, *murder isn't like that. It's horror and blood and pain. Noise and smoke and rending loss. It's not knowing who, the ache of never being able to stand above the stone and say, "There, it's over. He's paid. Rest easy".*

So, let Jordan play at seeking the truth, I decided. I could not. For Leslie Herrington. For Penelope Whiteside. For Anjanette Rousseau. For any and all who might have been or might be, I would find the answer. But I needed help. I needed Darnay . . .

The looming shadow fell across me as if I had summoned it up out of sheer desire. But when I raised my hand to shade my eyes from the encroaching sun, I realized it was not Darnay, but a member of the crew, blue-jacketed, standing stiffly to attention.

"Excuse me. Mrs. Lydia Tanner of cabin 205?"

"Yes. What is it?"

The boy—for that's all he was, a teenager, or twenty at best—was scaring me with his grave formality. So was the yellow cablegram he carried, gingerly, as if it might explode in his hand. I could see the word URGENT stamped in red across it.

I snatched the envelope out of his hand and ripped it open. The hole opening up in my gut felt big enough to accommodate the bus that had run us off the road that morning.

It was worse than I could possibly have imagined.

> JUDGE HAD MASSIVE STROKE THIS A.M.
> RECOVERY DOUBTFUL. COME QUICKLY.
> LAVINIA

23

The windshield wipers failed to keep ahead of the sheets of water that thundered down out of a crackling sky. The only saving grace was that I-95 was basically deserted at four-thirty in the morning. Aggravated at first when nothing else was available at the rental counter, I soon became grateful for the massive sport utility vehicle that rode high and sure above the torrents of rain pooling in the high-speed lanes of the interstate.

I flashed by the exit for Brunswick, Georgia, and gauged that I was probably still a good three hours from home. I yawned—a giant, jaw-cracking gape, then reached over to crank the radio up a notch. If I couldn't shake myself back to full alertness, I would have to stop somewhere and rest.

And I didn't want to do that. No time. I'd just spent the most frustrating twelve hours of my life, island-hopping until I found a direct flight to Miami, only to be grounded in Jacksonville by a series of severe thunderstorms. They had roared out of Alabama, spawning rare, autumn tornadoes and shutting down airports from Savannah to Raleigh, North Carolina.

I assumed the storms were also to blame for the continual busy signal that beeped in my ear every time I tried to reach any number in Beaufort County. Jordan had promised to keep trying to get through and let Lavinia know I was on my way.

Jordan had been nearly as shocked as I by the horrible news. She immediately threw herself into action, arranging transportation for me while I jammed some bare necessities into my carry-on bag. I was tearing down the gangway just as the crew began preparing to swing it on board. I spared a thought for Alain Darnay as the taxi sped me away from the docks. Jordan had assured me she would fill him in, as well as Trey.

I couldn't worry about them now. My whole concentration was fixed on the brief seconds of unobstructed vision before the wipers swept across the glass again. The repetitive motion threatened to hypnotize me. *Doubt–ful, doubt–ful,* my mind chanted in time with their beat.

It stopped raining a little north of Darien, and a faint, pale line broke the horizon off to my right as I neared Savannah. On impulse I pulled off onto the exit near Pooler and guided the big vehicle into a darkened McDonald's parking lot. I shut off the engine and dropped my head onto my hands. I needed to close my eyes, just for a moment. One more push—another hour—and I would be home.

I refused to think about what I'd find there. I refused to contemplate a world in which the Judge's gruff baritone no longer roared. I refused . . .

The lights of the restaurant sprang to life in one great, blinding glare. I watched an older gentlemen, somehow pathetic in the bright uniform more suited to the teenaged employees, flip the lock on the entrance nearest me and beckon me in. I climbed down, nearly tumbling before I remembered I'd been seated four feet off the ground, and dragged myself through the door he held open for me.

"We ain't open, not oh-ficially, for another twenty minutes," the old man said, "but you look like you could use some coffee. Be ready in a jiffy."

The sweetness of his concern and the warm smile nearly undid me. I mumbled my thanks and bolted for the ladies room. I threw cold water carelessly over my face, drenching the collar of my wrinkled polo shirt, and willed myself not to cry. I had a terrible feeling that once I started, I'd never be able to stop.

Jesse—or so his name tag read—set a steaming cardboard cup on the counter and returned to his opening routine. I really don't like coffee, but I needed something to jump-start my senses. I loaded it with three creams and two sugars and sipped while I fumbled in my purse for my calling card. But the public phone, tucked into the narrow hallway between the restrooms, was completely dead.

"Been out since last night," Jesse called from beside the end cash register. "You want somethin' to eat?"

I suddenly became aware of the tantalizing aromas floating out from the grill area behind him. Aside from the skimpy bags of airline peanuts and a couple of candy bars at Miami International, I'd had nothing since lunch the day before on the *Crystal Fjord*.

I paid for a sausage McMuffin with egg and a hash brown patty and collapsed into one of the molded fiberglass chairs attached to a table.

The Judge—*my father*—could not be dying. He was a tough old buzzard, I told myself, too ornery to die. He'd survived these strokes before, and he'd do it again. Somehow I just couldn't get my mind around the idea of my being the only one of the family left, that there would be no one in the world that carried the memory of my birth in his heart. Mine had been a pretty miserable childhood, filled with anger and shouting and pain. But there had been good times, too, sweet islands of calm when all the rest seemed only a bad dream. And at the heart of that sweetness there'd been Daddy, tall and laughing and . . .

"Here you be." Jesse's voice was low and soft as if he were afraid of spooking me.

I smiled my thanks for the plastic tray he set before me.

"You eat that up now, young lady, hear?" The mock severity brought another flood of memory. "Things allus look better with somethin' warm on your stomach." Jesse nodded in confirmation of his own wisdom and shuffled back behind the counter.

The food was hot and greasy and wonderful. By the time I'd wolfed down the sandwich and crispy potato cake, people were three-deep at the four registers, and the sun was glinting through the plate glass windows. I dumped the wadded up wrappers in the trash bin that said "Thank You" across its hinged door, and looked for Jesse. He was joking with a harried mother trying to juggle a handbag and two cranky toddlers, and I couldn't catch his eye. I hoped he knew how nourishing his kindness had been.

I mounted the Explorer and headed north.

I hit the worst of Beaufort's modest, morning rush hour and chained-smoked and fumed from my perch high above the crawling cars around me. At last I wheeled into the parking lot of the hospital complex on Ribaut Road and trotted beneath the sheltering live oaks into the hushed coolness of the lobby.

The kindly, gray-haired volunteer at Reception had no record of the Judge. He had not been admitted. I blustered and insisted, but she held her ground. Perhaps I should check with Emergency, she suggested, retaining her temper and dignity despite my abuse.

They'd sent him to Charleston—or Savannah where the hospitals were larger, more sophisticated. Maybe even to the Medical University of South Carolina. Those were the only possibilities I was willing to entertain as I tried not to race through the sterile, winding corridors to the Emergency Room entrance.

But I drew a blank there as well.

Where the hell is my father?

I wanted to scream my frustration as I stumbled out into the dazzling, sun-lit air and barely managed to get a cigarette lighted with nearly palsied hands. Ragged, half-sobs caught in my throat with each inhalation. I could feel panic, like a frenzied spring tide, rising to swamp me.

I tossed the half-smoked butt into the driveway and ran for my car.

Presqu'isle drowsed in the late morning glare, its drapes and shutters drawn tightly against the September heat. It didn't mean anything, I told myself.

In fact my labored breathing quieted a little at the lack of activity in front of my old home. This was the South. One of my father's stature and lineage did not "go gently into that good night". Death brought food and formality, condolence calls and a gathering of the survivors to comfort and recall.

I pounded up the sixteen steps of the graceful split staircase and burst through the doorway into the dark, cool foyer. The silence was total save for the muted ticking of the ancient grandfather clock and my own thudding pulse.

"Lavinia?"

It came out a hoarse croak. I cleared my throat, and the next try was a piercing scream that gave voice, finally, to all the pent-up fear that had lain tightly coiled in my chest during my long, desperate race for home.

"Lavinia!"

The sound of glass shattering against old wood came from the kitchen. I'd taken only a few steps when my father's housekeeper rounded the corner and stopped dead in the hallway. Her thin, coffee-colored hands worked at the faded apron tied around her trim waist, and the black eyes in her long face were wide with fear and, then, surprise.

"Bay? What is it? Dear Lord, girl, you scared me half . . ."

"Where is he?" I shouted, the long suppressed tears flowing unchecked now.

"Where is who?" Lavinia advanced toward me, hands outstretched. "Child, child," she crooned in a voice well remembered from tempests past, "hush now, hush."

The arms, frailer now, but achingly familiar, enfolded me, and gnarled fingers stroked my heaving back. Gently she guided me to the worn oak kitchen table and eased me into a chair. Shards of the broken tumbler glinted in the light flooding through the mullioned window as the older woman seated herself and took my trembling hands in both of hers.

"Tell me," Lavinia said simply.

Confusion mingled with the tears as I raised my face to hers. Why was she so calm? Why could I not detect some flicker of the fear and grief that must surely grip her heart as they did my own?

But Lavinia Smalls had always been the strong oak that had sheltered and protected my father and me. Why should it surprise me that she could weather this worst of blows with grace and dignity?

"Is he gone then?" I asked, prepared at last, under her caring gaze, to hear the worst.

"Is who gone? Whatever are you on about, child? And what are you doin' here? I thought you were off on a boat somewhere."

I barely had time to register the genuine perplexity in her voice when a soft hiss made me whirl around toward the door.

"What the hell's all the racket about?" the Judge demanded in his thunderous baritone as he and his wheelchair rolled into the kitchen.

24

The quality of the light slipping through the slats of the wooden shutters told me it was late afternoon. I rolled over into the familiar hollow my body had made over the years in the down-filled duvet.

I closed my eyes again, and, for a moment, eleven-year-old Lydia Baynard Simpson snuggled back under the safety of the hand-sewn quilt, hovering in that sweet space between waking and sleeping where dreams have faded, but reality has yet to lay claim.

Soon Mother would send Lavinia to rouse me from the "lie-down" she believed so essential for young ladies during the heat of the day. Unlike today, I had rarely slept soundly, my mind always darting from image to image until I would have been hard pressed to distinguish waking fantasy from dream or nightmare.

As if summoned from childhood, the creak of the floorboard just outside my door was followed by Lavinia's soundless glide into the room.

"I'm up," I said through half-slitted lids.

Her soft laugh echoed down the years of our shared memory. "Then let me see the whites of those eyes."

I wadded the pillows up against the headboard of the four-poster and hitched myself into a sitting position. I smoothed the long, white cotton nightgown, sprigged with delicate blue flowers, down over my legs. It was Lavinia's, its chaste femininity a revelatory contrast to the brisk efficiency of her daytime dress.

"Pretty," I said, fingering the lace edging the wide straps. "Thank you."

Lavinia nodded, then settled herself onto the tall, old mahogany bed. "Feelin' better?"

A whirlwind of conflicting emotions had assailed me in the stunned seconds after my father's sudden appearance in the kitchen. I had been close to incoherence, blurting out the story of the telegram and my mindless dash across the Caribbean in dis-jointed bits of sentences. Heart-stopping relief was followed swiftly by a numbed confusion, then blazing anger at whoever had orchestrated this cruelest of hoaxes.

Why?

That was the question we kept returning to as the Judge stormed and Lavinia brewed pots of the soothing, herbal tea that was her first line of defense against all life's trials. When we had at last exhausted the subject without arriving at any reasonable conclusion, the full weight of it all had come crashing down, leaving me drained and slumped over the kitchen table.

Then Lavinia had *shushed* my father and led me unprotesting up the wide, curving staircase to the second-floor bath with its old, claw-footed tub and pedestal sink. Tenderly she bathed my face and arms in cool water and helped me peel off the wrinkled, sticky clothes, before slipping her own sun-dried nightgown over my head and tucking me into my childhood bed.

I smiled now and answered her question. "I'm feeling much better, thanks. How's Daddy?"

"Madder 'n I've seen him in a while. And worried, too. He's been on the phone almost the whole time you've been asleep."

"It's working then?"

Lavinia nodded. "Came back on just before you came burstin' in. Lord, but you gave me a turn."

"I know. I'm sorry." I reached for her familiar brown hand, and she let me take it. It was the first intimate contact we'd had in the several weeks since she'd interrupted my tirade at the Judge on the verandah below. "Are we okay now? You and I?" I ventured, searching her face.

"I expect so."

"I still have questions. Can we talk about it?"

"Some day. When all this is behind us. And if the Judge is agreeable." She rose and crossed to the door, her carriage reflecting her dignity, her head high and proud. "I'd better get down there and tell him you're awake before he starts bellowing like a wounded moose again. Get dressed now, dinner's almost ready."

"What're we having?" I asked, flipping back the covers. I seemed unable to refrain from re-enacting all the old childhood rituals.

"Fried okra and peas," Lavinia answered, right on cue, naming my two least favorite foods. "And you're goin' to eat every last bite."

Cigar and cigarette smoke mingled with the sweet, dank odor of the tidal marsh as the Judge and I sat companionably on the back verandah. The old rocker I had curled up in creaked a little, but the rhythmic sound made an appropriate accompaniment to the cries of the tree frogs and the occasional screech of a swooping owl.

Lavinia had refused to join us, though both of us had urged her to stay when she delivered us a tray of iced tea and lemonade after our dinner of roasted chicken and fresh vegetables that had included neither okra nor peas.

"I finally managed to reach Jordan," my father said, sipping the tart fruit juice, tonight without benefit of alcohol. "It's easier when the ship is docked."

"They're in Charlotte Amalie, then." The memory of the magnificent harbor curving around the bustling capital city of the U.S. Virgin Islands drifted back on a tide of longing for Rob and the brief, sweet time we'd shared there: brilliant white days followed by soft, deep nights of tender lovemaking in a wide bed beneath a star-filled window.

It probably hadn't really been as idyllic as it seemed now, but no one was left to contradict my remembrance.

"Early this morning." The Judge broke my reverie. "She said they're scheduled to be there for another day." I heard the note of disapproval creep into his voice. "She's expecting you back."

"How did she take it?" I asked, ignoring his implied question. "About this whole thing being a . . ." I groped for a word adequate to describe the fake telegram, and failed.

"About as confused as the rest of us. The only certainty is that someone wanted you back here—fast."

"Or out of there. Maybe Jordan really is onto something with this Reyes guy. But how would he know enough about me—and you—to concoct such a believable message? I almost think it had to be somebody from here."

"Well, I did some checkin', and I don't think there's any way to find that out. Whoever it was probably charged it to his own telephone number, and Western Union won't give out that information to anyone but the sender."

"You mean it's impossible to track down this son-of-a-bitch?"

"Looks that way."

I rose and refilled our glasses, then used my lighter on the large citronella candles spaced out along the railing of the porch. With twilight would come the insects. I leaned my elbows on the weathered wood and watched the still waters of the Sound merge gradually with the blurring line of the horizon as the sun slipped away over the mainland. The sigh escaped and was lost in the growing hum and buzz and squawks of the night. I couldn't believe I would never be able to find out who had perpetrated this sick joke on me and my family. Or what its purpose had been.

"Did Jordan say anything about Darnay?" I asked finally. "Had she had a chance to explain to him?"

"Only about your leaving," my father said as I turned back to face him. He looked old and tired in the wavering light of the candles. "And a little about this suspect of hers. Apparently Darnay left the ship as soon as it docked this morning and hadn't returned by the time I spoke with her. I expect he'll be calling as soon as he hears." The cigar end glowed bright red in the growing darkness as the Judge drew on the forbidden panatela. "What did you think of him?"

"Darnay? He seems very . . . competent."

"And quite attractive to the ladies, as I recall." I heard the smile though I couldn't quite see it in the candlelight.

"What do you know about his family?" I tried for polite disinterest, but my father had too much experience reading nuance in a witness's voice.

"French father, American mother. Probably why his English is so good. Or were you inquiring about something more immediate? As in wife and children?" He took my uncomfortable silence for agreement. "Well, he has neither, so far as I recall. Married to the job."

I lit a cigarette I really didn't want to cover my relief. I hadn't realized quite how important the answer would be. Then something my father had just said struck me. It took a minute for me to pull it into focus.

"You aren't surprised he's on the ship, are you?"

I heard ice cubes rattle against the sides of the tumbler as he raised it and sipped. "I think I'm ready for a nightcap. Slop a little bourbon in here, will you?"

"Not until you answer my question. Alain is not a security consultant, is he? That's a cover. He's still with Interpol."

His silence would have to serve as my confirmation. If pressed, he could truthfully claim to have told me nothing.

"So they're already onto it," I said, more to myself than to elicit his response. "The pattern. While we've been stumbling around like idiotic amateurs, the pros have been two steps ahead of us. Why didn't he tell me?"

Looking back, it seemed that Darnay had had several opportunities to admit his real assignment, his true employer. Why had he lied to me? I had told him everything, secrets about Grayton's Race I had previously shared only with a dead man. Trust between us had been a one-way street. It surprised me how much that hurt.

"Orders," the Judge answered grudgingly into the soft, autumn night, "or so I would suppose."

"Not good enough."

I carried his glass down the wheelchair ramp into his former study and splashed in three fingers of whiskey from a crystal decanter on the sideboard. At least one of us would sleep tonight. I had just handed him his drink and stooped to brush his cheek with a goodnight kiss when Lavinia appeared on the verandah.

"Telephone for you, Bay," she announced, frowning at the dark color of the Judge's lemonade. "Long distance."

"Thanks. I'll pick up in the kitchen."

Though we had spent only a few hours in each other's company, Darnay sensed the tension in my voice as soon as I said hello. He fired questions about the Judge at me in short, staccato bursts, barely giving me time to take a breath between answers.

"He really is all right, then? You're certain?" he pressed.

"Of course I'm certain! Someone wanted me off the ship, and he picked the only sure-fire way to get me to race home without thinking twice about it."

"But why?"

"Don't you think I've been wracking my brain trying to figure that out ever since I found out it was a hoax? If I knew, *I'd* tell *you!*"

Darnay let the silence lengthen as I consciously reined in my temper. There was no point yelling at him. But he had caught the implied accusation in my words.

"I'm sorry you think I haven't been completely honest with you, Bay. I guess it's become a habit, not trusting anyone. Occupational hazard."

"So you are still with Interpol."

"Let's save this discussion for when I see you again. My *mea culpas* are always much more impressive in person." When I didn't answer right away, his next words shed the bantering tone. "You are coming back, aren't you?"

I could picture his wide brow crinkled in concentration as clearly as if he stood before me. How could someone's face become so familiar in such a short time? "What would be the point? Jordan and I hoped to uncover enough evidence to convince your employer to investigate the deaths of her mother and the others as possible homicides. You're already doing that, right?"

"Yes, but . . ."

"Then I repeat, what would be the point of my returning?"

"Well, for one thing, you've already paid for the cruise. Wouldn't it be a shame to miss the chance of seeing the rest of the islands on your itinerary?"

"I suppose so."

"And you could be a help to us—to *me*—in the investigation. The Countess tells me you've collected a lot of information about the three deaths."

"That's true. Although I didn't take any of it with me. I'd have to go pick it up from my house. Did Jordan talk to you about Diego Reyes?"

Darnay hesitated only a moment. When he answered, he swept away all my doubts about mutual trust. "Yes, and I've got the computer boys checking him out. Preliminary results look like he's what he claims to be, but we'll keep digging. Whoever is responsible for these murders is damned good at covering his tracks. We'll turn *Señor* Reyes's life inside out until we're sure about him, one way or the other. In the meantime, I've warned your friend to stay away from him. If he is our man, I don't want him spooked by a clumsy amateur."

I assumed his epithet extended to include me as well as Jordan, but I took no offense. It was a relief to leave it to the professionals. "Good," was all I said.

"So you'll come? I could really use your help, Bay. And besides . . ."

"Yes?" I held my breath.

"You and I have unfinished business, *ma petite*."

The endearment rolled off his tongue with the sensuous inflection only a Frenchman could give so simple a phrase.

"*D'accord*," I replied, and was rewarded with a soft laugh of pleasure as he hung up the phone.

25

I watched Dolores Santiago's round, olive face break into a wide smile when she spotted my cab pull into the driveway from her lookout post at the kitchen window. By the time I had paid the driver and slung my carryon bag over my shoulder, she and Mr. Bones had descended the steps to welcome me home. This time she didn't shy away from my grateful embrace, but hugged me back with an intensity that brought embarrassing tears to my eyes. I snuffled them away as she shooed me up the stairs ahead of her and into my house.

I dropped my bag on the floor of the entryway and reached down to stroke the striped fur of the cat twining in and out of my legs. His deep purring sent vibrations all up and down his back.

"Missed me, did you, old boy?" I asked as Dolores scurried off to the kitchen. "Well, don't get used to me quite yet. I'll be off again in a few hours."

It had taken some doing to arrange a flight that would allow me time to accomplish what I needed to do here and still reach Charlotte Amalie before the ship sailed again. But, as with most things in this life, if you're willing and able to pay, you can get pretty much anything you want. The airport shuttle would pick me up a little after four this afternoon, and I should be walking up the gangway sometime before midnight.

I'd left a message for Darnay about when to expect me.

I glanced briefly at the answering machine blinking furiously on the built-in desk as I walked up the steps and into the kitchen. Time for that later. Dolores bustled around, setting out a heaping plate of fresh fruit and a basket of warm biscuits on the glass-topped breakfast table. The blue china teapot already sat steeping under its worn cozy. Though Lavinia had plied me with food only a couple of hours ago, I didn't have the heart to turn down this welcome-home offering.

"The rolls, they are from the *mercado*, *Señora*. I have no time to make myself."

I waved off the apology and urged Dolores to join me as I spooned up ripe strawberries, glistening blackberries, and strips of juicy cantaloupe. She busied herself with pouring out the tea, then we both buttered the warm rolls and ate for awhile in companionable silence. I could tell she had something on her mind but, like Lavinia, Dolores believed food could, if not exactly solve all problems, then at least make them seem less insurmountable.

"It is *malo, muy malo, Señora*," Dolores said at last, refilling our cups. "When you call, I say to Hector, I say, '*mi pobre Señora*. What kind of *hombre* could do such a thing?'"

Dolores, an unwavering adherent to her Catholic faith, was as firm a believer in the reality of evil in this world as she was in the goodness of earthly saints like Mother Theresa.

"I may never find out who it was unless he decides he has some more surprises in store for me. Don't worry, *amiga*," I said, trying to reassure her, as well as myself. "I can handle it."

I helped her clear the table, then pulled out the chair at the desk and pushed the PLAY button on the answering machine. The first message was from Erik Whiteside, asking me to get in touch with him if I called in from the ship. A little knot of guilt formed in the pit of my stomach. I had completely forgotten about the young man from Charlotte whose website, as much as anything else, had helped to set me on this path as avenging angel for three dead women. I had promised to keep him informed and had, in all honesty, not given him a thought since I'd flown off to Grand Cayman.

Bitsy Elliott, my oldest friend and the catalyst who had brought Jordan and me together in the first place, tried for her usual light chatter, wondering if I had fallen off the face of the earth. But underneath I could hear the hurt in her voice at my having excluded her from subsequent events. I knew her breezy "Call me sometime when you drop back onto the planet" concealed a genuine rip in the fabric of our friendship, which I needed to mend—and quickly.

I didn't recognize Cissy Ransome's deep drawl right away, but she identified herself and moved on with breathless excitement. "Bay, I just got the most extraordinary call! You'll never believe! I heard you were out of town, but ring me the second you get back. This is just too good to keep! Bye now."

I couldn't imagine what tidbit of local gossip Cissy thought might possibly interest me enough to spend any of my dwindling time here finding out. I put her at the bottom of my list.

The fourth call, however, zoomed right to the top. Christopher Brandon needed to speak with me urgently. The attorney for Leslie Herrington's estate and the man from whom I'd received all the financial documents relating to the hardware store chain couldn't emphasize strongly enough, he said, how important this was. He reiterated this sentiment on the next message. And the next. I pulled out the telephone book, looked up his number, and dialed.

The pretty blonde receptionist I recalled from my visit to Chris's office got snotty with me when I insisted she interrupt his conference. My assurances that he really wanted to talk to me cut very little ice with this guardian of the gates who I now remembered had glared daggers at me when her employer had haltingly invited me to lunch.

I cranked up my best Southern aristocrat's hauteur and finally prevailed.

All trace of the endearingly bumbling young lawyer who had developed an instant crush on me had vanished. Chris Brandon was all business, and the business was a bombshell.

"Have you heard from the Macons?" he asked after the briefest of opening pleasantries.

It took me a second to catch up, so unexpected was his question. "You mean Dudley and Marilee? No. Why should they be in touch with me?"

"I heard you had lunch with them last week. Did they give you any hint of what they were planning?"

"I have no idea what you're talking about, Chris. We didn't part on the friendliest of terms, you know. All I wanted was for them to . . ."

The realization struck me like a slap alongside the head. Which is what I deserved. I didn't seem to be able to keep my mind on more than one thing at a time. How could I have forgotten . . .?

"Bay? Are you still there? Is something the matter?"

"What? No, Chris, I'm fine. Sorry. I just remembered that I gave the Macons a list of the missing documents from the pile you sent over. They promised to deliver them to the house on Monday, but they never came. I was so busy getting ready to leave town on Tuesday I completely forgot."

"And you're sure they didn't arrive after you left? Not that it matters now, I guess, but . . ."

"Hold on a second, let me check with Dolores."

I covered the mouthpiece with my hand and called for my housekeeper. She appeared from the guestroom, dust rag in hand and a quizzical look on her face.

"Did anyone deliver any papers after I left on Tuesday?" I asked. "Or did any packages or FEDEX envelopes come?"

"No, Señora, nada. Just the mail. Is on your desk in the office."

"Could you bring it to me please?"

She nodded as I turned back to the phone. "Chris? It doesn't look like it, but I'm checking the mail. I can't believe they would have mailed it. There were over a hundred things I asked for, including missing bank statements and tax returns. It should have filled a couple of boxes. Hold on."

Dolores handed me a thin stack of circulars and bills, nothing remotely large enough to contain what I had requested.

"Chris? No, nothing."

"It doesn't surprise me, the bastards!" he said with a fury I found all the more disturbing coming from the polite young man I remembered.

"Chris, what is this all about? Why are you so angry?"

"One more question, Bay. Did *anything* unusual happen after you had lunch with them? After you got home?"

"No, not that I remember. Why are you being so mysterious? What did old Dudley and Marilee do, abscond with the company pension fund or something?"

The silence on the other end of the phone was deafening. "Chris? Say something! You don't seriously mean . . ."

"Ask your housekeeper, can you? If anything happened after you left. I know it doesn't make much difference, but I'd like to know what spooked them. For my own satisfaction."

I could see I was going to have to play the game his way or I was never going to find out what he was talking about. "Did anything unusual happen after I left?" I asked Dolores, not bothering to cover the phone this time. "Anyone come by or anything like that?"

"No, *Señora*, no one comes while I am here. Only the man from the *seguridad*, he call me at home. But he say, no worry, he check. Is probably a *malevolencia*, is all."

Dolores smiled and turned to head back to her interrupted dusting. "Wait!" I called. "Let me get this straight. Someone from the security company called you? When was this?"

"*Martes.* In *la noche.*"

"So Tuesday night the security company called and said—what? That the alarm had gone off?" Dolores was nodding vigorously. "But they told you it was nothing to worry about, that it was probably a . . ."

"*Si.* A *malevolencia, Señora.*"

"A malfunction," Chris translated in my ear. "So that was it." I waved my thanks at Dolores and turned my attention back to the phone. "They tried to break into your house to get at the records, and set off the alarm. By the time the security guys got there, the Macons had been scared off, and the rent-a-cops assumed it was a screwup in the equipment."

"I'm afraid you could be right. So you're saying essentially that the Macons are gone, is that it?"

"Lock, stock, and every last penny out of the barrel. Cleaned out the operating accounts of all the stores, grabbed up all the stuff that was easily portable, and lit out for parts unknown. It all went so smoothly, I'm inclined to agree with your brother-in-law that they'd probably had it all planned out for a long time. Sergeant Tanner seemed to think they had devised a contingency plan in case anyone got too close to their operation. You must have done something to get their suspicions up. When they couldn't get into your house to find out what you had on them, they decided to cut their losses and run."

"This doesn't make any sense," I said, inching my bare toes out to where my tote bag sat on the floor, just out of reach. I managed to snag the handle and slide it over toward me. I realized it had been a long time since I'd had a cigarette—had even thought about smoking, for that matter—and wondered if maybe this was a sign I was ready to quit for good.

Nah, I decided as the first, dizzying lungful of tar and nicotine soothed all my ragged nerve endings at once.

"Look," I continued when Chris failed to respond, "let's think this through. If what you say is true, then the Macons had to be doing some serious embezzling to make it worth their giving it all up and bolting. Or else they were guilty of something else we don't even know about. I couldn't have proved they were stealing, at least not without the documents I'd asked them to supply and a lot more digging. From what I saw, it could have been chalked up to inept accounting practices or bad management. The IRS might have gone after them, but it would have been Leslie's estate that suffered any financial hits. She signed the returns as president of the corporation."

"She wouldn't have known what was going on. I'm convinced of that."

"Me, too. But she signed, whether she looked at the returns or not. That makes her liable. Does Red think there's any chance of catching up with the Macons?"

"He wasn't real hopeful. Oh, they'll put out an APB on the truck, but they'll probably ditch that as soon as they've put some distance behind them. Then they change their names and start over somewhere else. Red told me it wouldn't get a lot of priority attention. It isn't as if they killed somebody."

I tried not to analyze why that statement raised goose bumps along my bare arms. "So what are you going to do now?"

"I'm shutting down the stores as of the end of business today. We'll freeze all the records right where they are. Thankfully, payday was yesterday, and the checks had already been drawn on the special account before the Macons skipped. We're looking at a full-blown audit and a complete inventory, right down to the last nut and bolt in the bins. Want in?"

"No, thanks. Hire a firm that specializes in this kind of thing. They'll have the manpower to get it done quickly. I can recommend a couple of good companies, if you like."

"Thanks."

"Have you informed the Herringtons about all this yet?"

"Only Justin. He gave me the authorization I needed to lock the doors and lay off the employees. I had no idea how to reach Jordan and Trey."

"I'll be seeing them in a few hours. I'll have one of them get in touch with you."

"Make it Monday, will you? I'm heading for Jacksonville this weekend. First home game of football season for the Jaguars. A bunch of my buddies and I go every year."

"Have a good time. And Chris? Don't let all this get to you. There wasn't much you could have done, you know?"

"Yeah, I do know. But thanks, anyway. I'm just glad you weren't home when those two came calling. You take care now, hear?"

"You, too."

By the time the driver of the airport limo tapped his horn to announce his arrival, it felt as if I had spent the entire day on the telephone. I had smoothed Bitsy's ruffled feathers, promising a long, informative lunch when I returned from the Caribbean. I had reached Erik Whiteside at work, so we were unable to talk at length. Without disclosing any details, I let him know that Interpol was now on the case of his grandmother's murder. I could tell he was relieved, but the feeling had to be bittersweet. Being vindicated in his suspicions could never compensate him for the loss of his Granny Pen.

Erik brightened somewhat when I suggested we get together on Hilton Head as soon as the case had been resolved. It was high time we met face to face.

I gathered up everything I had related to our meager investigation—the printouts from Erik's website, the newspaper article Angelina had translated for me, and all the papers Jordan had received in her mother's personal effects—and placed it all in the calfskin briefcase I had last carried to my abortive lunch with Dudley and Marilee Macon.

Which reminded me that the one call I hadn't returned had been Cissy Ransome's. But after hearing Chris Brandon's shocking news about the disappearance of the two principal employees of the Bi-Rite Hardware Stores, I was pretty sure what juicy bit of gossip Cissy would have to offer. I could wait to hear her undoubtedly spicier version after I got back home.

Showered and changed into comfortable slacks, cotton shirt, and a lightweight jacket, I found Dolores leaning on the handle of the upright vacuum cleaner and gazing intently at the television in the great room. It had to be the Weather Channel, the screen filled with a large, swirling blob of orange on a bright blue background.

"I'm ready to take off, as soon as the limo gets here," I announced, but my words failed to elicit a response. "Dolores?"

"Oh, *Señora, perdo!* You see? The storm, she comes near where you are, no?"

I moved next to her and studied the map as the sonorous voice of the forecaster warned that Flora need increase in intensity only slightly to reach sustained winds of seventy-five miles per hour, the minimum level to acquire Class I hurricane status. While the estimated track would take it well north of the U.S. and British Virgin Islands, those areas were being put on alert for high tides and possible wind damage as the storm passed by in the next couple of days.

"Don't worry about me. See, it's staying north of where I'll be tonight and tomorrow. Then we head south on Sunday."

"This Flora, what if she comes here?"

The map showed a large ridge of high-pressure building off the eastern coast of the U.S., which would help to steer the hurricane off into the North Atlantic long before it approached any landfall, but I could see the genuine fear in Dolores's eyes.

"Don't worry," I repeated. "And if it does by some chance get close, just grab the cat and go. Everything else is insured. Just make sure you and your family are safe. That's all that matters."

"*Si, Señora,*" she said, but with a decided lack of conviction.

I cursed the weather forecasters and their tendency to hype every tropical disturbance as a potential Hugo or Andrew. The reason such disasters are so memorable is that they're so rare.

The horn sounded then, and I gathered my meager belongings together. The good part was that, with only my tote bag and brief-case to carry on the plane with me, I could skip the hassle of check-ing and reclaiming luggage. I hugged Dolores, promising to see her the following Thursday when we had originally been scheduled to return from the cruise.

As I greeted the driver and climbed into the brightly painted van, I felt a sudden surge of excitement quite different from the ap-prehension that had accompanied me when I'd last set out on this trip. The weight of carrying the threatening Grayton's Race docu-ments and the fear of what danger we might be sailing into in our quest for a serial killer were behind me. Ahead now were only the prospect of a relaxing, sybaritic vacation and the anticipation of completing the "unfinished business" Darnay had alluded to.

I smiled, conjuring up in my mind his tall, well-muscled body as I'd last seen it, encased in navy polo shirt and dazzling white shorts. I held onto that image throughout the next few, boring hours of plane changes, endless Diet Cokes, and talkative seatmates.

When at last I stood at the foot of the gangway and gazed up at the brightly lit *Crystal Fjord* docked majestically at the port of Charlotte Amalie, I had no way of knowing that I would soon look back with longing on those moments of boredom.

26

We stood at the rail on the topmost deck, our arms nearly touching as we leaned over to watch the huge ship being maneuvered away from the dock. A party atmosphere had taken over the hundreds of passengers who crowded around us. While only a few weary dock workers and port officials still wandered the nearly deserted quay, many slightly tipsy travelers waved and shouted, casting colorful streamers over the side as if we were the old Queen Elizabeth preparing to steam out of New York City in the opening scene of some 1930's movie.

Darnay had been waiting for me at the top of the gangway stairs. Our meeting had been awkward, neither of us knowing quite how to react, a handshake seeming too formal, an embrace, too intimate. In the end we had settled for a murmured greeting as Darnay took my briefcase and escorted me to my cabin.

Jordan had not made an appearance, either in our room while I freshened up and changed nor in the Aft Bar which had somehow become, in the matter of only a couple of days, our preferred gathering place. We had only a few minutes to sip our drinks before the deep-throated blast of the ship's horn had announced our imminent departure, and we followed the throng out onto the deck.

Darnay and I exchanged smiles, marveling at the ease with which Captain Bjornsen jockeyed the 40,000-ton behemoth away from its mooring. Using bow and stern thrusters, he slid the ship sideways, then turned her toward the sea. The sparkling lights lining the sweep of the protected harbor fell away behind us as Charlotte Amalie receded into the darkness. Soon most of the revelers drifted off to the discos and nightclubs whose music and dancing would go on until the last passenger had stumbled wearily back to his cabin, hopefully before dawn.

The wind hit us full force as we cleared the shelter of the bay, and we watched the pilot who had guided us safely out into the Caribbean climb down the precariously heaving ladder on the side of the ship to drop safely onto the deck of the pilot boat. With a wave and a short blast from his tiny vessel's frail horn, he headed back to his homeport and his bed.

"You must be exhausted," Darnay said, turning to face inward so his words wouldn't be snatched away by the freshening breeze.

We handed our empty glasses to a passing steward and waved away refills. Darnay pulled my arm through his as we walked companionably toward the stairway.

"Actually, I feel pretty good, all things considered. And I have about a million questions. Have you run across Jordan lately? I'm surprised she hasn't shown up yet."

"I saw her briefly at dinner. She and Grunewald have become quite an item. As have her brother and the famous lady writer. Those two haven't been seen most of the day."

I hoped Trey knew what he was getting into. While I had no trouble believing Jordan's wry observation that her brother would do anything to get backing for one of his projects, I had the feeling that Dame Margo Stanhope was more accustomed to being the one calling the tune. It was possible that the handsome, charming Trey Herrington had finally met his match.

"What?" Darnay asked, misinterpreting my smile. "Did I say something funny?"

"No, not really. I was just thinking that we've turned into an episode of *The Love Boat*. You know, 'Sail away and find romance on the high seas'?"

He pulled me closer as we strolled back toward the stern.

We took our usual table, and Luis immediately appeared from behind the bar, this time with Tequila Sunrises, the featured drink of the day. "And I make yours a virgin, miss," he assured me with a shake of his head at my peculiar tastes.

"So. Fill me in," I commanded as Darnay lit cigarettes for both of us.

He glanced casually around, as if he were not verifying that we couldn't be overheard. Though only one other table was occupied, and that on the other side of the bar, he hitched himself closer and leaned in, one arm draped negligently across the back of my chair.

"What do you want to know?"

I'd had a lot of time on the plane to think through the events of the past couple of days. I'd also taken the opportunity to leaf through all the documents I'd stuffed into my briefcase.

"Where did you go after you dropped me off at the ship on Wednesday? You said something about 'making things right'."

"I tracked down our friend Eddie Brown Shoes."

"How?"

"There was only one ambulance service on the island, so it didn't take much effort to find out where they'd taken him." Darnay chuckled and shook his head. "I understand he put up quite a fight. Seems he didn't want to be taken anywhere, but he couldn't drive with that wrist of his. Serves him right for hiring a car with a stick shift."

"So what happened?"

"They made him wait for the local *gendarmes* to show up. Of course he didn't want any police report filed, although his fake papers are probably good enough to fool most authorities doing a cursory examination. He convinced them to let him pay for any damages. I wouldn't be surprised if he spread a little cash around to the locals, too. At any rate, the ambulance deposited him at a small clinic on the edge of town. They'd just finished stitching up his head when I caught up with him."

"I wish I could have been a fly on the wall," I said, stubbing out my cigarette and reaching for the bowl of peanuts Luis had left on the table.

"Oh, it was all very civilized. I merely pointed out to *Mr. Keppler* that he had been mistaken in thinking that my dear friend Mrs. Tanner had anything in her possession that might possibly interest him, and that your trip to the bank had been for the purpose of making a deposit, rather than a withdrawal. I asked him to pass along a message to his employers, something to the effect that you had powerful friends now who would look most unkindly on any more 'accidents' befalling you, and that failure to heed this advice could be detrimental to their health, both physical and fiscal. I think, in the end, he believed me."

I started to inquire as to how Darnay had gone about convincing him, then thought I might sleep better *not* knowing. "Thank you" seemed grossly inadequate for an act that had probably guaranteed my security well into the millennium, but it was all I could think of to say.

"*Ce n'est rien*," Darnay replied, but we both knew it was a lot more than 'nothing'.

We accepted drink refills from the ever present Luis, and I looked up to find we were the only ones left in the open-air bar. A glance at my watch made me start in surprise. "Do you realize it's after three?"

"Maybe we should save the rest for tomorrow, eh? Or rather, later this morning. Your eyes look very tired, *ma petite.*"

His seemed to study my face with an intensity that had nothing to do with concern about my fatigue. Little crackles of electricity danced between us as his fingers idly stroked my bare arm. I talked to cover my nervousness.

"When do we dock in Tortola?" One of the larger islands in the British Virgins chain, it was our next scheduled port of call.

"We don't," he replied, easing back a little in his chair. "Dock, that is. Road Town has no facilities large enough to accommodate a ship this size. We'll be anchoring out in the channel and taking the tenders in. Wait! Hear that?"

I cocked my ear, but noticed nothing except the brisk breeze whistling through the narrow openings in the latticed panels that sheltered us. The piano player had long since gone to his bunk.

"No. What am I supposed to be hearing?"

"The pitch of the engines has dropped. We're probably approaching the point where we'll be dropping anchor. It's only a short distance from St. Thomas. That's why we sailed so late."

Now that Darnay had pointed it out, I did sense a lessening in the vibrations humming beneath my feet on the highly polished deck. Suddenly, I was overpoweringly weary.

"I think I will turn in now, before I collapse right here on the table," I said as Darnay hurried to pull back my chair and take my arm in that possessive manner that made my knees wobble a little.

Again I used words to hold my feelings at bay. "What did you find out about Diego Reyes?"

"Yes, do tell. We're all dying to hear."

We both turned, startled to find Jordan standing behind us. Her fey green eyes glittered with an emotion I couldn't quite identify. Beside me, I felt Darnay stiffen. Jordan's elegant, white crepe dress, cut almost to her navel in the front, clung to every curve, leaving no doubt that she wore almost nothing beneath it. She stood hip-shot, her body weaving rhythmically from side to side, although the ship had now come almost to a complete stop. Over her shoulder I could see a few lights sprinkling the hills of Tortola.

"I was just going to walk Bay to her cabin. She's pretty well done in," Darnay began, but Jordan cut him off.

"Oh, no you don't! I want to hear what you found out about that pretty-boy Spaniard. Luis!" she yelled, though the Jamaican bartender stood just a few feet from where she tottered. "Champagne!"

With a sigh of resignation, Darnay pulled out a chair, and Jordan collapsed into it. "Just a glass for the Countess," he instructed Luis under his breath. "Don't bring a whole bottle."

We settled back down at the table and watched as Jordan belted back half her glass in one gulp. "Don't be such an old stick, *Monsieur* Spoilsport," she slurred, "join me! I know Little Miss Teetotaler there won't."

"You're drunk enough for both of us," I snapped.

"Wait a minute," she said, carefully placing her glass on the table so that only a little of her drink sloshed out. She made an elaborate charade of touching the area around her mouth several times with a long, elegant finger. "Nope," she announced with a grin. "I'm not nearly drunk enough. I can still feel my upper lip."

With that Jordan downed the rest of the champagne and waved the empty glass at Luis.

"Don't you think you've . . ." I began when I felt Darnay's hand tighten around my arm. His look said, *Why bother?*, and I let the sentence dangle unfinished.

With a fresh drink, Jordan now turned her attention back to us. "So? What's the story? Is the jewelry salesman our man?"

"It doesn't appear so," Darnay replied wearily. "Everything you told me about him checks out so far. He's been in business for over twenty years, has homes in Brazil and Peru, and supports two ex-wives and three children. He uses the cruise ships to travel among the islands where he brokers the gemstones he buys all over South America. There's not one shred of evidence to indicate otherwise at this point."

Jordan sipped from the champagne glass and seemed to sober a little. "Well, I suppose you know what you're doing. It's probably just as well if it isn't him. I don't think he ever got back on the ship today. At least I couldn't find him anywhere. Deserted me just like everyone else has."

She looked around for Luis, but the bartender had caught Darnay's pointed expression and toss of the head and had disappeared a few minutes before.

Darnay seemed troubled by Jordan's revelation. I could feel his heightened tension run down along the arm he had kept proprietarily around my shoulders. Without a word, he again assisted me to my feet.

"It's time we all got some rest," he announced

"Just a minute." I looked down on Jordan now staring pensively into her empty glass. "Who else has deserted you?"

"Well, first it was you. But you're forgiven. You came back."

"Thanks," I said wryly.

"And Rolfe has been tied up all evening. He had to be on deck helping us sail out of St. Thomas. He was supposed to meet me afterward for a nightcap, but he sent some boy who could barely speak English to tell me he couldn't make it." Her pout made her perfect cheekbones stand out even more prominently. "He had to go into Road Town as soon as we anchored for some damned reason or other. I couldn't understand half of what the child was saying."

I could sense Darnay running out of patience with Jordan's alcohol-induced self-pity. "The man does have responsibilities," he reminded her.

Jordan ignored him. "And now Trey. He's my brother, even if he is a colossal pain in the ass most of the time. How could he just go off and leave me like this?"

"I know he's been sort of attentive to Dame Margo," I countered, asking myself what I was doing defending Trey Herrington. Maybe it was the little-girl-lost look on Jordan's normally haughty face. "But you yourself told me . . ."

"Oh, you don't understand anything! I don't mean he hasn't been around. I mean, he's gone. Over the side. Abandoned ship."

I must have looked as confused as I felt. "Where is he then?"

"On his way back to Hollywood, I suppose. All I know is he left a message with that Cockney steward of ours saying he was going to show Dame Margo-Bloody-Stanhope a Pacific sunset. No doubt as seen from the rumpled sheets of his king-size bed in the Malibu beach house. Men are pigs. Present company excepted, of course." She tried to wink at Darnay, but couldn't quite manage the requisite coordination.

"Come on, Jordan," I said, taking her hand and tugging her to her feet. "Let's get some sleep."

"You're right. The hell with all of them."

Darnay fell into step on the other side of her, but, strangely enough, she needed no assistance as we negotiated the deserted corridors and stairways on the way back to our cabin. I used my key, ushered Jordan inside, and quickly pulled the door closed as the clingy, white gown slid down around her feet, and she kicked off her shoes as she wove her way toward the bathroom.

I felt the hot flush of embarrassment begin to rise at my throat as I turned to say goodnight, but the look on Darnay's face sent all thoughts of parting straight out of my head.

This time there was no question of pretense as he swept me into his arms. The kiss touched a place in me I had thought locked forever against the pain and loss that loving had brought me. Suddenly none of that mattered, my fears swept away in a tide of desire, and I clung to him with a fierceness that shook me to my soul. When at last we reluctantly moved apart, the eyes I had once thought of as cold and hard gazed into mine with a longing that nearly stopped my heart.

"Come, *ma petite*," Darnay whispered. His hand, warm and strong in mine, urged me gently toward the stairway.

"No, wait! I . . ." Since Rob, there had been only one other, a man whose body I had taken with joy, but whose intent had been only to use and control me, a man whose charm and protestations of love had masked lies and deceit. I couldn't control the panic exploding in my chest like a hot burst of light. "I can't! I mean, it's not that I don't . . ." I stumbled over the words, trying to give voice to my confusion, but his finger against my lips silenced me.

"*Sshh!* It's all right, *mon amour. Nous avons beaucoup de temps.* I am a very patient man."

His next kiss barely brushed my lips, the sweet tenderness of it bringing a rush of tears to my eyes. Gently he wiped away the few that spilled over and reached out to open the door of my cabin. "Sleep well, *ma petite*. Breakfast tomorrow? At the usual place?"

I smiled and nodded, more grateful than he could ever know for his understanding.

"Do you think you can manage ten o'clock?" he asked, smiling.

"I'll be there."

"*Bien.*"

I watched his tall, angular back recede down the hallway, then stepped into my room. Something crackled underfoot, and I bent down to retrieve a letter-sized piece of paper and a small envelope addressed to Jordan in bold, black ink. Someone must have shoved them under the door during our absence, and I had failed to notice them when I'd let Jordan in. I set the envelope on the table between our two beds where she would be sure to see it when she emerged from the shower. I flopped myself onto the loveseat in the sitting room and studied the announcement printed on ship's stationery.

It was an advisory from the Captain. Flora had officially become a hurricane shortly before midnight. While all indications were that she would pass well to our north sometime during the day to-morrow, tropical storms tended to be unpredictable. All passengers, especially those planning on going ashore on Tortola, were advised to be alert for changes in the schedule that might come with very little warning. Should the weather necessitate it, our departure time, now set for six o'clock that evening, might be moved up or delayed as conditions warranted.

I placed this, too, on the nightstand for Jordan's perusal, peeled off my clothes, and climbed gratefully into my narrow bed. In the few seconds before I fell into exhausted sleep, while the memory of Darnay's lips still rippled along my nerve endings, I thought I felt a shudder pass through the great, steel hull of the ship as she rocked against the restraining anchor chains in a rising wind.

27

Darnay looked as if he hadn't slept at all when he joined me at the table on the stern of the *Crystal Fjord* a little after ten o'clock next morning. He had obviously managed a shower, his hair lying in damp tendrils across his forehead. He'd changed as well, the white pullover and yellow shorts a stark contrast against his darkening tan. He looked like a typical tourist who had partied too late the night before.

But his smile as he bent to brush my cheek with a kiss dispelled a lot of the exhaustion that had been tugging at his eyes. "*Bon jour*," he offered, signaling a passing waiter for coffee.

"*Bon jour* yourself. Didn't you get any rest? You look awful."

"Thank you so much. I am, however, unable to return the insult. By the way, your accent isn't bad. With a little training, I think we could make a passable Frenchwoman out of you."

If there was a *double entendre* there, I chose to ignore it. "So what's the game plan? You know, where do we go from here?" I elaborated when his puzzled look told me he wasn't familiar with the sports allusion. "Did you track down Reyes?"

"Not yet," he said. "There must be a hundred hotels on St. Thomas, not to mention dozens of little bed-and-breakfasts and rooming houses. The local police are checking it out. I expect to hear sometime this afternoon."

"But what if it's all perfectly innocent? I mean, suppose he just ran into some friends and decided to stay over for a few days? You'll never locate him if he's in a private home, will you?"

"Eventually. But if that's the case, what does it tell us? I'm seriously convinced that Diego Reyes has nothing to do with these killings. I've been on the phone with my superiors in Lyon, and the consensus is that this guy is a dead end. While he fits parts of the profile, he comes nowhere close in many others."

"You have a profile of the murderer? What does it entail? And how did Inter . . ." I caught myself before he had a chance to admonish me. "How did your office get onto it in the first place?" I amended.

Darnay reached over to steal a stem of grapes off my plate, then popped the sweet, green fruits one at a time into his mouth while he pondered my question. The gesture was at once casual and sensuous. I forced my mind back to the subject at hand as Darnay lowered his voice to answer.

"It was the computer, actually, although a human being eventually made the decision to review the data he was presented with. You see, we collect crime statistics from all over the world, on everything from drug smuggling, which is in our jurisdiction by reason of its very nature, to murder, money-laundering, and art theft if they involve the crossing of international borders. We gather information from all our member countries—over 170 of them—about things like aliases, fingerprints, MOs and so on. They all go into one huge database where any member nation can then access them. We've also got a new program that can scan the database and extract similarities in crimes based on any number of criteria, then produce a Modus Operandi printout."

"So someone asked for serial murders and Leslie Herrington and the others just popped out?"

"No, it doesn't work like that," he said, pouring himself more coffee and reaching for a melon slice on my plate.

"You want me to get you something?" I asked, and he laughed guiltily, swallowing the juicy cantaloupe before replying.

"I'm sorry. I promise, no more poaching."

I signaled our waiter, and over Darnay's half-hearted protests, asked him to bring a plate of fruit and some Danish from the buffet. When we were once again alone, he answered my question more completely.

"Actually, it was a piece of jewelry, reported stolen by a deceased woman's family, that set the wheels in motion. It showed up in loot recovered in a drug bust on a suspected trafficker in Lima, Peru. How it got to him, we're not certain. It may be that the man is telling the truth when he says he bought it from a guy he knows as a present for his girlfriend."

"Didn't you say Diego Reyes had a home in Peru?" I interrupted.

"Yes. It's another reason I haven't completely ruled him out. But he lives in Trujillo, not Lima."

"I'm sorry, go ahead. So you put the jewelry description into the database and . . . what?"

"It did an automatic search for matches—dead women, missing jewelry. When the computer spit out twelve names, our people got seriously concerned."

"Twelve? My God, this monster has killed twelve women?"

"Keep it down," Darnay cautioned, checking to see if anyone was paying particular attention to our conversation. Guiltily, I also scanned the area, relieved to find that, once again, we were the only ones left. Several waiters scurried back and forth, tearing down the breakfast buffet in preparation for the lunchtime cookout of hamburgers and hot dogs which would begin in just over an hour.

"Sorry," I whispered back.

"We were able to eliminate four of the deaths as having been outside our profile. You know, either the killer was known to the victim—a friend or family member—or the M.O. indicated a professional burglar who got surprised in the act."

"But that still leaves eight."

"Yes, it does. The Whiteside woman was among those eight, because her family had reported her jewelry missing and her death as suspicious. It wasn't until I got a call from your father, and he told me your theory about Jordan's mother and the Rousseau woman in Caracas that we were aware of their possible connection to our pattern."

"Did you really come all the way from France just because the Judge asked you to keep an eye on me?"

"Of course not. But with what he had to tell us, the regional office in San Juan decided it was time to put someone into the field. I'm the senior investigator for the Caribbean area, so here I am." Darnay lit my cigarette, then one for himself, and rose from the table. "I think these gentlemen want to clean up here. How do you feel about a jaunt into town?"

We moved away, nodding at the smiling waiters who pounced on our vacated table like cats on a day-old mackerel. The poor guys seemed to work twenty hours a day. I hoped they were well paid for it, although I assumed they made most of their money from the gratuity envelopes left by the passengers at the end of the cruise.

"So where does the investigation stand," I asked, as we strolled onto the covered promenade deck, "assuming Reyes isn't the guy?"

"I'm checking on some other leads," he said in frustratingly Columbo-like vagueness.

"Oh, no you don't. I'm in this thing up to my eyebrows, whether I want to be or not. If you want my help, you're going to have to level with me. Don't start with any of this 'need-to-know' crap."

"Okay, okay!" Darnay threw up his hands in mock surrender as we moved to the rail to allow a determined jogger to trot by us. I thought I'd read somewhere in the ship's propaganda that five times around the promenade deck constituted a mile.

Darnay pulled me back toward the bulkhead and into an alcove created by a recessed case containing a wicked-looking ax and a fire extinguisher. For a moment, I thought he intended to take up where we'd left off last night, but apparently he had only been seeking privacy.

"I'm waiting for a report on the crew."

"The *crew?* What on earth for?" I asked, stunned. It was the last thing I'd expected. "How could anyone from the ship possibly be involved with these murders? My God, these people work almost around the clock. I don't see how they manage to squeeze in time to sleep, let alone to follow passengers ashore and murder them in hotel rooms. Besides, all the dead women didn't travel on the same ship or even the same cruise line. Your theory makes absolutely no sense, Alain."

"So is this how it will be for us, *eh, ma petite?* When you are angry you will call me 'Alain'?"

The words, delivered in a soft, seductive voice, were followed by his strong, blunt fingers tracing the line of my cheek and jaw. His steel-blue eyes, only a couple of inches above mine, held me fast in their concentrated gaze as if he would pull the desired response out of me by sheer force of will.

"Back off, buster," I said, only half-jokingly, my hands planted firmly against his chest. His broad shoulders filled the narrow opening of the alcove as he hovered over me, his taut body nearly touching mine.

With a laugh at my foolishness, he stepped aside, and I stumbled out into the open air. I felt sheepish about that fleeting moment of panic when Darnay's face had filled my vision and his body had blocked my escape.

Escape? I asked myself, fumbling for my cigarettes while Darnay clicked his lighter. *Where on earth had* that *come from?*

It's all this talk of murder, I answered me. *Anyone would get the willies.*

In silent agreement we moved again to the rail, gazing southward at the Caribbean Sea stretching out before us. "They don't all work for the cruise line, you know."

The *non sequitur* threw me for a moment, until I picked up again on the thread of our interrupted conversation. "You mean, the crew? Who do they work for, then?"

"There are agencies—similar to those temporary office placement outfits—that supply crewmembers to almost every shipping concern in the area. They run the gamut from laundry workers to experienced officers."

"Why would a cruise line need that kind of service? Don't they maintain a full complement of people?"

Darnay raised his shoulders in that Gallic shrug I found so endearing. "They have peak times and slow times, just like any other business. It makes more economic sense to hire a temporary when you need one rather than keep on a full-time employee you might only need occasionally, don't you think?"

I had to agree. "So you think one of these 'temps' might be our man?"

"*C'est possible.* I'm awaiting a list from the purser as to how many are on board this ship now. A complete roster of agency employees they've used is being compiled by the home office of Royal Scandinavian, as well as all the other cruise lines that operate in this part of the world. It's going to entail a lot of crosschecking and digging."

Suddenly, almost shyly, Darnay lifted my hand from its resting-place on the salt-encrusted rail and raised it to his lips. "I'm sorry if I frightened you, *ma petite*," he said, his blue eyes boring into mine. I saw the question there and realized how stupid it had been for me to have had the slightest second of fear of this man.

"*Ce n'est rien*," I replied and rewarded him with the most dazzling, reassuring smile I could muster.

"Enough of this gloomy talk," Darnay laughed, reading my signals correctly. "I'm going back to my cabin and see if I have any messages. You grab the skimpiest, sexiest swimsuit you've got and meet me at the debarkation door in . . ."

He paused to consult his watch, and I leaped in. "Ten minutes!" I cried, turning for the stairway. "Last one there buys lunch on the beach!"

I found my suite immaculate and empty when I burst into the cool quiet, laughing and breathless from my sprint up the stairway. I had left Jordan snoring softly in the bed next to mine when I'd tiptoed out just an hour ago. She must have dressed quickly and gone in search of breakfast.

I pulled an oversized, straw bag from the shelf of the closet along with my wide-brimmed hat. Since all my swimsuits had been specially designed to cover my scars, I didn't have anything that qualified as 'skimpy'. I pulled on a white one-piece whose plunging neckline and gathered folds covered just enough of my breasts to avoid total indecency. I hummed to myself as I flung towels and lotions into the bag and tossed on a short, swingy cover-up that would preserve my modesty on the brief trip on the tender from the ship into the port of Road Town.

After adding my wallet, room key, and passport to the jumble, I crossed to the dresser to retrieve an extra pack of cigarettes and one of the paperback novels I had brought with me. My eye fell on the small envelope that had been slipped under our door last night, the one addressed to Jordan in heavy, black script. The folded note that had apparently been enclosed lay tossed carelessly on top. To this day, I don't know what made me commit such an unforgivable breach of manners, but without conscious thought, I picked up the letter and flipped it open.

I must have stood for some time staring at the innocuous message. "I want to show you my favorite island," it read. "Meet me at the tenders at 11:00. Don't disappoint me."

It was not these words that held me riveted, my breath coming in short, shallow gasps. It was the scrawled signature: *Rolfe*, the smaller letters nearly illegible, a series of bumps in an almost continuous line, overshadowed by the bold, flowing *R*.

I had seen that initial, written in just such dramatic fashion, before.

I dropped the card as if it were a match that had burned down to my fingers. In two strides, I was across the small sitting room. I grabbed my briefcase from behind the loveseat and dumped its contents out onto the bed. Frantically I pawed through the receipts and papers that had been Leslie Herrington's personal effects, until my fingers closed around the enclosure card I had so meticulously steamed away from the ship's programme in my kitchen less than a week before : *Until tonight, darling. R.*

The ink was still slightly smeared, but it would not take a handwriting expert to confirm my worst fears. The signatures were the same.

Rolfe Grunewald was Ramon Escalante. *Leslie's* Ramon.

He had murdered at least eight women in cold blood.

And now he had Jordan.

28

I beat Darnay to the debarkation deck, but only by a couple of minutes. I had no choice but to meet him there: I had never bothered to find out his cabin number. Nevertheless, by the time he jogged down the steps, swinging a canvas bag with the ship's logo emblazoned on it, I had worn a path in the dark green carpeting and had, undoubtedly, convinced the crew members manning the sea stairs that I had taken total leave of my senses.

Several passengers stood waiting for the next tender to return from the docks, and I heard one of the junior officers remark that the weather looked to be kicking up. Indeed, the ship did seem to be pitching more vigorously from side to side, but this elicited mostly good-hearted jibes, directed at those who were having some difficulty maintaining their balance, about having "drunk" their breakfast.

For me, it only compounded the urgency of the situation.

I threw myself at Darnay the moment I spotted him, hustling him off to the side, out of earshot.

"Bay! For God's sake, what is it?" Darnay grabbed me by the shoulders, but even his strong hands couldn't quell the trembling that shook my entire body. "What's happened?"

"It's . . . him!" I managed to blurt out, fighting to keep my voice to a low whisper. "Grunewald! He's Ramon!"

"Slow down, *ma petite*. Easy."

His calm tone helped to quiet me a little. I knew he had no idea what I was talking about, so I shoved the gift card into his hand, explaining in short, rapid sentences how I had come across it stuck to another paper in Leslie Herrington's effects and how I had managed to work it free.

"And now this!" I waved the note Jordan had received from Rolfe the night before. He took it from my shaking fingers and held the two side by side. I saw by the tightening of the hard muscle along his jaw that I didn't have to explain its significance.

"Wait here," he ordered.

"But . . ."

"Wait!"

He approached the two crewmembers and pulled one of them aside. The conversation appeared to be one-sided, with Darnay punctuating his rapid-fire questions with his index finger and the bewildered young officer mostly nodding in agreement. When he returned to me, his mouth was set in a firm line.

"They disembarked shortly after eleven. Thomas said he overheard them discussing snorkeling, and Grunewald had a duffel bag with him. It probably had his fins and masks and so on in it."

"So how many places can there be for snorkeling on Tortola? We just have to check them all out, and we'll find her. Come on."

"No, wait! Bay, damn it!"

I tried to pull away from the hand he had clamped around my upper arm, but his grip held me fast.

"Let go of me!"

We were attracting the worried looks of some of the passengers closest to us, and one of the officers had started to move in our direction when Darnay quelled him with a look and a brisk shake of his head.

"Will you calm down?" Darnay hissed in my ear, and I fought to control the panic washing over me. "That's better. Where are you rushing off to? All we have to do is wait for them to return to the ship. I'm not certain if the *Crystal Fjord* has a brig, but we can certainly arrange for Grunewald to be confined until I can get some answers out of him."

"So you don't think I'm jumping to conclusions? You agree he's most likely our murderer?"

Darnay reached down to pick up the canvas bag he'd dropped at my feet when he'd gone to interrogate Thomas, the young officer. From beneath the rolled-up towel, he extracted two sheets of ship's stationery covered with names.

"This list was waiting for me when I got back to my cabin. Sixty-eight out of the normal complement of six hundred fourteen crewmembers are temporaries."

The fourth name on the second page was Rolfe Grunewald, Acting First Officer.

"I need a cigarette," I said, looking around for an ashtray or any other indication that I could light up without being hassled by the people in my immediate vicinity, but I saw nothing that looked promising.

"Let's go back up on deck, get a drink, and discuss this rationally. We can't do anything until they get back on board."

"We can't wait for that! We have to find them! Don't you see?"

"No, frankly, I don't!"

A hum of anticipation rippled across the fifty or so people waiting near the open door as a gentle bump registered the arrival of a tender. That was followed quickly by the muffled tread of soft-soled shoes on the metal stairway that led up from the floating platform. We turned to watch as the crowd parted, allowing the few returning passengers to clamber back on board. Almost immediately crewmen began to usher debarkees down the stairs.

"Look," I said, staring straight into Darnay's eyes. "Number one, Jordan's out there somewhere running around with a man who has killed eight women that we know of, one of them her own mother. Secondly, she's been keeping him up to date on everything. I tried to warn her not to spill her guts to everyone she met, but I know she's told him a lot. In fact, she said it was Grunewald who sicced her onto Diego Reyes as a likely suspect. Why would he do that if he weren't already worried that someone was getting close to finding out about him?"

Then another thought struck me with the force of the wind whistling through the open door. "He sent me that fake telegram! It had to be him. He wanted me out of the way so he could take care of Jordan!"

"Now just hold on a second! You're losing control here, Bay." Darnay began to tick off his objections on his fingers. "First, if he is a killer—and that's still a big *if*—why would he want to harm Jordan? She's not even suspicious of him, is she? You weren't until just a few minutes ago. Why tip his hand by doing anything so blatant? Besides, it's not his usual M.O."

"How do we know what Jordan suspects?" I asked. "Maybe she's let something slip that's alarmed him. He can't know I'm back, can he? Maybe he thinks that with Trey gone, too, he's got an open field. Why take the chance on her realizing who he is?"

The last few passengers were moving toward the gangway. I saw Thomas raise his eyebrows in unspoken question to Darnay.

"Come on," I said, hefting my bag over my shoulder. "We'll discuss it ashore."

"Bay, I don't agree with your assessment. I think we should just wait . . ."

"You do whatever you want. I'm going to find my friend."

As I reached the bottom of the stairs and stepped into the rocking tender, I was relieved to feel Darnay's hand at my elbow. I turned to find his hard, blue eyes fixed on me in an expression I couldn't quite fathom. We made our way to the back of the small launch, staggering into the two rear seats just as it pulled away from the platform. The craft was only about three-quarters full, many of the *Crystal Fjord*'s passengers apparently opting to heed the Captain's warning and remain on board.

"Okay, so what's the plan? How do we find out where they might have gone snorkeling?" I asked. "Police? Harbor patrol?"

"How would Grunewald have known enough to send you such a convincing telegram?" Darnay asked, still back in our previous conversation. "How did he know about your father's health problems, and his housekeeper's name?"

"I don't know," I admitted, his questions echoing my own confusion. "Maybe Jordan told him. Or maybe he rifled our cabin while we were gone."

"Even so, it seems pretty farfetched for him to be able to . . ."

"Oh, I know it doesn't make any sense!" I snapped as the tender slowed, approaching the small ferry dock on the left side of the harbor. "Do you always analyze everything to death like this? Don't you sometimes just follow your gut?"

"Frequently," he announced with a grim smile, "although I generally try to have just the *tiniest* shred of evidence to back me up."

I ignored him and allowed a crewmember to assist me up onto the concrete pier. Directly ahead of us, the cruise line had set up an awning-covered rest area complete with chairs and a small buffet table on which plates of fruit and cookies rested alongside large vats of iced tea and lemonade. I accepted a Styrofoam cup of cold tea and walked past the knot of passengers waiting to board the launch for the return trip out to the anchored ship. Stepping out onto Waterfront Drive, I turned toward the north, across the green-crested mountains rising behind the little town, and stopped dead in amazement.

The heavens looked as if some schizophrenic child, unable to decide between blue and black, had a drawn a ragged crayon line through the picture he was coloring. To the left, only a few stray, fluffy clouds marred the clear azure synonymous with a bright Caribbean day. But to the right, far off in the east, it appeared as if night were already falling. The distant darkness seemed to roil and bubble, and angry cracks of sheer, vivid lightning ripped the sky as thunderstorms spawned in the outer rain bands announced the imminent approach of Hurricane Flora.

"We can't stay." Darnay spoke at my elbow. "The crewman says the storm is moving in too fast, and it's changing direction. We're in for a near-hit in about four to six hours. The ship will have to move."

I stood mesmerized by the awesome display before me, ignoring this urgent speech, although I did give him a brief nod to acknowledge receipt of the message.

"Then we'd better hurry," I said, shaking myself loose from the hypnotic pull of the sky. I moved onto the sidewalk and turned to look in both directions. "Which way is the police station?"

"Listen to me, damn it!" Darnay spun me around, both hands gripping my upper arms. "We're not going to the police station. We're not going anywhere except back to the ship on the next available tender."

We turned simultaneously as the brash horn of the launch sounded, and it edged away from the pier. It rode low in the water, jammed with more passengers than it was probably designed for.

This flouting of the rules did more to underscore the urgency of the situation than anything Darnay might have said. Still, he would not be able to convince me to abandon my quest. He should have known that.

"I'm going to find Jordan," I said with a quiet finality. "You do what you have to do."

I raised my hand and immediately a slightly dented, dusty minivan, executed a sharp U-turn from across the street and jerked to a halt at the curb just inches from my feet. The young, eager driver leaped from the right-hand side and slung back the wide, sliding door. "Police station," I heard Darnay growl just before he pushed me unceremoniously onto the long bench seat and jumped in the van behind me.

Half an hour later we stood outside the low, functional building, as I bent my head to Darnay's lighter. Although the sun still beat down mercilessly, the wind had picked up, sending small twigs and leaves swirling around our feet.

"Now what?" I asked as I nervously scanned the sky to the east. If anything, the darkness seemed to have deepened.

The local police had been most helpful, especially after the chief had an opportunity to examine Darnay's Interpol credentials. Although he had no official standing or jurisdiction, his requests had been honored with a dispatch I thought was probably unusual on this normally quiet, slow-moving island. But we had drawn a total blank.

Because of the approaching storm, the police had been out for the past several hours clearing the beaches of island tourists as well as the visitors off the ship. Away from the protected waters of the channel and the harbor, the sea was angry, large swells and waves pounding the shoreline. No one could swim in such heavy surf, let alone snorkel. And a call back to the dock where the tenders were scurrying to get all the *Fjord*'s passengers back on board revealed that Rolfe and Jordan had not returned.

We both turned at the sound of the door opening behind us and watched a grim-faced Byron MacGregor stride toward us. Despite the expectations his Scottish name aroused, the chief of police of Tortola was a towering black man, somewhere in his fifties, I had guessed, with closely shorn gray hair that accented his strong, chiseled features. He had a deep, resonant voice that perfectly matched his size.

"Nothing," he announced, shaking his head. "I cannot believe your friends are still on the island."

"But where . . ." I began, before Darnay took control of the situation.

"Where else might they have gone? And how?" he asked. He offered his cigarettes, and the chief accepted one and a light before answering.

"Virgin Gorda, if I had to make a guess," he said. "The Baths, a series of huge rocks and grottos just off the shore there, are world-famous for snorkeling, and they could have reached there quite easily in a hired boat."

"That must be it! Remember Jordan's saying last night that Grunewald was going ashore as soon as the ship anchored? He could have arranged for a boat then."

I had stubbed out my cigarette on the heel of my shoe, not wanting to drop the butt on the ground in front of the chief law enforcement officer of the island, and now I picked at the filter, shredding the white fibers as I spoke.

"But I have already explored this possibility," Byron MacGregor answered, flipping his own half-smoked Gauloises into the street where the wind sent it rolling. "No local firm has rented them a craft, and it is illegal for private citizens to do so. Besides, no one would risk the means of his livelihood to take to the sea today."

"Not even for a large sum of money?" Darnay asked.

The chief shrugged. "Perhaps. But word would have circulated among the other fishermen, and I have heard nothing. This is a very small island."

"How about a plane?" I asked, and both men looked at me as if they had just realized I was still there.

"We have a small airport on Beef Island, just to the east," MacGregor replied, pointing over his shoulder toward the darkening quadrant of the sky. "But Virgin Gorda has no landing strip."

"What about any of the other islands?" Darnay asked.

"In the BVI? Only Anegada, and they can accommodate only the very smallest aircraft. But that is out of the question."

"Why?"

Chief MacGregor regarded me with the same patient condescension he probably used with very small children and village idiots. "My dear Mrs. Tanner, look out there." Again he flung a hard-muscled arm toward the northeast. "Out there lies Anegada. The storm-trackers say they may already be feeling the effects of Lady Flora. No one flies a small plane into the teeth of a hurricane."

"Can you check? This is a desperate man, after all. He may not be acting entirely rationally." It was taking every ounce of self-restraint I possessed not to scream out my frustration. Why were we standing here calmly discussing the possibilities as if we had all the damned time in the world? But I sensed that only by proving I wasn't as crazy as I was accusing Grunewald of being could I hope to sway the stoic chief of police.

He looked to Darnay, his expression clearly saying, *Women! What can you do?*

A wave of gratitude washed over me as I heard Darnay say, "You're probably right, chief. Still, it wouldn't hurt to check. If it's not too much trouble."

"As you wish, Inspector."

"Thank you," I said to Darnay after Chief MacGregor had reentered his stationhouse. I collapsed onto a low, stone wall that fronted the ugly, utilitarian building and lit another cigarette. "He was about to tell me to run along home and bake some cookies and leave all this nasty business to the men folk."

Darnay's laugh was the first pleasant sound I'd heard in the last couple of hours. "Don't be too hard on him. He has been very cooperative, especially considering that I have no real standing here."

"Well, he can insult me all he wants, as long as he finds out where Grunewald has taken Jordan. I'm really afraid for her, Alain."

"Ah, *ma pauvre petite*, I know you are. How can I convince you that it's unnecessary?"

I lifted my eyes to find his filled with compassion and another emotion I wasn't yet ready to name. With gentle fingers he stroked the curve of my cheek.

"You can't." I reached up and captured his hand, pulling him gently down beside me. "Listen to me now, please. I know in my gut that Rolfe is a murderer, and I think you do, too. The signatures and the temp list only confirmed it. Think back to that first night at the Captain's table. The minute we were all introduced, Grunewald made straight for Jordan. Why? She certainly doesn't fit his usual victim profile."

Darnay settled back and lit a cigarette. I had his complete attention now as I marshaled my arguments and laid them out.

"First off, she's much younger than any of the others, by at least twenty years. Secondly, she's not traveling alone. Dame Margo Stanhope would have made a much more logical target for him, and yet he fastened onto Jordan. Why?"

"I have a feeling you're about to tell me," Darnay said with just a touch of sarcasm.

"Because he knew who she was. He recognized her name the minute he heard it."

"That's a pretty big assumption."

"No, it's not. Think about it. He spent a lot of time wooing Leslie over the course of the cruise and the few days in Rio. Surely she talked about her family. That would only be natural, no matter how strained her relationship with Jordan was. She probably even trotted out the pictures of the grandchildren. And from everything I know about Leslie Herrington, she wouldn't have passed up an opportunity to brag about her daughter, the Countess, and her international lifestyle."

It seemed to be taking Chief MacGregor a long time to check out flights from what had to be a tiny airport, but I couldn't worry about that now. I needed this chance to plead my case with Darnay. I had to convince him that Jordan was in danger, otherwise my determination to rescue her would end up being a solo endeavor.

"So you're saying he deliberately kept Jordan close so he could monitor what you and she and Trey were up to."

"Right! I mean, looking at it from his perspective, he had to be in a panic. It couldn't be a coincidence that the daughter and son of one of his victims just *happen* to show up on the same cruise he's working. Not to mention their nosy friend and a security consultant that attaches himself to their little circle."

I was warming to my theory, and I could feel Darnay's initial resistance bending a little my way.

"He tried to sic us onto Diego Reyes, but he had to know that wouldn't stand up to any kind of intensive investigation, so he sent me a telegram to get me out of the way, and devised a plan to get rid of Jordan."

"There's where your theory falls apart, Mrs. Holmes." Darnay rose to his feet and began pacing along the cracked sidewalk before us, stopping to peer through the glass doorway into the police station before he turned again to me. "What about Trey Herrington? And me? Even if you were gone, he and I were still around."

"Yes, but Trey was preoccupied with Dame Margo. Rolfe must have thanked the gods when the two of them decided to skip off to California. As for you, as far as he knew, you were just a consultant for the cruise line. He probably thought you were there to check out the viability of their security measures for protecting valuables and for keeping unauthorized people from gaining access to the ship. He couldn't have known you're from Interpol, because I didn't tell Jordan. Unless you did, or he got it from someone else?"

Darnay shook his head. "Not even the Captain was informed of my real status. No one on board except you knew the truth."

"So, go ahead. Knock down my assumptions. Believe me, I'd be thrilled to be wrong. I'd like nothing better than to run back to the ship and sail the hell out of here, away from that storm. I'd like to wake up tomorrow morning and find that none of this has really happened."

Darnay resumed his seat and drew me close with a strong arm around my quivering shoulder. "Everything you say makes a kind of sense, darling. Everything except why you're so convinced that Jordan is in danger now, this minute. And why Grunewald would pick the middle of an oncoming hurricane to make his move."

"I can't explain it any better than I already have," I replied, plucking his *darling* out of the grim conversation and slipping it away to be examined later. "It's a feeling as much as anything. I don't think he's entirely sane, Alain. How could he be and do the horrible things he's done? And I think the storm makes a perfect cover. A boating mishap, an accidental drowning? Blame the weather, and who could argue with him? Especially if there aren't any witnesses. I just know we have to find them before it's too late. I *know* it!"

The wind swirled as the door to the police station opened, changing the currents around us. Chief MacGregor reached us in two powerful strides. I read the answer on his face before he had time to voice it.

"Grunewald hired a plane, a small Cessna. He made the arrangements early this morning. He is a licensed pilot and flew the plane himself. He and your friend landed at the airstrip on Anegada about an hour ago, got into a waiting car and drove off. No one has seen them since."

29

The rain held off until we were nearly upon the low, flat island. Actually, the first things I noticed as we approached were a few scrawny palm trees swaying in the rising wind and the naked masts of a dozen sailboats rolling at anchor in the small harbor.

Darnay and I had been huddled up on a hard, board seat that had once been padded, but whose stuffing had disappeared over time through the many rips in its faded vinyl cover. We had just scrambled into the bright yellow slickers Chief MacGregor had urged on us when he'd introduced us to our guide and captain, Kenneth Bleeker, and reluctantly sent us on our way.

The captain turned now from his place at the wheel, his crooked yellow teeth still a sharp contrast to the deep ebony of his weathered skin, and flashed us a smile of reassurance. A native Anegadian, Kenneth made the trip from his home to Tortola twice a week, occasionally ferrying supplies and locals between the two islands. We'd been fortunate, the Chief had informed us, to have caught up with him. No one knew the dangerous reefs around Anegada better than Kenneth. It was said he could navigate the treacherous waters on a moonless night without so much as a compass.

The goods he was carrying back to the isolated island were lashed securely in the stern and covered with a tattered tarpaulin. Scattered around them in the well of the boat were all the trappings of his profession: line and fishing tackle, nets and lobster pots, and big plastic buckets that I was certain, to judge by the lingering smell, usually contained bait.

Darnay tightened his arm around my shoulder as the trim, wood-hulled fishing boat slowed, and the swells sent her rolling in the heavy surf. I tried to muster up a smile, but my face felt as if it had been painted onto the front of my skull. Darnay's thick, brown hair was plastered to his head and caked with salt spray, and I was afraid I looked as bedraggled as he did. With the roar of the twin, outboard engines and the wind screaming past our ears, we'd had little opportunity to talk. Once Kenneth negotiated the deadly coral heads that punctuated the shallow entrance to the harbor and set us down on firm ground, we had no clue as to how we would set about locating Grunewald and Jordan.

We'd made an unspoken pact not to reveal the reason for this madcap dash across the Caribbean in the face of an approaching hurricane, and Darnay had asked Chief MacGregor to keep it to himself as well. We had no real proof, other than my own gut instinct, that Rolfe was a dangerous serial killer. Even if we had been able to convince the Chief, he had neither the facilities nor the manpower to launch any kind of armed sortie to rescue my friend.

Stealth and surprise seemed our best allies.

The quaint, thatched roof of the restaurant and bar attached to the island's only hotel suddenly materialized through the thin current of misty rain as Kenneth Bleeker maneuvered us closer to shore. In the brief time it had taken us to move slowly out of the public dock on Tortola and set off on our harrowing, two-hour journey, the garrulous Kenneth had told us it was the Anegada Reef Hotel where he would be setting us down, and that it was the favorite gathering place for locals and visitors alike. He had also managed to slip in a little native history, recalling how, on old navigational charts, Anegada had been called Drowned Island, probably because its treacherous reefs had been the cause of more than three hundred shipwrecks over the centuries. Many of them still lay just offshore in the clear, Caribbean waters and were a mecca for divers and treasure hunters.

The moment the engines died as Kenneth eased his boat up to the hotel dock, I caught the ominous roll of thunder echoing across the open waters to the north. We were totally surrounded now by the heaving, black clouds, the warm sunshine of Tortola a dim memory. I took Darnay's hand as he pulled me up onto the rickety, wooden pier.

We shook hands with Kenneth Bleeker, and Darnay tried once again to press a folded wad of bills on him, but he politely refused to accept more than the few BVI dollars he normally asked his passengers to contribute toward the exorbitant cost of his fuel. As we turned toward the hotel, several young boys, clad only in faded shorts, jogged by us and began to help Kenneth off-load his cargo of supplies.

The outdoor bar was deserted, the white resin chairs and round tables stacked neatly and lashed with heavy rope to a nearby palm tree. Other than that, we saw no preparations for the approaching storm. We walked through into the enclosed restaurant to find about a dozen people grouped in a loose semicircle of chairs around a fairly new, large-screen TV set, tuned I could see, to the Weather Channel. The bright red, swirling blob of Flora danced just to the north of a series of tiny dots that represented the Virgin Islands. She appeared to be almost on top of us.

Conversation ceased and twelve heads swiveled in unison to regard us, shivering and dripping onto the green tile floor. We must have looked like a couple of drowned cats. For a long moment no one spoke. I felt as if we had interrupted some sacred, secret rite and half expected one of the tanned, leathery faces to erupt in a shouted demand that we be cast back out into the gale.

Then Darnay shook his head, scattering water in all directions like a soggy St. Bernard, and a small, sprightly man detached himself from the group and made for us. His hand outstretched, a smile of genuine welcome lighted his craggy face. " 'allo, there! You must be the folks hitched a ride over with Kenneth just now. Welcome! I'm Nigel. Nigel Henry. Own the place, don't ya know!"

His voice had that same Cockney lilt as Gordon, our cabin steward back on the *Crystal Fjord*. The thought of the ship made me shiver, wondering if she had set sail yet to escape the coming hurricane and just where she'd end up. I sent up a silent prayer that we'd be able to get back to her before long—*all* of us.

" 'ere now, you're shakin' like a leaf! Soaked through, you are," our host remarked as he shook hands with Darnay and helped us off with our slickers. He hung them on a series of wooden pegs ranged along the wall near the door and ushered us into the small restaurant.

Everyone there seemed to know each other, and their faces carried identical creases wrought by too much sun and wind, undoubtedly a result of years of observing life from the rolling decks of the beautiful sailboats moored in the harbor. Still they seemed friendly enough, though I would never be able to attach names to all of them. They spread out a little, making room for two more chairs to be pulled into the circle as Nigel set out two steaming mugs of tea. Only Darnay took advantage of the bottle banged down on the table next to us, splashing a generous measure of rum into his mug.

"Off the ship, then, are ya?" Nigel asked as all eyes turned again to the muted television screen. Though they appeared to ignore us, I could sense the communal held breath as they waited for an answer.

"Yes, that's right," Darnay replied, sipping his fortified tea with apparent unconcern.

Somewhere along the line I had unconsciously decided to leave the details to him. Now that I'd gotten us here—through sheer stubbornness and force of will—I had no idea what to do. This sort of thing was Darnay's *forte*. I felt completely justified in letting him call the shots.

"They'll be moving her right about now," one of the sailors said over his shoulder. He had a white brush cut and alert, gray eyes over a lean, well-muscled body. American, I thought, probably ex-military to judge by his bearing.

"Right you are, Charlie," Nigel answered, providing the name I couldn't come up with. "Probably out into the channel is all," he assured us, warming our tea from a battered tin pot. "Soon as this lot blows over, we can get you back out there, don't worry."

"Is it going to hit us?" I asked.

"Not likely," the laconic Charlie responded. "Kenneth Bleeker says no, and I put a hell of a lot more store in his predictions than I do in these pretty-boy meteorologists."

"We'll get a few bangs and knocks, but nothing too bad," Nigel agreed. "Safest place to be right now," he added, surveying his property with pride. "The old girl has stood up to a lot worse storms than this little pisspot. Beggin' your pardon, ma'am."

"We were supposed to meet some friends," Darnay said into the chorus of soft chuckles that abruptly ceased with his announcement. "They flew in this morning. We got our signals crossed and missed the flight. Sort of expected to find them here."

It wasn't exactly a question, but he let his voice rise at the end of the sentence. The click of his lighter sounded like a rifle shot in the silence as he held it first to my cigarette, then to his own.

"Reg didn't say he was expecting anyone." Charlie finally turned far enough in his chair to be able to look Darnay square in the face.

I hoped the smoke rising in front of us managed to conceal the surprise I was certain Darnay felt as much as I did. *Reg?* Did Grunewald have yet another name, another identity he could he put on and throw off like most of us changed our socks?

"Yes, Reg," Darnay replied without missing a beat. "Actually, it's his companion who invited us along. Great friend of Ms. Tanner here. Old school chums, and all that. Met up with her on the ship, quite by accident. Asked us to join them at his place for a few days."

I had to force myself not to stare in bewilderment at this absolute fairytale Darnay was spinning. Where had he gotten the idea that Rolfe had a house here? Or that Rolfe and Reg were for certain the same man? Although logic dictated that there couldn't have been *two* idiots who had flown small planes through a gathering hurricane onto the island in the past few hours.

Somewhere in the space of the next several, silent seconds, the group apparently decided we were harmless, and probably exactly who we claimed to be: a pair of not too bright tourists who had set off on a holiday in the middle of a raging tropical storm. It still amazes me how protective small communities are of each other, even of a member who only spends an occasional few days in residence.

"You'll need a car," Nigel said.

* * * *

Sometimes now, when I'm sitting safe and snug inside, with a storm raging against the shutters and a fire crackling cheerily in the hearth, I remember that wild ride along the south coast of Anegada with a driving gale trying at every turn to force us off the narrow dirt road and into the sea.

I had ducked into the ladies' room for a quick repair while Charlie brought the ancient Fiat around to the front, and Nigel and Darnay huddled over a rough map drawn on the back of a cocktail napkin. My mission proved hopeless, my salt-encrusted hair an impenetrable helmet unwilling to yield to comb or brush. I gave a quick thought to dunking my head under the trickling faucet, then decided I could accomplish the same thing just by stepping outside into the rain. I did manage to rinse off my face and hands, and straighten my damp, wrinkled cover-up. The swimsuit underneath felt glued to my skin.

Darnay and I had each donned our drying slickers, then hefted our bags over our shoulders. He had given me the list of temporary employees, which I had tucked inside the waterproof case I carried my cigarettes and lighter in. His canvas tote was almost soaked through, the once neatly rolled-up towels now scrunched down into the bottom.

A few hands were raised in dispirited farewell, but no one really seemed to mourn our departure as Nigel walked us out to the thatch-covered overhang by the bar. Charlie had pulled the car as close as possible to where we stood, then bounded up to join us, leaving the motor running.

"You can't go too far wrong," he remarked, grabbing eye contact with Darnay and holding it. "Only the one road. Just be careful when you get to the end. It's not a long walk to Reg's place, but it's exposed. Not a lot of cover."

It was a strange remark, and something decidedly out of character for Charlie, if the baffled look on Nigel's face was anything to go by. But the two taller men continued to stare into each other's eyes, some unspoken understanding seeming to pass between them.

"Thank you, sir," Darnay said at last with a grin that seemed to exude relief. "Major, was it?'

"Colonel. Special Ops. I'll be here until the storm passes. Why don't you and your lady stop back here for a drink? Say, about eight? Phones are out, so that way we'll know you made it okay."

"Yes, " Nigel chimed in, "the derelict old system goes down the second there's a breath of wind, otherwise I'd ring up Reg and have him be on the lookout for you."

'Thanks all the same, but I think we'll just surprise him." Darnay and Charlie exchanged another meaningful look before the quiet American turned toward the restaurant, and we made a dash for the car.

It took only a few minutes to travel the three miles from Setting Point, where the Anegada Reef Hotel and its occupants had hunkered down to wait out the hurricane, to the tiny village called The Settlement where the majority of the island's one hundred fifty or so permanent residents made their homes. The narrow streets were deserted as we chugged through the quaint hamlet, then back out into the open where the winds lashed the little car from all directions. Far from being a typically lush, tropical Caribbean paradise, Anegada was dry and scruffy with stunted vegetation, and, Kenneth Bleeker had informed us, there wasn't a spot anywhere higher than thirty feet above sea level, including the hotel and most houses which were all only one story tall.

Any kind of significant tidal storm surge, and we'd all be treading water in a damn big hurry.

To this day I don't know how Darnay kept the Fiat on the winding road. The winds from the outer bands of Flora swept out of the north and raced unhindered across the narrow neck of the east end of the island. Rain was being driven through the crack of the rear quarter window on my side where the glass failed to fit properly. Darnay snapped at me when I suggested using one of his towels to block up the gap, so I smoked and sulked and watched the road anxiously. When the dirt track took a slight jog to the right, then petered out a few yards farther on against a high dune crowned with a few scrawny tufts of pampas grass, I knew we had arrived at our destination.

Neither one of us spoke as Darnay turned off the ignition. Sheltered a little behind the dune, we could hear the erratic ticking of the cooling engine above the muffled whine of the wind. The windows immediately fogged up.

"Now what?" I asked.

"What do you mean?" Darnay shot back. "You wanted to find Jordan, so let's go find her."

"Wait a minute!" I grabbed his arm as he fumbled for the door handle. "What's the plan? I mean, we can't just go marching up to the front door and ring the bell."

"Why not? Our cover story's as good as his. We came exploring, got stuck in the storm, heard from the locals that he had a place here, and came seeking refuge. Once we're inside we can assess the situation and decide from there."

"That's ridiculous! In the first place, we're supposed to think his name is Rolfe, so how would we have located him when everyone here knows him as Reg? Secondly, there's something going on here that you're not telling me. You've been dead-set against this from the beginning. Now you're prepared just to walk in and brazen it out? Did it never occur to you that old Rolfe, alias Ramon, alias Reggie might be armed?"

"Why should he be? According to your theory he smothers helpless old ladies in their beds. He doesn't need a gun."

"What's the matter with you, Darnay? You've being acting weird ever since you and Charlie back there got into a pissing contest trying to stare each other down. He was trying to warn you about Rolfe, wasn't he, with all that talk about 'no cover' and being 'exposed'? That didn't have anything to do with the weather. What is he, an ex-cop?"

Darnay tried very hard to hold onto the stony glare he'd been directing at me, but he couldn't quite control the brief flash of admiration I saw light his eyes just before he looked away.

"I'm right, aren't I? You're trying to pick a fight with me so you can jump out of this car in righteous indignation and leave me behind! I had no idea you were so devious!"

The corners of his mouth twitched involuntarily, then he sobered. "Look, we don't know how this guy is going to react to someone pounding on his door in the middle of a hurricane. Let me go first. If everything's under control, I'll come back for you. Give me fifteen minutes. If I don't show up, turn this thing around and get the hell out of here. Head for the hotel. You'll be safe there until the storm blows over."

"Not on your life!" I put as much determination as I could muster into it, then shivered as the possibly prophetic meaning of the words registered. "I'm not sitting here alone while you go playing hero!"

I leaned over in my seat to retrieve our bags, which I'd set on the floor at my feet. Darnay lunged after me, one powerful hand locked like a vise around my wrist. We were staring hard at each other, bent nearly double in the steamy cocoon of the tiny car, when the windshield exploded in a shower of glass.

30

I thought I heard the whine of the bullet as it ripped through Darnay's empty headrest and imbedded itself somewhere in the cracked leather of the rear seat. Immediately the storm poured through the shattered window, attacking us with needles of rain and scouring our exposed skin with wet, wind-driven sand.

"Stay down!" Darnay yelled, barely audible over the combined noises even though his mouth was just inches from my ear. My eyes were screwed shut, one arm flung across my face in an effort to protect them, but I felt his hands tearing at the soggy canvas bag at my feet.

"What are you doing?" The wind grabbed the words the second they were out of my mouth and flung them away into the sea.

"Stay here!" was all I heard, then the unmistakable *click* of a round being chambered in a semi-automatic pistol and the crash of the door as it blew shut behind him.

I hunkered my five-foot ten-inch frame in the tiny well under the dashboard for what seemed like hours, the cramps in my legs growing until I began to lose feeling in my feet. Kenneth Bleeker had been wrong. This had to be the heart of Hurricane Flora, lashing the island with the full force of her fury. The Fiat rocked from side to side, and I later swore that at times her wheels lost contact with the shifting sand. Debris bounced off her battered doors and fenders, those shuddering *thuds* the only sounds that penetrated above the raging storm.

At almost the precise instant when I could bear the pain in my twisted legs not one second longer, the screaming wind dropped to a bare whisper, and an eerie silence settled around me. I hesitated, confused, my ears ringing with the sudden lack of sound. Then I remembered Charleston and Hugo, and I realized this was the eye passing over. How long this lull would last, I had no idea, but I knew it was only a respite, a soft temptress waiting to lure the un-suspecting out into the open, only to snap her jaws shut when the back side of the hurricane slammed ashore. I shook off the few inches of sand that covered my back and head and scrambled out of the car.

I stepped down into a pool of calf-deep water and nearly toppled face-first into the muck. I stared, unbelieving, around me. The landscape had been totally altered, the sparse vegetation looking as if a giant fist had pounded it to splinters. Most of the dune behind which we had sheltered just a short while ago now lay piled across the hood of the Fiat along with shredded fronds and the twisted limbs of stunted pines.

I forced my thudding heart to slow, straining in the unnatural quiet for any sound that might tell me in what direction the danger lay. The shot that had shattered the windshield had come from the front. I bent low and scrambled up what remained of the sand dune, peering cautiously over the top.

The cottage lay just to my left, nestled on a small rise amid a protective screen of sea grape. The weathered wood siding, silvered with age and exposure to the relentless assault of the sea air, made the compact building almost invisible. It looked to be intact, unscathed by the onslaught of the storm.

Nothing moved in the barren emptiness except for the angry, roiling sea. A few yards offshore, ten-foot breakers slammed into the fragile reef sending plumes of spray rocketing high into the gathering dusk. Frantically I searched the hillocks of sand and swampy pools of standing water for some sign of Darnay. Even a glimpse of Grunewald with a high-powered rifle slung over his shoulder would have been a welcome sight. I felt like the last survivor at the end of the world.

I don't know how long I crouched in the wet sand, shivering in cold and fear. It was the merest brush of air across my filthy cheek, the lightest finger of wind lifting my sweat-soaked hair that sent me scrabbling down the dune, heedless of whatever man-made peril might lie in my path.

Flora was on her way back.

I stifled the urge to scream out Darnay's name, moving instead in a zigzag pattern toward the house. I stopped frequently, taking cover behind the few, sparse torchbushes still clinging stubbornly to the ground and behind scattered mounds of old conch shells piled high in what might have been native totems built to appease the gods of the sea. If so, they had failed miserably. The breeze was rising inexorably, the sand I kicked up swirling away in counter-clockwise eddies that mimicked the motion of the looming storm.

Another few minutes and twenty more feet to the right and I would have missed him. At first I mistook his low moan for a trick of the wind, but it came again just as I prepared to launch myself across the last, exposed yards of beach to the relative sanctuary of the thick stand of shrubbery surrounding the house. I turned and staggered in the direction of the sounds, nearly stumbling over his outstretched legs as I rounded the largest of the shell mounds. He lay spread-eagled on his back, arms outflung, the pistol still clutch-ed in his right hand.

A widening pool of bright red saturated the sand beneath him.

I dropped to my knees beside him, my hands groping frantically for the source of the bleeding. His skin felt clammy, cold and spongy, as if he were already dead. But his heart continued to pump out his lifeblood as I rolled him gently to the right and nearly fainted at the sight of the gaping hole in his left side. The bullet had ripped away a huge chunk of flesh, the wound already contaminated with sand and debris from the murky water rising around us.

I had to stop the bleeding. Whether unconscious or in shock from loss of blood, Darnay made no sound as I pulled away the tat-tered remnants of his shredded polo shirt from around the gash. Propping him up against my knees, I whipped off my jacket and pulled the flimsy cover-up over my head. In the movies—and probably in Dame Margo Stanhope's romances—the heroine al-ways rips up her petticoat to bind the wounds of her rescuer. The sodden mass of cotton refused to yield so much as a thread, even at the seams, as I pulled and twisted it in helpless fury. In the end, I stuffed the entire wad of cloth against the raw flesh, pulled the drawstring from the bottom of the slicker, and used it to secure the makeshift dressing by knotting it securely across his chest.

The wind was back with a vengeance. I knew we had to get under cover fast before the fury of Flora's eastern side hit us head-on. I slapped Darnay gently on both cheeks, hoping I could rouse him at least enough to walk a little on his own. Though I am certainly not a small woman, I knew I would never have the strength to carry—or even drag him—all the way to the house. I gave no thought as to who or what we might find once we got there. I only knew I had to get him warm and dry, or he would never survive.

Faced with a choice between the elements and Grunewald, I decided to take my chances with the force I had any hope of being able to reason with.

Maybe.

I slipped the handgun into the pocket of my slicker.

Somehow I managed to communicate the urgency of the situation to Darnay, who wandered in and out of coherence as I helped him struggle to his feet. With his right arm draped around my shoulder and his left one clutching the bandage to his side, he leaned heavily against me as we set off. In a shambling, stumbling lope, I half-supported, half-dragged him through the trees, bent nearly double in the roaring wind, and up to the snug little cottage. With a final push that drained both of us of our last ounce of strength, we crawled up the four wooden steps and across an open porch covered with blowing sand.

From my knees I reached up to twist the tarnished brass doorknob with my left hand. The right I kept firmly locked around the grip of the handgun in my pocket. The windowless door swung open, and I tumbled onto a soft, blue carpet, into a world of warmth and dim lantern light. I pulled Darnay the rest of the way in, my battered senses prepared for a shout of challenge, even for the whine of another bullet. My finger twitched nervously against the trigger of the Glock. But all that greeted us was a profound silence, followed by the sharp crack of the door as the greedy wind sucked it shut behind us.

I don't know how long we lay huddled together on the floor. My watch, along with my shoes and all our other belongings, had been ripped away in our frantic rush to the cottage. The full force of the storm lashed us now, the hurricane shutters fastened tightly over the windows groaning under the attack. Despite the cold and wet that seemed to have settled into my bones, I could have curled there on the carpet and slept for a week.

Darnay's incoherent mumbling brought me back.

I urged and prodded and mostly dragged him until he finally managed to collapse onto the cushions of the chintz-covered sofa pulled up in front of a wood-burning stove. The fire had gone out, but enough warmth still radiated from it that some of the chill began to seep out of me. I knew I should get him out of the rain-soaked clothes plastered to his body, but I also knew the effort was beyond me. Besides, my makeshift bandage seemed to be holding, and I didn't want to start the wound bleeding again.

The cottage appeared to consist of this one large room. Somewhere in my foggy brain it registered that the interior looked more like an English library than a Caribbean beach house, with shelves of books lining two walls and a tiny, galley-type kitchen tucked into one corner. Then I spotted the doorway that must lead to a bedroom, and I darted through it.

Jordan lay sprawled across the rumpled sheets.

For one, heart-stopping moment, I thought she was dead.

Then, by the dim light of the glass-topped hurricane lamp, I saw the gentle rise and fall of her chest. I flung myself across the bed, screaming her name as I grabbed her naked shoulders and shook her furiously. Her black-capped head rolled from side to side, but her green cat's-eyes remained tightly closed.

Clad only in a scanty pair of ivory satin briefs, Jordan's smooth skin seemed almost pearlized in the soft lamplight. Quickly I checked for wounds or injuries and found none. This had to be a drugged stupor which, hopefully, she would soon sleep off. I pulled the light blanket up over her, grabbed the heavy comforter that lay crumpled on the floor at the foot of the bed, and raced back to Darnay.

He had begun to shiver, the involuntary spasms sending his entire body into paroxysms that shook the sofa on which he lay. I tucked the bedspread around him as tightly as I dared, making certain he was covered from his chin to his filthy bare feet. Back in the bedroom I ransacked the drawers, pouncing on a heavy black sweatshirt and matching pants along with a pair of white athletic socks. In the surprisingly large adjacent bathroom, I peeled off my soggy swimsuit, toweled myself off, and pulled on the blessedly warm, dry clothes.

Back in the living area, I draped my discarded yellow slicker over the arm of a Queen Anne chair. The weight of the handgun I'd slipped into its pocket banged against the delicate curve of the hand carved leg. Reluctantly my trembling fingers locked around the grip as I slid the Glock into my hand. Then I curled up on the floor next to Darnay and laid my head on the cushions beside him.

The screaming wind assaulted us from all sides, but the sturdy cottage held its own. The noise had become almost soothing, the incessant whine broken only occasionally by the hard *thump* of some dislodged limb or other debris being flung against the weathered walls outside. I might have dozed, or perhaps I'd become mesmerized by the dark and the wailing storm. I don't really remember now.

My one, burning recollection is of the scream of terror that leaped into my throat when the door suddenly flew open, and Hurricane Flora blew the bloody, tattered nightmare that was Rolfe Grunewald into the room.

Backlit by continuous flashes of lightning that ripped the pitch-black sky behind him, the man who had charmed with urbanity and wit, then ruthlessly murdered eight elderly women, stood framed in the doorway like a vision from hell. Blood dripped from an open wound on his temple, the redness fading to pink as it mingled with the rain blowing around him in sheets. As he forced the door closed, I saw the reflected gleam of metal in his right hand.

Frozen in fear, I could only stare helplessly as he advanced into the room. Our eyes locked in the glow of the lamps, and I remember thinking he didn't look like a madman, despite his battered appearance. In fact, his expression was one of sadness, a reluctant, but caring parent about to administer punishment to a well-loved child, I thought, as I watched his right arm rise inexorably toward me.

"Hello? Is anybody here? Rolfe?"

The innocuous words, half-whispered from a raspy throat, jerked Grunewald's eyes toward where Jordan, wrapped in a sheet like an avenging spirit, stumbled into the room. I watched as, in slow motion, his arm swung the yawning muzzle of the gun in her direction.

Gently I eased my hand from behind Darnay's head, wrapped my left one around the right. In the cold, dead calm at the back of my brain, I heard Sergeant Red Tanner saying, *Now don't pull the trigger. Squeeze it. Gently. That's it . . . squeeze . . .*

The explosion was deafening, blotting out even the shrieking wind of the dying hurricane. For a lifetime Grunewald stood motionless. Then slowly his head swiveled toward me, that look of regret now mingled with shocked surprise. He teetered for a moment on wobbly legs, then folded gracefully onto the soft, blue carpet, blood pulsing briefly from the gaping hole in his heart.

It took awhile for me to realize that the screams I was hearing were my own.

31

I wiped a tiny rivulet of sweat from the side of my face as I twisted the plastic tie around the bulging, black garbage bag and stood up, massaging the tightness in my lower back. All I needed to do was haul this load out to the driveway, and the cleanup effort would be complete. Proudly I surveyed my yard, now neat and free of the dozens of palm fronds and twisted limbs that had littered it in the aftermath of the storm.

A weakened Hurricane Flora had followed me back across the Caribbean, skirting the South Carolina coast just north of Beaufort. Damage had been minimal, most of it caused by flooding rains, but there had been no injuries, no loss of life. The winds that had lashed us the night before had been no worse than those we occasionally experienced from the spring thunderstorms that normally plagued us in March and early April.

I dragged the bag of debris out to join the half-dozen others piled ready for the landscape crew to pick up, then reached for a cigarette before I remembered I'd purposely left the pack inside. Even if I still wasn't ready to go cold turkey, I could at least get back to my initial game plan of cutting back.

I gathered the rakes and shovel, stripped off the cotton work gloves that hadn't prevented blisters from forming on both my thumbs, and carried them into the garage. I washed up, poured myself a well-earned tumbler of iced tea, and settled onto my favorite chaise on the shaded deck. As always, my eyes went immediately to the sea, calm and sparkling in the late September sun. The dune had taken a beating in the storm-heightened tides of the last few days, but the fragile, yet tenacious sea oats still danced lazily across its crown in the gentle morning breeze.

As it had during all the few quiet moments I'd been able to snatch from the harrowing week just past, Alain Darnay's face leaped immediately into my mind. My last glimpse had been of his salt-encrusted lips pressed tightly together as Charlie and Nigel and the others who had ridden too late to our rescue placed him gently in the back of a Land Rover and sped off over the ruined road toward the airstrip. I had begged to go with them, afraid not only to leave his care to these strangers, but terrified that the brief glance of his pain-dulled blue eyes might be the last I'd ever have.

They had to pry my hand out of his.

Flora had dealt the island only a glancing blow, or so they told me. I shuddered now, remembering the screaming wind and pounding surf, and prayed fervently never to experience the full force of a storm such as she. Charlie, whose last name I never did discover, had taken charge then, covering Grunewald's body and whisking a still groggy Jordan and me back to the Anegada Reef. Within hours we were settled into a small, secluded hotel on Tortola, our neatly packed bags appearing miraculously from our cabin on the *Crystal Fjord*, now steaming blithely toward her next port of call. If she operated less smoothly without her missing First Officer, I never heard.

Police Chief Byron MacGregor surprised me with his compassion and his unyielding belief in my version of the events on Anegada. Between them, he and the mysterious Charlie managed to bulldoze their way through the formalities that usually accompany violent death. Formal statements, inquest, verdict, exoneration—all sped by in a blur of strange faces and unfamiliar procedure. Less than seventy-two hours after shooting to death Rolfe Grunewald, alias Ramon Escalante, alias Reginald Montgomery, I was huddled in a first-class seat next to a wan, subdued Jordan Herrington von Brandt, heading home.

Now I lit a cigarette and swallowed hard, commanding the tears that rose unbidden into my eyes not to fall. Darnay had disappeared without a trace into the bureaucratic maw of Interpol. All efforts to determine where he was, *how* he was, were met with the sort of stonewall of politeness the French are so adept at erecting. Even the Judge who, along with my brother-in-law Red Tanner were the only people who knew the true outcome of my ill-fated voyage, found himself unable to crack the perimeter of silence surrounding Alain Darnay. My attempts to locate his family in France met with similar frustration. It was only from Charlie that I had been able to obtain answers to any of the thousands of questions that plagued my mind as I had waited to board the small turbo-prop on the first leg of my journey home . . .

The most reassuring information he had provided me was that the man I had killed with that one, incredibly lucky shot had indeed been a murderer. Jordan, whose careless chatter had led Grunewald to believe she knew more than she actually did, had been scheduled as victim number nine. She'd had no inkling as they sipped champagne after making love to the sounds of the storm's fury that her glass had been laced with Valium.

Charlie also shared with me the few tidbits he'd been able to glean from the horde of Interpol agents that had descended on Anegada just hours after we'd been whisked away. Evidence of bank accounts and other hideaways in several South American countries, along with passports in various names had turned up in the East End cottage. Several pieces of jewelry were also recovered, their descriptions sent off to be compared with the lists of that reported missing by the families of Grunewald's victims. No one seemed to doubt they'd found their killer.

According to local gossip, the professionals had reconstructed the scenario something like this: waiting for the drug to take effect on Jordan, Rolfe had heard the engine of our Fiat and come outside to investigate. Realizing who we were and guessing at our mission, he had panicked, firing through the windshield. When Darnay had leaped from the car, the two had stalked each other, exchanging shots and wounds. Grunewald's, a graze across his temple, had left him unconscious long enough for me to find Darnay and drag us both into the cottage.

The only thing Charlie couldn't—or wouldn't—tell me was that which I most needed to hear.

"They'll take good care of him, you know," he'd assured me as we stood in the noonday heat on the tarmac of the airport on nearby Beef Island. "They look out for their own. He'll get the best."

"But why can't I know where he is? Why won't anyone tell me if he's even alive or dead?" The obvious anguish in my voice failed to move this enigmatic man with the military bearing and the hard, gray eyes.

"Alive, when we put him on the plane on Anegada. Torn up, but alive when Nigel delivered him to his people in San Juan. Former RAF, is Nigel. He got him there as fast as anyone could have."

"But then why . . .?"

"Need to know, Mrs. Tanner," he said gruffly, touching an imaginary cap in a half-salute as he turned away, "and you don't. Have a safe trip."

I had watched him stride out of my life without a backward glance before I trudged wearily up the stairs and into the plane . . .

The phone rang in the kitchen, and I stubbed out my cigarette and sprinted inside. Any interruption was welcome if it managed to hold back my growing fears about Darnay.

Jordan sounded subdued, that frantic gaiety and reckless daring that had been so much a part of her charm, now muted and repressed. Perhaps it had come from her brush with violent death. Or perhaps she was finally growing up. In any case, she had displayed a serenity of spirit in the last few days that became her well.

I knew she was calling to say goodbye. She had decided to take the step she had proposed to her mother barely one month of days, but a lifetime of grief and experience ago: Jordan von Brandt was going back to Europe to reclaim her daughters. If she won, she would bring them to Natchez, to their grandmother's house, to their grandmother's heritage.

"Good luck," I said, as we both fought back tears. "Kick ass over there, kiddo. Don't take 'no' for an answer."

"It's funny, you know?" Jordan said with a strained laugh, some of her old, wicked humor peeking through.

"What?"

"How I always thought Leslie was such a crappy mother, and how I always swore I'd never be like that with my kids. It took her dying to make me see that's exactly what I'd done: repeated every mistake she'd ever made with me. I wonder if she knows."

"Beats hell out of me," I answered, "though I'd like to think so. Take care, and keep me posted. Get a computer so we can e-mail."

"The girls already have one. I'll get them to teach me how to use it."

The emotional silence threatened to overwhelm us both. The bond forged between us in a darkened room on a far-away island as we stared down at the body of the man I had just killed would bind us together in a way few people ever experience. Suddenly words seemed unimportant, inadequate to convey the feeling.

"Goodbye," I said softly. "Be well."

"You, too," I heard Jordan whisper as I hung up the phone.

My swim had been necessarily brief, but the rapidly cooling ocean and a freshening northeast breeze had invigorated me and loosened up the kinks my unaccustomed yard work had left in my back and shoulders. Showered and dressed in lightweight slacks and a long-sleeved cotton sweater, I let down the top on the Zeemer and headed for Beaufort. I had several appointments to keep.

Christopher Brandon's secretary greeted me with the same lack of enthusiasm she had demonstrated on my first visit, but ushered me into the young attorney's office within a few minutes of my arrival. The light in his eyes and the warmth of his handshake reminded me of his earlier, stumbling infatuation, so I kept the meeting short and business-like.

"I understand the Herringtons have been in touch with you," I began when he'd held the visitor's chair for me, then seated himself behind his desk.

"Yes, I've talked with all three of them in the last few days."

"How's the audit of Bi-Rite going?"

"Slowly, but we're getting a handle on it. The Macons weren't really very clever. You would have zeroed in on their scam as soon as you had those missing documents you asked them for. The auditors told me the work you did in organizing everything was a big help. Speeded up their investigation a lot."

"Thanks."

Chris Brandon had sent someone to retrieve all the boxes from my office-bedroom the day after I'd returned from the Caribbean. Dolores had been as delighted as I to be rid of the clutter.

I pulled from my purse the envelope that was the reason for my visit. "Here's Jordan's power of attorney, signed and notarized. Anything relating to the estate or the sale of the stores I'll be reviewing and signing off on for her until she gets back in the country."

"Great! We've got a potential buyer, a big Atlanta outfit, waiting in the wings. As soon as the financial mess is straightened out, I think we'll be able to make a deal."

"Any word on Dudley and Marilee?" I asked.

"Not a whisper. They seem to have done a first-rate job of disappearing off the face of the earth." Chris Brandon leaned back in his big swivel chair, his hands clasped behind his head. "I have this wild picture in my mind of the two of them tearing up I-95, with their truck piled high with stolen weed trimmers and chain saws."

I joined in his laughter, then rose from my chair. "I have to be going now, Chris. Thanks for all you're doing for the Herringtons. You'll be in touch when you need my signature, I assume?"

The crestfallen look on his face forced me to bite back a smile. "I've heard from Justin out in Dallas," he blurted out, trying, I thought, to postpone my leaving. "He's managed to locate copies of all his mother's investment documents, so the estate settlement can proceed pretty quickly now. Maybe we could discuss it over dinner?"

"Sorry, that's where I'm heading now, out to *Presqu'isle*." It was only a small fib. "Command appearance before the Judge. But thanks anyway."

As he walked me through the reception area and out into the hallway, his mention of Justin Herrington triggered the doubts that had plagued me ever since Jordan had relayed the same information a few days before. I'd been so sure the burglary at Leslie's Natchez mansion had been tied somehow to her murder, but Grunewald's death had certainly proved the fallacy of that supposition. Rifling his victims' homes had never been part of his M.O.

So who would benefit from possession of Leslie's private papers? Her son Justin handled all her personal finances. Had he been cheating his own mother, siphoning off assets or playing fast and loose with her funds? If so, he'd had two weeks to cover his tracks. His chubby, ingenuous face floated up into my mind, and I shook my head in sadness. I really hated to believe it of him, but logic dictated I probably must. Yet, the fact that he was now willing to turn "copies" of all the documents over to the estate lawyers pretty much precluded our ever being able to prove anything, even if Jordan and Trey had been willing to pursue it.

We had reached the top of the stairs. "Look, Bay," Chris Brandon said, his lightly tanned, boyish face turning pink with the effort of what sounded almost like a prepared speech, " I'd really like to get to know you better. I mean, I'm very attracted to you, as you may have noticed, and I really do admire you a lot. May I call you?"

I didn't need this complication, no matter how flattering, in my life right then. Every unguarded moment of thought was filled with Darnay's pale, battered face. But a good Southern upbringing seeps into the bones, and politeness is its skin. "I may be out of town for awhile," I said, extending my hand with a smile, "but try me in a few weeks, okay?"

"Okay," he beamed, releasing the handshake, "I'll do that."

Back on the sidewalk, I dropped a couple more quarters into the parking meter on Bay Street and darted around light traffic to the opposite side. My luck held as I strode purposefully past the bookstore, casting a glance inside without turning my head. The last thing I needed was another interrogation by Cissy Ransome. Despite my best efforts, I had no doubt she'd have the entire story of my harrowing trip out of me before I knew what hit me. I was determined not to become the subject of local gossip and speculation again if I could help it.

In all fairness, though, I thought, as I pulled open the door to the Fig Tree and stepped into its welcome gloom, Cissy had managed to help solve one of the puzzles surrounding the events of the past few weeks. Had I responded to her message during my whirlwind trip back to Beaufort, perhaps I might have seen the truth long before I did.

For it was Cissy Ransome who had provided Rolfe Grunewald with the information he needed to make the emergency telegram so believable that I had left Jordan alone and vulnerable and come racing back home. He'd apparently gotten the name of the bookstore off the covers of the novels I'd left stacked in plain view in my cabin on the *Crystal Fjord*. Even though he was a foreigner, the urbane serial killer knew a lot about small towns. He had called, claiming to be an old college flame trying to track me down again after years of pining away for our lost love. Cissy, whose favorite reading material graced the shelves of her Romance section, had chattered on for twenty minutes, imparting enough personal data to make it easy for Grunewald to construct a sure-fire ploy to lure me away from the ship.

Her breathless message on my answering machine had been meant to alert me to the return of this bogus lover back into my life. Had I only called her, maybe I might have been more prepared for what happened, maybe I could have changed the outcome so that Darnay . . .

I shoved that thought away as I stopped at the nearly deserted bar. At three in the afternoon on a workday, only a couple of determined drinkers and a few tourists were scattered around the low-ceilinged room. Gilly Falconer left off washing glasses in the deep, narrow sink under the bar, wiped her hands on the ever-present apron, and walked over to where I stood.

"Hey, girl," she said with her usual irreverent grin, "your date's waitin' out on the porch."

"It's not a date, Gilly," I countered, glancing through the windows toward the tables facing the river. I couldn't see anyone sitting out there. Maybe he was behind one of the pillars. "It's business."

"Yeah, right," she laughed. "You decide you don't wanna deal with that 'business', you just send him on in here to me, you got that?"

"Has he been waiting long? What's he drinking?" I asked, ignoring the innuendo. "Maybe you should take him a refill."

"This is definitely your kinda man, sugah," she drawled, again displaying her suggestive smile. "Iced tea, can you beat it? I left the pitcher and a glass for you so's I wouldn't have to interrupt y'all. Now go on, git out there." Gilly shooed me with her apron as if I were a balky child.

The door creaked a little, and he turned in his seat. His blonde hair, cut short, but not buzzed, was almost white, and his eyes were a deep, dark brown. I noticed broad, muscled shoulders in a plaid sport shirt as he rose at my approach. In faded jeans and deck shoes, he was almost exactly my height, with youthful good looks and a disarming smile. I guessed his age at somewhere in the middle twenties.

"Bay Tanner?" His low voice held just a trace of North Carolina in it.

"Yes," I said, extending my hand. "And you must be Erik Whiteside."

I'd felt he deserved to hear the story in person, to watch my face as I gave him the facts about how the man who had murdered his grandmother had died. I'd selected the Fig Tree as neutral territory for our initial meeting, unsure how awkward or uncomfortable we might turn out to be with each other, considering the nature of the events that had first drawn us together.

But I needn't have worried. Erik Whiteside had a charm and ease of manner that belied his twenty-six years. I had no qualms when, having finished off two pitchers of iced tea, I finally convinced him to come stay with us at *Presqu'isle*. While I used the pay phone to alert Lavinia to our imminent arrival, Erik took care of the check and went to retrieve his car from the lot behind the local motel where he'd intended to spend the night. Gilly gave me a lascivious wag of her eyebrows as I waved goodbye.

Erik Whiteside drove a huge, four-wheel drive sport utility vehicle. The gleaming, black monster looming just off the rear bumper of my little, sea green convertible made me feel like a bug waiting to be squashed. In tandem we negotiated the swing bridge onto

Lady's Island, then St. Helena's, and finally down the long avenue of oaks to my childhood home. I smiled at Erik's low whistle as he jumped down from the cab of the Expedition.

"Wow!" he said with unfeigned enthusiasm, "you actually live here? It's like something out of a movie. Or a history book."

"Well, I don't anymore. Live here, I mean. It's my father's place. He's very eager to meet you," I added as we mounted the sixteen steps onto the verandah. It was again only a small fib.

When I'd first broached the subject of this half-formed scheme, the Judge had looked at me as if I'd finally lost my mind. But his opposition had been only token. I could tell, as the discussion continued long into the night, that the idea had excited him almost as much as it did me. We would, after all, be working together, a father-daughter team of discreet inquiry agents, as the British called them. No tacky PI stuff for Simpson and Tanner, no stalking unfaithful husbands or digging up dirt for sleazy defense attorneys to use to get their equally sleazy clients off. Instead we would concentrate on more cerebral investigations: financial larceny, embezzlement, perhaps an occasional missing person. I was not unmindful that I still had done little to help Adelaide Boyce Hammond locate her long-lost brother, Win.

We would have no office, print up no business cards. What clients we deigned to take on would be referrals from those whom we trusted. With an informal pipeline, should we need it, into local law enforcement via Red Tanner, I knew all we lacked was an entree into the daunting, but vitally useful world of the Internet. Erik Whiteside had already proved he could gain access to places he wasn't meant to see. That had certainly been helpful in the past; it would be invaluable in our new endeavor. The young computer wizard whom we hoped to put on retainer had just passed my job-screening interview, but he had yet to make it by the wily old curmudgeon who was my father and future partner.

Lavinia had outdone herself with dinner. Erik declared that she had hit upon every single one of his favorite dishes and prepared them better than anyone since his Granny Pen. The introduction of that lady's name into the conversation cast a brief aura of sadness over what had been an otherwise pleasant meal, but we soon recovered our good humor as the Judge regaled our visitor with charming stories from his days as Beaufort's leading attorney. Lavinia and I, of course, had heard them all a thousand times before, but I couldn't help noticing how fondly her lined, but regal face regarded my father in the muted light of the crystal chandelier.

I helped Lavinia clear, then allowed myself to be chased out of the kitchen. When I wandered into the study, I could tell that the concentrated cigar smoke was beginning to get to Erik Whiteside, so I offered to show him the grounds. There wasn't much to see in the falling dusk except the soft shades of pink and orange riding gently on the surface of the Sound and the blurred silhouette of *Presqu'isle* fading into the night. Having caught the almost imperceptible nod from the Judge as we'd made our escape from the smoke-filled room, I used this opportunity to put our proposition to Erik Whiteside.

"Gosh, I don't know what to say," he stammered as we stood at the end of the wooden pier and listened to the night birds calling to each other across the water.

"You don't have to give me an answer right now," I said, pulling a cigarette from my pocket and lighting it myself. "Sleep on it. We can talk about it over breakfast in the morning."

"I'll need to get going pretty early," he reminded me. "I don't like to be away from the store too long. You know how kids are these days. I don't really trust them not to screw everything up while I'm gone."

I hoped the twilight covered the smile twitching at the corners of my mouth. "I understand. Shall we say seven?"

"That'd be great. I really think I want to do this. I mean, you're not even asking me to give up my job or move or anything."

"Not yet, anyway," I cautioned him, "though it might come to that, down the road."

"Well, I'll let you know for sure tomorrow, but right now I'd say you can count me in."

We shook hands solemnly, then I escorted the charming young man back into the house. At the foot of the staircase we said goodnight, and I retreated back into the study to inform my father that we appeared to be in business. I found that he had wheeled himself onto the back verandah, so I followed him out and settled into my usual rocking chair.

"Tell me something," I said after a long silence during which both of us smoked and concentrated on the now-dark water at the foot of the property.

"We seem to do an awful lot of soul-searching out here on this ol' porch," my father remarked, "and not all of it pleasant. I'm afraid to ask what it is you want to know."

I blushed a little then, remembering the confrontation we'd had just a short time ago, and the revelation that had sprung from it. We still hadn't entirely resolved that issue. It was something we'd have to work on in the months to come. But all that had nothing to do with what I wanted to ask him now.

"Well, it really is none of my damn business, and I know that's what you'll want to say the minute the question is out of my mouth, but if we're going to be working together from . . ."

"Let me guess," the Judge interrupted me. "You want me to tell you about Jack T. Herrington's death."

"How did you know?"

"Seems to me you've pretty much tied up all the other ends of this Herrington mess you got yourself into, except for that one. And I also know that you'll keep worryin' at it like a coonhound with a rib bone until you get an answer."

"So what happened? Was it really just an accident?"

"Yes," my father responded and sipped from his glass of warm, diluted whiskey and lemon. For a moment I thought that was all he was going to say. "Jack T. was drunk. It wasn't all that unusual a condition for him. He lost control of the car and slammed into the river. Wasn't wearing a seatbelt. Doc Hopper said he died instantly, or near enough as to make no difference."

"Then why all the secrecy? People die from driving drunk every day, and surely no one . . ."

"Let me tell it, all right?" he snapped. "The reason we kept things quiet was that there was someone with him in the car."

"That's no secret either. Everyone in town pretty much knew about Jack T. and his women. Unless . . ."

"It wasn't a woman. Nor a girl either, before you ask me that." I saw his jaws clamp tightly around the dead cigar stub in his mouth as he turned away toward the Sound.

"But then who . . .?"

And then I had it. Of course. No wonder his friends had been at such pains to protect his family from the details of Jack T. Herrington's final night. "Who was he?" I asked.

It took a moment before my father replied. When he did, his voice held a weariness born of years of concealment and a sadness I could tell held no condemnation now. "He was a hitchhiker, some teenager Jack T. had picked up along the highway a few days before. Kid was belted, had hardly a scratch on him. We never did find out for sure who propositioned who first, but it seemed a safe bet this wasn't the first time it had happened. Luckily the sheriff himself was the first one on the scene. Hustled the kid out of there and called me. I got hold of Charlie, Law, and Boyd and together we convinced the youngster it was in his best interests to take the money we were offerin' him and just go on about his business. He was on his way before sunup, and that's the last we heard from him."

"He didn't come back and try to blackmail you for more money? That's surprising."

"We thought so, too. We were prepared in case it came to that, but it never did. Boyd always maintained that Sheriff McCray musta threatened that boy with somethin' that scared the bejeezus out of him, 'cause he just disappeared for good that very night." I heard the click as he unlocked the brake on his wheelchair. "I'm turnin' in, Princess. Don't stay up all night."

I heard the screen door bump shut behind him as he rolled down the ramp. I lit a cigarette and exhaled into the cool, night air, wondering how Dudley and Marilee Macon had managed to stumble onto Jack T.'s secret life. How easy it must have been for them to turn the shameful knowledge into a blank check.

I shook off the sadness and smiled into the dark. *Princess.* My father hadn't called me that in thirty years. I sighed, wondering if we'd ever be able to recapture the closeness we'd once shared, if this new venture of ours would be enough to chase the demons of the past out of this wonderful old house—and out of my life altogether.

The distant shrill of the telephone broke the heavy silence. I waited, hoping Lavinia would pick it up, but she must already have gone upstairs. From the bathroom adjacent to my father's study, I heard running water. Cursing his foolish stubbornness in refusing to have an answering machine installed, I trotted into his room and grabbed up the receiver.

"Yes?" I snapped.

"*Bon soir, ma petite. C'est moi.*"

The weak, but steady voice settled over my heart like a soft, warm blanket. In that moment, I finally expelled the breath of fear I'd held tightly inside me for more than a week.

"Darnay, where the hell are you?" I yelled joyfully into the telephone.

About the author

Kathryn R. Wall wrote her first story at the age of six and hasn't stopped since. She grew up in a small town in northeastern Ohio and attended college in both Ohio and Pennsylvania. She acquired her love for words from her mother, a teacher of English and Latin, and her love for numbers from her father, the controller for an automobile conglomerate.

For twenty-five years Wall practiced her profession as an accountant in both public and private practice. In 1990 she and Norman, her husband of thirty years, established a manufacturing tooling distributorship, the sale of which led to their retirement to Hilton Head Island in 1994.

Wall continues to work part-time in the accounting field and mentors at a local public school. She is also a founding member of the Island Writers Network. She has two stepsons and four grandchildren.

Her first mystery novel, *In For a Penny*, has achieved both commercial and critical success. The third book in the series, *Like a Bad Penny*, will be available in late 2002. All the novels feature widowed financial consultant Bay Tanner and take place in and around Hilton Head Island and the surrounding South Carolina Lowcountry.

Colophon

Tabby Manse™

Coastal Villages Press is dedicated to helping
to preserve the timeless values of traditional
places along our nation's Atlantic coast—
building houses to endure through
the centuries; living in harmony
with the natural environment;
honoring history, culture,
family and friends—
and helping to
make
these
values
relevant
today.
This
book
was
completed on
January 19, 2002, at
Beaufort, South Carolina. It was
composed using Corel Ventura 8
and set in Adobe Garamond, based on a typeface
designed by Claude Garamond in Paris in 1530.

Order form

Coastal Villages Press
2614 Boundary Street - Office B
Beaufort, SC 29906

Please send me the following book(s):

(   ) copies of *And Not a Penny More* by Kathryn R. Wall, 312 pages, paperback, published by Coastal Villages Press, ISBN 1-882943-12-0, at $14.95 each $_____

Plus postage at $1.50 per copy   _____

Total: $_____

Your name: _____

Address: _____

City, State, Zip: _____

Your phone number: (_____) _____

Date: _____

Additional copies of *And Not a Penny More* and all the other exciting volumes in the Bay Tanner Mystery series are also available at your favorite bookstore and from your online book retailer.

Visit the author on her website at www.pennynovels.com and the publisher's website at www.coastal-villages.com.